The Outcast Prophet of Bensonhurst

A novel by
Marco Manfre

This book is dedicated to all of those who have no voice
and no one to speak for them.

One fire burns out another's burning,
One pain is lessen'd by another's anguish.
(Romeo and Juliet 1.2. 42-43)

THE SICK, WEAK WEED

He used to look up at people through the spaces between his fingers, and know. It was a gift and an affliction.

***

Anthony Caricetti stood stiffly before the judge and explained that he wanted to change his name to Roosevelt in honor of the great statesman who had led his country during its darkest days but had not lived to see the final victory. He wanted an American name. He declared in nervous, carefully measured tones that, unlike most of his cousins, aunts, uncles, and other assorted relatives, he had been born in America, not in "the old country." He was a veteran too. He tugged at the sleeves of his worn, pin-striped suit as he recounted how he had spent 18 of the worst months of his life as a Marine, island-hopping from one hot, diseased hellhole in the Pacific to another in defense of his beloved country.

He had earned the right to the name of his choice.

Roosevelt was the name that he wanted for his sons.

The fact that, in October of 1945, when he appeared before the judge, he did not have any sons was of no consequence to him. He would have sons, and soon, and they would proudly be called Roosevelt.

The judge respectfully denied the petition.

Never one to be bound by the opinions and decisions of others, Anthony began using Roosevelt as his family name.

During the next four years, without any great passion or excitement, he and his wife, Lucia, brought four sons into the world. In fact, she had been five months pregnant with her first when Anthony had stood before the judge that day.

He named his sons George, Ronald, James, and, of course, Franklin. He refrained from using the name Theodore. He had never liked the looks of that president as he appeared in photographs. Something about his teeth.

Then, one night, three years after the birth of Franklin, unexpectedly, and to the obvious dismay of Anthony, who was quite satisfied with what he had, Lucia whispered to him, "We're gonna have another one."

Anthony and Lucia's fifth son was born in November of 1952.

Anthony named him Anacleto.

If he had given the boy pretty much any other name, it could have been Americanized. If he had been named Vincenzo, he could have been called Vincent or Vinnie or Vin; Salvatore would have become Sal. Normal names. A normal beginning in life.

When Anacleto was about six years old, the boys in the neighborhood, who had more common names, began calling him Antiseptic and Anaconda. Anaconda led to Snake and Snaky and, sometimes, Slimy. Amused at first, Anacleto laughed. A shy, insecure child, he didn't mind the reptilian nicknames. Then, a few days after the non-stop name calling began, Anacleto looked directly into the eyes of the boys as they bellowed, "Slimy, Sneaky Snake, Snake, Snake" and "Anaconda Asshole" and other alliterative variations on Anacleto. What he saw chilled him. The bleak, cold smiles and hateful grimaces that accompanied the flood of shouted alterations of his name revealed their loathing. Even at that age, he understood: this was to be part of his life.

Shocked and bewildered, he put his head down and covered his eyes with his hands. The sounds around him became just so much incoherent buzzing and static. He understood nothing except for the fact that he was despised.

Shaken and confused, he attempted to regain his composure. He approached the boys, and asked them to stop. That led to more odious variations on his name. He tried using Catholic guilt—timidly informing them that, according to what his father had told him, Anakletos, the original Greek form, had been the name of the third pope. It meant "invoked." He didn't know what that meant, but, it was a pope's name.

The boys began calling him Pope and then Pop and, eventually, Pup and Puppy.

The misery caused by the continuous name calling pushed the boy into a dark, cold, isolated crevice of existence. He refused to tell people his name. He did not speak unless he was cornered. In school, he kept his head down, squinting at the pink and gray squares of linoleum through the spaces between his fingers. He spent so much time stooped over that when he walked he had to remind himself to straighten up. His hunched appearance, so much like a tree branch bent by the weight of winter ice, led to more name calling.

He never once asked a question or made an unsolicited comment in class. Rather than causing a teacher to ask, "Yes, Anacleto?" or, worse than that, to say, "Anacleto has something to share with us," he stayed down, covering his face with his hands, his right hand sheltering his left, and remained silent.

Safe within the cold darkness of his tomb.

No one seemed to notice his withdrawal from the world around him.

Teachers benignly enjoyed addressing him in the very formal "Mr. Roosevelt," as in "Mr. Roosevelt, please cover your mouth when you sneeze" or "You really must attempt to use better penmanship, Mr. Roosevelt."

Once in a while, he would be referred to as "Mr. President."

He knew they were not attempting to hurt him. It was just his lot in life.

Every year, despite his mute but clearly apparent discomfort, he was nominated for the post of class president. He never needed to hear the final tally: it was always a glowing, unanimous victory for his opponent. He sensed, rather than heard, the annual announcement of "Thirty-four votes for (whoever ran against him) and no votes for Mr. Roosevelt."

Since the rule seemed to be that only two students could run for class president, whoever was nominated was automatically the winner because Anacleto was always the other nominee. His brothers were often nominated for posts in their classes, and each of them won once or twice.

Then there was his hair. Steel-spring tight brown-black ringlets. His mother thought his hair was "so bee-u-tee-ful that it's a cryin' shame to cut it."

Why didn't she know that his wild, kinky hair was one more humiliation to bear? He wanted a then-fashionable crew cut, but his mother reacted to that suggestion as if he had told her that he wanted to cut out his eyes.

From time to time, he thought about doing that.

One more thing: a minor birth defect caused his left hand to be a little shorter, thinner, and weaker than his right. Even though he used his right hand for eating, grasping, and for covering his mouth when he sneezed and coughed, if he remembered to do so, he always preferred his unusual left hand.

It was more like him.

Little by little, he slid further back, away from the world of smiles and laughs and friendships to his dim, cold habitat. He became used to the solitude. It comforted him. There, he was able to take refuge in his thoughts. His brain was home to a million dizzying, rapidly changing, contradictory, confusing ideas and bizarre contemplations. They flashed and whizzed and snapped and crackled across his synapses.

He called it his *head fog*.

When he was compelled to confront the bright light of the alien world, to mingle with its inhabitants, he hesitated and stuttered, attempting to latch onto one thought, only to lose it; then he attempted to grasp another one. He knew that he was being stared at. He was expected to say something. He usually remained mute. When he did venture to speak, he stuttered and mumbled and lisped something odd, fragmented, and totally inappropriate to the question he had been asked.

"The...wittle....boy in...the story...he...wikes...uh, uh...he wikes...his pr...prob....problem is...my dad...he...the b-boy...he has a good...his prob...I dunno."

He would pray during class. No,...not pray talk to, have mental conversations with God and with Jesus. He would beg, plead, make arrangements, promise to do anything to be saved from having to speak.

God, please...I will stop eating chocolate ice cream...and Oreos...I won't watch "Roy Rogers"...I'll pay attention at Mass on Sunday...Please don't let her call on me.

Slowly, surreptitiously, his head would sink down until it was almost completely hidden by his school desk. He would slowly, secretly make the Sign of the Cross, hoping to ward off the assault from his teacher. He would cover his face with his hands. Then, cautiously moving his fingers slightly apart, he would look down, and then to his left and his right, searching for signs, messages in his environment.

LJ-478 B. Where did I see that? Boycott. Where did I hear that? Nouns, verbs, adjectives, adverbs, nouns, verbs...

He would carefully and slowly twist his torso so that he would be able to see the tops of the classroom windows. He told himself that, if he were to look at a particular classroom window through the spaces between his fingers, and if he saw that the sky was cloudy, that would mean he would be safe. Or...if he were to slip a textbook from his desk and open it without looking, if the page number he spotted was even, that would be a sign: he would be able to sit up and remain unnoticed and unmolested for the rest of the school day.

Each of these futile attempts at comprehending and manipulating the strange, frightening world left him feeling bitter. Who was this God who was unwilling or unable to protect him?

Each of his teachers expressed concern. They had all seen shy, peculiar children who refused to talk, but this one was different. His second grade teacher, Mrs. Goldstein, referred him to the school speech therapist, straight-backed, angular, musty-smelling Miss Callahan. That rigorous lady sat at her polished oak desk on which every sheet of paper, every pencil and paper clip lay aligned in perfect symmetry, and peered down at him through thick-lensed tortoise shell glasses. He sat on a small wooden chair next to her. Miss Callahan repeatedly attempted to engage the boy in conversation.

"Anacleto, what do you like best about yourself?"

Unable to latch onto a thought, he remained silent.

"Anacleto, please repeat the following phrase." Her diction, phrasing, and pronunciation were old-world, precise, serious. "Anacleto, please say, 'My little friend loves to eat licorice.'"

Head down, hands covering his eyes, he tried to repeat the phrase.

"M...my wit...tle fw...fwiend w...woves to e...eat wic...wic... o...wis."

She patiently and repeatedly exhorted him to "Climb, climb, climb, Anacleto—just as Hillary conquered Mount Everest, so too can you reach the summit."

The clarity of his speech was unimportant to him, but Anacleto did feel guilty about not trying harder to improve because Miss Callahan put so much effort into attempting to correct his diction.

Two years of twice weekly speech lessons taught Anacleto how to use his lips, tongue, and vocal cords properly so that he could pronounce the initial *l* in words. Miss Callahan smiled austerely and applauded when he reached that verbal hilltop. It was a very helpful skill when he had to say hello and goodbye to his Aunt Lillian.

Miss Callahan's ample abilities, however, were not potent enough to help Anacleto to overcome his chronic stammering and stuttering or to reach the jagged precipice of his self-imposed isolation. She and his fourth grade teacher, Mrs. Cunningham, after a long, whispered discussion, decided that the source of his communication problems was deeper (or, to be more exact, higher in his head) than his lips, tongue, and vocal chords.

They referred Anacleto to sweet, bewigged Mrs. Collazo, who taught third grade and who acted as the unofficial school guidance counselor during some of her lunch breaks. He was overwhelmed with a cold, sweaty panic the first time he sat in the tiny custodial closet-turned office that Mrs. Collazo used for her sessions. The wildly expressive primary color paintings crafted by the children in her classes from year to year that covered the faded, cracked walls of that little room did not help the boy to overcome his alarm as he sat in the small, enclosed space. In fact, the dizzying designs added to his confusion. The lingering odors of ammonia and old paint, mingled with the aromas of whatever he and Mrs. Collazo had for lunch, aggravated his feelings of suffocation and exacerbated his inner turmoil and pushed his brain into overdrive.

Monday, Tuesday, Wednesday...

The only ventilation came from a small rectangle of grating at the bottom of the gray steel door that led to the basement-cafeteria-gymnasium of the elementary school.

Mrs. Collazo talked. And talked. She believed that if she talked enough, she could exorcise the demon that controlled the child's brain. He knew there was no hope. His peculiar brain was in full control of who he was, a thing to be despised.

However, after a while, Anacleto began to take comfort in Mrs. Collazo's lovely sing-song grandmotherly voice as she described meals that she had prepared and shopping trips she had made. She told him wonderful stories about her twin daughters and their husbands and the many grandchildren who brightened her days.

Listening to her non-stop conversation relieved some of Anacleto's tension and allowed him to focus.

Anacleto sat across from her, a small, round wooden table between them, his head down, his hands covering his eyes. She instructed him in the appropriate way to sit for meals: straight against the back of his chair, head erect, arms at his sides or folded in his lap. She placed blue and red plastic dinnerware pieces on the table and explained how to hold utensils and how to cut food with a knife.

She said, "You're supposed to hold your fork in your left hand and cut your meat with the knife in your right hand. Then you have to carefully lay down your knife and switch the fork to the right hand for eating."

Anacleto pictured Mrs. Collazo in her home, enjoying a Sunday dinner, except that in his scrambled mental renderings of the scene all of her family members sat at small school desks, their hands folded on their laps, while she stood before them, tomato sauce-stained wooden spoon in hand, instructing them in table manners.

Occasionally, she would narrate a travelogue about one of her many "lovely trips to Italia." She was good. The boy could picture the ancient mountain villages and the goats and the crumbling old churches. He smelled the cheese and the wine.

He also smelled the rotting corpses under the altars.

She hugged him a lot too. He didn't mind. But he didn't respond.

They role played with dolls. One of them, a Raggedy Andy, had a damaged left hand. Anacleto chose that one. Mrs. Collazo used Raggedy Anne. Raggedy Anne talked and talked and talked. Raggedy Andy listened, his eyes fixed on his companion, his two hands at his sides. Anacleto held Andy on his lap and stared at the top of his wooly head.

***

Anacleto was never placed in the "Dumb Class" because, despite his peculiarities and his crippling inarticulateness, his grades on written work were always very good. He used to look at the boys in that class as they walked into the building from the schoolyard ahead of the other classes and wish that he was on that line. At least, there, he would have a friend or two…maybe. He understood that he did not deserve friends or even acceptance. It was appropriate that he was shunned. He was a sick, weak weed rotting in a far corner of the school garden where the wind-blown trash collected.

The place of decay.

Then, to his surprise, he did have a friend for a few weeks during this period of his life. Robbie Feinstein moved to the neighborhood from Westchester and, before he met the rest of the boys, he latched onto Anacleto. Robbie was quiet and shy. Unlike the others on the street, who lived to compete in fierce, boisterous, riotous blood sports, Robbie liked playing in his house. His mother and father had filled every space in his cramped room with mechanical toys, games, action figures, and building sets in an attempt to make up for the fact that they had moved their only child from the large rooms and the spacious wooded backyard of their suburban house to the urban tightness of Brooklyn. Mr. Feinstein's commute to lower Manhattan, where he worked as a bank loan officer, had become too much for him, so they had decided to move into the city. They had chosen to rent the upstairs apartment of a house on the street where Anacleto lived.

They played together every day. Robbie did not mind Anacleto's silence. When he was with Robbie, Anacleto did not cover his face with his hands. Sometimes, they would sit on the carpet of Robbie's bedroom, silently playing with the collection of little toys that he kept in a small glass fishbowl. They would dig into the bowl and take out flexible rubber cowboys, Indians, soldiers, rigid plastic airplanes, and metal battleships. Raging battle scenes and airplane flights played out as they sat on that carpet. Robbie provided the dialogue and most of the sound effects. Anacleto heard only his head fog static…his secret sound track.

One day, at Robbie's house, Anacleto committed his first sin. Robbie was in the bathroom. Anacleto stared covetously at a perfect miniature reproduction of the *U.S.S. Nautilus*. He had begged his mother (the only one with whom he spoke full sentences) to buy a box of Rice Krispies just so he could have his very own Nautilus.

"It's fr…free…in the box, M…mom," he explained.

"But, you don't eat the cereal—nobody in the house does," she replied.

"But it's…fr…free. They sh…show it on TV—you o…open the b…box, and it's there!"

"No Rice Krispies."

"B…but, Ma, it fl…floats and, if y…you put ba…baking so…soda in it, it sub…submer …submer…goes down, and then it—"

"I said no!"

But, now, there it was, sitting in front of him, proud and lovely in naval gray, perfectly miniaturized. Real. To Robbie, it was just one of a hundred little toys that he owned. To Anacleto, it was perfection itself.

He slipped it into his pocket.

When Robbie returned from the bathroom, Anacleto mumbled that he had to go. Robbie watched in surprise as Anacleto bolted from his house.

He ran home, unlocked the door, rushed to the bathroom, and hurriedly turned on the bathtub taps, remembering to place the rubber stopper on the drain. Then he went to the kitchen and searched in the cabinets, pushing aside bottles of spices and packages of pasta until he found a box of baking soda. He brought it to the bathroom and locked the door.

As the tub filled with tepid water, Anacleto carefully removed the plastic plug at the bottom of the submarine and shook some baking soda into it. Then he replaced the plug and waited for the water in the tub to reach just the right level.

Satisfied that he had created a deep enough ocean for the world's first nuclear powered submarine, he shut the faucets. Then, on his knees, leaning forward against the side of the tub, he placed the tiny craft on the surface of the water.

He watched it float and then gently bump against the far side of the tub and then come to a stop. He carefully flicked it with a finger and watched it sail to the other side. Excited and proud, the boy knew it was real. With his keyed-up heart beating furiously in anticipation, Anacleto carefully grasped the streamlined little vessel with two fingers and, holding it under the surface, he rocked it from side to side. Then he brought it to the bottom of the tub. He released it. He held his breath. The submarine bobbed to the surface and floated. Then, after a few seconds, it submerged…and then it resurfaced, and submerged…

Anacleto's heart was full; he thought it would burst. He smiled. The little beauty was his. He began planning long distance voyages for it.

The phone rang, startling the boy. Just one ring.

He thought of Robbie and the fishbowl and of confession.

A searing pain radiated through his already overwrought brain; his stomach suddenly felt leaden and sour and twisted in knots. His hands turned icy cold. He washed the remaining baking soda from the toy and dried it, placing it in his pocket. Then he drained the tub and walked back to Robbie's house.

Anacleto stood in the doorway. Robbie's mother said that her son had gone out.

"I….haf…have….Could I….I…I th…think my k…k…key…"

She let him in. He walked to Robbie's room, pretended to look for his house key, and then guiltily returned the submarine to the fishbowl.

Robbie never knew. No one knew…except for Father Shandlin.

***

They were in the back of Anacleto's house in a two-foot wide space between two garages, pulling out tree branches, old boards, and rocks. They wanted to build a fort. Bending down and looking backwards and upside down through the space between his legs, Anacleto heaved a large rock to Robbie. As he looked forward to search for another piece of building material, he heard a thud and a cry.

He turned around. Robbie was holding his hands to the top of his head. Blood trickled down to his startled face. It fell in heavy drops to the ground.

Then Robbie ran home.

Anacleto stared at the pool of blood.

Blood....flood....dead...blood out...blood in...

A neighbor drove Robbie and his mother to the hospital.

As Anacleto stood on wobbly legs in front of his house watching the car speed to the corner, Mrs. Rinaldi, a childless neighbor, cast a wizened, venomous look his way and told him that he was a bad boy: "...always playing with rocks and sticks and hurting other children."

Not true. Not me. Other boys, dirty boys do that. Not me.

It wasn't fair that she thought of him in that way. He covered his face. The old lady wasn't there anymore. She had never been there.

If I look in a mirror, I won't be there.

Sixteen stitches were needed to close the wound on Robbie's scalp. He forgave Anacleto, but Robbie's mother would not allow them to play with each other. A month later, Robbie and his family moved away.

***

One Fourth of July, when he was ten, Anacleto was drawn from his house by the rhythmic booming of a drum—many drums—coming from the street. He ran to the corner, just in time to see a combined Boy Scouts, Sea Cadets, and Army Reserve parade. His bony body vibrated in rhythm with the loud percussion and squeaky brass of the bands. He felt the music travel from his head to his groin and down to his feet. It pushed the static from his brain.

Later, he asked his mother if he could join the Boy Scouts.

"What you wanna do that for?" she asked.

"I...dunno. I...th...think it's n...nice."

"No. It's not for you. I don't want you going there."

"But, Ma—"

"No. It's not for you. You don't need that."

That Christmas, she bought a bright red, white, and blue cloth jacket for him. It was two sizes too big so that he would be able to fit into it for a few years. He wore it every day, even during the summer. When he outgrew it, his mother bought an identical one, again two sizes larger than what he needed.

James and Frank, the two brothers who were the closest in age to Anacleto, wanted to know why he got a new jacket when they always had to wear Ronnie's and Georgie's cast-offs. Their mother told them that Anacleto needed to have the special jacket.

"Anacleto, look at yourself in your bee-u-tee-ful new jacket in the mirror. Go ahead…go in my bedroom."

He dutifully walked into his parents' bedroom, but he did not look in the mirror. He waited for a few seconds, staring at the bed…the bed where he had been made; then he returned to his mother.

He never looked at his reflection. Why would he want to? He did not want to…know.

***

Lucia told people to leave Anacleto alone and to stop asking questions about him. She complained that all of the attention caused her child to act strangely.

She assured Anacleto that she loved him and that he was fine the way he was.

One day, she told him, "This whole family…it's a little nuts."

She would laughingly explain to people that, sure, the boy was a little odd, but she wasn't concerned.

"He'll snap outta it when he discovers girls," a neighbor replied.

"God forbid," Lucia exclaimed. "He don't need no girls."

Anacleto could not imagine that there was anything about girls worth discovering. Besides, he hadn't figured out boys his own age.

I wasn't meant to live with people. I like cats, dogs, birds, all animals, but Mom won't let us have pets—not since Buddy died.

Buddy had been the family parakeet. He had sleek, smooth feathers—emerald and lemon and cobalt with a trace of snowy white; he almost talked. Lucia had bought him because her favorite cousin, Renee—the boys had to call her "Aunt Renee"—a hard, beautiful, chain-smoking renegade who cursed like a sailor, seemed to derive so much pleasure from her parakeets. Renee waved away a cloud of cigarette smoke and said, "Lucy, look at my beautiful boys: they are so fuckin' smart. Listen to them talk, the little bastards."

Lucia was always shocked at Renee's easy use of that kind of language; she would slap her knee and laugh. She used basically the same language, but only when she was angry, which was three or four times a day. Even though Anacleto was rarely the cause of his mother's anger, since he spent so much time at home with her he always believed that the red-hot storms of vituperation and obscenity that exploded from her mouth were directed at him.

She bought Buddy. After about a week, no one else in the family even looked at him, so he became Anacleto's pet. The boy happily walked through the house with the little bird's delicate, cold claws wrapped tightly around an outstretched finger. His smooth beak would gently peck and then rub against the boy's cheek.

He's my buddy. He makes me safe. I make him safe.

Buddy shed feathers and cracked seeds and seemed to be continuously defecating, and Anacleto did not always keep the cage clean. He used to let Buddy fly around the kitchen when they were the only ones home. Anacleto loved the rapid fluttering sound that Buddy's wings made as he darted from curtain rod to curtain rod and from the top of one kitchen cabinet to another. The sound obscured Anacleto's head static.

Buddy always came to Anacleto when he called. When Anacleto's finger brought Buddy to the door of his cage, the bird would unhesitatingly jump in and land on his perch. Buddy understood the arrangement.

Anacleto was not always diligent in his efforts to wipe up the spots of speckled white gel that Buddy released as he flew about the kitchen. Lucia, upon discovering a hardened lump on her stovetop or on a windowsill, would threaten to let the bird fly—right out the window.

"B…but he l…likes to fl…fly in the k…kitchen," he tried to explain to his enraged mother.

"He can *fly*. Let's see how he likes flying in the middle of the winter in Brooklyn," she threatened.

That is why, when Anacleto came home from school one day and found Buddy stiff and motionless in his mother's hand he did not, could not believe that she had found him dead at the bottom of his cage.

Anacleto took the cold, lifeless bird from his mother and cupped him, bringing the little body to his face. He inhaled the strange, familiar odor. Turning from his mother, he touched his lips to Buddy's velvety feathers.

Don't be dead. All my other prayers didn't matter. This one does. Please don't let him be dead. I love him. I'm a good boy. Please…

Inconsolable with grief for days, Anacleto mourned this loss with a dark, bitter sadness, one that was colder and more desolate than what he had felt when both of his grandfathers had died within a week of each other.

More even, than the death of his father.

He slipped a little deeper into his isolation.

***

Anacleto's father died on the boy's eleventh birthday. He had been sick. Anacleto knew that, but, in the way that children ignore what they do not comprehend, he never imagined that his father would actually die…go away from his life.

When Anacleto arrived home from school that day, he started to tell his mother that he had to go to the library to borrow books for a research report. Unlike most of the other children in his class, Anacleto was looking forward to doing it.

Anacleto's spinster aunts, two of his father's five sisters, were sitting at the small kitchen table with Lucia, crying. Anacleto looked down. Their sobs told the story. Even so, when his Aunt Marie stood up, put an arm around his shoulders, and walked with him down the long hallway, Anacleto was surprised by the heavy weight of another layer of reality.

She held him close and whispered, "Your father's gone."

His legs buckled, but she held him.

After an hour of attempting to combat the jumble of ideas, the new static that crisscrossed his brain, the sense of unreality that was more potent than it had ever been, he fell asleep. He awoke to the sounds of people...talking, sobbing, crying.

"Oh, no…I can't believe it! Oh…"

"Such a shame! I'm so sorry."

Anacleto watched cartoons on television.

"It's ok. Leave the boy."

The next few days were a blur.

Sweet flowers. Dead sweet. Like a dead cat…in an empty lot, but sweet. The cat on the shed roof...the dogs snarling…

Two grandparents…now his father. The grim news, the twisting in his stomach, spinning in his head; the wake, the funeral Mass, the burial, the food-laden table on the return from the cemetery were dismally familiar to him by now.

Heavy memories.

This one, his father's, a scar.

During this period of grief, the president was murdered.

Lonely woman…sad horse…a world of coffins.

Anacleto's brothers, who were supposed to take turns caring for the boy, continued to take turns ignoring him, hoping that one morning they would wake up to find that he had disappeared in the night.

They did not need to worry. He had never appeared.

He missed his father, not because they had ever had an intimate relationship. They had never came close to knowing each other. But, over the next few days and weeks, Anacleto missed him, especially at dinner time. He had always been fascinated, no, mesmerized by his father's ability to simultaneously eat, talk, and direct his wife as she brought food to the table while he tore through the pages of the *Daily News*. He would grunt and chew and talk and furiously turn pages, knocking over salt and pepper shakers, bowls of grated cheese, occasionally allowing the edges of his paper to fall into his food as he concentrated on a story that had caught his attention. The rest of the family had to squeeze close together, moving themselves and everything that was on the table, except for his food, away from him so as to avoid collisions with the flying pages of his newspaper.

He and Lucia and Anacleto's brothers talked and laughed during meals. Anacleto ate in silence. Then, with an upraised index finger, the anchor of the family would, without any preamble, read a headline. That meant he had found a story that he considered educationally beneficial to his boys, and he was going to read it to them. His notion of what was educational was…different. He read and expounded upon every salacious story that referred to movie stars and politicians. Also articles about bloody car accidents and plane crashes. Anacleto listened in horror to descriptions of savage stabbings, industrial accident maimings, and horrific burns suffered by victims of house fires. The boys smiled, while their mother frowned, as their father read and commented on the extramarital affairs of people in high places. He ignored most articles that dealt with government, politics, international relations, and almost everything else. Oh, yes...he read aloud every article having to do with the Yankees, especially his beloved Mick. He bitterly cursed the *Lost* Angeles Dodgers and gloried in their every loss. He skipped over news stories about their victories.

He greatly admired President Kennedy. He loved the man's youthful zest and the fact that Kennedy had served in the Pacific during the war, as he had. He always denied that he was proud that Kennedy was Catholic, but the boys knew that he was. And yet, their father had not, in their memory, ever been in a church except for funerals, first communions, and weddings. On a few occasions, Anacleto had asked his mother why that was, but she had always given vague replies. The boys had gone for religious instruction and they attended Mass every Sunday with their mother while their father slept late. When they arrived home, they would always find the sections of the Sunday paper spread haphazardly on the kitchen table, which also held their father's breakfast dishes and several cups, each partially filled with cold coffee. For some reason, when he was home alone, their father would fill a cup with coffee, drink some of it, put the cup down, and then fill another cup, sip some coffee, and put it down, until he had repeated the process four or five times.

No one ever understood why he did that.

SANTO

Anacleto did not need anyone, least of all the boys on his block. They could have their games and their jokes and their rivalries. They could also have Santo.

Santo Faricola.

Santo was the biggest and the oldest of the group of boys on the block where Anacleto lived, so he was in charge. All of the boys who were within a year or so of each other in age played together. Occasionally, boys from different age groups played with each other, but that was rare. More often than not, they just taunted each other. There was even more tension when it came to boys who lived on other blocks. Sometimes, there would be stickball or punch ball or softball challenges; they generally ended in heated arguments or bloody fist fights.

Santo had moved to the neighborhood recently. Even though he was more than a year older than the boys whose group Anacleto was nominally a member of, he spent most of his time with them, rather than the boys his age. None of the younger boys dared to protest. Since Anacleto generally hid out in solitary contemplation in his room, he was not concerned about this.

Santo was the organizer and the enforcer and the arbiter of justice as he saw it. When Santo made a decision, only the foolhardy dared to disagree.

One hazy summer day, Santo announced that he was forming a club. Anacleto had been hanging around at the fringes of the group all morning because his mother was cleaning the house and she didn't want anyone in her way. Santo announced that everybody would meet on the corner right after lunch and that each boy had to bring a dime as an initiation fee. Since his mother had finished cleaning when he got home, Anacleto decided to stay in. He never wanted to be with the boys. Besides, even if he had wanted to, where would he come up with ten cents?

At a little after one, Anacleto's doorbell rang. His mother answered it. She returned, red-faced, her mouth a twisted, angry weapon.

"Santo says you owe him ten cents. He says go to the corner. You shouldn't borrow money…or hang around with that sonofabitch. He's gonna get you in trouble some day."

She rummaged through her pocketbook and handed Anacleto two nickels.

"I…I…didn't…"

One look from her stopped him cold.

He met the others at the corner. After Santo had checked to make sure that each boy had his initiation fee, he started walking down the street. The other boys followed him, bubbling with excited conversation. Anacleto trailed behind, enveloped in a fog of anxiety and dread, cold sweat drenching his hands.

Santo stopped in front of Tischman's, the local candy store, and told the boys to turn the money over to him. Then he stepped inside.

When he emerged, he started walking again, and they followed. He led them to a large empty lot that abutted an abandoned freight rail line. They picked their way through the hilly, weedy woods, one of the last places in Brooklyn where large stands of trees could be found, except for those in parks. Finally, Santo stopped at a fallen giant, and sat down. The rest of the boys sat on either side of him. Anacleto remained standing.

"What do you have? What did you buy, Santo?" Albie asked.

"I'll show ya." Santo took from his pants pocket a pack of L & M cigarettes. After gently tapping it three times on his knee, he unwrapped the package and plucked a cigarette from it; then he placed it between his lips, struck a match, and inhaled deeply.

"Ok. You guys light up."

All of the boys did as they were told.

Anacleto sat on the ground, a few paces in front of them, his lips tightly closed, his head down.

"Come on, Anaconda. What are you, a baby snake?" Santo grinned at him through a cloud of smoke.

The others broke into raucous laughter as they exhaled ragged white clouds. One of them farted.

"Pig!" Santo shouted, and laughed, and then he farted.

This broke them all up. Then they competed with each other to see who could create the loudest blasts.

Anacleto smiled, his head still down, purposely not looking at the boys.

They can't see me. No one can.

"Come on, Puppy, take a drag."

He kept his lips shut.

"We know you're weird. This just proves it, Puppy."

Anacleto sensed, rather than saw, that Santo was holding his lit cigarette toward him. He scooted on his backside, moving away, and extending his hands to protect his multi-colored jacket from the ashy cigarette. Then Santo got up from the log and, standing in front of Anacleto, he waved the cigarette back and forth in front of the boy's face. Anacleto liked the smell, but he kept his head down, his hands covering his face.

Santo returned to his spot. The other boys talked and laughed and smoked. They were enjoying this forbidden pleasure. After a while, they began to blow smoke rings. Then they lit a small fire of twigs and roasted a variety of insects.

Anacleto looked at Santo through the spaces between his fingers; he was shaking his head and saying, "Poor kid. He oughta come outta his shell. And take off that fuckin' jacket! I tell ya he's a snake. Else he'd be dyin' of the heat."

Anacleto closed his fingers more securely over his eyes and tried to convince himself that he was alone in a dark, isolated corner of an abandoned house in a deep forest, far from the sounds and smells of people. He knew he could be happy there.

After sitting in the self-imposed darkness of that corner of that house for what seemed like hours, the head-buzzing static and the blurry noises around him, along with the strong smell of burning tobacco, sickened the boy. He felt weak and dizzy. He tried to stand, but couldn't. He slumped down. Then he slowly rose. Unsteadily, his head spinning, he looked at the group of boys. He turned and stared at the railroad tracks below. They were weed-covered, as was the rest of the landscape. Still, they led somewhere.

When he felt better, he turned back to the group and, grabbing a cigarette from one of the boys, he took a drag. His head fog thickened and intensified. He felt himself being lifted off the scrubby ground. He pulled himself back to earth and sat, hunched over, his hands on his face for another long while, lost in a maze of confusing thoughts.

Santo announced that it was time to go.

As soon as Anacleto walked into his house, he knew that his mother knew.

"Ma. They s…sm..smoked. I d…did too. I sh…should…sh…shouldn't—"

"What'd you say?"

She bolted from the house.

The next day, when he went out, he learned where his mother had gone. She had informed the mothers of all of the boys about their smoking club activities. She managed to argue with each and every one of them.

The boys wouldn't even let Anacleto stay on the fringes of the group for the rest of the summer. Not that he cared.

They all continued to smoke, some of them with their parents' approval, just to spite Lucia.

***

He had actually collided with Santo before the older boy had moved to the neighborhood. Anacleto had been in a stationery store, buying a ballpoint pen to give to his teacher as a Christmas present. As he walked from the store to his bicycle, which was parked in front, he heard and then saw, a short distance down the sidewalk, a large boy with long, filthy black hair being slapped repeatedly on his face by an even larger man. The boy crouched, covering his face with his arms.

The man stood over the boy and began punching, full force with both fists, the top of the boy's head. When the boy covered his head with his hands, the man slapped his face. Anacleto turned away and hunched over near his bicycle, holding his hands to his face. The repeated hammer-like thuds vibrated in his brain, short-circuiting the already jumbled electrical impulses. He shivered. After what seemed endless minutes of this sickening sound, it stopped.

Still crouching, he pivoted slowly and looked through the spaces between his fingers.

The man spat on the sidewalk near the still cringing boy and warned, "Next time I tell you to do something, you do it. No back-talk to me or your mother!"

Then the man smoothed back his hair with both of his hands and walked toward Anacleto. The dazzling early winter sun peeked through a break in the cloud-filled sky behind the approaching man and shone directly into Anacleto's eyes. Then, through the spaces between his fingers, he saw: the man glided toward him, propelled by the photons, bathed in the light. He was covered in blood—his hands and arms, his face, his white shirt were dark red, wet, glistening in the sunlight. Then, as the man came closer, walking now, Anacleto saw that there was only one small red spot of blood leaking from a perfectly formed hole on the left side of his shirt, over his heart. Blood trickled down. When the man passed, Anacleto saw that there was an identical spot on the back of his shirt in line with the other one. Blood oozed from that hole too, down his shirt, his pants, his shoes. The twin rivulets left an intertwined red trail on the sidewalk.

Anacleto understood that he was having one of his fuzzy, confused breaks from reality. Each time one of these episodes occurred, he knew who he was and where he was and when he was, but he felt that he was looking down from a distance…and not believing that what he saw was real. What was happening around him and to him was dream-like and ephemeral. He perceived the brightness of the real world from a place of coldness, blackness. He looked at it through a peephole.

I am Anacleto. I am on the sidewalk. This is real. It is Saturday. I am Anacleto…

It was always paralyzingly frightening; he would feel light-headed and chilled by these alarming breaks from the real world, the world around him.

People on the sidewalk looked at him disapprovingly. Their expressions and gestures revealed the depth of their disgust. They blamed Anacleto for what had happened to the boy. They felt that the man should have been hitting Anacleto.

That wasn't fair. None of them had helped the boy or tried to stop the man. The man with the bloody holes. But still, Anacleto felt guilty. He tried to tell himself that he couldn't have stopped the man.

Still crouching, Anacleto looked at the boy through the spaces between his fingers. He knew that the boy would kill his father some day.

"What the fuck you lookin' at?" It was the boy.

Anacleto didn't know what the right answer was, so he turned and began unlocking his bicycle chain. He sensed that the boy was moving toward him. Instantly, he was up and back in the stationery store. The boy followed; his sneakers squeaked as if they were wet. Anacleto moved quickly from aisle to aisle as the boy tried to grab him. The owner of the store, a little man with a German accent, told them to take it outside. Anacleto ran out. The boy followed. Anacleto dashed into the pizzeria next door, where he and the boy continued their frenetic ballet, this time around tables of people who were eating, drinking, and looking at them. The men behind the counter laughed and said something in Italian, and then one of them pushed Anacleto out the door and held the other boy behind for a minute.

I am Anacleto. This is real…

He had never been in a situation like this. Even though he was often teased and ostracized by other children, no one had ever pursued him like this.

He ran along the sidewalk, frantically trying to decide whether to head into another store or attempt to outrun the boy to his house. Anacleto worried that if he ran away, the boy might damage his bicycle. Of course, if he didn't run away...

For a big boy, he was quick. With one large hand that grabbed a bunch of jacket at the back of Anacleto's neck, the boy stopped Anacleto's forward motion and jerked him to a painful stop. He slammed Anacleto—hard—against the side of a parked car. The window glass was cold, hard. His nose and cheek hurt; a bitter stream of mucous dripped down the back of his throat.

Red vinyl upholstery...black rubber floor mats. Fuzzy dice hanging from the mirror.

The boy pressed his bulk against Anacleto and breathed into one of his ears, "You think it's a laugh that my asshole father slapped me around?" The smell of animal sweat and moldy clothes was overpowering.

Please, God, I don't want to get punched. Please…I'm not this bad…

"I…didna, I did…didn't…laff."

The boy pulled Anacleto from the car and turned him as if he were a toy so that now their faces were inches apart. Anacleto saw that the boy's cheeks were bruised and inflamed. He squinted: his cold, red eyes drilled into Anacleto's brain.

Into my darkness.

Anacleto looked down, saw the boy's old, worn-out sneakers. He wanted to tell the boy that one was missing a lace. The bath of cold sweat that slowly dripped from his neck to his crotch froze him.

I am Ana...

The boy lifted Anacleto's chin and slapped his cheek, but not hard.

"I bet your old man beats the crap out of you, and you cry."

Anacleto raised his hands to his face and peered from between his fingers.

I know...his pain, but I can't tell him I understand his shame.

"Well?" the boy sneered.

Anacleto knew that he had to say something, but he did not have the will or the strength to talk. He was in cold, murky, deep water and he didn't have the energy to swim. It was so much easier to stop moving and just sink to the frigid depths, and rest.

But he still had breath in his lungs.

"I bet you get on your knees and beg like a girl."

He tasted the water. Salty, sour, cold.

The boy punched Anacleto's arm. It hurt. Anacleto opened his mouth. The thought of drowning terrified him.

"I...don't have a f....father.....D...dead," he whimpered.

The boy relaxed his grip. He pried Anacleto's hands from his face. He examined his left hand. Then he looked at the other hand. He pushed Anacleto back to the parked car. Then he turned around and walked off down the sidewalk.

About a month later, Santo, his sister, Anne, and their mother moved into the downstairs apartment in Albie's house, next door to where Anacleto lived. For the first couple of weeks, whenever Anacleto was out and he saw Santo, he hunched over even more than usual. He hoped Santo would not recognize him. After a while, it was clear that Santo either did not remember their first meeting or that he had other things on his mind.

Santo's father appeared three or four days a week, always in the late afternoon, except for Saturdays, when he would arrive in the morning. He was never there on Sundays and he never spent the night in the apartment. Anacleto recognized the coughing sound of the man's old Buick as he started it, always at around 11 p.m.

Anacleto would lie in bed and wonder where he went.

***

One Saturday afternoon, when Anacleto was alone in his house, in bed reading, he heard the front door open and then quickly close. Then the inside lock clicked in place. He assumed it was one of his brothers. If it had been his mother, she would surely have called out to find out who was home. He didn't want to talk with anyone, so he continued to read. A short while later, he heard a vicious, heavy pounding on the door. Then more pounding. Louder and louder.

Anacleto went downstairs. Santo was crouching on the floor in a corner of the little foyer near the door, trying to appear small. He looked at Anacleto menacingly, then with a softer look. More pounding. The doorknob was being jiggled from the outside. More pounding.

"Open the door. Santo, come outta there! You're gonna get a worse beating if you don't open up."

Anacleto shivered with fear; then he looked at Santo, who mouthed, "Please." He turned from the boy hiding in the corner and looked at the door. The hammering became more violent.

The house, viciously slapped, was being ripped from the ground. Hot, rough-edged static blazed through his brain, paralyzing him. That and Anacleto's remoteness prevented him from moving a muscle even though he felt a degree of sympathy for the big boy who was cowering in the darkness of the entrance hall.

All he had to do…all that he could do was…to not do anything. He looked down at the floor. He felt weak. He sank down, crouching. He looked at Santo. The big boy was frightened. Angry. Ashamed.

The pounding continued. The sound reverberated in Anacleto's head, mixing with the painful electric rasping of his head fog. He covered his face with his hands. Then he looked at Santo again, this time through the special lens formed by the spaces between his fingers. He knew that something was going to happen; he sensed that it would be life altering. His heart throbbed in syncopation with the hammer blows on the door.

Santo squeezed himself lower to the floor and deeper into his corner.

Anacleto forced himself to stand; then he walked back up the stairs to the room that he shared with his brother, Frank, and lay on his bed. After a while, the pounding stopped. Then he recognized the sound of Santo's father's car starting and driving away. A few minutes after that, he heard the door being unlocked, opened, and then softly closed.

***

How strange it is that, of all people, Santo should have been the one who, in his brutish way, pulled Anacleto one small step up from his world of darkness to that of people.

It began on a breezy, cool, sparkling Saturday in April, the beginning of the baseball season. The New York Mets were beginning to attract what would become an impassioned following. This was exciting news for those who hated the Yankees; and for all of those who had still not healed from the injury caused by the middle-of-the-night desertion by the Brooklyn Dodgers, this was a new group of underdogs to love.

But baseball meant nothing to Anacleto.

He read books and newspapers and watched the news on television. He was terrified and fascinated by the violence and brutality of the world around him. It haunted him as he lay in bed at night in the small room.

He retained the image of the smiling, young president—dead.

Anacleto was eleven and a half.

Early afternoon. Anacleto was in the schoolyard because, after eating his lunch, his mother had insisted that he go out. Since there was nothing else to do outside, he had followed the neighborhood boys to the schoolyard. He didn't plan on playing ball. He never did. He listened, fascinated by the quick, foul-mouthed give and take of the boys as they played stickball. It was faster and more inventive than the dialogue in the books that he borrowed from the public library and consumed on a weekly basis—*Robinson Crusoe*, *The Good Earth*, *Wuthering Heights*, most of Dickens, all of them chosen from a list of summer reading books that had been given out in school one June. Occasionally, he read newer books with no enduring literary value. A trashy one that he read a number of times was called *The Tattooed Man*. It was a strange little paperback that he relished because he had bought it at a school book fair—one of the few times he had been given money by his mother for anything.

The usual, all-day stickball games were in progress in the schoolyard. Each group of boys took practice swings and threw grounders, all the while guarding the section of wall and schoolyard that they had chosen for their game. Santo hadn't shown up yet, but the triplets, Ralph, Bobby, and Carmine, after excitedly watching other groups of boys begin their games, had decided to start playing without him. Jimmy, Philly, Mike T., Mikey B., and Albie nervously looked in the direction of the schoolyard gate.

"Come on, retards, let's start the game," Ralph commanded.

When Santo wasn't around, the triplets, who were a few months older than the rest of the boys, took charge; of the triplets, Ralph was the oldest (by two minutes).

Anacleto marveled at their easy use of language. He felt that he was still a learner. He pretended he was the one yelling "Asshole!" or "Shit-for-brains!" or "Douche bag!" He sat against the chain link fence of the schoolyard, hands to his face, listening to the banter. About halfway through the game, Santo bulled his way past some younger boys who stood talking at the schoolyard entrance, and walked deliberately toward the boys from the block and their stickball game. The angry welts that bordered his red, puffy eyes told the story of why he was late.

Without a word, Santo walked up to Bobby, who was standing, stickball bat in hand, in front of the strike zone that had been white-chalked on the wall of the school, and kicked him in the rear so hard that he lost his balance and fell to the ground, dropping the bat. The boys watched it fall and roll away. None of them looked at Bobby as he rubbed grit from the palms of his hands onto his jeans and laughed nervously as he got up.

They all looked at Santo.

Santo's fiery glare ignited all of the other boys in the schoolyard. Anacleto watched in horror as they screamed and rolled on the ground, frantically trying to put out the flames. He held his breath as the last one stopped moving. Wispy orange flames and ashy smoke rose from the prostrate bodies. The smell was overpowering

What could I do? How could I stop it?

Then, with his red eyes almost closed, Santo counted, although this was hardly necessary; there were always eight boys. Santo made nine. It was usually Jimmy, Philly, Albie, and the two Mikes against Santo and the triplets.

"You, Puppy, you asshole, c'mere!" Santo lit a cigarette and took a long, deep drag.

Even though he was looking down, Anacleto knew Santo was talking to him.

"You…Shithead!"

Anacleto pretended not to hear.

I am Anacleto…

"Here, you fuckin' Anaconda. You're playin' today!"

He played. He joined Santo and the triplets. He was so overcome with cold, sweaty panic that he could barely stand. His surroundings were a blur, his body was limp, and his connection to the task at hand was nonexistent. He struck out six times. He dropped every ball that came his way. The more errors he made, the more confused and frightened he became.

"You suck, you fuckin' mad dog!" Santo snarled, and then spit on the ground.

What is this place? Who am I? Anacleto. Anacleto. Schoolyard…ball. Today, now… sweat…cold. I want to go home. Mom.

About halfway through the game, Anacleto told Santo that his stomach hurt and that he had to go home. Santo administered a lightning-fast punch to Anacleto's midsection, which doubled him over. Santo diagnosed his illness as "Puppy bullshit."

I just want to go home…to my bed…to my walls.

Anacleto's team was up. He leaned against the schoolyard fence, dreading the time when he would be called to bat again. He prayed for deliverance. He prayed to all of the gods and goddesses that his team would be out so he could be spared that frightening, confusing ordeal. The air was warm. He was soaked with sweat. The others were in tee shirts, their jackets in a pile by the fence. Anacleto's jacket was suffocating him. He unzipped it, allowing a feeble breeze to cool his chest.

He looked at the zip-out lining. It was composed of a fuzzy red material. He moved the zipper that held it in place a few inches. Then he scanned the ground around him until he spotted a jagged piece of green bottle glass. He picked it up and carefully sawed at a small section of lining, easily cutting through the nubby part, past the white cottony insulation, and through the other side. He pulled out the piece of lining, slicing off a few remaining threads. He held it in the palm of his weaker hand. It was soft and damp. Then he pushed the fragment of glass through the chain link fence, watching it fall and splinter on the sidewalk.

His palm was bloody. He dabbed the blood with the piece of lining. Then he carefully folded it into a small square and placed it in his jeans pocket. He removed the sweat-saturated jacket and laid it carefully on the ground next to the fence.

The game went on. Since Anacleto couldn't escape and because he hated the vile curses directed at him by Santo, he knew he had to try to play better. He attempted to stand straighter, to look more directly at what was around him.

During his next time at bat, he popped up. Then, in the field, he managed to stop and hold onto an easy grounder that came right to him.

"You suck, but not as bad as before," Santo commented matter-of-factly.

Anacleto was grateful for the break from the stream of angry profanity. He prayed that it would rain or that one of the boys would get hit in the face by a pitch or that a fight would break out somewhere in the schoolyard, but the game went on without interruption.

Finally, Santo decided that it was time for a run to the candy store. Anacleto didn't have any money, so he stayed outside, guarding the pile of jackets, stickball bats, and the ball that lay at his feet. He held his jacket in his hands.

The stickball bats were easy to come by; they were just broom handles, usually with black electrical tape grips. But the pink rubber Spalding balls that were referred to as *Spaldeens* cost fifteen cents each. During the course of a stickball game, it was not unusual for a hard-hit ball to be knocked over the schoolyard fence. Sometimes it was easy to find—under a parked car or in a front yard, but there was always the possibility that it would be lost forever—down a storm sewer or out of reach on a flat roof or…just gone. Sometimes a ball would split on its seams. What followed were cursing, threatening arguments about who was going to pay for a new one. If, at the beginning of the game, the owner of the ball had called "chips," all of the others would have to "chip in" to pay for a new one.

While the others were in the candy store, Anacleto patiently waited. He hoped that when they emerged, one of them would offer him a sip of Coke or a bite of a pretzel stick. The triplets came out first, followed by the others. They walked down the street, back to the schoolyard, sharing their sodas and nibbling their snacks. Anacleto followed, wishing he could go home. The boys sat in a shady spot near the rubble of the fenced-in school vegetable garden that, somehow, every summer, sprouted corn that someone—they never knew who—had planted. Anacleto sat near them, examining the cracks in the asphalt. The boys ate their pretzels and Three Musketeers and drank their sodas and ignored him. Then Santo reached into his zippered jacket, the one that he had put on right before he had entered the store, and pulled out two bags of potato chips, a package of Oreos, a few twists of black licorice, a pack of Marlboros, and a new *Spaldeen.*

Where? How? How could...his soul...his eternity...

The boys laughed and shared in the booty.

Anacleto thought back to the time, a year earlier, when he had been accused of stealing. A few of the people on his street received regular deliveries from a soda truck. The big truck would double park in front of a house; the driver would jump down from the cab and roll up one or two of the sliding doors on the side of the truck, revealing racks of wooden boxes filled with soda—cream, ginger ale, black cherry, and bottles of seltzer. He would load a few of those boxes onto a handcart and wheel it to the houses of the customers. He would return with empty bottles that he would load onto a different set of racks in the truck.

When the truck would pull up, the other boys would continue playing. Anacleto would watch the delivery man. One day, while the man was at someone's house delivering soda, Anacleto noticed a small, yellow rubber cowboy perched on the lip of one of the empty soda boxes that was in a rack on the side of the truck.

"Howdy, pardner," he seemed to be saying.

Anacleto pried him loose from the box. The cowboy was grateful. He moved slowly and warily from one soda box to another. He walked along the side of one of the craggy rises, looking for his horse. It had run off during the night. The cowboy climbed higher to get a better...A sharp bolt of lightning shot from Anacleto's buttocks to the back of his head. He dropped the cowboy and put his hands to his rear. As he started to turn around, he saw the delivery man's foot coming at him for a second blow. This one caught his hands and the small of his back. He hurtled forward, falling to the street.

"You stinkin' little thief." The man roughly put the empties and the handcart in the truck. Then, looking at the prostrate boy with contempt, he climbed into the cab and drove off.

Anacleto stood up and gently rubbed his sore back. The other boys, who had stopped to look at the comical scene, shook their heads and laughed.

The yellow cowboy lay scraped and blackened on the street, a casualty of a rear tire of the big truck. Anacleto's back hurt him for three days. He did not tell his mother.

He kept the yellow cowboy.

"Hey, Pup…you in this world?"

Anacleto hunched over more and began to cover his face.

"Pup, you want some?" Santo held out the bag of cookies.

Anacleto looked up at Santo and smiled.

"You gotta do something. You gotta stop that face-covering bullshit. You ain't a little kid no more."

They all looked at Anacleto.

"Leave him alone, Santo. Don't give him a hard time." Albie had a soft heart.

"I'm not! I wanna help the kid. You're twelve, right?"

Anacleto slowly, deliberately lowered his hands and shook his head no. "S…sev…seven m…months…N… Novem… ber," he said.

"Look," Santo continued, "if you wanna get over this bullshit, do it now, and you can be one of us."

"It's his name, Santo," Albie explained. "He hates it, so he hides his face."

"It's a pretty shitty name," Santo observed, with a smile.

They all laughed. One of them said something about Anacleto's left hand. Then someone shushed him.

"If we give you a new name, you gotta stop being weird. Okay?" Santo asked.

Anacleto looked at Santo.

"It's Anacleto Rooz-velt, right?"

Anacleto shook his head.

"They don't never call you anything else, just Anacleto, right? Something short, like …Cleto?"

No. Just Anacleto.

He waited, knowing that there was no other name.

"Anna?" They all laughed. "No. That's like my sister's name—Anne. No good. … Annabelle?" They laughed again.

Then, looking very pleased with himself, Santo smiled and said, "I got it…"

Anacleto peered through the spaces between his fingers for what he hoped would be the last time. As he looked, he knew Santo would die in prison.

"Clete," he announced, "…like Clete Boyer. He ain't a champ, but you ain't neither. How about it? If we call you Clete, can you stop being a jerk?"

I'll try, but I'll always be a jerk.

***

After Anacleto's father's death, his mother never entered a church again except for weddings, confirmations, and other life cycle events and she never pressured her sons to go. Anacleto's brothers stopped attending Mass immediately. He continued to go. He prayed that he could believe in prayer. He waited out the long, tedious service in the old neighborhood church, not permitting himself to walk out until the end, trying to convince himself that it all meant something.

Then, one Saturday afternoon, after reading a chapter in a history book about the abuses of the Roman Catholic Church and the beginnings of the Protestant Reformation, he asked the shadowy image on the other side of the partition in the dark of the confessional booth whether he thought that Martin Luther was burning in Hell. The priest, after a few seconds of reflection, answered, "No."

Anacleto began leaving before Mass was over. He would walk home slowly, stopping every so often. Then, one Sunday morning, after his twelfth birthday, he walked right past the church. He sat on a park bench for an hour. Then he went home.

He didn't tell his mother, not that she would have cared. Her attitude was that Jesus had taken her husband, the love and the rock of her life, so she didn't need Jesus. Anacleto did not tell her because he wanted his decision to be part of his life, without the involvement of anyone else. His secret.

Anacleto's mother respected secrets. To her, almost every word in every conversation was a secret in and of itself. It didn't matter whether they were her words or if she was simply holding them for others. If it could be verbalized, there was a good chance that it was a secret. She considered some of the most mundane details of her life classified. Her age. If anyone ever discussed her age, she would be transported into red-faced, steaming, screaming fits of rage and run away from the conversation. What she ate for dinner. That was always to be kept within the family. She never told anyone what she spent for…anything, from a house repair to a head of lettuce.

She had become even more secretive after her husband died.

So, it came as no surprise that she would not answer Anacleto's questions about what was in the attic of their crumbling old house. Anacleto burned with curiosity to discover what lay in that unknown place above his head.

Perhaps, if he had been a more typical boy, with friends and activities to occupy his time, he wouldn't have been so curious.

Then his story and what happened to Santo would have been very different.

***

One day, after school, while his brothers were out playing and his mother was at work at the clothing factory where she was undoubtedly bent over her sewing machine, concentrating on her work and keeping her family secrets, Anacleto opened the hall closet, the ceiling above which had a wooden hatch that led to the attic. He squeezed the ladder that he had taken from the garage into the closet, pushing it against the shelves that were laden with disorganized piles of towels, stacks of canned goods, cleaning supplies, and boxes of bills, receipts, and other papers. He carefully climbed the ladder until he was right below the wooden hatch. It was heavy. As he lifted it and pushed it into the attic, a shower of dust fell on him and into the closet. He climbed to the top step of the ladder and entered another world. Outside, the air was fragrant and warm, but in this place, it was cold and the smell of decay was strong. He pulled the cord on the light fixture, but the bulb was dead. Some rays of light from the gable vents filtered in through the dust that he had raised.

There was roof sheathing above and rafters below. Nothing else. The house was old, so there was no insulation. A dusty, chilly, musty wasteland. Anacleto boosted himself up and sat on a rafter, propping his feet on another one, and closed his eyes. Unlike the basement of his house, which was to him a source of unending fear, this place soothed him. After a few minutes, he shifted his legs so that they hung down the opening.

Then he saw it. An old, narrow wooden cheese box was wedged in the space between two rafters a few feet from where he was. Slowly, carefully, he inched toward the box and lifted it. Heavy. Then, sitting as he had before, he brought the box to his lap. It was grimy with dust. The lid would not slide open. He placed it near the attic hatch; then he swung his legs down the opening and onto the top step of the ladder. He retrieved the box and, holding it against his chest, he moved down a couple of steps, closed the hatch, and climbed down. He decided to put the ladder away and clean off the dust that had fallen into the closet before opening the box. He pushed it under his bed.

He needed a screwdriver to force open the lid, but his father's tools were in the basement. He shivered as he descended the splintery, creaky wooden stairs, all of the basement lights on, a lit flashlight in his hand, calling out, "Here…I…I am. I'm c-c-coming d-down."

I'm…fine…this is silly. It's just a creepy old basement.

Back in his room, as conflicting feelings of heady excitement and heart-thumping anxiety coursed through his body, he slipped the screwdriver into one of the spaces along the side of the lid, and slid it open. He saw a lumpy, filthy blue rag, folded over and tied with a frayed cord. He removed the heavy cloth bundle from the box and laid it on the floor. He slowly, patiently untied the knot in the cord, and spread open the cloth.

There were three small metal pistols.

Cap guns!

He picked up one of them. It was silver colored and cold and heavy. The hammer was hard to pull back. He managed, with great effort, to lock it in place. There was a hole in the breach where he imagined a cap of some sort could be placed. When he pressed the trigger, the hammer slammed down hard.

Clack!

The hard metal-on-metal sound was brutal and harsh; it was too dangerous sounding for a cap gun. He began to think they might be real pistols.

He wanted to show them to a friend, but what friend?

Who…? Do I really want to be close to someone?

He wondered whether he would have to talk to his friend each time he saw him. Would they always have to do something? What about when others came along? Would those boys have to join them and would they be his friends too?

His head hurt more than usual, thinking about this.

He wrapped the guns in the cloth again, placed them back in the box, and hid it in the garage. He decided that he would return it to the attic the next day after school. He was filled with the dark, heavy feeling that he should not have brought the box down from the attic. It was a dusty relic that did not belong to him...it was a connection to a world he should not enter...even touching it may have been a mistake.

That evening, as the family sat down to the usual Friday night meal of breaded, desiccated flounder and mushy vegetables swimming in tomato sauce, Lucia announced that she wanted to tell them about a dream. The boys knew that when their mother began a sentence with those words their lives were about to change. Anacleto remembered the dream that she had related a couple of years earlier; in that one, she and one of her cousins were in a theater in Long Island watching *Casablanca.* In this version of the movie, Ingrid Bergman was in love with Mr. Santorino, the man who sold fresh eggs at the farmers' market on 86th Street. In the dream-movie, the two lovers ate popcorn while they watched themselves on the screen in the theater. Then they choked on their popcorn. This intersection of the sublime and the mundane was, to their mother, a clear warning: the boys were not to go to the movies.

For about two weeks, Lucia enforced the movie ban, but then she seemed to forget about it.

Almost every Saturday, Anacleto's brothers would spend the day in one of the local movie theaters with the rest of the boys who were their friends. Coming up with the half dollar each for admission, candy, and a drink was hard work but almost guaranteed if they followed the script. Of course, they should have had their own money—they all had part time jobs—but they always seemed to have empty pockets. What they did was, beginning on Friday night, they would tell their mother about the wonderful movie that was being featured the next day, and then they would ask for money. She would refuse. On Saturday morning, they would beg and promise the world to her. She would adamantly shake her head. At noon, the two younger ones would cry and the two older ones would complain that everybody had nicer mothers than they did. After a few minutes of that, she would unhappily open her pocketbook and give each of them two quarters, repeating the reminder that no one should know how much money they had.

Anacleto went to the movies only when his brothers invited him to go along with them. That happened on those occasions when it was clear that they were not going to get any money from their mother in the usual way. One of them, usually George or Ronnie, the oldest ones, would whisper to her that Anacleto needed a day out.

"Mom," one of them would say, "Look at the little guy. He doesn't do anything but watch cartoons and read all day."

They would all look at him, shaking their heads sadly.

"You know, we're his only friends."

Lucia would complain that work was slow that week and she couldn't afford to part with the money, now $2.50 since Anacleto would be included in the excursion to one of the movie theaters that was within walking distance of their house. She was lying, of course. When work at the garment factory was slow, she collected union benefits and unemployment insurance. Besides that, she received a Social Security check for each of her sons each month.

The week before her latest dream revelation, they had used the "poor Anacleto" ploy to wring money from her.

"There's a good movie playing, Mom. It's *Zorba the Greek*. It's history. It's good for our brains." George tapped his forehead with one finger, and winked.

"I don't know. I don't have no money to throw away."

"It's about the Jews, Mom. You always tell us to be smart like the Jews."

"No. You're trying to fool me. You said *Zorpa the Greek*, not *Zorpa the Jew*."

"It's Zor-ba. He's a Greek Jew. There's Jews in Greece."

"I don't know. I don't have—"

"Come on, Ma. You know you're gonna feel bad if Anacleto spends the day in the house."

They all looked sympathetically at Anacleto.

"I'll give you the money for the movie, but that's all. No candy. Use your own money."

She gave a quarter to each of the boys.

All the way to the theater, Anacleto's brothers tried to convince him that they should hold his money. This, of course, was in preparation for their running ahead of him into the theater and leaving him behind without a penny. This had happened a couple of times before. He had not minded because, on the few occasions that he had sat through a Saturday feature, the noise and tumult and the assorted smells always upset him. The assault on his senses brought on a prolonged, agonizing break-with-reality event. He would sit low in his seat, looking at the screen through the spaces between his fingers, not comprehending the action of the movie.

I am Anacleto. I am here. This is a movie. I am Anacleto...the movie's not real...I'm real.

The best efforts of the white-haired, white-uniformed, flashlight-armed "matrons" who patrolled the aisles in an attempt to keep order were no match for the hundreds of raucous, candy-throwing boys and girls who filled the theater.

While his brothers immersed themselves in the chaotic atmosphere of the movie house for four or five hours, watching a double feature, cartoons, a nature documentary, and coming attractions, all the while joining in the revelry, Anacleto generally lay on his bed, reading. Sometimes, he would sit in the local library, embraced by his jacket, transported to other, better worlds.

But he wanted to see this movie because he had read the book. He held his money tightly in his hand.

When they reached the theater, Anacleto's brothers strolled in to see *Bikini Beach*. Surprised that *Zorba the Greek* was not playing there, Anacleto remained in place for a few minutes. Then he walked home.

"I'll tell you about my dream"

Lucia closed her eyes and smiled sweetly.

"I was with your father, may he rest in peace, and your father's cousin, Connie. You know, the one with the dyed blond hair and the crooked teeth. So, we were on a, on a, you know, where you walk…by the beach…"

"A broadwalk," George offered.

"Yeah, a broadwalk."

"It's *boardwalk*, Mom," Frank corrected.

"What? Oh, yeah. Well, we were walking and eating hot dogs. They were soooo good!"

"Let's have hot dogs tomorrow," James suggested.

"What? No. I'm making roast beef tomorrow. Anyway, we were having such a good time. But then, it's kinda confusing, but, all of a sudden, we're in front of the church and I'm ashamed about the hot dog. I don't know why. But then, Father DeCosta is there. You know,…the priest that disappeared one Sunday before Mass and no one never heard from him again. He says to me—Connie is out of the dream now—he says, 'No more hot dogs.' Then, you know how it is in dreams, he's not Father DeCosta no more...he's Mr. Weintraub...you know, the old man with the Jewish hat down the street."

The boys waited for the interpretation of the dream, but, at this point, their mother started eating her fish.

"What's it mean, Mom?" Frank asked.

"Okay, I'll tell you. It was a regular hot dog, not a kosher one."

With that, she smiled knowingly and resumed eating.

"What do you mean?" two or three of them asked at the same time.

"It means we're supposed to be Jewish."

The only sound was that of their mother chewing her dry fish.

"What?" George looked stricken.

"Look, our name's already Jewish—Rooz-velt. Your father never talked about it with me, but I always thought he was a Jew. After all, how many old-timers like him had a circumcision?"

Anacleto's brothers were mortified. He was curious. He knew he was circumcised; he had always thought that what he and his brothers had was what every boy had. He had never known that *it* could look a different way, that it could be uncircumcised. And he had never heard about the Jewish connection.

"I don't want to be Jewish," Frank whined.

Their mother just smiled and pulled a fish bone from her mouth. Anacleto suspected that his brothers' talking, the week before, about how Zorba was Jewish was what had inspired their mother's nighttime revelation that they should join their Hebrew neighbors in their spiritual journey to the Promised Land.

The family conversion did not mean very much. They still had fish on Friday nights and they celebrated Christmas and Easter. None of them went to church anyway, except when they had to for family occasions. Anacleto still liked the atmosphere in church and the smell of incense; he held onto a remnant of his former spiritual connection to God there, but not enough to attend Mass.

However, since, by their mother's edict, they were all Jewish now, she *schlepped* (her word) the boys along with her as she shopped around at the synagogues in their neighborhood. At each one, the rabbi or the president of the congregation explained to her that she would have to learn how to read Hebrew and know how to pray in a synagogue. After that, if she was serious about conversion, the rabbi would explain the procedure. Her boys, she was told, would have to attend Hebrew School. All of them would have to go to Friday night and Saturday morning services and observe all of the religious traditions.

Their mother asked if there was a shortcut.

One rabbi, a bent little man with a salt and pepper beard and a colorful yarmulke on his shiny bald head, laughed, and in Yiddish-accented English said, "You know, my dear, you vant to make the chicken soup, you can do it the rrrr-ight vay or you can open a can of Campbell's."

Lucia, without losing a beat, told him that Campbell's was good enough for her. The rabbi, laughing again, told her that Campbell's wasn't kosher.

When he explained how much lessons for her plus Hebrew School tuition for the boys and membership in the synagogue would cost, she told him he was a *ganif.* She hadn't lived in a mixed neighborhood for over twenty years with her ears closed.

Walking home, she told her sons that eating matzoh every so often and saying that they were Jewish was sufficient. She had never understood much about her Christian faith, so being an uninformed and unobservant Jew fit right in with her religious practices.

Anacleto had gone to school with Jewish boys and girls his whole life and he knew something about their beliefs. But now, he wanted to know more. He thought that this might be what he needed to help him to navigate the treacherous waters of his life.

He read a few books about Jewish holidays and practices and got halfway through a basic Hebrew book, having learned the alphabet and a few words, before deciding that the amount of effort required to learn a language that he would never use was too great. But he still wanted to learn about being Jewish.

One day after school, he sat in the neighborhood library leafing through a copy of *Genesis* in English and Hebrew. It was part of a leather bound set of *The Five Books of Moses.*

"You want to be one of us?"

Anacleto looked up. It was Stanley Alperovitz. He lived around the corner. On occasion, the boys on the block would allow Stanley to play stickball with them because he could throw a knuckleball and a slider.

Anacleto lowered his head and started to cover his eyes with his hands. Then, with a purposeful effort, he put his hands on the book, lifted it up and pretended to read. He hoped Stanley would go away. Instead, the boy plopped down a big pile of books, sat down across from Anacleto, and began writing in a notebook.

After a minute, he stopped writing, looked up, and said, "It's okay, you know."

Anacleto raised his head a little, and saw a smile.

"I...I'm just r...reading," he explained.

"I can see that."

"I...it...it's n...nothing."

"No. It's good. I know a lot about being Catholic."

Stanley didn't say "Cat-lick," as did most of the people Anacleto knew, his family included. Just about everybody Anacleto knew was either Catholic or Jewish. Actually, they were either Italian-Catholic or Jewish. Since he read widely, he knew there were other kinds of people. He even knew, that, contrary to what the boys in his neighborhood believed, Italians and Jews did not comprise most of America's population.

That level of understanding had astonished Carl Larsen. He and Anacleto had been among the few in class one year during the Jewish High Holy Days. About half of the students at their junior high had stayed home for religious reasons. James and Frank, having decided that they would stay home on every Jewish holiday that classes were in session, were absent from high school that day. Anacleto could have done that too, but he wanted to maintain his perfect attendance. George and Ronnie had both graduated from high school by that time and were working, waiting to be drafted.

Carl mumbled a few words about what a waste of time it was being in a half-empty class. They had never spoken with each other before, but, of course, Anacleto did not speak to anyone in school.

"You, know," Carl confided, "I'm not Italian and I'm not Jewish."

Anacleto, forcing his hands to stay down by gripping the sides of his desk, replied, "I k...know; you're Luth...Luth...eran—Norwe...we... wegian."

Carl almost fell out of his chair.

In a neighborhood in which the typical name was Bruni, Parelli, Braunstein, or Levy, "Larsen" seemed exotic. No one had ever shunned Carl, but he knew that he did not fit in with the others. His pale, freckled skin and white-blond hair marked him as different—although not as much as Anacleto's weirdness stigmatized him and kept him apart from the others; Anacleto's uniqueness, the visceral, instinctive distaste that his very appearance engendered in most of the people whom he encountered was obvious and talked about, as in "There's Anna-clee-to! Don't let him t...t...touch y...you."

It was who he was.

Even though Carl's white bread appearance was starkly different from that of the majority of students at the school, most of whose ancestors had fled the Mediterranean and Eastern Europe to enter this land of opportunity, he was treated politely, but from a distance. No one could imagine him eating a slice of pizza.

It was the same for the four or five Hispanic and Asian students at the school. The half dozen or so "colored" students, however, inhabited a peculiar netherland: the two boys were respected athletes and the girls seemed to walk and talk with a rhythm that was in harmony with the soul music that was fast becoming the favorite of every white boy and girl in Brooklyn. Most of the white students in the school, with the exception of a few bottom dwellers, treated the black students like fascinating visitors from a distant and exotic country. They were smiled at and invited to sit and talk. But, once the bell rang at the end of the day, the black students traveled home together, apart from the rest of the boys and girls. It was unthinkable for white and black students to actually be friends. The black kids knew that. Perhaps they didn't want white friends.

But, poor Carl: it was clear that he wanted in. It was not to be; at least, not now. Anacleto assumed that *he* would never be let in.

He wasn't knocking.

Stanley continued, "I've been in church a few times. It's kinda creepy, but it was nice at the same time."

Anacleto had been in Stanley's house when he was younger. He used to go to other boys' houses then. He had also been invited to birthday parties before the boys began to think that he was too bizarre to be around. Stanley's family kept a kosher kitchen, but Stanley ate whatever the other boys ate when he was out of his house. Once, when Anacleto was at Stanley's house for lunch, he had asked for a glass of milk; Stanley's mother looked at the hamburger on his plate, and frowned. He was also there on a Friday afternoon in the winter, when sundown came early, and Stanley's father asked Anacleto to turn on a light for him. He didn't understand why he had been asked to do that, but he knew it had something to do with the yarmulke that Mr. Alperovitz wore when he was in his house. He had an office job in Manhattan.

Manhattan—the city—was a wondrous, alien place. On the occasions when Anacleto had been there, around Christmas to visit Saint Patrick's Cathedral and to see the tree in Rockefeller Center and the magical department store windows on Fifth Avenue, the people he saw seemed so different from the ones in his Brooklyn neighborhood. They looked American. They could have been actors and actresses. Some of them probably were. Anacleto understood, from the clothes that they wore and the confidence with which they strode down those busy sidewalks, that many of them had money.

Of course, he saw wretched people too; they horrified him. Some of them were obviously intoxicated. Some slept right on the sidewalk. Police officers, in their blue double-breasted uniforms, would rap their night-sticks on the ground next to the sleeping people to rouse them or else they would roughly push them from the busy sidewalks into alleyways.

There were unusual people on the subway platforms and on the trains. There were blind people with white-tipped canes, their unseeing eyes covered by dark sunglasses; some of them held the leashes of large, obedient seeing-eye dogs; one man played a saxophone. He had a tin cup for donations clipped to his belt.

There was a man with no legs who used his hands to propel himself along the length of the subway car, riding on an old wooden dolly with screechy wheels. Anacleto had seen many lost souls who argued with invisible adversaries. He looked with great sympathy at those unfortunates. He did not cover his eyes with his hands.

Then there was the man with the swollen tongue. Anacleto had been alone at the Canal Street station the first time that he had seen him. The man's tongue, or maybe it was his bottom lip, was red, inflamed, distended. It protruded from his face, looking like a swollen, erect penis. He was the saddest-looking man Anacleto had ever seen. Anacleto glanced at him and then turned away to wait for his train. He knew the man wanted to be left in peace.

The second time that he saw him, months later, Anacleto was with his mother. They were coming home from a visit to Aunt Renee, who lived in the Bronx. The man entered the subway car. All of the other passengers seemed to be aware of the man's presence from the second he walked through the doorway. They looked, some scarcely able to disguise their feelings of shock and revulsion. Anacleto gave him a fleeting look. The man wanted to be left alone. Anacleto understood that. After a few seconds, everyone turned away from the man. Everyone except for Anacleto's mother. Her eyes, riveted on the man, were large and round and her mouth was open wide. The tip of her curled tongue extended from her mouth, almost as if she were attempting to imitate the man's deformity.

Then, a sound, low and hissing, emerged from his mother's still open mouth. Anacleto looked at her in horror. Everyone turned. The man froze in his tracks as he was about to take a vacant seat.

Then she began to howl and scream, pushing her hands to the sides of her head as she bellowed.

"Oh, oh, oooh!! My Gawddd!! Oooooh!!! Yow! Yow! Ah, ah, ahhhh!"

For a few seconds, Anacleto sat frozen. Then he acted.

Despite his desperate, strenuous efforts to control her, his mother continued her paroxysm of animal-like yowling for close to a minute, during which time the disfigured man slouched in his seat and raised his newspaper to cover his face.

Everyone else in the subway car moved away from Lucia and stared apprehensively at her, frightened and repelled by her feral shrieks.

After a while, she quieted and then whimpered. Eventually, she fell asleep.

The movement of the subway as it traveled along its underground tracks always excited Anacleto. The clattering sound, the rocking speed, especially during the jarring turns, the on-off-on flashes of the overhead lights, and the sizzling sparks rising from the tracks shot through him, amplifying the regular buzzing in his brain. He held himself tightly to his seat at every curve. He thought that, one day, a train in which he was riding would fall off the tracks; if it was on an elevated section, it would crash down to the busy street below, killing everyone on board and obliterating everything on which it landed.

He always looked at the windows of the apartments that were level with the track and wonder who inhabited them and try to imagine the lives they lived. He felt sorry for those people—not because of the sound of the trains that ran past them day and night, but because he imagined apartment living to be cold and anonymous and dangerous. He supposed the tenants felt vulnerable.

He never got used to the smell of the crowded stations, especially the busy subterranean ones in Downtown Brooklyn and in Manhattan—ozone and dust and sweat, along with hot dogs and the fragrance of fresh-squeezed orange juice. The oncoming trains wailed and squealed as their steel wheels screeched on the tracks to lurching, grinding stops.

Anacleto was always relieved when his trip was over and he was out of the station. But he always liked his trips to Manhattan, where the women who walked along the busy sidewalks looked elegant and the men wore suits. Stanley's father was the only man in Anacleto's neighborhood who wore a suit to work. He was an accountant. His mother was a teacher. They used to go on vacations, sometimes by plane.

"So, do you wanna know about my religion?" Stanley asked brightly, as he peered over his stack of books.

Anacleto stood up and put *Genesis* back on the shelf. Then he walked home.

He thought it was interesting that his family could now be considered lapsed Catholics and unobservant Jews at the same time.

WAITING FOR HIS LIFE TO CHANGE

During all of his elementary school years, Anacleto walked to and from school, alone most of the time. He generally enjoyed the solitude. On occasion, he would walk behind groups of boys, listening to their conversations, pretending that he was taking part. He always went home for lunch. Even when one or two of his brothers were in the same school as Anacleto and they stayed there for lunch and to play punch ball in the schoolyard, he would trek home. After his father died and his mother had to start working, he ate lunch alone. Who wanted to eat in the smelly, noisy cafeteria and ask permission to use the even more malodorous bathroom?

Anacleto continued going home for lunch when he attended junior high school.

During nice weather, the students were allowed to go into the schoolyard or to the adjoining city park after they had finished eating lunch. The park was small, but heavily wooded and nicely landscaped. However, the several hundred twelve- to fourteen-year-olds who swarmed into it turned that bucolic paradise into a near-riot zone. Boys and girls monopolized the swings, monkey bars, and slides, performing dangerous stunts meant to impress each other. The mothers of preschool children knew to stay away from the park during that mid-day period. The harried park employee who ran the refreshment stand usually sold out everything that was on his shelves within fifteen minutes of the arrival of the first of the lunchtime school crowd. When the latecomers learned that there were no more candy bars, potato chips, and sodas, they complained to and cursed at the now agitated park employee. At some point, before the teacher who was assigned to the park during the lunch period blew his whistle (it was always a male teacher) as a signal that it was time to return to school, a fist fight or two would have broken out somewhere in the park.

Rather than proclaiming the park off limits to the students because of their unruly behavior, one year, the principal assigned a half dozen of the toughest, meanest, most troubled ninth graders, seniors, to be monitors. They became known as the Park Patrol. Miraculously, those boys, who previously had started most of the lunchtime fights, managed to maintain a shaky peace that lasted all year. At the graduation ceremony that June, those boys were awarded Certificates of Merit for Outstanding Service to the School. Those were the only awards they were likely to ever receive.

***

After Anacleto's father died, the family car collected dust in the garage for a year. At that point, her husband's family told Lucia that she needed to learn to drive. They said it was either that or give up the car. Since she never gave away or threw away anything that still had any life in it, she agreed to learn. Anacleto suspected that her in-laws were tired of being called upon to drive the family to places that were too difficult to reach by bus or subway. Each of his father's eight siblings took turns giving driving lessons to Lucia.

Somehow, she passed the road test on her first try.

Once the State of New York via this major error in judgment had granted Lucia a license to drive, she told her children that they were not going to touch the steering wheel of her car—ever.

Anacleto's family had lived without a car until right before his father became ill, when a friend from work offered to sell to him, cheap, his cream-colored 1951 Studebaker. It was elegant. Both the hood and the trunk ended in lovely, rounded projections that were circled with gleaming chrome. Anacleto's father had driven it only a dozen times before prostate cancer transformed him from the buoyant, robust life-of-the-party that he had always been to the wraith who did not have the strength to leave his hospital bed.

Lucia was a terrible driver. For one thing, it was obvious to everyone in the family that, despite the fact that she had passed the road test without them, she needed glasses; she refused to have her eyes examined. Besides that, she never really understood the right of way rules or how to squeeze past double parked cars. She drove away from numerous fender benders without stopping and without getting caught.

She did have one serious collision—with a car driven by a teenage girl. The girl was so upset that she had damaged her father's car that she let Lucia yell and curse and threaten without defending herself. The girl just cried and repeatedly said, "I'm soooo sorry!" She had struck the rear bumper and the rear quarter panel on the driver's side of Lucia's car. It hadn't been her fault because Lucia had cut in front of her, from the right, as the two cars approached an intersection. No one called the police. Lucia, who instructed the girl to write down her name, address, and telephone number, refused to provide the girl with any information about herself. She directed George to call the girl's house that night to demand that her parents pay for the damage to the car.

They paid.

Lucia became friends with Joe, the body shop man who repaired the car. Joe came to the house a few times. He and Lucia would drive off in his car, returning hours later. Later on, she would mutter, "His wife's a son-of-a-bitch-bastard…He's too good for her." Anacleto understood, but the thought was so upsetting that he pushed it out of his head.

On the first day of summer vacation two years after Anacleto's father had died, his mother announced that she had arranged a part time job for him at Joe's body shop. Since Anacleto was not quite 14 years old, he would work off the books starting the following Monday. Mornings only.

That first morning, shaking with fear and anxiety, he walked to Joe Zitto's Auto Body. When he got there, he saw two very thin black men sitting on the sidewalk, reclining against the front wall of the shop. One of them looked him over.

"Ain't open 'till eight."

"I...know."

"Boy, you too young to own a automobile."

"I...I'm s...s...sup...posed to w...work here."

They looked at each other. Then they smiled and shook their heads in amusement. He stood a few feet away from them, near the large double garage doors, and listened to the men talk. They laughed a lot. He could not understand more than an occasional word of their conversation. At one point, one of them said something to the other about how they were doing their part...something about a sit-down strike. That broke them up for almost a full minute. He understood that. Their language was English, but it wasn't. He liked the flow and the rhythm. He hoped, if he worked with them for a while, he would be able to understand them better.

When Joe pulled up to the shop in his shiny black Eldorado, the two men stood and followed Joe to the side door, which he unlocked. Anacleto trailed behind them into the shop.

Paint and body filler and gasoline fumes.

"You're...your name...one of Lucy's boys?"

"Ye...yes. I'm C...Cl...ete."

"Okay. First job...Take this money and go to the corner store and get us three coffees, two regular, one strong and sweet, and three danish. And a box, not a pack, of Marlboro. You can get something for yourself."

Anacleto ordered four coffees. He had never eaten any but Italian pastries, so he did not know what kind of danish to buy; he chose four rectangular ones with sugary coatings.

When he returned to the shop, all three men were hard at work removing a damaged hood from a Ford truck. Anacleto stood, holding the paper bag, trying to decide where, in the midst of half a dozen cars in various stages of repair, spare parts, tools, grease, and filth to put it down. Joe looked up and told him to leave it on the cluttered desk in his office. The coffee smelled good and Anacleto wanted to taste his pastry, but, since the others weren't stopping their work to eat, he put the bag down. When he came out of the office, Joe pointed to a metal bucket filled with carburetors, and told him to clean them.

He struggled to lift the heavy pail.

"How sh…sh…sh…should I c…c…clean them?"

"Gasoline. Over there. Take that brush." Joe pointed to a red metal can and a black-stained, short-handled brush. "Do it out back," he barked. As Anacleto walked, the heavy bucket filled with greasy carburetors in one hand and the gasoline can and grimy brush in the other, Joe and the two helpers placed the damaged hood on the floor, straightened up, and admired the new one that they would install on the truck. Then they disappeared into Joe's office.

The sunny backyard was scrappy and weed covered. There were two or three junk cars and a broken windshield and other dead car parts back there. Anacleto emptied the contents of the pail onto a bare spot; then he knelt on the still-dewy weeds, poured some gasoline into the pail, placed a carburetor into it, and started scrubbing. After the first two, which he brushed until they were sparkling, he began to feel nauseous. The summer sun was powerful even though it was only a little past eight-thirty. He cleaned the next couple in a perfunctory manner. His head was spinning, his eyes burned, and his throat felt parched. He stood up…too quickly.

I'm Ana...

He stopped himself; then he quickly moved away from the pail and sat in the shade of a spindly, twisted tree. After a few minutes, he returned to work. He found that, if he took a break every so often, he would not feel sick.

When the last carburetor was more or less clean, he dumped the dirty gasoline onto the ground, put the carburetors back in the pail, making sure to place the cleanest ones on top, and brought everything back into the shop.

Joe took a fast look at his work and told him to start sanding a car that was parked out front.

"C…can I h…have my c…coffee f…f…first?"

"Your coffee? Oh, that was yours? Sorry, kid. I drank it."

It wasn't until Anacleto had started walking out the door, sandpaper in hand, that Joe called to him, holding the paper bag.

"C'mon, kid. Have your breakfast. And, by the way, no more prune danish!" He made a face. The two other men laughed as they worked.

He worked until noon. Walking home that first afternoon, he felt hot, dirty, achy, and tired. And resentful. He imagined that all of the other boys on his block had slept late and lounged around while he had been laboring like a man sanding an old Buick in the hot sun and lugging car parts from the storeroom to the men working in the shop. None of the boys Anacleto's age had jobs. Of course, all of his brothers had summer jobs, but they were older.

Anacleto worked all that summer in the body shop, four hours a day, five days a week. Joe paid him $20.00 cash weekly. He thought he should have gotten more, but, when he saw Joe's dark scowl, he remained silent.

Joe and the two workers, Sammy and Shoe, got along well. Joe was grumpy with them in a joshing way...Anacleto couldn't understand it, but the men seemed to find everything that Joe said very amusing. There was only one time that he saw Joe flare up. Sammy and Shoe had been installing a windshield on a station wagon. Smoke lazily drifting from the cigarettes hanging loosely from their lips, the men lifted the heavy glass and gently settled it in place. Then they carefully examined every inch of the rubber gasket that they had just glued into the frame, to make sure the windshield was tucked in nicely. They stood back to get a better view of their work. Then Sammy pushed the glass in, all along the perimeter—slowly, ever so gently.

They all heard the crack. Everybody in the shop—Joe, Shoe, two customers, Anacleto—they all looked at the now useless windshield. Joe cursed and howled and stamped his feet.

Sammy stood there, his hands covering his eyes.

Anacleto understood.

It was not a happy summer. Anacleto was bored and, for the first time in his life, he felt lonely. He read a lot. He liked *The Once And Future King* and *The Agony And The Ecstasy*, but *Fail Safe* upset him. The book brought to mind the missile crisis of October 1962, which most of the other boys Anacleto's age had seemed to ignore. Recollections of those dark, frightening days still haunted him three years later as he lay in bed at night. Then he saw *Dr. Strangelove*. Images from the movie added to his fears. He wondered where he would be when the first missiles struck. Everyone said that New York was a top priority target. Anacleto studied maps of the city, trying to imagine where a missile might detonate. Manhattan would be the bull's eye, but he calculated that his part of Brooklyn was only seconds away from the blast zone. It wasn't fear of death that kept him up at night. It was the vision of desolation that would follow the short, vicious nuclear war that left him sweaty and sleep-deprived as he tossed and turned in his sweltering bedroom that summer. He thought of the *Twilight Zone* episode called "Time Enough At Last." In it, a weak, bookish man who is tormented by his shrew of a wife for his love of reading emerges from the vault of the bank at which he works, where he had spent his lunch hour, reading, to discover that he is the lone survivor of a nuclear holocaust. At first, he is astounded, confused, and inconsolable. Then he comes across the ruins of the public library, and realizes that its thousands of books strewn across the steps leading up to the shattered building are his and his alone. With no job to draw him away and no wife to restrict his freedom and no other people to interrupt him, he finally has the time to read to his heart's content. Then, as he bends down to reach for a book, his glasses fall from his face and shatter on the ground.

Anacleto tried to push those disturbing thoughts from his brain, but he was powerless to do so. As he lay in bed at night, at times, he became teary-eyed, thinking about the dead president. He thought about his widow and his children. The sounds and images of the funeral—the riderless horse, the steady martial drumbeat, the family in black—were burned into his brain.

One Saturday morning, Anacleto's brother, Frank, asked if he would like to go to the beach with him. Frank was the only one the brothers who ever paid attention to Anacleto and, since his two best friends were counselors at a sleep-away camp for the summer, he used his Anacleto as a back-up companion. Anacleto didn't mind.

***

Anacleto poured his heart into writing poetry and short stories most afternoons after school that next year. He imagined people, places, and worlds that were far different from his reality.

After what seemed a long, tedious, lonely year, he graduated from junior high school. He looked forward to entering high school in the fall. He would be a sophomore since the last year of junior high was ninth grade.

He endured another dreary summer of reading, writing stories, working at the body shop, and waiting for his life to change.

A BETTER ME

Anacleto liked what he saw when he looked in the barber's mirror—he no longer feared seeing his reflection, but this was the first time that he actually liked what he saw. Luckily, his mother was seated when he walked into the house shorn of his wild curls.

He decided that he had to build up his scrawny body; he found that task incredibly difficult because he had no one to advise or encourage him. No one to tell him that he could do it. He was alone when he ran, first, unenthusiastically, as he circled the block, a distance of about a half mile, and then greater and greater distances until he could cover five miles without a break. He struggled with the set of weights that his brothers had used to develop their rock-hard, muscular arms, chests, and abdomens. He lifted. He curled. He suffered through dozens of sit-ups and push-ups each day.

At the beginning, he was so sore he thought the pain would last the rest of his life. After a month, he felt stronger and looked bigger. His usually pallid complexion took on a rosy glow. His dull brown eyes seemed a bit brighter. Even his weak left hand had grown and become firmer. It throbbed with pulsating blood vessels.

He persevered. He felt a marked improvement in his physical strength by the time he started high school in September.

It's still me, but a better me….maybe.

He "accidentally" left his red, white, and blue jacket on a city bus on his way to school the first day that it was cool enough to wear it. When his mother's torrent of expletives petered out, he told her that he would buy a new jacket. He bought a pea coat from an Army & Navy store. His mother was so surprised that he had actually saved enough money to purchase a coat that she was speechless when he wore it for the first time.

He threw out the little square of jacket lining that he had kept in his wallet for years.

For the first time in his life, he had money in his pocket. He was supposed to deposit gift money, along with all of the money that he earned at the body shop, into his savings account at the Williamsburg Savings Bank. For years, he did that. Then, on occasion, he started holding back a dollar or two, which he hid in an empty paint can in the garage. He enjoyed knowing that some money was his, even if he had to keep it hidden. If his mother had known about the secret stash, she surely would have been catapulted into one of her enraged fits of cursing and apoplexy.

Every morning, he would throw his damp ham on Wonder Bread or peanut butter and jelly sandwich into the first garbage pail that he passed on his way to school. He bought the school lunch and ate it at a different table every day. He had never eaten cafeteria food before, except for the few times that his mother had taken her boys to a Horn and Hardart Automat in Manhattan. As dried out as the school hamburgers were, as over-toasted as the grilled cheese sandwiches may have been, they were better than what had been in his paper bag.

His mother would have been furious if she had known that he was throwing away her food. To Lucia, every slice of bread had value. She worried about money all of the time. Four years after her husband died, she was still nervous, adrift, and confused. So much had changed. She had gone back to work after years of being a full-time mother and housewife. Now, besides taking care of the house and her sons, she had to handle the bills and face new and challenging responsibilities alone. She never felt complete or competent without her husband.

In school, Anacleto made a concerted effort to keep his hands down, look people in the eye, and exchange a few words with them. He didn't make any friends, but he didn't feel like a total outcast either. His grades were good, as usual, especially in English and history. Since he always went straight home from school and stayed in for the rest of the day, he had honed his study skills to perfection. He was always ahead of the rest of the class, and, sometimes, the teacher in terms of knowing the material in the textbooks. When he wasn't studying, he read, wrote short stories, worked out, and ran.

He was the first one out of the building after the last period every day. He had no reason to stay; he knew that, in the midst of a crowd, he would be alone.

Wherever I am, there's me…no one else.

When school ended that June, he returned to the body shop. He hated the job, but he liked having money. Joe gave him heavier work to do now and more hours, so he did not need to lift weights that summer. As he sanded fenders and lifted and lugged heavy car parts, the muscles on his arms, shoulders, chest, and legs grew, as did his desire to be a part of the world around him.

GRASPING THE EXTENDED HAND

Near the end of his junior year of high school, Santo became his friend.

The boys on the block had finally understood that Santo stayed with them because his peers had rejected him. They didn't know why and they didn't care. Once they saw that Santo was a "loser" and that he didn't have anyone else, they stopped thinking of him as a leader. They banded together against him. One day, when Santo attempted to take charge of a street stickball game, they rebelled. He puffed up and pushed Albie, fully expecting the boys to cave in to his size and ferocity. Instead, he faced eight pairs of angry eyes and ready fists. He laughed scornfully; then, when he understood that his reign was over, he smiled bitterly. He called the boys "cocksucker babies" and said that he should have stopped hanging around with them long before. He walked off, combing his hair and whistling.

That's when Santo began talking to Anacleto. He knew that Santo was using him, but when the older boy extended his hand, Anacleto grasped it. At first, Santo had just nodded to Anacleto in the hallways in school between classes. Then, during the spring semester, they were in the same hygiene class. Based on his age, Santo should have graduated that year, but he had been held back in junior high school.

"You know, you're real smart," he informed Anacleto one cold afternoon as they walked down the steps of the school to the sidewalk. At first, Anacleto didn't realize that Santo was talking to him.

"I wish I could do better in school, but it ain't my thing."

"You're…sm…smart in…oth…other ways, Santo."

Either because of Anacleto's reply or just the fact that he did reply, Santo stopped walking, and stared. Anacleto stopped walking too, and looked at the sidewalk.

"What do you mean?" he asked.

"Well,…you always s…solve pr...problems…with ball games—"

"Oh, you mean when there's too many guys or we don't have a place to play a game?"

"Yes. And the b…boys listen to you." Anacleto knew they had broken with him, but he decided to spare Santo's feelings.

"They used to because they knew I'd break their asses if they didn't. I don't hang around with them no more." He laughed and then resumed walking.

Anacleto caught up to him.

"Oh. I d…did…didn't know."

"What? I didn't hear you. You said it too fast and too quiet. Say it again."

No one, except for his teachers, had ever asked Anacleto to repeat anything that he had said.

"I said th...that...I d…didn't know about that."

"Oh, yeah?"

They walked along the busy streets, passing the hardware store, the TV repair shop, the shoemaker, Doc Heller's pharmacy.

"Hey, let's get a soda. I got some money," Santo offered.

Anacleto didn't allow his surprise to show. His head spun and his heart felt swollen with gratitude and affection as they walked into the drug store and sat at the counter.

Doc was wary. He had dealt with Santo before.

"Gimme an egg cream, Doc," Santo said with a smile as he lit a cigarette and inhaled deeply.

"And you?" Doc asked.

"I'll h…have one t…too."

Doc began to mix milk and chocolate syrup in each of two tall glasses. Then he squirted seltzer into the mixture, allowing a little of the foamy head in each one to slowly drip down the outside of the glass. Anacleto enjoyed watching the reserved old man work. Doc had owned the pharmacy forever, mixing and dispensing medications and even bandaging minor injuries. Besides fountain drinks and candy, he sold toys, comic books, newspapers, and paperbacks.

"Angie Boscalli got knocked up." Santo announced this news as they sipped their egg creams.

Anacleto felt sick; he squirmed on his stool as his genitals shrank.

"It was Larry…You know…the Irish kid with the red hair."

"Wh…what's going to h…happen?"

"Well, either they get married or she fixes it."

After a minute, Santo asked, "You ever do it?"

Sure…lots of times…in bed at night, silently, with Frank snoring in his bed a few feet away.

"I didn't think so. Ya' gotta remember to wear a rubber. I keep one in my wallet."

"I know about that," Anacleto stated.

"Yeah. Everybody knows, but somehow, they forget to use 'em."

Anacleto agreed, shaking his head wisely.

He had seen them…stretched, yellowed, lying in the street next to the curb. He knew he would never have the courage to buy a package. Doc Heller would stare disapprovingly at Anacleto through his thick glasses, so he would have to go to a drug store where no one knew him. What if a woman were behind the counter?

Why would I be buying them?

"I guess Larry got careless. Now she's ruined."

"They c…can't get m…married. Too y…young."

"He's almost eighteen. He can quit school any time he wants, and get a job on the docks."

"Sure. That w…would be g…good."

"No. It stinks. If it happened to me, I'd get it taken care of. I ain't gonna marry a girl who's been used."

"But—"

"Yeah. She's some gorgeous piece of ass. Maybe—"

"N…no. I mean…They've been g…going out—"

"Yeah. I know. Well, it's their problem."

It was an embarrassing problem. It was a devastating problem. Anacleto decided that it was better to be alone than have to face that kind of situation.

"Did you hear what happened last week between the old professor and Fat Marie, Victoria's mom?" Santo smiled as he asked this question.

Anacleto knew, but he said he didn't.

"The sneaky old Pollack down the block's been doin' it to Victoria, Fat Marie's daughter. The old bastard, Professor What's His Name, the one that sits in his front room typing all day, he's been giving Victoria lessons a couple of times a week. He don't take no money for the lessons… in fact, Victoria's been getting a few bucks a week from him since she's been twelve."

Anacleto remembered the ugly confrontation between the elderly Mr. Kolchesky and Fat Marie, Victoria's mother. She had pounded on the old man's front door with a hammer. He had reluctantly opened it—only a few inches. Marie had grabbed the doorknob and tried to push the door open wider, but a thick security chain had held it in place.

She screamed at him and hit the door repeatedly with the hammer, denting and cracking it.

"You filthy old man—pig—Pollack bastard! You put your hands on my daughter! I'm gonna call the cops on you!"

He tried to placate her, assuring her that he had never touched the child; he had only instructed her in history and math.

"You fucking liar! You bastard!"

She screamed and hammered. Flakes of white paint and splinters of wood exploded from the door with each blow.

He tried to reason with her. He whimpered. He told her that he had been a good neighbor for years and that he would never touch a child.

A group of people had gathered to watch. No one said a word.

Marie cursed, threatened, and hit the door repeatedly. Mr. Kolchesky begged Marie to calm herself. He swore on all that he held holy that, to him, Victoria was an innocent child.

"All I do is give her a little help with her homework. You have to believe—"

"I know you had your hands on her! I find out you ruined her, I won't call the cops! I'll cut your fucking throat when you sleep!"

At that, she grabbed the edge of the door and tried to push it open. The chain held. Marie, who was wearing a large shapeless housedress over her immense, shapeless body, hit the chain with her hammer, but that just yanked the door closed, catching the head of the hammer and cutting into her hand. Mr. Kolchesky screamed and moved away from the door, deeper into his foyer. All that Anacleto could see of him was his white beard.

Marie's dark curly hair was wild. Anacleto stared with fascination and revulsion at her bare, man-sized blue-veined feet. She held the door open with one hand and shoved one large knee in the space between the door and the jamb. The hammer, in her other hand, repeatedly hit the chain.

She cursed and sputtered and spit. The old man moved further into the dark house; he was invisible now.

A few people hesitantly suggested to Marie that she should go home. She turned, her eyes hot and fierce, and, waving the hammer at her neighbors, told them that she was going to break his bones. Then she would go home.

She continued pounding on the chain.

Anacleto turned and walked away from the revolting scene.

Victoria stood in the doorway of her house, across the street, looking at the commotion from behind her partially open door. As Anacleto passed by, he could see that she was smiling.

Santo continued talking, saying, "She's fourteen now—old enough and experienced enough. Maybe I'll lay her some time."

With that, he finished his drink, pushed thirty cents toward Doc, and stood up.

Anacleto followed.

"You know…I never forgot how you covered for me that day my ol' man came lookin' for me."

Anacleto wanted to tell him that he understood…the need to hide.

"You know, I learn a lot from you. You hold your tongue. A lot o' guys around here talk big all the time. You don't," Santo remarked with admiration.

"I…d…don't have m…much to s…say."

"You do. You're just unsure of yourself. You gotta get out more. You can't be a hermit and stay in your house. You oughta play ball."

"I'm n…not good at sp…sports. You know th…that."

"So what! You gotta try. Life's a game."

At that moment, Anacleto wished he was Santo. Learning to do well in school was easier than learning how to live.

"Can we go to your house?" Santo asked.

"I…don't know. My m…mother doesn't like us to bring k…kids over."

"She ain't home, right?"

"No. She's w…w…working, but my br…brothers—"

"I know your brothers. They bring over their friends."

They did. They smoked and played music and talked on the phone when their mother was out. They all had brought girls to their rooms at one time or another. George and Ronnie were in the service, but James and Frank, who were both in college, still lived at home.

Anacleto nervously unlocked the door and let Santo follow him in. His heart was pounding, sure that his mother would come home early and catch Santo in the house. They watched television and talked. Anacleto helped Santo with his math homework.

Anacleto wanted to do something to show that he trusted Santo, that he was a friend. While Santo sat at the little desk in the room that Anacleto shared with Frank, struggling with *Tom Sawyer*, Anacleto took the ladder from the garage and climbed into the attic. He brought down the box and nervously showed the guns to Santo.

"They look real," Santo exclaimed.

"I…know, b…but they…they aren't."

"They look like starter pistols, you know, for a race. Let's show them to Albie's dad. He knows a lot about guns."

"No! They have to go b…back in the at…tic. They have to st…stay there. My…m… mother d…doesn't know—"

"Come on. We'll just show them. Then you can put them back."

Santo pulled back the hammer of one of them and, aiming at the map of the United States that had been pinned on the wall of the bedroom for as long as Anacleto could remember, pulled the trigger. The snap of the hammer gave Anacleto an instant headache.

They brought the box of guns to Albie Caspari's father, who, they knew, would be in the shed behind his house. He spent hours there, making birdhouses, cleaning and organizing fishing equipment, and smoking his pipe. He was the only man in the neighborhood who went hunting and fishing. He would load up his station wagon with gear, place his rowboat on the roof, and go off, sometimes with Albie, for long weekends upstate or in Pennsylvania.

Mr. Caspari always liked to have Albie and all of the other boys around.

They listened to him, wide-eyed: "Next summer, Albie and I are going bear hunting…in Pennsylvania. Yeah, hunting is a man's sport, boys. So is fishing. I've got the best fishing gear money can buy. Now, the rest of you boys wouldn't know anything about hunting rifles, the way Albie does. Maybe Albie will bag a bear. Wouldn't that be great?"

He would clap his hands and cheer when he heard the familiar screech of tires and the crash of metal as cars collided on the corner of the street. Even when the stop sign was in place, which wasn't often because it was a favorite target of late-night vandals, at least once a week, some car would speed past the corner and hurtle into the intersection. Then there would be the sickening sounds of rubber scraping on asphalt and metal crumpling and glass breaking. And screaming.

"That sounds like a good one. Let's go, boys," Albie's father would say, rubbing his hands together. Anacleto went with the others most of the time. He tried to justify his voyeurism by telling himself that he wasn't contributing to the misery of the accident victims by viewing the carnage. That didn't help: standing there, he felt dirty. The sight of crying, bleeding people upset him.

Anacleto knew that if he were an animal, he wouldn't be a fox or a wolf.

He remembered one especially violent crash. The two cars were bound together by the twisted metal of their hoods. Both windshields had shattered. The man and woman in one car were holding their hands to their bloody faces and the man in the other car was slumped forward, unmoving, against the steering wheel of his car.

A woman from one of the houses nearby brought a glass of water to the scene, but she just stood there, holding it.

A police car arrived. The officers examined the vehicles and the victims with dispassionate exactness, and then one of them talked into the two-way radio in his patrol car. Albie's father would always talk with the cops—there was some sort of connection.

Santo showed the box of guns to Mr. Caspari. After he had carefully examined one of them, Mr. Caspari said that they were real single-shot pistols and that he thought he had ammunition for them. Holding onto the pistol, he went into his house. Anacleto remembered from a time that he had been in Albie's house that Mr. Caspari kept rifles, pistols, and ammunition in the basement. He also had, mounted on one wall, large fish that he had caught and heads of animals that he had hunted.

"I knew I had it," he said as he emerged from the house, holding the pistol and a box of cartridges. He also had a cloth and tools to clean the pistol.

"These things can backfire if they haven't been cleaned," he said as he put the cartridges on a wooden bench next to the box with the other two pistols. The cartridge box fell, spilling the small bullets to the ground.

"Albie!" he called.

Albie and Santo scooped up the cartridges, dropping them into the box and putting it back on the bench next to the cheese box.

Mr. Caspari carefully cleaned the barrel and the chamber of the pistol. Then he placed a round in the chamber. The boys from the block, who had been playing with Albie in his backyard before Santo and Anacleto had come, watched in silent fascination. Then, pointing to an empty Coke can that was in a garbage pail next to the shed, Mr. Caspari told Albie to bring it to him. He placed it on a tree stump, and then he walked back to the boys. When he was sure that all of the boys were out of the way and paying attention, Mr. Caspari aimed at the soda can and pulled the trigger.

The crack hurt Anacleto's ears. The acrid smoke burned his eyes.

The can lay on the ground, punctured, jagged. Dead.

Anacleto wished he had not brought Santo to his house.

The boys ran to Mr. Caspari to examine the still smoking gun. He let each of them have a turn holding it. Then he took it back.

He announced, "This kind of pistol was used in a bank robbery in the Bronx years ago."

Anacleto grabbed the pistol from Mr. Caspari's hand, threw it into the cheese box, slid the cover closed, and ran home. When he got to his house, he hid the box under his bed.

***

When his mother came home and throughout dinner, Anacleto was tense, certain that she knew that Santo had been in the house.

She told the boys about her boss at the garment factory where she worked, saying, "Mr. Morris, he lets the girls go for unemployment if the work gets slow. I'm going next week."

"Does that mean we'll have less money?" Frank asked.

"Don't worry. He'll let me work a few hours off the books. Just don't spend any money 'cause I can't give you any. And…don't none of you touch your bank accounts." She looked at Anacleto when she said that.

As soon as he finished eating, Anacleto checked on his secret stash hidden in the garage. It was untouched. The next day, when he was home alone after school, he pulled the cheese box out from under his bed and, without opening it, he put it back in the attic.

***

A couple of days later, a Friday, Santo told Anacleto that he was going to teach him to catch and hit a softball.

“Tomorrow. We’ll go to the schoolyard. The two of us. I’ll teach you. Come to my house at nine.”

The next morning, Anacleto woke early. He ate breakfast. Then he waited. At 9 a.m., he walked down the alleyway alongside Albie’s house and rang the doorbell that was next to the side door. Francine, Santo’s mother, came to the door. He smelled tobacco…and lilacs. Anacleto struggled to make small talk with her. She was wearing a faded blue bathrobe that was only partially closed. He could see most of her pale pink brassiere and the rounded flesh that peeked above it. He realized that she saw he was looking, so he averted his eyes. She smiled; then she closed her robe.

“I’m glad you’re Santo’s friend now. That’s nice.” She stroked his cheek.

Lilacs.

He wanted to ask her where her husband went every night. Then Santo came to the door.

“I’m going out, Ma.”

“Hi, Clete.” It was Santo’s sister, Anne.

“Looky. It’s Anne and Anna—cleto.” Santo smiled.

“Santo, remember what your father told you.”

“I know, Ma.” Santo frowned.

The schoolyard was already a busy place when they arrived. They staked out an area that was near the unoccupied softball field, and Santo started throwing a softball to Anacleto, who was using a glove that belonged to one of his brothers. After Anacleto missed or dropped the first few, Santo walked over.

“You can’t be a retard. You’re 17. It ain’t hard to catch a ball, even with a bum hand. Watch me.”

He proceeded to toss the ball into the air, underhand, and make basket catches. Then he threw the ball higher, overhand, and, moving swiftly to remain under it, he caught it every time.

“Okay. Now you.”

He gently tossed the ball into the air a few times, and Anacleto didn’t miss. Then he threw the ball higher. Anacleto didn’t move fast enough. It fell next to him.

Santo repeated this a dozen or so times, giving directions to Anacleto about where to move and how to hold his glove.

"That's better. Now, I'm going back over there. Remember what I showed you. And remember, life's a game…a serious game. If you act like a rag, people treat you like a rag. You gotta be a rock. Now, don't let the ball push you around."

For the next hour or so, they practiced. Anacleto improved. Then Santo taught him the right way to hold and swing a baseball bat. Santo was patient. He lobbed underhand pitches to Anacleto.

"Okay. You got a swing. Now put power into it. You ain't no girl."

This was harder than catching and throwing. Anacleto was strong enough, but the aggressiveness that is needed to wallop a ball was just not part of who he was.

The sun was high. It was warm for a late April morning.

Anacleto underhanded pitches to Santo. No matter how or where he threw the ball, Santo hit it. His squinted eyes followed the trajectory of the pitches and his body moved so that he was always in the best position to make contact. He swung for the fences every time, and Anacleto had to run to the end of the schoolyard to retrieve his blasts.

They stopped playing, and walked to the candy store for drinks.

"You know, my sister likes you."

Warmth rose from Anacleto's stomach to his cheeks.

"I hear you put your hands on her, and you're dead!"

"I…I w…wouldn't."

Anacleto never thought about Anne. In each of his fiery nocturnal fantasies, he was older, making love to his future wife in their spacious Manhattan apartment. He always pictured some girl who he had seen at school, a quiet, unadorned one who slunk along the sides of the hallways during passing, hugging the walls, avoiding the mad rush of students. Sometimes, his late night fantasies turned into dreams. Sometimes, the dreams were pulsatingly real. He could not imagine that happening in the real world.

"It's okay, Clete. I like you. Just don't ruin my sister."

He had no intention of even talking to her.

When Anacleto and Santo returned to the schoolyard, they stood near the fence, watching some boys play softball. Then, when the inning was over, Santo lit a cigarette and walked over to the boys. Anacleto stayed near the fence.

It happened in a flash. One of the boys, about Santo's age, but taller, heavier, with long black hair, shoved him. Before the boy's hands left him, Santo snatched the cigarette from his mouth and flicked it at the boy's face. The boy smacked his baseball glove across Santo's cheek. Santo covered his face with his arms to block the next blow and, lowering his trunk, he plowed into the boy. They grappled, punching each other's backs. As the other boys cheered and then cursed at and threatened Santo, the two fighters separated and exchanged a few punches, most of them missing vital spots. They circled. Santo's face was red where the glove had hit him. The other boy's tee shirt was torn and his long, straggly hair was wild. Santo swung his right fist—hard, catching the boy on the ear. Stunned, the boy held the side of his face and bent over. Santo waited. A couple of other boys moved from their circle and shoved Santo. The long-haired boy straightened up and waved off the crowd.

Anacleto wanted to run home. He wanted to punch one of the boys. His heart was beating painfully fast and his hands were cold and damp. He turned away, covering his face with his hands. Then, turning back and looking through the spaces between his fingers, he watched the fight. The schoolyard was awash in blood, bodies floating on its slimy surface.

Anacleto picked up the equipment and slowly approached the crowd of screaming, cursing boys. He knew he had to be a rock. He tried to swagger. He was sure it looked more like a waddle, but no one noticed him.

Santo had the boy in a headlock. The boy was punching Santo's chest. Santo kneed the boy in the abdomen and then he threw him down.

Anacleto worked to gain control of his composure, his place, his gravity.

When the boy stood up, Santo punched him in the stomach, doubling him up.

Still bent over, the boy steamrolled into Santo, but he was ready—Santo kneed the boy in the face. Blood gushed from the boy's nose and mouth. It dripped onto the asphalt, forming a crimson puddle. Santo stepped back, eyeing the crowd. A couple of the others were talking to their friend, asking him whether he wanted to continue fighting. He shook his head, indicating that he wanted to, but his legs were rubbery. His friends sat him down by the schoolyard fence. He held his tee shirt to his bloody face.

Santo, still stepping backward, reached Anacleto. Then he turned around and started walking to the schoolyard gate. Two boys broke from the group and followed Santo. Anacleto didn't think; he just moved—right into the path of the two boys. They stopped short and then one of them, a large, square hulk who needed a bath, roughly pushed Anacleto out of the way. He stumbled, spun around, and fell, hitting his forehead on the asphalt and dropping the softball equipment. He closed his eyes, expecting a punch or a kick, but none came. He touched his forehead. His hand came away bloody. He sat up. Then, slowly, he stood.

The two boys had cornered Santo at the handball court, where they traded punches and kicks with him. The others, who had been sitting with their injured friend, left him and ran to the new fight. There was a loud smack. Santo held his cheek. Both boys, one in front of him and one behind, began punching Santo. Santo kicked the one who was in front of him between his legs—hard. The boy went down. Then, turning quickly, Santo encircled the waist of the other boy and pushed him down. The boy landed on his back, with Santo on top. Santo grabbed the boy's head with both of his hands and knocked it to the asphalt. Then he climbed off the moaning boy and looked warily at the angry group that now surrounded him. The circle closed in, but Santo punched first, catching one boy on his nose. The boy yelled and put both of his hands to his face.

Two others lunged for Santo. One of them wrapped his arms around Santo's waist, but Santo managed to break free and run out of the schoolyard. The two new attackers chased after him.

As Anacleto walked, quickly, out of the schoolyard, he counted…three here, one other one, the original fighter over there. They were all sitting or lying on the asphalt. Three were holding their hands to their faces, blood dripping from between their fingers. The other one lay in a fetal position, his hands cradling his crotch.

Anacleto ran down the street, clutching the bat and ball and gloves. His head hurt. He stopped, pulled a handkerchief from his pocket and held it to his forehead. He felt blood soaking through it.

Henry Fleming. Smoky, burning woods.

The two boys who had followed Santo had been stopped by a police officer who regularly patrolled the neighborhood. Anacleto slowed down as he passed them. A block later, he caught up with Santo. They walked quickly, turning around from time to time. They knew that the others would try to follow them to find out where Santo lived. They would try to catch him another time when he least expected it.

They moved rapidly, detouring down side streets several times, and then ran into a church. It was a different kind of church. The sign read Saint Michael's Episcopal Church. Inside, it was cool and dim and silent. They walked down the aisle to a small alcove behind the altar. Anacleto had never been behind a church altar. When he was ten, he had thought about becoming an altar boy, but when he spoke to a priest about it in confession, he asked Anacleto whether he attended the church school. Anacleto told him no. He asked Anacleto whether he knew Latin. He told Anacleto that Catholic school students made the best altar boys.

They hid in the dim hallway for about twenty minutes. Both of Santo's cheeks were swollen, his lips were cut, one puffy eyelid was bleeding, and there were specks of blood on his nose and ears. His bloody tee shirt had been ripped down the front, almost in half.

Anacleto held his handkerchief to his head.

"Those fucks!"

Anacleto couldn't believe that Santo was cursing in a church, even if it wasn't a Catholic church. They peered out the back door. As they carefully surveyed the street and then warily trotted home, Anacleto's mind kept returning to Santo's sacrilege. Why was it that no one else seemed to take to heart the reality of sin? Non-Catholic, non-Jew that he was, he often thought about sin and his relationship to God. His belief in God...his skepticism about God.

When he was younger, it used to amaze and frighten him, on the rare occasions when he would walk home from Saturday afternoon confession with boys from his block, that they would use foul language and talk about sex. The worst offenders were the triplets—and they went to Catholic school. How were they going to receive communion the next morning? Would they do it in a state of sin? Would they be able to absolve themselves of those sins? How could they not care? He would have told them that they were supposed to remain pure, at least until they had received the Sacrament the next day, but they would have just renewed his membership in the Bush Club.

The Bush Club: If a boy had never been inducted, the others would ask, "Do you wanna be a member of the Bush Club?" By the time a boy was seven, he knew what that meant, and he would try to run away before they could push him—roughly—into whatever landscaping bushes or shrubs he was passing. When Anacleto had been inducted, it had been summer, and his face and bare arms and legs had gotten scratched by the woody branches of some woman's old hedges. His membership had been renewed a dozen painful times after that. Once, the owner of the house whose bushes had entrapped him ran to the sidewalk, screaming at him as the other boys ran away. The woman held Anacleto by the back of his neck as he directed her to his house, where she proceeded to yell at his mother, telling her what a destructive boy he was. Lucia let the woman have it with both barrels. For a while, it looked as if they were preparing to tear each other's eyes and hair out.

By the time the enraged woman marched home, threatening to call the police, several of the neighbors had come out to witness the embarrassing scene. Even though his mother knew it had not been Anacleto's fault, she punished him by ordering him to sweep the basement.

The source of many of his nightmares.

Anacleto told Santo that he had a lot of courage.

"It ain't courage. It's survival. Nobody gonna put me down without me putting them down first. You gotta be your own man."

Survival.

That night, lying in bed, Anacleto's brain played back the sounds of flesh smacking flesh; he heard the grunts, the curses, the cries. He saw the blood. His head throbbed. He replayed his part: blocking the path of two of the attackers and being knocked down, his forehead colliding roughly with the asphalt.

The blood on my handkerchief—like the red badge of courage. The church. Dim, quiet, holy place. Santo cursing in that sacred place...He doesn't understand boundaries. There are lines that should not be crossed. Life is dangerous. He's doomed.

Anacleto had ignored his mother's frantic questions when he came home; he had thrown the bloody handkerchief into the bathroom sink, slowly and carefully washed it and then his face. He had dabbed his wound with iodine—the ragged burning of the medicine did more than protect him from the chance of infection; it was his penance.

His thoughts shifted: what had happened at Santo's house when he had gotten home? He had been in fights before...plenty of times. He had once proudly displayed a raw gash on his knuckles.

"Yeah. His tooth was in there. I pulled it out and threw it down the sewer. He was bleeding like a pig."

All of the other boys had admired Santo's bloody wound.

***

Santo's attackers never did find out where he lived or, if they had, they did not act on the information. Anacleto was disappointed. He had hoped they would come. That day in the schoolyard had aroused in him a burning rage the likes of which he had never felt before. He wanted to see all of those other boys bloodied, shredded, howling. He knew that, despite any lingering animosity that the boys from the block still held toward Santo, they would have defended him, full force, from trespassers from another neighborhood. Even the group of boys who were Santo's age, the ones who had long excluded him, would have stood by him, if the intruders had come.

Anacleto would have stood at the point of the group.

***

The next night, Sunday, Anacleto felt energized. He lay in bed for hours, remembering the fight, as well as how to catch and hit a softball. He went through the steps over and over again.

Be a man, not a rag. Survival.

Then his thoughts slowly shifted. He imagined a step-by-step fantasy scenario involving a bland girl with nice teeth who he had seen at school. They spent every night wrapped in each other's arms, aflame with hot, unquenchable passion. With half-closed eyes, he squinted at the clock on his night table. He had to be up for school in three hours, but he was too deeply involved in the fantasy to bring down the curtain and try to sleep.

Then…Anne's face was there. It was still the other girl, but it was also Anne. It was Anne as she might look in a few years. It was Anacleto as he hoped to look one day.

THE DANGERS OUTSIDE

When Anne smiled at him in school a few days later, Anacleto resisted the urge to turn away. He felt uncomfortably warm, but his fingertips were like chips of ice. He pretended that he did not see her.

He and Santo had been eating lunch together every day and spending time together after school. One day, at lunch, Santo asked to borrow some money. Anacleto told him that he didn't have much. In truth, his stash had swelled to more than four hundred dollars.

"W…what's the money f…for?" he asked.

"I can't tell you. It's a situation with my mother."

"Oh."

"My father's such a bastard." Then Santo smiled darkly. "Bastard. Ha."

"Why d…does he hit y…you?"

"He's nuts. And…there's another reason, but I can't tell you."

"Oh."

"See you later," Santo said.

Santo stood up, leaving his untouched hamburger and fries, and walked to another table. He sat down and began talking with some boys who, everyone said, belonged in jail.

***

Anacleto didn't see Santo in school or on the block for the next few days. One afternoon, after he had finished the bulk of his homework, he went to Santo's house. Anne answered the doorbell and told Anacleto that her brother was not home. They stood in the doorway, talking. Then she asked him if he wanted to go for a walk. His stomach was in knots and his fingertips were icy cold again. He didn't say yes. He just stepped into the alley; Anne walked out and closed the door.

As they walked and talked, Anacleto forced himself to look at her: her long, lovely midnight-black hair, her translucent skin, her skinny, but nicely proportioned shape.

They stopped at a little park a few blocks away.

"He's different. I don't know if it's the fight he had or what, but he's angry and worried," Anne said, sighing.

"He did seem to b…be c…con…cerned about m…money."

"Money?"

Anacleto shook his head.

"What's the money for? Do you know?" she asked, searching his face.

"He did…didn't say."

"Were you in that fight too? Your head looked…kind of bruised when I saw you."

"I just tried to st…op some of the oth…er g…uys."

"You're a good friend, Clete."

The next day, Anne caught up to him as he walked home from school. He tried to be less serious than he had been the day before. He felt more relaxed as they talked. She smiled and gently poked his arm with her elbow a few times as she told him a funny story about school.

Her smile is for me.

He thought about reaching for her hand, but he knew that would be wrong. They were just friends. Santo had warned him. He had to think of her as a sister.

"When I graduate, I'm going to get a job in the city…and live there." She stopped to smooth one of her stockings.

"You h…have another y…year to g…go. Same as me."

"I know, but I think I'll try to get a job in Manhattan this summer."

"Doing w…what?" he asked.

"Anything."

"It's hard to g…et jobs in M…Manhattan."

"Maybe not. Jenny works in her father's office on Fifty-Seventh Street. I can probably get a job there too. I'm sick and tired of Brooklyn…and my father."

"Is he t…tough on y…you too?"

She remained silent for a long while. He thought he had said the wrong thing.

"He's not a bad man. Life's tough for him, for all of us."

As much as he wanted to know about her father—where he was when he was not with them and why he seemed to be so crazy—he held his tongue.

"How's your mother?" she asked.

"My mother is n…neur…neurotic. It's because she still m…misses my father and sh… she does doesn't know how to get along without him. My father… was c…cr…crazier."

They both laughed. She put a hand on his arm and looked at him.

That smile.

He lightly touched her shoulder for a second and then withdrew his hand. She looked at him and opened and closed her mouth without saying anything.

"You're funny, Clete. Life is funny."

"I g…guess."

"I want you to help my brother. He's in trouble."

"What d…do you m…mean? What k…kind of tr..trouble?"

"Ask him."

"I d…don't even know where h…he is."

"He's cutting school. He's going to flunk out. He should have graduated by now. I've been covering for him, but, sooner or later, my father's going to hear about the cutting—"

"Wh…why? Wh…what sh…should I d…do?"

"He's been going out every night. When he goes out tonight, I'll ring your bell. I want you to go with him."

"I c…can't. My mom doesn't l…like me to go out on s…school nights. She'll go c… crazy."

"And I thought my family's nuts. Come on. Please!"

"I…I want to…cause Santo's my fr…friend."

"So?"

"You don't un…der…st…stand. I—"

"Clete. You're not a kid anymore. You'll be seventeen in a few months."

"I know, b…but…I don't—"

"I need your help."

He wanted to tell her that he would do whatever she wanted, but his mother couldn't find out about it. Then she grabbed his hand, his weaker hand. They stopped walking. Her eyes were sad, dark…his brain was on overload.

"You can go, can't you?"

"I…u…usu…ally d…don't."

"Tell your mom that we're going out for a walk. When Santo leaves, I'll ring your doorbell. Be ready to come out, right away."

They walked the rest of the way home in silence. She had not released his hand. He held hers firmly, grateful that, for once, his was warm and dry.

He couldn't concentrate on his homework. He felt stimulated, aroused. But that was not what he wanted. He did not want to be tempted. He wanted to think. He lay on his bed, playing out the possible scenarios: upsetting his mother by going out. What would happen? Staying home…What would that lead to? Going out with Anne…His pulse quickened.

Such a pretty smile. Standing naked before me…

Frank stood in the doorway. Anacleto looked up.

"Boy, you were in a world of your own. Was it a nice place?"

He knew he had to stop day dreaming. He had to concentrate and decide what to do. He had an obligation to Santo. If he tried to help him, maybe his life could change.

*Maybe **my** life will change.*

That night, shortly after dinner, he approached his mother as she watched television. He knew he couldn't wait for Anne to ring his bell.

"I'm g…going out."

"What? I want you home."

"Mom, I'm not a baby. Other boys g…go out all the t…time."

"Where are you going?"

"Out."

"Who are you going with?"

"Anne."

She looked stricken. She expelled gas. Then her face turned red and, with her eyes closed, she told him that he was not going out with any girl.

"She's j…just my f…friend."

"She's a girl. You're not going."

He began to float…his feet left the floor…his head was spinning. Then he thought of what Santo had said about being a rock. He pulled himself down.

"I'm going out. I w…won't be late. Why don't you ever g…give my br… brothers a hard t…time when they g…go out?"

"They're older," she said.

"Yes, but they…"

"You're diff…different. You need to be watched."

"I can…take c…care of myself."

"I know it's no good…no good if you go out. There's things you…" She pulled down on her cheeks stretching her face into an unnatural frown. "You remember the time you opened the black umbrella in the house?" Her eyes, stretched to a deviant hugeness, bored into his brain.

Of course he remembered opening the umbrella in the house. He also remembered the little compact case mirror that had broken when he dropped it.

"It's bad…dangerous…bad luck. Things happen. Dirty things. It's not for you. Oh…son-of-a-bitch-bastard!!! Oh…No!! Oh my God…Protect my boy." She released her face and put her hands together, as if in prayer.

He walked to the door, shaking. He escaped while his mother alternated between vile curses and desperate prayers. But he knew she was right. He belonged at home. He used to wonder why other boys…and girls did risky things. Got themselves in trouble when they had plenty of chances to avoid it. He thought of the ones who called out in class or confronted teachers. It never ended well for them. Maybe it ended the way they knew it would end. And driving...He had known that Philly's older brother, Ed, would wreck his car. It was a gleaming yellow 1957 Chevy Impala convertible. He had washed and buffed it every day. He'd made sure that everyone on the block could hear its ear-splitting unmuffled power for a full five minutes before he peeled out and raced down the street with dangerously revved-up abandon.

Everybody on the block seemed to be astounded when they heard that Ed had crashed it into a tractor trailer and that it was a total loss. He'd gashed his arm and broken his nose. It was one month to the day after he had bought the car with five years of savings.

Anacleto knew that life outside of one's own home was dangerous. Why was it such a surprise to everyone else?

Outside, on the sidewalk, he shivered as he waited for Anne. Fear? Yes, but a sensation of having overcome an obstacle…a sense of …victory. He thought about his mother, alone in that big, old house. She hated everything. Her life had turned out to be such a disappointment. She had nobody. Anacleto's brothers didn't think about her. Anacleto could hardly stand talking to her. Her brother hadn't spoken to her in years and her husband's family had never really liked her.

What am I doing? I should be home, studying, reading.

Then Santo emerged from his apartment and walked quickly toward the corner. Anacleto waited for Anne. Santo was halfway down the block. Anne was nowhere to be seen. Anacleto ran to catch up to Santo, who turned, startled.

"What are you doin' out?"

"Oh, I was s…supposed to t…take a walk with Anne, but I guess she's n…not c… coming."

"Yeah. She wanted to go out, but my dad was holding her arm, bawling her out about something."

"Where are you g…going?"

"I would tell you, but—"

"Oh. H…how come you've b…been out of school s…so much?"

They stood at a bus stop at the far corner of the block under the weak glow of a street lamp. Santo pulled a pack of cigarettes from a knapsack that hung from one shoulder. He lit up. At that moment, with the smoke trailing from his lips, he looked tired, troubled.

"I got problems. I told you…money."

"I know. I w…want to help y…you, Santo."

"You can't."

"I th…thought we were fr… friends. I want to help you."

"You can't," he repeated.

"Can I go with you?"

"If you come with me, Clete, you gotta know…it's gonna change your life."

"What do…? What…ever. I w…want to help y…you."

They looked at the approaching bus. When it stopped, Santo stepped up, turned, and looked back. Anacleto got on. They paid their fares and sat in the back. The bus was empty. They rode in silence for a few blocks.

"Life sucks sometimes, you know," Santo whispered.

"I k…know."

"You have it rough too."

"I guess. I get con…fused a lot and I…don't know h…how to b…be with people."

"I know. All you need is confidence. You're hung up on your hand and how you talk."

"It…it's not m…my hand—"

"Look…I'm not ragging you…Everything's screwed up."

Anacleto looked out the window and wondered how many of the people on the sidewalks and in the stores were happy. How many of them were afraid and how many ran home from school and work to empty houses and loneliness?

"You know…everybody h…as problems. You…you've helped me. I w…want to help you."

Santo smoked his cigarette and looked out the window. He rubbed his eyes a few times. Anacleto watched him for a full minute, wondering if he had said the wrong thing.

"I'm gonna tell you because you're the only one I trust and you're gonna find out some of this sooner or later."

He dropped the cigarette stub to the floor and stepped on it. Then he withdrew another cigarette from his pack and lit up.

"You want a smoke?"

Anacleto shook his head.

"I told you, my father's crazy. What I didn't tell you is my mom can't stand him no more. He's draining her. She wants Anne and me and her to go away, but she don't have ten cents. All he gives her is a few bucks for food and the bills. She wants to go to my Aunt Rita. That's her sister. It was all arranged, but…"

Anacleto waited. He wanted to know, but, as Santo spoke, he began to be afraid of what he would hear. More than wanting to know the rest, he wanted to help Santo. He wanted to thank Santo for being his friend and for opening up to him.

"My mom's gonna have a baby."

"That's g…good, isn't it?"

"Listen. If I tell you this, you gotta keep your trap shut. You're my friend, but if you...I swear, if you breathe a word, I'll kill you." As he said that, Anacleto pulled away and sat back in his seat.

Santo pulled the cord above his head. The bus driver responded by swerving to the next bus stop. They used the rear exit, and walked down the street to a wooden bench that was between two large, ancient, leafy maples.

"This ain't my stop, but I gotta tell somebody. Anne don't know this."

Santo looked at Anacleto long and hard. Anacleto forced himself to stare back; he swore that Santo's secret would die with him.

The secret that Santo heartbrokenly and angrily shared with Anacleto that night in that little spot of greenery on that street in Brooklyn formed the beginning of a deep bond between the boys. It was a link in a chain that would drown Santo and bring Anacleto to within a hair's breadth of sinking with him.

THE STORY THAT SANTO TOLD

They sat, and Santo told the story of the sad, frightened girl, Francine, who would become his mother. How she came from a home of drinking, of fighting, of filth. She would flee her house every chance she got and walk and walk until she was too tired to walk anymore. Then she would return home, too drained to be kept awake by the monstrous alcoholic rages and vicious cursing and clawing of her parents. Her sister, Rita, seemed to be able to hide in her room all night, playing loud music on her phonograph and pretending to ignore the chaos, but Francine could not do that. She felt that every shouted curse and every smashed object hitting a wall was tearing her to pieces. Santo told Anacleto that Francine ran away when she was sixteen. She stayed with her mother's sister, her Aunt Bess, but after a few days, her parents found out where she was; they came to Bess's house in the middle of the night. When Bess didn't answer their violent pounding on her front door, Francine's father punched his hand through a window, pulled out the shards of glass, and entered the house through the shattered frame, monstrously howling that he wanted his Francine. He unlocked the front door for his wife. Then, when Bess tried to block his way, he grabbed her by the throat with a bloody hand and repeatedly slapped her face with the other one. Then he pushed her to the floor and kicked her head. Francine's mother watched her sister being beaten. Then she and her husband dragged Francine home.

Anacleto's eyes did not leave Santo's dark, troubled face; he hadn't shifted his gaze or moved a muscle from the second that Santo began talking. He felt weighted down. He was a part of the bench on which he sat. The dim, leafy spot was a room in Bess's house and he was with Francine and her beastly parents. He looked down on Bess, bloody and whimpering. He, not Santo, was telling the story.

"I can't tell you no more. I…want to, but…"

A sudden breeze slashed through the canopy of leaves above them. Anacleto looked up, past the leafy branches; above, all was black, jet black, speckled with minute sparkling gems, smaller than grains of salt. His head, and then the rest of him began to ascend. He looked down on the two boys on the bench. Then he gazed upward, past the visible pinpricks of light in the numbingly cold expanse of the night sky. Was there someone else, somewhere else in the vastness who was suffering because of the violence and despair of that tortured night of violence? Of another night?

"Did sh…she die?"

"Who? You mean Bess? No, I don't think so. My mom wasn't allowed to see her again. I don't know anything about her…about her now."

"That's too bad—"

"Listen. I'll tell you the rest. It's about my dad. But not now. You gotta promise to keep it to yourself."

"Okay."

"This is stuff Anne don't know. It would ruin her if she knew."

"Okay," Anacleto repeated.

"If you wanna go home, it's okay." Santo stood up, scanned the dark, deserted street, and starting walking back to the bus stop.

Anacleto waited. He knew Santo would return.

Santo came back, sat down, and moved his anguished face close to Anacleto.

"You gotta swear."

"I s…swear."

"No. You gotta say that you'll never tell. On whatever you hold holy and on your mom and your brothers and your whole life."

Anacleto repeated, more or less, what Santo had asked him to say.

"My Aunt Rita, my mom's sister, she was gonna take us all in—my mom, Anne, and me. She was gonna sell her house and we were gonna go off to California, where my dad can't find us, where he won't make my mom crazy. And so Anne don't find out." He turned his head away from Anacleto. He wiped his face with his hands. Then he turned back to Anacleto. "I swear to God, if we stay here, he's gonna make me hurt him some day."

I know that. I've seen it happen.

Santo looked up, as if he was expecting someone to appear above him in the tree branches. Then he squeezed his eyes tightly closed.

"I told you my mom's pregnant. It made my aunt mad. She won't talk to my mom no more. I couldn't understand it. I called her—my aunt—a bitch." Santo rubbed his eyes, then he lit another cigarette, inhaling deeply. "At first, my Aunt Rita, she won't tell me why she's so pissed off at my mom. All she said is my mom can't make up her mind about my dad—whether she wants to leave him or stay. I mean, if she wants to leave him, which she says sometimes to me and Anne, why'd she…you know…let him get her pregnant?"

"I guess sh…she l…loves him."

"Yeah, maybe. He's not bad to her most of the time, but there's a big strain."

Santo told more about his mother when she was a young woman. She quit high school and left home. She couldn't stand another day with her abusive parents. It pained her to leave Rita behind, but she had to run to save her own life. She stole money from her father's wallet. Santo told how she got a job in a diner in Queens. She became friendly with an older man who was a regular customer. He took her out. She became pregnant. She moved to a better apartment that the man paid for. He couldn't stay with her and he couldn't marry her.

"Why couldn't he m…marry her? Who was the m…man?"

"Boy, are you stupid," Santo laughed. Then he became serious again. "The man was…is my father. She was pregnant with me. Then she had Anne." He smiled, but there were tears in his eyes.

He flicked his cigarette to the street, stood up, and rubbed his face with his hands. Then he sat down again and lit another cigarette. He took a long drag. He exhaled a cloud that enveloped his head, partially obscuring his grief-stricken face.

I will not lose control. This is not my family.

"My aunt, she told me all this. She told me my dad couldn't marry my mom... or stay with her 'cause he was already married." Santo looked at Anacleto. Then he put his head down. He waited for Anacleto to respond. "He's still married," he continued. "He's got kids, grown kids. I think he has grandkids. He goes home to his other family every night. His real family."

Anacleto couldn't breathe. Santo sniffled; then he snorted and sent a gob of spit toward the nearby street.

"Aunt Rita got mad at my mom for getting pregnant. Like I said, I got mad at Aunt Rita. I didn't know why she was so pissed off at my mother. I yelled at her and told her she promised to help my mom and us. Then she told me the whole story. Rita says that mom can't leave him now...not with a baby coming. My mom, if she didn't get pregnant, we all coulda left and went to California—all of us. It woulda been nice."

All of Anacleto's thoughts remained trapped in the buzzing and sparking confusion of his overloaded brain.

"Aunt Rita says his…wife, his legal wife, she found out about us a long time ago...years ago. She yelled at my mom over the telephone, I think. I was there when my mom was on the phone. I could hear a woman yelling on the other end, but I didn't know what was going on. My mom looked like a ghost when she hung up."

"D…does Anne—"

"No. I don't want her to know. I can't stand this. I think she would kill herself if she knew she was a…bastard. That's what we are, you know. My little brother or sister is gonna be a bastard…a little bastard." Santo laughed.

I feel his pain. Unwanted...a mistake...like me.

"He's never gonna be there for us. What do we do if he drops dead in our house one night? Do we call his real wife and tell her? How would we know who to call? What if he drops dead there? Are we ever gonna know? Is my mom gonna be able to go to the funeral? I ain't going, no matter what."

Then Santo told Anacleto about the many times his mother had planned to leave, only to give up the thought because of a lack of money or because she really did love this man who belonged to another family.

"I don't even know if Faricola is his real name. Maybe he made that name up to make it harder for his wife to know about us, his other family." Santo sobbed. His misery at that moment transcended Anacleto's usual fog of despondency and confusion.

With a great effort, Anacleto said, "That does…doesn't mat…ter. My name is…isn't really Roosevelt."

He was trying to be reassuring. He felt that he had to try to act confident and assertive. Everything was different now.

After a while, Santo spoke: "It's not the same thing. Look…I need money to get my mom and Anne away so they can have a better life. Understand?" He stood up and began walking to the bus stop. "Now you know. Do you wanna go with me?"

"Where're we g…going?"

"Listen. I didn't want you mixed up in this. I told you I gotta make money for my mom."

"But—"

"You don't wanna go where I'm going. I don't wanna go. Go home."

They walked to the bus stop. When the bus arrived, Anacleto followed Santo up the steps.

***

The half-filled bus moved swiftly as it carried them to a neighborhood, a part of Brooklyn that, although not so far away, seemed earth-shatteringly distant and different from the place where they lived. As Anacleto stepped off the bus, he knew that he wanted to be home.

"Th…there are s…so m…many Negroes here."

Santo ignored the comment for a few seconds, and then, with a smile, he replied, "There are only Nee-grows here."

As they walked quickly along the busy sidewalk, passing people hurrying home from work or going in and out of the stores that lined the street, Anacleto thought of what his mother would say if she knew that he had gone into a "colored" neighborhood. She would not say anything; he pictured her screeching and screaming and pulling her hair and squeezing her face. She would flail her arms sputter about guns and—

"This is it. Come up with me. This guy's my friend." Santo opened a chipped, cracked blue wooden door between two storefronts; Anacleto followed him into a small, musty-smelling alcove with four flat brass mailboxes on one wall. Each one had a small white button above it. Santo pressed one.

"Who?" A scratchy voice came from a metal speaker above the mailboxes.

"It's me, Santo."

There was a buzzing sound; Santo quickly turned the knob on a door leading out of the alcove and walked into a hallway. Anacleto followed.

***

Back on the bus, Santo asked, "You know what this is?" Keeping his knapsack on his knees, he unzipped it a little, revealing the top of a plastic bag. Then, looking around him, he opened the bag. He gestured for Anacleto to smell it.

"I know."

"You ever try it? Naw. How would you?"

Anacleto wanted to tell him that he didn't need to smoke a joint to feel afloat…or cut off from reality.

"Everybody lights up now. Like I said, I need the money."

"Why don't you get a j…job?"

"That's the sucker way of makin' money. Besides, I need a lot."

They stared out the window of the bus for the last few minutes of their ride together. As the bus approached their stop, Anacleto realized that the few black people who had been passengers earlier had all gotten off. He stood up and walked to the rear exit. He looked at Santo, still sitting, holding the knapsack on his lap. Santo winked at Anacleto as he descended the steps to the sidewalk. Anacleto watched the bus move from the curb and slowly disappear.

Anacleto walked along the silent street to his house, where he would be invisible, safe. He thought about how he should have looked at Santo through the spaces between his fingers, but he was trying not to do that anymore. Besides, what was the point? Santo wouldn't have listened to what he would have told him. Anacleto did not think that he could save Santo any more than he could save himself.

***

He wanted to tell Santo that he would help him. He needed money, and Anacleto would give it to him. Santo had no reason to be ashamed about his situation. What were families? Anacleto's mother and father had been married. His father was dead. His mother was alone, as if she had never been married, as if her husband had never existed. What did that mean? Was he anywhere now? Was he anything more than a decomposed remnant of a once-living thing? Anacleto didn't want to think of his father that way. What about all of the married couples who hated each other? How many of them couldn't stand the sight, the smell of each other? He had heard violent, sickening screaming fights between husbands and wives on occasion—mostly at night—in the summer, when the windows were open. And what about the husbands who sneaked around. There had always been talk about that. He had not understood what was being said when he was younger.

"Yeah, Richie has a…you know, a cousin; he visits her two, three times a week."

People didn't talk about it much, but there were wives who cheated on their husbands too.

Anacleto felt close to Santo.

He's more my brother than any of my real brothers are.

***

The next day, when Anne asked Anacleto about his night with Santo, he lied. He told her that they had talked for a while and then Santo had said not to bother him anymore. She asked what they had talked about. He told her that Santo was angry about how his father treated him. She was more worried than ever about her brother.

"He goes out every night and he doesn't come back until morning. Then he sleeps all day. I think he's stopped going to school. My mother says she understands...that Santo needs time."

"What does your…father…say?"

"Well, they had a big fight. My father slapped Santo and Santo raised his fists to him."

"What happened?"

"Nothing. They don't talk." Then Anne looked at him and smiled.

"What?"

"Nothing. Just tell me something," she said.

"What sh...should I tell you?"

"Anything. What did you eat for dinner last night?"

He laughed.

"What's so funny?" she asked.

"Oh, my mother. Telling what we have for dinner is a secret with her."

Then Anne smiled again. "You know what? You practically don't stutter anymore."

He had not actually stopped. However, at times when he felt very relaxed, he was able to speak a few words at a time without the jarring paralysis which had been a part of him for as long as he could remember. If he was very nervous, he might occasionally stammer and struggle to latch onto the next word, but he felt more confident and at ease than he had ever been.

Anne kissed his cheek.

"You're getting better and better every day."

Flushed with embarrassment, he stammered, "I...I'll talk to Santo again."

***

He waited for Santo outside of his house that night. When Santo emerged, at around seven, carrying his knapsack, Anacleto walked with him.

"What's happening?" he asked, forcing a smile.

Santo looked tired. "Nothin' good."

"How's your m…mom?"

"You know how she is. Pregnant. Besides, you see her. I know you see Anne every day."

"She's just my f…friend, Santo."

"I know. I don't care. Just don't hurt her or get her knocked up."

"It's n…not like that."

When they got to the corner, Santo crossed to the other side of the street and waited for the bus. Anacleto followed.

"Where are you going?" Anacleto asked.

"Same place I go every night."

"You're going to get in tr...trouble selling pot."

"Yeah, maybe, but I got other problems now."

Anacleto waited.

"For one thing, I told her I was gonna have some money soon, but she don't want to leave my father. For another, it turns out…I owe a lot of money."

The bus approached. Santo turned to Anacleto.

"Listen, Clete. It's all right. You're my man. I…I know you're a good friend, but don't bother me now."

When the bus stopped, Santo mouthed, "Go home." Then he got on, paid his fare, and walked to the back. The bus pulled away from the curb.

Anacleto watched until it disappeared in the early evening traffic.

THE MISSING GUN

Anacleto decided that he did not want to work in the stink and heat of Joe Zitto's body shop again, so he looked in the classified section of the *Daily News* for a summer job. An ad for a job selling magazine subscriptions caught his attention.

One day in June after school, he took the subway to the address that was listed on the ad. It was an old storefront in Brooklyn Heights. After he filled out an application, two men in suits explained that, after he had been trained, he would go door-to-door in a different neighborhood each day with the newest issues of magazines such as *Time* and *Life* and a pad of order forms. They paid $10.00 per week plus $1.00 commission for each subscription that he landed. They said that some boys earned as much as a hundred dollars some weeks.

Even though he was worried about his stuttering, Anacleto was eager. They told him to report to the office on the first Monday of summer vacation at 9 a.m. As he stood up to leave, the phone rang. One of the men motioned to him to sit.

The man picked up, listened, and then he said, "Okay" once or twice. Then he hung up.

He spoke to the other man. "That was Rowley. He said we don't have to hold onto the applications from those colored kids. He said we should just throw them out."

"Okay, kid," he said to Anacleto, "One more thing: you have to dress nice for this job—slacks, button shirt, shoes. Got it?"

Anacleto stood up and shook his head. Then he left.

On the first day of vacation, he woke up early and walked to Joe Zitto's Auto Body.

***

That summer was a particularly fertile one for Lucia's life-altering dreams. Saturday mornings were about the only time all week there was a chance of James, Frank, and Anacleto being together, which was necessary before she would describe her dreams, not that any of the boys wanted to hear about yet another confused bit of nocturnal insight.

George and Ronnie were both in Vietnam. James, who had changed his major from sociology to education, was entering his senior year at Brooklyn College, and Frank was going into his third year at City College, majoring in chemistry. They had two summer jobs each—as afternoon lifeguards at Coney Island and at an electronics warehouse at night.

They heard the dreaded announcement just as they sat down to breakfast: "Let me tell you about my dream."

This was the third such declaration that summer, and it was only the middle of July.

Lucia's dream, which she had needed a couple of days of thought to interpret, involved the usual neighbors, relatives, and priests and, since they were Jewish, a rabbi made a quick, confusing cameo appearance.

"And so, it means we have to move."

James and Frank were panic stricken.

"What? What are you talking about, Ma?" Frank asked.

James wanted to know whether this was necessary.

"Of course it is," Lucia cheerily answered.

"Where? Still in Brooklyn?" he asked.

"I don't know," she answered. "Maybe another country—like Connecticut."

None of the boys cared to correct her error. They were too stunned.

"But all my friends are here. I can't move now. I…we have to finish college." James was dark with anger.

Lucia smiled cherubically and sipped her coffee. Anacleto laughed at the irony of it. Before, he would not have been concerned about moving, as long as he had food and a bed and a library within walking distance. Now, though, he had Santo, although he didn't really have him. But he knew that Santo needed him. And he had Anne, although he didn't have her either, at least not in the way he wanted her.

Now that I care about people, I'm about to lose them.

Lucia said that she had spoken to a realtor, who had taken her to see a few houses in various parts of Brooklyn, Queens, and Staten Island. She said that some of them were nice, but she wanted to look in "other countries that are not around here."

James and Frank looked at each other gloomily. They looked to Anacleto, hoping that he would attempt to appeal to her.

But, then she said, "The agent, he wants to list our house. He wanted to come in here and look the place over. I told him no. I don't need no stranger in my house."

Anacleto knew then that they were not going to move.

But Lucia didn't know. She started cleaning out closets and packing vases and figurines and extra sets of dishes that she had not looked at in years.

"While I do this, you clean the basement," she ordered.

The boys spent all of that Saturday morning gathering the junk and assorted refuse that had accumulated in the cold, dank, dark basement during the many years that their mother had lived in the house.

When the brothers had deposited onto the sidewalk in front of their house piles of dusty, moldy lumber, broken cinder blocks, boxes of damaged toys, loads of broken tools, Christmas lights with frayed wires, and more junk than all of their neighbors together could have amassed in their combined lifetimes, they thoroughly swept out the now empty basement. All that was left, besides the giant, cylindrical fuel tank and the boiler, was their father's old workshop, neat for the first time in years.

"Now, get me the ladder."

Those words sawed into Anacleto's brain: a flash of light blinded him and jagged hot slivers of metal sliced through his skull. He could not draw a breath. Then, reassuring himself that he had replaced the cheese box in precisely the same location in the attic from which he had taken it, he relaxed a little.

"What's the matter? You don't look so good." Frank stared at Anacleto with concern.

"I'm okay."

After showering, Anacleto sat on his bed, reading *Crime and Punishment*. A repeated, dull metal on metal clanking emanated from the basement.

Prison cell doors banging shut.

"We got trouble."

Anacleto squinted at his mother, surprised that he had dozed off. He rubbed his eyes and wiped saliva from his lips. He took the still-open book from his chest and laid it on the bed.

"Who…what do you m…mean, Ma?"

She sat on the bed, next to him. Her tired brown eyes fixed on his face. He wanted to reach up and hug her, but didn't.

"The box…in the attic. Did you touch it?"

His cross-wired brain buzzed.

Yes. No. What box?

He focused on the illustration on the cover of the book. Sorrowful eyes... window to the soul...a man...troubled...points of light...punishment for his crimes.

"I know it was you," she sadly accused. "The others wouldn't think of lookin' up there."

"I j…just l…looked at them. I p…put them b…back."

Then the screaming, cursing, howling began. She slammed her hands on the bed and pulled at her hair.

"Where's the other one? Son-of-a-bitch-bastard!!!"

"Wh…what d…do…do you m…mean?"

She squeezed her face between her palms and cursed. He wanted to laugh, but he also wanted to cry. She walloped him on his shoulder so hard that he almost tumbled off the bed.

"There were three guns in that box. I know there were. Now there's two!"

She pounded her head with her fists. Then, placing a pointed finger to one of her temples and folding her hand into a gun, she fired. The room filled with smoke…She collapsed onto Anacleto. Blood seeped from the wound on her head onto his lap.

"There's trouble. What did you do? Where is it?"

He stammered and stuttered and told her about showing the pistols to Santo.

"So, he has it?"

"No." Then he told her how they had brought them to Albie's father and how he had brought a box of cartridges up from his basement and how he had fired the gun. "B…but only …once."

"Once? He shot the gun? Jee—sus! I…I told you…you don't give away secrets to strangers!"

"It's okay. I t…took the b..box and put it right b..back in the at—"

"But one's missing. Where the hell is it?"

"I d…don't know."

Then, forcing herself, Lucia spoke in a calmer voice, explaining to Anacleto that the pistols had belonged to someone who his father had known. There had been three pistols. She had wrapped them in the blue cloth and put them in the box and given the box to her husband. She had seen him put it in the attic. That had been when they were first married.

"There were two guns when I took the box from the attic, and they weren't wrapped in the blue cloth. I just broke them up with a hammer. You gotta ask Santo where that other gun is."

Anacleto stood up and told her that it would be all right, that he would take care of it. As he walked the short distance to Albie's house, to Santo's family's apartment, he played back the mental recording of Mr. Caspari's firing of the pistol that day. He remembered that Mr. Caspari had examined the gun after he had fired it. Anacleto had understood then that it had been a mistake to show the gun to Santo and more of a mistake to show it to anyone else. He had grabbed the pistol from Mr. Caspari's hand, surprising him. Anacleto remembered how he thought he had given people one more reason to think of him as weird, but he hadn't cared. He had put the pistol in the box, under the blue cloth, and closed the box, and brought it home. He knew that there had been three pistols. He had not bothered to check the box. He assumed that the other two had been in there when he put the one that had been fired back into the box. He had been too frantic to check. He didn't think Santo had it, but, where else could it be?

Anne came to the door. She was combing her hair. Wet, long, black, lustrous. He imagined her leaning over him and being enveloped in the moist fragrance of that luxurious growth.

"I…talk…I have to t…talk to Santo."

"He's sleeping."

Her father called out, asking who was at the door. Anne smirked, and ignored him. Anacleto could hear her father and mother talking.

"W…would you wake him up? It's important."

"No point. He won't get up."

"But—"

"I'll tell him to see you when he gets up."

"Okay. Thanks."

"Sure." She stared at Anacleto for a few seconds before she closed the door.

He knew…He thought he knew how she felt…but he didn't know how to be sure. He asked himself what he was thinking. Of course she didn't like him that much. No girl could. It came down to her sorrow. Her father cast a pall over her life. He wondered whether she knew. Santo had said that she didn't. She could not wait to get away. Just like her mother when she was young. She smelled Anacleto's sadness as he smelled hers. Just as animals could identify members of their group in the dark recesses of a forest or a jungle by the familiar odor.

Once I take care of this mess with the pistol…maybe…

Where could it be? He didn't want to ask Albie or his father. He hoped they had both forgotten about that day. When Anacleto had taken the pistol from Mr. Caspari's hand, he had looked surprised. He must have thought that Anacleto had no manners. Mr. Caspari didn't live with the fear of making mistakes, as Anacleto did. As soon as he heard that sharp crack and smelled that harsh smoke, Anacleto knew he had done the wrong thing. He had given away a family secret.

Maybe Mr. Caspari knew about that. What had he said? Guns like that had been used in a robbery in the Bronx.

My father never...He had been a gentle, wacky soul.

He thought about his uncles, older cousins, his deceased grandfathers. Tough men... big hands, worker's hands. Hard…scarred. Hands that worked long hours. Those men provided for their families. They had all saved their money and improved their lives. They drank strong, tart homemade wine made from grapes that grew in the backyard of his father's parents' house in Gravesend, a short distance away. There was a wine press in the basement.

Years before, his mother's mother and father moved from the Bronx to live with them in Brooklyn. He used to refer to them as "my real grandma and grandpa," even though he had loved his father's parents too.

His "real grandpa" had smoked his whole life. After he had been diagnosed with cancer and Anacleto's grandmother had taken every penny from his pockets so he could not buy cigarettes, he bummed them from neighbors. When the neighbors refused to give cigarettes to him because Anacleto's grandmother, in a mixture of broken English and Italian, had told them how sick he was, he walked up and down the streets of the neighborhood, eyes down, scouring the gutter, searching for discarded butts that did not look too dirty. Anacleto's grandmother yelled at her husband and alternately cursed and looked to heaven to ask Saint Peter to intervene, but Grandpa just smiled sheepishly and sucked in the smoke. He became sicker and sicker. His eyes and skin turned yellow. After a short stay in the hospital, he was brought home to die.

One day, when Anacleto was alone in his house, his grandfather in bed in the dim, cramped downstairs apartment at the back of the house, he heard a thump and then a cry, a plaintive meow. He ran downstairs and entered the apartment. His grandfather lay on the floor, clothed only in a wrinkled, soiled pajama top, and nothing else, one hand cupping his genitals. He moaned in a high-pitched warble that now sounded more like that of a wounded bird than a mournful cat. He had fallen on his way to the bathroom. Anacleto stood, confused and helpless, while his grandfather moaned; then the old man started to cry. Although Anacleto felt faint, shaky, nauseated, he concentrated on helping his grandfather, promising himself that he could be sick later. He lifted and pushed the emaciated old man into a sitting position, averting his eyes so that he would not see his genitals, so he would not shame him. Then, crouching behind him and slipping his arms under his grandfather's arms and wrapping them around the old man's shrunken chest, Anacleto locked his hands together and tried to lift him from the floor. He pulled him up a couple of inches, and then sat him down on the floor again. His grandfather whimpered. Anacleto tried again, but he was not strong enough.

"You just a little boy. You get-ta help."

Anacleto gently put his grandfather down so that he was lying on the floor, and placed a pillow under his head; then he ran to Albie's house. He rang the doorbell. His fists pounded on the door. Nothing. He ran to the back of the house, to the shed. Mr. Caspari was there, sanding a roof that would cover a birdhouse.

"M…m…my gr…and…fath—"

"My God, boy. Get the freakin' marbles out of your mouth. You'll never get into college talking like that."

"My...grand...f...father fell."

Mr. Caspari continued to sand.

"He...he's on the floor. I can...can't g...g...get him up."

Mr. Caspari ran his fingers along the clean smoothness of the miniature wooden roof. Then he held it up to the light, inspecting it. Then he sanded a bit more. When he was satisfied that it was ready for painting, he put it down, threw the sandpaper into a wastebasket, and walked from the shed toward Anacleto's house. He picked up the old man, who had by now soiled himself, and laid him on the bed.

"I can't be called over her to help you all the time. You better look after your grandpa, young man," he instructed, and left.

His grandfather was not able to leave the convertible couch in the small living room of their apartment for the last few weeks of his life. His grandmother had moved her husband from the bed that they had shared for sixty years, the one that had been in their tenement apartment on Elizabeth Street in Little Italy and then in their large old house in the hills of the Bronx and now in their little bedroom in the apartment at the rear of the house that they shared with Anacleto's family. She had convinced him to relocate to the convertible so that he would be able to watch the television that was in the living room, but Anacleto knew the real reason was that she did not want to sleep next to him because of the smell that emanated from his dying body. She fed him and gave him medicine and cleaned him, but Anacleto never saw her kiss him. She never touched him in a loving, reassuring way during his few last weeks.

A week after his grandfather had fallen, Anacleto was alone with him again. He had been panicky when his grandmother had said that she was going grocery shopping.

"What if h...he has tr...trouble br...breathing, Grandma?"

"Don't-a you wor-ry. He's-a okay today."

"He's br...breathing ver...very rough."

"What you mean?"

"I mean...I mean h...he has tr...trouble."

"What you say?"

Anacleto never understood why his parents and grandparents had never taught any of the boys how to speak Italian. They used the language like a secret code when they didn't want anyone to know what they were saying. Despite the fact that he and his brothers had picked up hundreds of words and phrases in Italian, they understood little of what they heard.

Speaking very slowly and accentuating his words, even using the phrasing that his grandmother used when she spoke English, even adding vowel endings to some words, he said, "Gr…grandma, Grandpa, he no breathe-a…you know…" He demonstrated inhaling and exhaling. "He no breathe-a v…ver…very good."

"Oh, don't-a you wor-ry."

His grandfather slept all afternoon. Then his chest began to expand and contract rapidly and a snorting, whistling, rattling sound escaped from his toothless mouth with each of his labored breaths. His chest lifted and fell with each series of choking inhalations. He gasped and struggled for air. Anacleto stared, unable to decide whether to go to him or call a doctor.

Within seconds, the gasping, strangled efforts stopped.

Anacleto walked to his grandfather and whispered in his ear. He touched his face. It was tepid and unresponsive. He knelt by the old man's bed and asked forgiveness for not having held him as he suffocated. Then he ran from the house, down the street to the corner, and seven blocks to the church rectory. He rang the bell that was next to the large oak door. After two more rings, a small, tidy-looking woman wearing a floral print apron opened the door. He told her he needed a priest; she invited him into the foyer and asked him to wait. Minutes passed before Father Bearden, a short, heavy, balding man, approached Anacleto. He had bread crumbs on his face.

"M…my g…gr…grand…grandfath…er just died at h…home. My grand… m…m… mother and my m…mother will come home s…soon. I know…they're b…both going to f…faint and become hys…hys…t…terical. Could you c…come?"

The priest checked his watch. Looking disappointed, he told Anacleto that he needed a couple of minutes. Anacleto waited. He feared that his grandmother might be finished shopping. He worried that one of them might arrive home before he and the priest got there. He waited in the dark foyer, fighting the urge to leave.

Finally, the priest emerged, holding a black leather bag. They got into his car and Anacleto gave him the address. Candy bar wrappers and a couple of issues of the *Post* lay on the floor. Anacleto had never thought about what priests ate or read.

They pulled up to the house and entered the room where his grandfather's body lay. It had cooled and begun to look waxy. He and Father Bearden looked at it for a moment. They heard a key in the lock.

His grandmother walked in. She took in the scene—her dead husband, the priest, Anacleto, and raised her hands heavenward and began to howl.

Father Bearden looked at her and then at the body, and decided to tend to the living. As Anacleto's grandmother sobbed and shook and choked, the priest, holding her shoulders, kept repeating, "It's all right, mother, it's all right."

Then, without a sound, Lucia slipped into the quiet room and, standing next to her mother, she starting yelling and pulling her hair. The priest was so shocked and frightened that he pulled Anacleto's grandmother away from Lucia. Anacleto put his arms around his mother and held her. She calmed down and kept repeating, "Now he's dead. Now he sleeps."

Father Bearden settled the two women onto the heavy, old couch. He asked them to pray with him. Anacleto's grandmother started to kneel, but the priest told her to remain seated. "Jesus wants your prayers. He does not want you to faint, mother."

They prayed. Lucia and Anacleto remained mute.

"Won't you join us, children?" Father Bearden asked.

Anacleto, who had been holding his mother's hand, felt it tense. She took in the priest with her bloodshot eyes. Then, standing, she picked up the can of pine-scented room deodorizer that had been on the little table next to the old man for the last weeks of his life, and she sprayed the room as Father Bearden and her mother prayed.

After that day, whenever Anacleto smelled pine trees, he thought of his grandfather's slow, painful, lonely descent into death in the little apartment at the back of his house.

WHAT HE SAW IN THE PARK

Anacleto caught up with Santo as he was leaving his house that night, and asked about the missing pistol.

"Yeah? So? I don't have it."

"My mother is r…really upset. It's m…my fault. I never should have—"

"Don't be such a baby. Be a man. Tell her it happened. The gun is lost."

"But, where is it?"

"How the hell should I know?" And he stormed off.

Anacleto knew he had to talk to Mr. Caspari. He didn't want to because the man would enjoy the fact that Anacleto was in trouble. It wasn't that he disliked Anacleto. He didn't dislike anyone. Or like anyone, for that matter, except for Albie and maybe his frail, sick wife. When he looked at people, it was with the scrutiny of a laboratory scientist examining bacteria under a microscope.

As Anacleto stood on the stoop of Albie's house, with his finger poised to ring the doorbell, he weighed the possibilities: Mr. Caspari might have some ideas about the location of the missing pistol or who might have taken it or what happened to it, but, no—if he had seen someone touching it, he would have said something. He was a lot of things, but he was not reckless about firearms. He wouldn't have kept one of the guns either. He wasn't a thief. Besides, he had pistols, shotguns, rifles, the least expensive of which was better than that single-shot starter pistol. Anacleto didn't want to open himself up to ridicule or to rumors about the guns that the Roosevelt family had hidden away and that their idiot youngest son had shown to the world. Mr. Caspari would surely wait for an opportunity to ask Lucia whether she had found the missing pistol. He would do that because he would know that talking openly about it would drive her crazy.

Anacleto came down from the stoop and began walking to the corner. He needed to think. The wet, warm, heavy air was suffocating. The cloud-filled sky was darkening by the minute, choking off the last traces of summer sunlight. He moved slowly down the sidewalk, thinking.

How is it that trouble follows me? Me! I don't lie or steal. Most other people are so dishonest. But they have sunshine, while I live under a perpetual, leaden cloud. Then there's Santo. In the midst of a storm. His father. Part of Santo's problem. He has to find another way to get money, to live his life. I used to be better at knowing what to do. I used to stay in my room.

Find the gun…stay in my house…simple life.

He walked for a long while, not thinking about where he was going. He found himself a good distance from his house, by the stretch of promenade and park at the

Narrows, near the Verrazano Bridge. The nearby trees were shades of gray and black as he walked along the promenade overlooking the bay. The choppy water was steel gray, with explosions of white when the waves broke against the rocks below. He sat on a bench, looking at the gloom, feeling grateful for his solitude. His head hurt and he was drenched with sweat. He knew his mother was sitting by one of the front windows, raking her fingers through her hair and pulling down on it, frantic, convinced that something had happened to him.

Good. She deserves to worry. But she's had a terrible life...but she can't treat me like this anymore. Of course, it's my fault the gun is lost. But, whose were they?

He stood up to leave. The sky was completely black now. He could not determine where, in the distance, it met the water of the bay. He walked along the promenade and through the park until he reached the sidewalk. A bus stopped a short distance down the street and discharged its passengers.

Santo, carrying his knapsack, emerged from the bus and headed to the park that Anacleto had just left. Anacleto reentered the park, immediately losing sight of Santo amidst the thick, dark foliage. He walked faster. He spotted Santo walking on a footpath and then opening a wooden gate and disappearing into a thicket. On the gate was a sign that read PARK EMPLOYEES ONLY. Anacleto hesitated briefly before opening the gate and entering the fenced-in area. He walked off the path to a section where the growth was wild; in the dim light, it was difficult to walk without stumbling over split branches and tangled undergrowth, so he moved slowly and carefully. He saw a small, gray wooden shed, partially visible amidst the trees in the beam of a bare light bulb. Near it, sitting on a bench, lighting a cigarette, was Santo.

Anacleto stood behind a tree in an area of particularly thick growth, watching Santo. He felt guilty, but he was unable to tear himself away. He knew, but he needed to see it. After a while, he began to feel hungry, but the need to satisfy his curiosity and the idea that he could help Santo kept him rooted to his spot.

A few minutes later, three boys approached Santo. He greeted them, but Anacleto could not hear what they were saying. Santo gave a cigarette to one. As the boy lit up, Santo pulled a small clear plastic bag from his knapsack and handed it to one of the other boys. One of the boys handed some cash to him. Then the boys left.

This happened a half dozen or more times during the next few minutes. Anacleto thought he recognized some of the boys and girls, but, in the dim light, he could not be sure. Several of Santo's customers were men and women.

A tall, thin girl approached Santo. They talked; Santo shook his head "no." They talked a while longer; then they kissed for a long time.

Anacleto needed to urinate, but he hesitated because he was sure that Santo would hear the sound if he did it right there. Then Santo released the girl and said something to her. She looked around and then she unbuckled his belt and pulled down his pants and undershorts. Anacleto felt his throbbing head lift from his body and, turning around, he started to move out of the thicket, but he stepped on a branch; it snapped. He froze.

"Who the hell?"

Anacleto slowly, carefully took a few more steps, but not before Santo, hurriedly buckling his belt, caught up to him.

"What the fuck you doin' here?"

"I have to talk…to—"

"You already talked to me. I don't know where it is."

"I…I…know. It's—"

"Listen. This is private. You stay away." He looked back to the bench, but the girl was gone.

"Shit! Shit!" He glared at Anacleto.

"I'm…sorry. I—"

"Shit! My stash!" He raced back to the bench, looked around frantically, and then he ran off. Anacleto heard him crashing through the underbrush, calling out, cursing savagely. When Santo returned to the bench, Anacleto walked over to him.

"Did…sh…she steal it?"

"The bitch!"

"Who is she?"

"How the hell do I know?"

"You mean, she would d…do that just for s…some p...pot?"

Santo glared. Then he lit a cigarette and smoked quietly.

"I really h…have to pee," Anacleto said through clenched teeth.

"So, there's about five billion trees here. Pick one. And why don't you jerk off while you're at it?"

Anacleto moved a few feet away from Santo and relieved himself. It always amazed him that Santo and most of the other boys he knew talked about *that* so casually. He had held off for a long time, torn by the polar opposites of his bright, hot, almost continual state of arousal and his dark, cold fear of eternal damnation. The memory of the anxiety and dread that had always overcome him in the dark of the confessional had been strong. Once he had finally given in to his seemingly inescapable need for self-gratification, he decided that it was too blissful and personal to discuss with anyone.

"What did you mean 'she would do that'?" Santo asked when Anacleto had returned to the bench.

"I…I don't know."

"Listen, Clete, I like you. If you were anybody else, I'd punch your face in. I got girls comin' onto me for me. This one, she wanted…"

Anacleto waited.

"Listen. I tell ya, you don't belong here," Santo said, kicking a stone.

Two young men appeared. One was a tall, well-built black man. The other was white, thin with long, messy blond hair.

"I don't got any more tonight, guys."

"What? It's only nine o'clock," the white man said, incredulous.

"Sorry. Come back tomorrow."

"What the fuck?" The white man looked spectral in the muted light.

"What the hell can I tell ya? It was a busy night."

"I need this, Santo," he whined.

They left. Santo pulled a wad of bills from his pocket, and counted.

"I'm in trouble, Clete. I need money."

"You have so much."

"I owe a fuckin' boatload."

He told how he had stopped going to Brownsville. He met someone who knew someone who…

"You mean you're buying from *those* people?"

Santo laughed, but only for a second. "They're businessmen. They're part of the community. They dress nice. They live nice. They're real gentlemen."

Then, as someone else began walking their way, Santo said, "Oh, shit," and he led Anacleto through the underbrush and out of the park.

They went home by bus.

"Listen. I really need money now. You'll get it back."

"I don't understand." Anacleto suppressed the urge to tell Santo that he had a choice because it was clear that he was hurt, broken. He needed support.

"Okay, Santo. H…How much?"

"Two hundred."

"What? How m…much pot did you buy?"

Leaning so close to Anacleto that he could taste Santo's stale-tobacco breath, he whispered, "My life's in your hands. I been dealin' dope. I owe."

Anacleto's face grew warm and his fingers felt cold. He thought of *Naked Lunch.*

"Y…y…you aren't—"

"I'm not that stupid. I just sell it."

They rode the rest of the way home in silence. The brightly lit storefronts and the street lamps that they passed did not dispel their gloominess. A transistor radio being held by someone on the bus was playing "Paint It Black." Its jarring sound compounded Anacleto's unhappy, depressed mood.

When they arrived at Santo's house, Anacleto asked him what he planned on doing.

"That's my problem. I have to raise the money."

"What happens if you don't p…pay them?"

"Number one, they slap me around. Number two, they don't give me anymore to sell and they still want their money, and more."

"They ch…charge you interest?"

"Yeah, big time. But this ain't a bank. They collect or you won't see me no more."

"I have the money, but—"

"What?"

"I feel bad helping you buy dr…drugs…you know…to make people s…sick."

"Listen, you been a hermit so long, you don't know how many people are begging for this stuff. Everybody graduates from weed to something else. Junk ain't no different."

"It's d…different. Did you see that guy…tonight? He was sh…shaking. He's sick from the drugs. It's b…bad."

"You gonna help me or you gonna come to my funeral?"

Sparks zapped through Anacleto's brain. He wished he were bigger than Santo. He would wrap his arms around him and bring him to his house and tell his mother to lock him in.

"I'll g…give you the money, but it'll have to be tomorrow. I can't get it t…tonight."

"You gotta. I need it now. I can straighten out with my…friends. It's early. I can maybe make back what I lost."

Anacleto didn't want to hear that. To give Santo money to protect him from trouble was a sacrifice he was willing to make, but the thought that he would be staking him for another round of drug dealing made him sick.

"Santo, only once. I'm n…never…never doing this again."

"It ain't gonna happen again. Besides, if you weren't sneakin' around, spying on me, this never woulda happened."

"I'm s…sorry. I was worried about the g…gun."

Anacleto saw Santo's face grow dark; then he smiled, and said, "Hey, it's okay. You know what? If you hang out with me, I can get you laid. How's that?"

"No…no. I'll get the money for you."

"You know, if you're 'saving it,' you're a prick. Girls ain't saving it. What's gonna happen is, the first girl who lets you touch her tits, you're gonna be so grateful you're gonna think you're in love."

Anacleto looked at him without responding.

"Then, you know what's gonna happen?" Santo asked.

When Anacleto remained silent, Santo continued: "You're gonna get hurt. You'll be home alone, thinking you found true love, and she'll be screwing some other guy who don't give a damn anymore than she does."

"If you w…want the money…"

Santo followed Anacleto. When they got to the garage, Anacleto put a finger to his lips, although he didn't need to do that. Santo, big as he was, walked like a cat. Anacleto slowly swung open the old garage doors just enough to squeeze through. The ancient, rusty hinges squeaked. A window at the back of his house opened.

"Anacleto…An-a-cle-to, is that you?"

He jumped.

Poking his head out of the garage, he said, "Y…yes, Ma. It's m…me."

"What the hell are you doing? Where have you been? You missed dinner. I was so worried."

"Shhh, ma. I'm okay. I lost track of the t…time. I—"

"Come up here, right now."

"I'll be there…in a m…min…minute, Mom. I'm fine."

"I was scared, oh so scared." And now, she started to cry.

"Mom, I'll be up in a minute. Go in, p…please. Please don't cry."

He never should have said that.

"What do you mean? I shouldn't cry? I thought you was dead. I sent your brothers out to look for you. They're still out. I'm all alone. Ever since your father died—"

"Ma, stop crying. I have to get s…something. Then I'll be right up."

She stopped crying. Now she was curious. "What are you doing? Who's that?"

"It's Santo. Ma, I promise you…l…leave me alone f…for one minute."

As she cursed and sobbed and called out questions from the window, Anacleto walked further into the dusty garage, squeezed past the car, and, reaching up to the shelf, took down the paint can. He opened the lid and counted out two hundred dollars. Santo stood behind him. He shoved the money into Santo's outstretched hands, and replaced the can.

Outside, Santo bear-hugged Anacleto, and then he jogged down the driveway to settle with his gentlemen business partners. Anacleto dragged himself to his house to settle with his mother. As he stood before the door, trying to convince himself that what he had seen that night was real, he sensed that he was being observed. He turned, and saw Santo's father sitting in his car, smoking a cigarette.

As he lay awake that night, despite his black worries and the bitter sense of doom that enveloped him, Anacleto felt strangely empowered. Because his mother had been so relieved to see him alive, she had not questioned him; she just asked him to call the next time he was going to be late returning home. She did not say a word about the missing pistol.

She also said that they were not going to move, at least not now.

His brothers, when they returned home, said they had known that Anacleto was all right. Frank, in fact, after looking him over, said, "Good for you." James told him that it was about time he started breaking a few rules. They play-fought with him and said that he should go out with them one night.

If they think I've jumped some sort of coming-of-age hurdle, I won't disappoint them.

In truth, he felt strong. He had enjoyed the sense of freedom, except for the dread that overpowered him when he thought about Santo; he didn't need to look through the spaces between his fingers—now he was entangled in the dark, rough-edged gloom that was Santo's life, and he knew that misery awaited his troubled friend.

Me too.

He also thought about his money that took so long to accumulate—holding back gift money, sanding cars, breathing in noxious paint fumes. Handing his money over to some men who dressed like gentlemen. He had seen them. At least he had seen men who other people had said were them, were "connected." It was hard to know. A lot of men in his neighborhood dressed like them and walked and talked like them and drove cars that were as flashy as their cars were. So, who knew? Somehow, Santo knew.

And now, his money was being used to buy poison.

What if Santo got caught by the police? Would he tell them where he had gotten the money to buy the drugs? Would he tell his business partners? Would they come looking for Anacleto? Would people who bought the drugs from Santo die? Whose fault would that be? Whose soul would be blackened?

The next afternoon, Santo paid back the two hundred dollars. He held out twenty more as a gift, but Anacleto turned it down.

"You know I'm not going to l…lend you money again."

"That's okay. I'm okay now. I just wish I could find my friggin' knapsack."

"Santo. How long are you go…ing to do this?"

"I dunno. I ain't going back to school."

"You'll n…never get a g… good job, you know."

"Don't tell me what to do. You keep stepping over the line. I don't like it."

"You know why I do…it."

"Yeah. I know. You're my only real friend," he said, smiling.

"Listen, Santo…quit. Keep the money you m…made. Give it to your mother. Go back to school. I'll help you study every d…day."

"It's too late. Don't sweat it. Look…I gotta make tracks."

And he was gone again.

***

Although Anacleto looked for him, he did not see Santo again for the rest of the summer.

THE DIAMOND-SHAPED WINDOW

During his last year of high school, Anacleto's mother told him what she had told each of his brothers: "You can get a job, you can get drafted, or you can go to a city college."

He worked harder than ever in school. He also got his driver's license…against his mother's wishes. She had refused to give him lessons. James had taken a teaching job in Manhattan and was sharing an apartment there with a friend, so he was rarely around. Frank, who was still living at home, agreed to teach Anacleto to drive. Anacleto actually knew how. He had observed the moves of every driver of every car that he had ever been in. The first time he sat behind the wheel of Frank's Super Sport, he adjusted the mirrors, started the engine, checked for traffic, and pulled out as if he had been driving for years. After only two lessons, he took the test and passed.

Of course, he had no car and nowhere to go.

Tired of living on the periphery, he decided to join an organization or club in school. He also told Joe that he would take him up on his offer to work at the body shop on Saturdays. He wanted to earn as much money as possible.

He decided to join the track team, but the coach told him that he never took seniors unless he needed replacements, which he didn't at that time. He told Anacleto that he should have thought about trying out well before his senior year.

"Let me give you some advice," he said. "When you want something, you go after it—today, not tomorrow and you grab it and you hold it."

Anacleto thought about joining the literary club, but when he reviewed all of the stories and poems he had written over the years, he decided he couldn't share them with anyone because they were too personal...too sad...too desolate. He tore them up and threw them in the garbage.

He ended up joining the art club, not because he was particularly creative, but because he had heard that the people in the club were different—outsiders, as he was. Anacleto had been trying not to think of himself in that way anymore, but it was an effort.

When he had to pose for his graduation photograph, he sat up, forced himself to smile, and looked right into the camera lens. That was also an effort. When the yearbooks were handed out in May, people with whom he had barely exchanged two words thrust their yearbooks into his hands and asked him to sign next to his photo.

Of course, by the time the yearbook was being circulated, Anacleto had become a celebrity because of Rudy Kaufmann and the sculpture.

***

One night, around midnight, as Anacleto was ready to turn in, the phone rang.

"What? Who's calling? It's the middle of the night!"

"Go back to bed, Mom. I'm sure it's a wrong number. I'll get it."

It was Anne—frantic, almost out of control. Her mother was going into labor. She didn't know what to do. Would he come over?

He didn't knock when he got to Anne's door; he walked in. Francine was moaning in pain, leaning over an arm of the living room couch, straddling a puddle.

"I've ruined the carpet," she moaned.

"We've got to get her to the hospital!" Anne looked wild.

"I guess your dad left for the night. Can you reach him?"

Anne shook her head.

"Should I c…call an ambulance?"

"The baby'll be out before then," she cried.

She held her mother and told her not to worry.

"Should I ask Albie's dad?"

"No! We owe rent. He was down here before yelling at Mom. I think that's why she's in…It's okay, Mom."

"You want me to c…call for an am…am…balance?"

"There's no time. Clete, you have to drive us."

"What? How?"

"Take your mother's car."

"I…c…can't…"

"Yes you can. What's she going to do…call the police?"

He looked at the anguish and fear on Francine's face and the pleading look on Anne's. He thought of Santo mouthing "Please" as he cowered in the foyer.

When he reached the house, his mother was asleep. He thought she would have been sitting at the kitchen table, ready to pounce on him, but she hadn't been like that for a while. She seemed to have finally become resigned to the sad reality that her youngest son had changed.

He fished the car key from her pocketbook, but then he thought of the narrow, twisting driveway that he would have to negotiate, in reverse, in the dark, to get to the street. Then he saw Frank's keys. He had gone out with friends; one of them had picked him up. Anacleto snatched the keys and ran back to Anne's house. They were waiting right inside the doorway. He and Anne led Francine to Frank's car and sat her up front. Anne scrambled into the back, and Anacleto, shaking harder than he would have believed possible, sat behind the wheel. He carefully, deliberately adjusted the mirrors, started the engine, and put the car into gear. As he was beginning to pull out, a big Cadillac appeared out of nowhere and shot past them. Anacleto jammed on the brake pedal, and froze.

He wiped the sweat from his eyes, checked for cars, and pulled out. He drove slowly, old man slowly, student driver slowly. By the time they reached the hospital, he was cold-wet with perspiration and his hands hurt from his death grip on the steering wheel. He double parked, and they walked Francine to the emergency entrance. Anne brought over a wheelchair, and they pushed her in.

They spent the night in the maternity waiting room. They talked about Santo.

"It's as if he never existed," Anne said, mournfully.

"I know. I can't believe it. I saw him every day. Then, a couple of times a week. But…since this past summer, nothing."

"He's gone. I don't know where he went."

At around 5 a.m., a nurse told them that that Francine had delivered a healthy baby boy. She was fine, but she needed to sleep.

"You can come back in a few hours to see your new brother."

Anne smiled; then she looked worried.

"I don't know how to reach my father."

"I...know. I mean...uh...What about your Aunt Rita?"

Anne swallowed hard. "I guess I'll call her later."

As Anacleto drove, Anne next to him, he felt the warmth of her body.

"I don't know how my mom and I can ever thank you," Anne said to him.

"It's okay. We're friends. I hope you know…you c…can always depend on me," he answered.

He parked the car in the same spot as the one it had been in when he had taken it. He wasn't surprised that it was vacant. In that neighborhood, most people were in for the night by 11 p.m. or so.

He walked Anne to her door.

"So, what's she going to c...call him?" Anacleto said.

"I guess Peter. That's the boy name she wanted."

She unlocked her door.

"Do you want me to…ch…check the house?"

"No, Clete. It's okay."

"Good night."

"Thanks, Clete."

Anne reached for him. She kissed him lightly on his cheek. She entered her house and closed the door. He walked away. Then he stopped and turned.

He could see her, standing in the dim foyer, looking out at him through the little diamond-shaped window in the door.

RUDY

The art club at school did not start until mid-October because the advisor, Mr. Randazzo, had spent the summer and part of the fall teaching a class at a college in Italy. The actual name of the organization was The Creation Club. It met every Wednesday from 2:30 to 4 p.m. in one of the art rooms. There were seven other members, five boys and two girls. Mr. Randazzo asked them to introduce themselves and explain why they were there. Most of them said they wanted guidance or advice about how to develop their talent. One of them glumly explained that he thought he had ability, but was not sure. He shyly held up a painting he had done for the others to see.

One boy, Rudy Kaufmann, sat cross-legged on a desk, and said nothing.

Anacleto wanted to say that he had joined because he needed to do something other than just disappearing into his house every afternoon, and this club seemed to be the least threatening.

"Hi. I…I'm Clete Roosevelt. I…I'm a…senior. I don't have a p…portfolio because I have never drawn or painted anything worth k…keeping." At this point, several of the others applauded.

"Yeah. That's right. Art is about creation, not collection." That was Vinnie, a senior.

"Anything else, Clete?"

"No…Thanks."

Mr. Randazzo explained that, since the club was starting so late in the year, he wanted the members to begin thinking immediately about the big project for the year; he also wanted them to try a new approach.

"In previous years, as the returning members know, we've worked on individual forms of artistic expression. We've visited museums and galleries and exhibits for inspiration, and then we've worked on paintings or drawings or…sculpture individually."

Anacleto looked around the room. Easels, blocks of wood, clay, brushes, paint…what he expected to find.

What am I doing here?

"When we collaborate, when we incorporate, we open our minds to new concepts. We are…forced to examine the ideas of others and they are compelled to learn from us and, if we are lucky, really lucky, we find out what we are capable of. This year, I would like you to work with each other in groups of two, three, whatever, to create your big projects."

Mr. Randazzo explained that they would spend the afternoon looking through each other's portfolios and questioning everything.

"I am not a teacher...not on Wednesday afternoons. I'm a fellow artist. When you examine my work, do not hesitate to question and criticize. If you think it's good, tell me how it could be better. If you think it's shit..."

Anacleto didn't hear the rest. He was too shocked to listen.

"By the time you leave today, you should have taken each other's phone numbers. Of course, many of you know each other from previous years, but it would be fruitful for you to know each other better. I'm hoping that, by next week, each of you will have paired up with at least one other member to begin thinking about the long-term project. We will present the finished works at the school Expo in the spring."

At first, as they examined each other's work, most of the students were reluctant to say anything other than "That's nice" or "I like that" or "You're really saying something with this." But then, Rudy, a large, messy-looking boy dressed in a stained flannel shirt, baggy jeans, and scuffed black boots, broke the ice. Actually, he pulverized it. He was completing a slow, detailed examination of the work of Melinda, a skinny girl with stringy blond hair and red-framed glasses. As he held her last piece, he groaned.

"Ugghhh!!"

Everyone looked at him. He placed the piece down on a table and looked at Melinda. Then he proceeded to rub his large hands up and down his face.

"This is dreck! Garbage! Shit! Diarrhea! You should burn all of it!"

Melinda started to cry. The other girl in the group, Carrie, held Melinda and told her that Rudy was wrong...and crazy. A couple of the boys told Rudy that he shouldn't be so hard on Melinda.

"Are we here for art or for comic books? She has a good idea—every one of them starts out well, but then she commercializes it!"

Vinnie said, "That's your opinion. It's not bad. In fact—"

Rudy pointed to Vinnie's portfolio. "And...do you think any of that crap in your bag of tricks is art? I don't think so."

Then someone defended Vinnie, and Rudy tore apart *his* work.

"This is the work of spoiled, fat, middle class, second generation fascist American Guineas and Yids!" Rudy spat out.

"Hey, wait a minute—"

"None of you would last a minute in the world of art...You would faint if you came across a black man in dreadlocks who smears his excrement on canvas—"

"You're an idiot!" That was Carrie.

"Oh? A lone voice from the enslaved female section of this so-called Creation

Club. I'm surprised you have the balls—that's right, you don't have balls—to speak up."

"We're supposed to be talking about art, not politics, Rudy," declared Vinnie.

"Art is politics…politics is art…the war, racism, feminism, queers…all of it is art and all of it is real."

After a minute or two of this, Mr. Randazzo entered the fray.

"Instead of arguing, why don't you question Rudy? What is it exactly that he doesn't like? Ask him. Go over each piece. Let him show you what he would have done."

"No. Let's look at Rudy's work," Vinnie suggested.

"You want to see it? Look," Rudy challenged.

Still sitting cross-legged on a desk, he began taking pieces from a large battered valise; there were dozens. There were small oil paintings, collages, huge pieces of cardboard carelessly folded in half and covered with poetry and paint, small wooden and clay sculptures, a totem pole carved from a tree branch. He displayed and explained them; as he finished his description of each piece, he carelessly dropped it in a large cardboard box that was at his feet.

"This is what I really see when I look at myself—hair, piss, shit, and sweat."

He plopped the small canvas into the box on top of the other pieces.

"This is real—I used my own blood...and dirt from the street."

It went in the box. He pushed his long, messy hair back from his face. Everyone in the class, Mr. Randazzo included, was spellbound by Rudy's performance.

"This is called *America in Vietnam*." It was a collage of photographs of broken bodies and deformed faces, victims of shrapnel and napalm pasted on a large American flag. He waved it, and then he dropped it in the box.

"Now, my next to last creation…"

He took out a small sheet of plywood. It had been painted midnight black, with a small, round mirror, probably from a cosmetics compact, in the center.

"This is called *The Face of Despair and Revulsion*." He passed it around. They all looked at their own reflections in the mirror that lay amidst all that black. When it was returned to Rudy, he dropped it into the box. Then he put his head down; the ends of his unkempt hair touched the worn fabric of his pants.

They waited.

"Are we going to see your last 'creation'?"

"I thought you would never ask." Rudy sat up and reached into his pocket and pulled out a small can. They smelled lighter fluid. Before any of them realized what he was doing, Rudy rapidly squirted fluid into the box, lit a match, and dropped it in. The box and its contents exploded in flames. They all backed away as Mr. Randazzo ran for a fire extinguisher.

Rudy remained seated on the desk, Buddha-like, staring at the flames as they flickered, inches from his face.

***

Mr. Randazzo stopped Anacleto in the hall, a couple of days later.

"Clete, I would like you to be Rudy's art project partner."

"I th…thought he was being sus…suspended from school."

"Yes, but since the fire was confined to the box and…it was part of his presentation, it's only a two-day suspension."

"D…do you really think the f…fire was part of his project?"

"I know him. At another time in another place, he might be…lauded for that … demonstration."

"Oh. I guess."

"Do you know, there are artists who create small sculptures, and then smash them, and then put them on display?" Mr. Randazzo said.

"Why?"

"Oh…I guess they're trying to say that creation and destruction are really two sides of the same coin."

"Oh."

"So, will you be his art partner?"

"Why me?"

"Because, even though I don't know you well, I believe you are…non-judgmental. Anyone who works with Rudy will learn a lot, but he will have to put up with a lot."

"I don't know—"

"Look. He's a troubled young man. I won't deny that. He's had problems all his life—and he's never had a friend."

"It sounds l…like you're talking about me."

"Do you think your problems are unique?"

"Well…I guess, when I think about h…how I've always been…alone. Actually, I have…had a friend—"

"Everybody has problems. Family, health, anger, weight, bad breath."

"I guess."

"His are worse. I'm afraid he's at a crossroads. He needs a stabilizing presence. I think you and Rudy will get on well. He needs a partner…and a friend."

"I guess it's because I'm weird. Is that why y…you th…thought of me?"

"You are not weird. You're a loner…that's all. I also think that you have a gift—great insight—artistic and otherwise. I think you see reality…without being influenced by what others think. You have your own honest perspective. That is a gift."

"Some gifts are really pr…problems. You know 'Tommy'? You know, the song by *The Who*, the singing group? I sometimes think that song is about me, ex…cept I'm not a pinball wizard…or any other kind of wizard. I'm just odd."

"You're wrong. You're a healthy young man with vision. Your problem is you think too little of yourself."

"I…Yes. That...th...that may be true. I never know if I'm d...doing the right thing."

"Do you think everyone else is so secure?"

"It s…seems that way."

"Some are, but, most people…cover…They try to look secure."

"Maybe."

"You have artistic sensibilities…I listened to your comments the other day."

"I don't have a port…portfolio."

"I know. Why is that?"

"I've always just thrown out ev…everything I've drawn or written. I can't. I m...mean they just never seem good enough."

"Ah. You're not that different from Rudy in that way, are you?"

***

Anacleto began talking with the other members of the art club when he saw them in the hallways between classes and at lunch. They were different from him—they spent hours a day painting or drawing or sculpting at home. Some of them attended private art schools on weekends. But he made a connection with them.

"You could have told Mr. Randazzo that you wouldn't do it, you know," Melinda said.

"I know, but, it's okay."

"It's not okay. He's unstable. What if you two spend weeks creating a project, and, at the end, he sets it on fire?" she asked.

"I won't let h…him."

***

The next Wednesday, at the art club meeting, to everyone's great relief, Rudy was a no-show. Mr. Randazzo showed slides—Mary Cassatt, Alexander Calder, Manet, Monet, Van Gogh, Gothic cathedrals. Anacleto liked all of it. He thought about that. He wondered why he liked just about every piece of art, almost every bit of writing that was read aloud in every class, virtually every book that he had ever picked up, except for ones that he could not understand. What was there that prevented him from disliking the work of others? He used to think that he was just very accepting of everyone and everything, but…

Suddenly the door opened and then hit the wall hard. Light from the hallway spilled into the darkened classroom.

Rudy stood there, looking lost and bewildered for a few seconds.

"Hi, Rudy. You're here. Good."

Anacleto couldn't see Mr. Randazzo clearly in the semi-darkness, but light from the hallway eerily reflected from his glasses.

"Why don't you shut the door and have a seat? We just started."

Rudy walked in. Then he went back to the door and gently closed it.

Mr. Randazzo continued the presentation. His method was to show a slide, identify what was on the screen, and then wait for comments. Sometimes people said nothing, in which case he would tell a little about it or ask a question.

"Why do you think the objects in this scene are so askew? Do you think Van Gogh wasn't able to get it right or did he have some other idea in mind? What makes this an example of art that endures?"

Silence.

Then, from the back of the room, Rudy called out, "His craziness was his art."

No one else said a word. Anacleto had a thought, but he felt that he had talked too much already. After about thirty minutes, Mr. Randazzo shut the projector and asked for the lights to be turned on.

"Okay. Did you like the presentation?"

Silence.

"Why do you think I showed those pictures to you?"

At first, no one spoke. Then Rudy mumbled, "To bore us to death."

"Were you bored, Rudy?"

"That's what I said."

"What, exactly, bored you?"

"It's all been imitated so much that it's boring as hell."

"Interesting. Any other thoughts?"

They all waited.

"Okay. Let's talk about the long-term projects. Who has made a decision? What are the teams?"

A couple of people raised their hands. Mr. Randazzo reminded them that this was a club, not a class. They didn't have to raise their hands—they should just speak, as they would in any other social situation. Two boys said they planned to create a large mosaic on a school wall, if they could get permission. Mr. Randazzo asked them to submit to him a copy of what they had in mind, along with a list of materials they would need and possible locations. The two girls were working together to paint a huge mural. Two other boys described their project as a series of small sculptures that would be part of a larger whole to be displayed on a unique table that they would build.

Mr. Randazzo looked from Rudy, who was sitting, cross-legged on a desk again, to Anacleto and then back to Rudy.

"What about you two?"

"I have an artistic vision, but I choose to work alone," Rudy sneered.

"Oh. I won't say you can't, Rudy, but I was hoping that each piece would be a collaboration."

"I work alone."

"Clete, what about you?"

Anacleto had assumed that Rudy would have a plan and that he would simply be an assistant. He didn't have a thought.

"I'll have to…think some…some more."

"That's okay. We have time." Then, turning back to the others, he asked, "Okay. What have you been working on this week?"

A few of the members displayed small watercolors or oil paintings. A couple had done charcoal sketches.

"Doesn't anyone ever do anything original?" Of course, it was Rudy. Everyone looked at him.

"What do you mean, Mr. Hot Shot?" Bruce, who was well over six feet tall and heavily-built, leaned over Rudy. Rudy coughed. Bruce covered his face with his hands and backed away, snorting.

"Disgusting!"

"You're a pig!"

"Ugh, what a slob!"

Rather than apologizing, Rudy continued: "Original…not done before."

"Like what, Rudy? Everybody would like to know." Mr. Randazzo worked to defuse the situation.

Rudy drew his hands through his hair and looked up, his bloodshot eyes bulging. Then he jumped from the desk and rummaged through his knapsack, removing a book of poetry by Ezra Pound. He put it down. Then he walked to one of the classroom closets. He filled his arms with art supplies and dumped them on a desk.

He spread a large sheet of paper over four desks that he had placed together, and taped down the corners. Then he opened jars of tempera paint: red, white, blue. He poured sloppy globs of each color onto the paper and, using his hands, mixed them together. Then he hastily wiped his paint-smeared hands on edges of the paper. Next, he ripped pages from the book of poetry and placed them, at different angles, on top of the paint. Finally, removing one of his heavy, black boots, he plunked it down, over and over again on the paper, making wet, messy footprints on the pages and on sections of paper that were covered with wet paint. Then he rubbed his face, leaving streaks of red, white, and blue on it.

No one spoke.

Finally, Rudy said, "I would piss on it, but I'd probably be suspended again."

Only Mr. Randazzo smiled.

"It's hideous!" Melinda actually shuddered.

Carrie agreed.

Vinnie commented that his baby brother did the same kind of artwork, saying, "He finger paints too."

"Do you appreciate it?" Rudy asked.

"What?" asked Vinnie.

"I asked you whether you appreciate it or whether you don't understand it."

"What's to understand? He smears paint. You just did the same thing."

No one spoke.

Then Mr. Randazzo said, "I think I understand what Rudy means. Just because something appears to be easy to do or from left field or by an unknown, does that mean that we should ignore it?"

"What do you call it?" Anacleto asked.

"I call it crap," Tom dryly remarked.

"I call it *American Values*." Rudy ran his fingers through his hair again.

"You know…you're pushing it." Bruce did not lean over Rudy this time as he spoke.

"Relax, Bruce. This should be a discussion, not a fight," Mr. Randazzo cautioned.

"Yeah? Well, my brother is over there…in Vietnam, and this reject is trashing our country. I didn't say anything about the way he desecrated the flag last week."

"The flag...Hah!...*it's* a desecration!" Rudy proclaimed.

That comment upset several of the students. Mr. Randazzo looked alarmed. Anacleto was distressed.

"In this piece, I am only pointing out the trash—"

"What?" Bruce and two other boys had looks of bloody murder on their faces.

"What do you think, Clete?" Mr. Randazzo, trying to calm the waters, asked.

Oh, no. Not my opinion.

"I'm not sure. I don't know…if I like the idea of the red, white, and bl...blue, but…it is different. And…he has a right to his opi...opinion."

Rudy turned to Anacleto. His look was inscrutable.

***

That night, right after dinner, the phone rang.

"Clete? May I please speak with Clete?"

"It's Clete. Who…who's this?"

"Oh…Hi…It's…you know…it's Rudy…from the club…the art…club."

"Hello."

Rudy was silent. Anacleto waited.

"What a bunch of losers…Huh?"

Since Anacleto did not reply, Rudy continued: "I mean…I don't know why I go to that thing. I could go to an art show or stay home reading or…"

Anacleto remained silent.

"I guess I shouldn't have called you."

"Why *did* you call me?"

"I…thought that you…you see, you…"

Anacleto waited. He was not about to make it easy for Rudy.

"Do you want to do a big, a really big project with me?"

Anacleto didn't, but he didn't have a grain of an idea about what kind of art work he could do alone. He could have asked one of the other groups to take him in, but he hadn't. He liked the idea of belonging to the art club...the slide shows, the museum trips, and Mr. Randazzo. He wondered whether he could remain a member of the club and not do a project. He probably could have, but he would have felt like more of an outsider. That was the ugly aspect of his life that he was trying to change.

"No. I didn't think you wanted to collaborate with me. That's perfectly all right. I work better alone," Rudy announced.

I know about being alone.

"No. I'll work with you. But…we have to talk first."

"Oh. About what?"

"Well, I think you're t…talented. I like your…your…boldness. I admire your c...courage. But, I don't agree with your politics. I like traditional art also. I don't think that art is b…bad just because it's been done before."

"Well, there we disagree," Rudy said.

“I know. That’s okay, but, I don’t like it when you put peo…ple d…down.”

“It makes you nervous, right?”

“N…no. Not ner…vous.”

“You’re nervous now. I’ve noticed…you stutter only when you’re nervous. Do I make you nervous?”

Anacleto did not answer.

“Okay. I’ll be quiet for a minute,” Rudy said. “What should I do? Not voice my point of view because you’re afraid I’ll hurt somebody’s feelings?” He sounded exasperated.

“No. You can do whatever the hell you want to d…do, but...”

“But what?”

“But, if we’re going to w…work together, I don’t want people to th…think I hate them the way you do.”

“I don’t hate them. I despise them. There’s a difference.”

“What’s the difference?”

“I don’t hate mosquitoes. I despise them. They don’t do what they do because they think about it. When they bite me and suck my blood, they do it out of ignorance. They are ignorant. I despise ignorance,” he said.

“And, I sup…pose only you aren’t ignorant?”

“No. You are not ignorant.”

In the end, Anacleto told Rudy that he would meet with him at lunchtime the next day.

***

Rudy sat across the cafeteria table from Anacleto and unrolled a rough sketch of what he had in mind for the big project. It *was* big. He had drawn a picture of a huge tubular sculpture that, according to the figures he had penciled on the sketch, would stand about three stories high.

“What will it be made of? It’ll cost a fortune.”

Rudy smiled. “It will cost close to nothing. It will be fabricated from metal clothes hangers, held together with wire and electrical tape.”

“Oh. And it’s on a ply…plywood base?”

“Yes.”

“But how will we…I mean you—”

“We. We, my friend, will build it in the small schoolyard. You know the section that nobody goes into because the asphalt is broken up? There are two small buildings, an old equipment shed and a part of the school building that has a flat two-story roof.”

"Oh. I think I know what y…you mean."

"We'll use stepladders. Then, when it is too tall for stepladders alone, we'll stand on the roof of the shed. Then, when the height of our structure requires it, we'll move it a few feet, and stand on the other roof. Then…we'll stand on the stepladders on that roof. When we're done, it will be thirty-five or forty feet tall."

"Wow. That will be some…thing."

Anacleto examined the sketch.

"Clete, keep that down. I don't trust—"

"Nobody's going to copy your idea. No…body wants to."

Rudy looked hurt.

"I don't mean it's not good. It's great…maybe even brilliant. I mean…nobody wants to do a project except for the people in the art club…and they have their projects."

"Even so…" Rudy looked around. Then, leaning across the table, he whispered, "You can never be too sure about people."

MR. RANDAZZO

The next day, Rudy and Anacleto spoke to Mr. Randazzo about the sculpture. They showed the sketch to him and explained that they would need access to the small schoolyard. He said he would make all of the arrangements.

That afternoon, they bought two 4 by 8 sheets of thick plywood; four 2 by 4s, each one cut in half, giving them eight four-foot-long pieces; a gallon of black exterior gloss paint; paint brushes; and paint thinner. They transported the materials to the little schoolyard using an old red wagon that Rudy had found.

Mr. Randazzo had managed to not only reserve the little schoolyard for them, but he had also obtained a key for the lock on the gate that enclosed the small, unused section of school property, as well as a key to the supply shed that stood there.

They placed the two sheets of plywood on the ground, next to each other, with the long sides touching, as near as possible to the shed and the small section of the school with the low, flat roof. They connected the sheets with steel fasteners that Anacleto had taken from his father's basement workshop. That created an eight-foot by eight-foot base. Then they placed the eight sections of 2 by 4s on the plywood, arranging them in a large, roughly circular arrangement near the perimeter of the plywood. Using a manual hand drill, they made holes in the 2 by 4s and screwed them to the base. That formed the circular foundation on which they would begin to build the sculpture.

It was a cool, bright afternoon. In the hour or so of sunlight that was left, they applied a coat of black paint to the top side and to all of the edges of the plywood and to the foundation circle. The next day, they turned the heavy structure over and applied a coat of paint to the underside. They applied two more coats to each side during the next few days. The board had to be protected because it would be exposed to the elements from then, late October, until the school Expo in May.

They also began collecting black wire coat hangers, which they stored, along with two stepladders, rolls of black wire, a large work light, a hammer, a box of heavy-duty u-shaped fasteners, and rolls of black electrical tape, in the shed. The shed had not been used in years; it was dusty and smelled of mildew.

The next afternoon, they placed the first course of coat hangers, standing upright, along the outer edge of the 2 by 4 foundation on the plywood base; they hammered them in place using the u-shaped fasteners, which they drove into the outer edges of the circle formed by the 2 by 4s. All of the subsequent courses of hangers would be attached to the previous ones using wire and electrical tape. Anacleto watched Rudy work. His fingers were strong and dexterous. He could skillfully and effortlessly complete more work in seconds than Anacleto could in ten minutes of struggling. After two hours of work, they had wired and taped together twenty rows of hangers, rising eight feet from the base.

Anacleto was pleased. Rudy was not. Standing back a few feet and looking at their work in the glare of the work light, he complained that several hangers were askew and would have to be removed and reset.

"What? I don't see where, Rudy."

"If you can't see, then you should get glasses."

"Hey. This is not go…going to w…work, if you're going to sh…sh…shoot your mouth off every time you think something—"

"Save your fetid breath. We'll look at it tomorrow."

They were both tired, so they put the tools in the shed and locked it. Then they walked out of the small enclosure, locking the gate behind them.

In the week or so that Rudy and Anacleto had spent collecting materials and beginning the project, they had said very little to each other. That day, on the short bus ride home, as a way of initiating conversation, Anacleto told Rudy about his plans.

"This summer, I'm n…not working at that body shop. I'll get a job…any job…in the city. Maybe, I'll work in an office."

Rudy silently looked out the window.

"What are…your p…plans for the summer?"

"I don't make plans. I just live."

"Did you apply to c…college?"

He did not answer, so Anacleto continued: "I took the SATs. Now I'm waiting to hear."

"I do not plan on attending college. What would I learn there?"

"Oh...What would you do instead? You'll get drafted."

"Let those racist, fascist pigs try! I welcome the fight!" A few people on the bus looked disapprovingly at the boys.

"Maybe they w…won't get to you."

"Whatever. I want to have a show at a gallery somewhere, maybe in the Village. All I want is enough money to move out of my cesspool of a house and be left alone!"

"Oh, is it tough at your house?"

Instead of answering, Rudy asked, "Is your home life so good that you want to stay forever?"

"It's not good either, but I need to go to college before I move out."

"Well, I need intellectual stimulation and artistic freedom, and all my mother ever says to me is 'Don't stick out like a sore thumb. Act like other people,' or something like that."

"I under…stand."

"What do you mean?" Rudy asked.

"I mean…I understand wh…what your mom wants and I under…stand what you want."

"No, you do not. I'm a solitary voice crying out in the intellectual and spiritual wilderness of this dead zone called Brooklyn."

Then Rudy stood up and moved into the aisle of the bus; he raised his arms, and fixed his eyes on a spot on the ceiling. He stood there, transfixed. Everyone on the bus stared at him. Some smiled. A few people told him to sit down. He ignored everyone.

"Rudy, sit down. Come h…here."

Anacleto felt that everyone was looking at him because he was with Rudy. His face burned. He got off the bus two stops before his usual one, leaving Rudy as he was, wherever he was.

***

Little by little, Anacleto learned more about Rudy. His father had worked as a comic book illustrator. He wasn't a creator, just one of the people whose job it is to fill in the backgrounds. Rudy denied that his father's talent had inspired his own love for art.

"He was washed up before he hit thirty."

"That's too b…bad."

"No. It's good. That's how he educated me—I'll never cave in to the system; I'll never be a working slave."

"I don't see it that way. Is he happy?"

"He draws and paints and sleeps and farts a lot," he commented dryly.

Anacleto laughed.

"I'm serious. He's fifty-seven years old. He married my mother when he was forty. She was thirty-six. She used to work as a secretary. She hasn't done a damned thing in years. They're both old farts."

"Well…that w…would explain the farting."

Rudy smiled.

He did not mind being different from everyone else; in fact, he gloried in it. If he could have instantly and painlessly transformed himself so as to be able to conform to the rules of appearance, behavior, and sensibilities of those around him and been assured that those changes would have led to freedom and artistic acclaim, he would have made his hair messier, his clothes dirtier, and acted more peculiar than ever. He reminded Anacleto of a cartoon that he used to watch on TV in which gremlin-like characters repeat, "We're happy when we're sad; we're always feeling bad."

Anacleto tried hard to fit in. He spent time out of school with some of the people from the art club. They went into Manhattan together. They saw *Jules and Jim* and *The Shop on Main Street* and everything that Ingmar Bergman had made up to that point at the close of 1969. They visited the Museum of Modern Art and the galleries on Fifty-Seventh Street. Anacleto's new friends were stirred by what they saw and hoped to be recognized someday. He was happy being recognized by them.

One afternoon, while working on the sculpture, Anacleto told Rudy that he had done well on the SATs and would surely be starting Brooklyn College in the fall. Rudy's reaction was as Anacleto had expected it to be: "You'll be one more shitty little cog in the great education industry wheel…you'll allow your thoughts and dreams, along with those of the rest of this generation, to be ground down to dust."

Anacleto laughed.

"You sneer, but you will discover, in ten or twenty years, that my assessment is right. You will be a pitiful working stiff, living in the segregated suburbs and hating your life and your obese wife and your spoiled children."

"And…what…about y…you?"

"I…" At this point, Rudy, standing on the stepladder, waving a bunch of hangers that were in his hands, declared, "…I will be a drug-addled artist, living with women of all shades and complexions, fat with my children growing inside of them…I will be creating and destroying…pointedly shunning wealth and commercialism…doing the work of the people and shitting on the awards that a needy, ignorant, gross public will attempt to bestow upon me."

Anacleto was speechless. They resumed their work.

***

The sculpture, after having been torn down and started three times, now rose twenty feet. It had a diameter of almost eight feet at its base and was sturdy and graceful. Even Rudy was pleased with it.

But they were almost out of hangers.

"We need more to complete my…our artistic vision," Rudy proclaimed.

"I know. But…where c…can we get them?"

"Scour your neighborhood," Rudy commanded.

"I have…twice. You know that. You have to g…get some."

Rudy closed his eyes and thought for a minute.

Then he said, "We have to be as creative in collecting hangers as we have been in building our sculpture. We'll spend the next two days collecting hangers. There's no point in coming here without them. We need hundreds more!"

That afternoon, Anacleto asked his mother to bring home hangers from the factory where she was working.

"Why? What you need hangers for?"

If he had told her the reason, she would have refused to get them.

"It's for a science project for school. It's actually for a cl…class I'll be taking in college next year."

She was proud that James had finished college and had become a teacher, Frank was to graduate soon, and Anacleto would be starting in September. She worried about George and Ronnie in Vietnam. George was supposed to be rotated out in the spring.

Many of the students in Anacleto's school were vehemently anti-war, almost to the point of open rebellion. They wore *Peace* buttons and attended demonstrations; some refused to stand for the *Star Spangled Banner* and would not pledge allegiance to the flag. Anacleto hated the war, but, since George and Ronnie seemed to profess, in their infrequent letters home, a love for the service and pride in their mission, he refused to attend the demonstrations.

Besides, he still felt uncomfortable in crowds.

His mother said that she would bring home lots of hangers. He stressed that they had to be black wire hangers.

"I know what you mean," she said.

And she did. In fact, she gathered more hangers than she could carry. When his mother arrived home from work the next afternoon, she made the extraordinary announcement that Anacleto should drive the car to the factory after school the following day so that he could load the hangers into it. She normally walked to the clothing factory at which she worked.

Now they had more than enough hangers to finish the sculpture. Rudy and Anacleto worked on it every afternoon that the weather permitted, often into the night. It was so high that they had to stand on ladders on the flat roof of the small building that adjoined the rest of the school in order to add more rows. When they stood at the tops of the ladders, their hands were forty feet above the ground.

Rudy announced that it was not high enough.

"Are you out of your freakin' mind?"

"Are you upset?"

"Yes!!"

"Then fucking curse like you're fucking upset!!"

"Okay! Screw you!! It's h…high enough!"

"Not a real curse. You're so repressed."

"Maybe, but you're out of control. It's high enough."

"It is not. It will be high enough when it makes the statement that it is intended to make."

Anacleto told Rudy that if they tried to build it any taller it would fall.

"And? So?"

"And? So? Are you kidding? What's the point of building it if it's going to f…fall?"

"Up, down, erect, flaccid…it's all the same thing. It's the struggle…the statement that matters. There are no guarantees…No…that's not true. Life is shit—that's a guarantee. Do you lie awake at night and worry that you won't die in your own damned bed?" he asked, a manic smile on his lips.

Anacleto looked at the sculpture, then at Rudy. Then he walked home.

The next day, Rudy strode up to the table in the school cafeteria at which Anacleto was sitting, plopped down on the bench next him, and interrupted his conversation with Carrie and Melinda.

"I have to talk with you…It is of the greatest—"

"Not now, Rudy."

"What? You have to talk with me…now!"

The two girls turned away from him.

"If it's about the project, I…I'm not inter…ested."

"It *is* about the project." Then, whispering, he asked Anacleto whether he had told anyone about it.

Anacleto told him that everyone knew they were partners.

"I mean, have you told people about our project?"

"Oh, you mean about…?" Anacleto said that in a loud voice that caught the attention of the girls. Rudy looked upset. Then, more softly, Anacleto said, "No, Rudy. I haven't breathed a w…word."

"May I talk with you privately?"

"I'm not getting up, if that's what you m…mean."

"Very well. Make it difficult for me."

"I don't make it difficult for you. You make it difficult for you. You're rude and unpredictable. You insult people…including me. You think that r…rules and regulations are meant to be broken—"

"That's true. So?"

"So…don't complain when things don't g…go y…your way."

"I have every reason to complain."

"And why is that?"

"Because I have vision, and no one else does."

"Well, isn't it hard to bear that burden of…uh—"

"Being illuminated?"

"Call it what you want, Rudy. I don't c…care."

"Oh, but you do. I've seen your eyes. You are inspired by our work. You want to see it through to the end."

"I did. I'm not so sure now."

"But, but…you're not going to abandon me now, are you?" Rudy looked as if he was about to cry.

"I don't know."

"We have only three weeks in which to complete our creation."

"It's ours, huh?"

"It is and it has always been."

"Well, I'm n…not so sure now."

Rudy, his eyes red, his face drawn, leaned closer to Anacleto.

"I…need your help," he whispered.

"Why?"

"Because this project is too much for me. Because…I have liked working with you." His sad, tired eyes blinked as he waited for Anacleto's reply.

"I'll have to think it over."

"But—"

"Rudy. Stop. Don't say anything else. I'll th…think about it."

Rudy ran his fingers through his greasy hair. Then he stood up and stepped over the bench, losing his balance, and beginning to fall. Anacleto caught him.

"Thanks. I knew I could depend on you."

Then he walked out of the cafeteria, attracting the unfriendly stares and the contemptuous remarks of all who saw him.

***

The phone rang. Since it was almost midnight, Anacleto ran to pick up the receiver. Of course, Lucia called out from her bedroom, "Who's that? Who's calling so late? Is it a problem? Who is it?"

"Give me a second, Mom." He put the phone to his ear. "Hello."

Silence.

"Who is it?"

"Clete?"

"Yes."

"I need to talk to you." The connection was poor and the voice sounded as if it was underwater.

"Who is this?"

There was a long silence. Then a sigh, followed by a click. The line went dead.

***

Anne and Anacleto sat next to each other on the city bus to school the next day.

"How's your mom?" he asked.

"She's okay."

"How is she able to cope with it?"

"She prays a lot. Mostly, we don't talk about him, though."

"Thank God she has Peter."

"Yeah. The other night she said that Peter must have Santo's soul."

Anacleto refrained from asking her whether that was a good thing. Instead, he told her that anything was possible.

***

Three straight days of rain and occasional sleet gave Anacleto the opportunity to put off his decision about whether or not to continue working on the project. It had been a mild winter, with very little snow. He and Rudy had been able to work on the sculpture almost every afternoon. Crazy Rudy was probably there right now, he thought. He was probably dangling from the top of a ladder, in the rain, adding to the height of the…thing.

It is something, though. I've never enjoyed working on anything as much as this. Wouldn't it be great if we won at the Expo? Would it? Why would it matter?

Finally, Anacleto decided that he did not really care. He was through—with the sculpture and with Rudy, so he skipped the next meeting of the art club. Mr. Randazzo sent for him the next day.

"What happened, Clete?"

"He's impossible to w…work with."

"And?"

"I'm not an artist."

"What is an artist?"

"Well, I…would nor…mally say it…it's a person who paints or draws or writes or creates a product that is…art."

"But?"

"But, I think y…you must have some other idea in mind."

"Why are you concerned with my idea?"

"I don't want to…be rude, but…you're my teacher, and—"

"And so you think you have to say what I want you to say?"

"Not ex…exactly."

"Tell me."

"I know you're try…trying to help me to realize something…" Anacleto looked down as he spoke.

"Yes. Can a creative, thoughtful person who shares ideas but who does not make a product be considered an artist, Clete?"

Anacleto thought about that. Then he looked up. "I guess…if you stretch the definition. Look, I…I have to get to class."

"I'll write a pass for you. Missing a few minutes of—"

"Business Law—my one easy class."

"Right—it won't crimp your grades."

Anacleto waited.

"So? You are that person. You are gifted in ways that you don't see. You are an artist. But, more than that, Clete, you have another gift. Do you know what it is?"

He shook his head.

"I think you've walked through fire…and survived. I won't say unscathed because I think you've suffered, but you're better for it. You understand people. You know what they're thinking and feeling..."

How does he know that? I haven't done that in a while. Never again.

"…and people are inspired by you. You can be a…a source of strength for people because you listen and you don't judge people. You can be the one who others call out to when they are lost. You have something to offer."

"I don't know."

"Help Rudy. He needs to succeed. There are things about him that I'm not allowed to tell you, but, believe me, he needs you. He's calling out to you."

***

Anacleto joined Rudy that afternoon. When he walked into the little schoolyard, the height of the sculpture was…breathtaking.

Rudy sat in its shadow, his head down.

"It looks gr…great." Anacleto avoided looking at him.

"Oh. The prophet has arrived."

"Yes, that's me, Anacleto, the pro…phet."

"Can you see the problem?"

Anacleto looked. Other than the fact that the top row did not end in a rounded shape, as it appeared in the sketch, it looked fine. "I guess it needs about ten more courses of hangers, bringing the top to a dome-shape. Then, it will be finished."

"No. Keep looking."

"I don't see…uh oh." A breeze kicked up. The tower swayed and creaked and rocked back and forth.

"Do you th…think it will fall?" Anacleto asked.

"In a strong enough wind, yes."

"I guess you do care about that...So, what d…do we do?"

"We need to brace it better to the base and we have to attach another layer of hangers to the entire outer structure of the tower."

"What? You're talking about…thousands of hangers. It'll take us weeks, and the Expo is in two weeks."

"Seventeen days."

Since Anacleto knew that Rudy's appearance and demeanor were not suitable for the job, Anacleto visited every dry cleaning store in the neighborhood. In every one of them, he pleaded for hangers. Most of the owners were willing to give a few. One or two handed him full boxes, but he and Rudy needed hundreds more.

He managed to convince his mother to allow him to use her car to pick up more hangers for what she believed to be his science project. He gathered more from the factory at which she worked. Then he traveled to adjoining neighborhoods, Bay Ridge, Borough Park, Gravesend, and then farther and farther from home, Sunset Park, Cobble Hill, Carroll Gardens, places he had never visited.

He came up with the idea of telling people that the hangers were for a United Nations project, an attempt to bring the benefits of modern American products to poor souls who lived in underdeveloped countries, people who had never seen clothes hangers. That appealed to the sense of humanitarianism in quite a few store owners. One Vietnamese store owner actually ordered a dozen boxes full of hangers and had them delivered to the school, believing that they were destined for his embattled homeland. Anacleto felt guilty about the lie, but not enough to return the hangers.

They had to work as many hours a day as possible. If he and Rudy did not complete the sculpture in the next fourteen days, they would not be ready for the Expo.

Since they did not have enough hangers to form a complete new layer that would cover the exterior of the entire structure, they decided to reinforce every other course. That seemed to work and it added an interesting, alternating series of bold, denser, darker rings to the spiral sculpture. It tilted slightly to one side. Rudy smiled enigmatically and said that was fine.

They worked hard and quickly during those last days—balancing perilously on the ladders, repeatedly turning the entire base and then weaving new hangers into the sculpture, ever fearful that the wind or the weight of the mammoth structure would cause it to collapse. That made him think of Santo…how his life must have collapsed.

Where can he be? I don't know where to look.

Anacleto suggested that Rudy should be the one to complete the tower. His hands were magical. Rudy did not simply create a dome to top off the towering cylinder of steel—he crowned it by building what looked like a giant mushroom cap. Anacleto held the ladder that was on the roof of the small building as Rudy wired and taped the final hanger in place.

They brought the two ladders down from the roof and placed them and all of the leftover materials in the shed. Then they moved back a few yards and admired the tower. It stood close to fifty feet tall.

"It's going to not only tower over, but utterly obliterate every other project and all of the rotten ideas of this even more rotten society."

"Is that…wh…what you want?" Anacleto asked.

"That and so much more."

THE TOWER

The sky on the day of the Expo, a Saturday in early May, was gray and threatening at dawn. Anacleto had told Joe, the week before, that he wouldn't be at work that day. He showered and dressed quickly, gulping a cup of coffee before leaving the house. Then he caught the bus. When he arrived at the school, the sky had cleared and the sun hung brightly in the sky.

The Spring Expo was a lively event. All of the students and teachers were encouraged to take part whether or not they were affiliated with clubs or organizations. Besides the hundred or so drawings, paintings, sculptures, and assorted works of art, large and small, that had been brought to the school that morning, there were puppet shows, musical performances, sports clinics hosted by puffed-up athletic team members, cheerleading competitions, exhibits of science experiments and inventions, and dramatic presentations, as well as food and drink vendors and amusement rides. It seemed to Anacleto that just about every student and teacher, along with hundreds of neighborhood residents had come to the athletic field and the large schoolyard for the annual celebration.

Anacleto checked on the sculpture. He was baffled when he saw what Rudy had added to it late the night before. Rudy had called him on the phone at midnight and, in a triumphant, maniacal voice, announced that he had gone back to the schoolyard and added an important touch to the tower. He also proclaimed that he had thought of a new, more fitting title for the sculpture than *Spiral Tower*, the name that he had submitted for the brochure that had been printed by the school for the Expo. He would not reveal it to Anacleto.

"Let it suffice to say," Rudy had shouted into the phone "that, unlike the so-called Great Bard, I believe that an appropriate name makes all the difference!" He followed up that comment with an angry laugh.

"Okay. If you say so."

Anacleto swept the area around the sculpture and left the gate to the little section of schoolyard open. A few people wandered in and expressed their admiration for the giant black spiral.

Anacleto wondered where Rudy was. He thought that the praise would do him some good. Perhaps that was all he needed to begin to act in a more rational and normal manner.

After half an hour or so, Anne and Francine, wheeling Peter in a stroller, came along.

"Oh, Clete, it's...really something." Anne's eyes sparkled.

"It's beautiful, Anacleto. So, it's called *Spiral Tower*." Francine patted him on the shoulder as she admired the sculpture. Peter babbled and dribbled and made faces. They all laughed.

"What are those two round things at the bottom supposed to be?" Anne asked.

"It…it's just part of the design…Rudy's grand design. In fact, he made them last night…k…kind of a last minute idea."

Anne laughed. "It looks sort of like—"

"Like what?" Anacleto looked up at the tower, at the mushroom cap top, and then down to the large round structures at the base.

She covered her mouth with her hands and shook her head.

Anacleto looked at it.

It sort of…No…!

It's like a big…thing…you know…" Anne's face had turned red. "A tall…black… penis." Anne covered her mouth and, losing control, started to laugh.

"Oh…no…Oh, it sort of d…does," Anacleto admitted, shocked and embarrassed.

"I don't think it does," Francine said.

"Don't tell Rudy. He would love the idea. He always tries to p…push cr…crazy ideas in people's faces. Oh…maybe no one else will think it does. How did I not see that?"

"He's a degenerate," Anne remarked.

"No. He's strange, but…he didn't do this on purpose."

"He's disgusting. Where is he?" Anne grimaced.

"He's sup…posed to be bringing a sign with a more artsy name for it."

"He's disgusting."

"I'm surprised at you. You n…never judge people you don't know."

"There are some people who you only have to hear about, and you know they're awful."

Anacleto nervously scanned the crowd, looking for Rudy.

"Well, do you have to stand here all day? Can't you walk with my mom and me?"

Where the hell is he? He probably expects me to wait for him. He's probably arguing with someone about the civil rights movement or the war in Vietnam or why he doesn't take baths…and I'm standing here. And Anne…

Anacleto felt the familiar confusion and panic rising up. He pushed it down.

"Okay, let's go," he said.

They walked into the main schoolyard.

Francine bent down and took Peter from the stroller. Then, holding him against her shoulder and wheeling the stroller, she walked to a display of homemade dolls. Anne and Anacleto talked with Mr. Rolando, one of the science teachers, at his booth, "Science Experiments for Fun and Profit." Anacleto felt the buzzy beginnings of his head fog. He was barely able to follow the conversation.

They examined other exhibits. When he and Anne reached the athletic field, Mr. Randazzo stopped to ask where Rudy was.

"I…don't know. I saw him yes…yesterday."

Mr. Randazzo looked worried.

"I need to find him. If you see him, please…send him to me," Mr. Randazzo said.

"Wh…what is the mat…ter?"

"He called me last night…late…very late. He seemed to be over the top…out of control," Mr. Randazzo replied.

"Isn't that the way h…he al…ways is?"

Mr. Randazzo scowled.

"No. I…I guess y…you mean he was worse. I spoke with him. He was—"

"He said crazy things…frightening things," Mr. Randazzo explained, looking around.

As Mr. Randazzo walked away, he looked like a father searching for a lost child.

Why am I always hooked up with people with problems?

Anacleto felt he should get back to the sculpture. When he got there, a small group of people had gathered at the entrance of the section of school yard enclosing the tower.

What? What the hell...

On the fence was a white board with black lettering:

BLACK MANHOOD UNCHAINED
BY RUDY KAUFMANN and CLETE ROOSEVELT

Anacleto pushed his way past the others. Rudy was standing on the platform, draping a large, heavy, steel chain over the bottom of the sculpture.

Anacleto pulled him away.

"What the hell are y…you d…doing?"

Rudy's enflamed eyes bulged from his head. He was dirtier and messier than usual and his body odor was repulsive. His fixed grin was frightening.

"The sign! What does it mean?" Anacleto shouted.

"It means that we have won! WE HAVE WON!"

"Won? What the h...hell are you talking about?"

People were pointing at the spiral, laughing, pushing each other. Two boys were holding their crotches and pointing at the tower. A few older visitors were visibly upset. Mr. Carlson, one of the black teachers, looked sad; he shook his head and then he walked away.

"We c…can't l…leave that sign—"

"Oh, yes. Don't you see…" Rudy held Anacleto by his shirtfront; flecks of saliva flew from his mouth as he exclaimed, "It…is the fulfillment of the dream… Nat Turner… John Brown...Martin Luther King…Malcolm X—"

"What? N…no. Rudy, we have to t…take it down—"

"Touch the sign, and I'll fucking kill you!" Rudy threatened.

Anacleto walked to the sign. Rudy had wired it to the fence.

"Give me the pliers," Anacleto demanded.

"Touch it…and you die…you fascist traitor!"

"Rudy, y…you n…never talked about this—"

"Touch it and I'll cut your heart right out of you!"

As Anacleto reached up to untwist one of the wires, Rudy grabbed the back of his shirt and pulled. Anacleto turned and pushed him off. Rudy fell. In an instant, he was up again. This time, he pushed Anacleto, hard, against the fence. It knocked the wind out of him. Anacleto doubled over in pain.

"Fight! Fight!" A crowd had gathered around the two boys.

Two male teachers grabbed Rudy and held him. His eyes were wild and his arms flailed. He broke loose and swung wildly, punching one of the teachers, Mr. Rosen, on the jaw. The teacher held his face. The other teacher struggled to maintain his hold on Rudy. Then Mr. Rosen grabbed Rudy around his waist. The other teacher, ducking under Rudy's punches, managed to grasp one arm, and then the other, and pin them behind Rudy's back. Then, all three of them fell. The two men held Rudy down while he struggled and shouted.

"Calm down, son. Take…take it easy."

"You FUCKERS! RACIST FUCKERS! The whole world is watching!"

The two men, flushed, scraped, and visibly upset, maintained their hold on Rudy.

"Someone, call for help," Mr. Rosen shouted.

Anacleto warily approached the figures on the ground.

"Rudy…Rudy… It's o…okay…."

Rudy thrashed about, groaning and growling.

"Rudy…if you calm down, they…they'll l…let you go."

"Fuckers! Fascist fuckers! You—"

"What, Rudy?"

He stopped resisting. With heart-breakingly sad eyes, Rudy looked at Anacleto, and croaked, "You were supposed to be my part…partner…my friend…"

The neighborhood cop, Officer Sudano, pushed his way past the crowd to Rudy and the two teachers. Kneeling down and holding Rudy's arms behind his back, he told the men to stand up and move away. Then he whispered in Rudy's ear. Rudy shook his head in agreement. Officer Sudano released Rudy and stood up. Rudy slowly got to his feet. He swayed from side to side for a few seconds. His face was bruised and one pants leg was torn at the knee. He looked at Anacleto, and then he hung his head. The police officer placed an enormous hand on one of Rudy's shoulders, and led him away. Anacleto stood there, motionless, lost, empty. The now-silent crowd began to disperse. Anacleto could not look at the tower. He was ashamed.

Mr. Rossman, the principal, approached him.

"Are you responsible for this?" he asked, pointing at the sculpture.

Anacleto shook his head in silent assent.

***

For the rest of Saturday and all day Sunday, each time the phone rang Anacleto was sure it was the police, the principal, Mr. Randazzo, or anonymous callers wanting to curse at him for his part in the project.

The only call that came for him was from Anne.

"How are you?"

"I guess I…I'm st…still in shock…and so em…bar…embarrassed. I guess th…this sounds stupid, b…but I just thought it was a sp…spiral tower with a mushroom-shaped top and two round things at the bot…tom."

"It was. When I said that it looked like a…penis, I didn't think it was supposed to be."

"I th…think nobody would have realized what he had in mind—"

"Without the sign?"

"Yes."

"Are you feeling bad, Clete?"

"I'm feeling crappy."

"Do you want to go out?"

"No. I have some homework."

"Clete, you can take a break…you can get a B in a class."

He laughed. "I get a B now and then."

"Not many. Come on over."

"No. Thanks. Not tonight."

Monday morning, as soon as Anacleto arrived at school, his homeroom teacher told him to report to the principal's office. His stomach dropped.

When he told the secretaries in the school office who he was, they exchanged a knowing look and asked him to wait. After a few minutes, Mr. Rossman came out of his office and gestured to Anacleto. He walked, on unsteady legs, into the principal's office. After Mr. Rossman had closed the door, he sat at his desk and pointed to a chair that was facing him. Anacleto sat.

"Clete, I must inform you that this will be our only informal discussion. After this it becomes official. Do you understand?"

"No. Not r…really."

"No?"

"I m…mean I un…derstand what y…you mean by this be…ing informal and—"

"Calm down. Take a breath and then explain what you mean."

Anacleto breathed deeply and, tightly gripping the arms of his chair with his cold, claw-like, nervous fingers, he tried to control his agitation.

"I mean, *what* becomes…official?"

"Why, the incident…the prurient, radical, pornographic nature of your so-called artwork."

No. How is this happening? I won't graduate…College? Oh, no. No.

"Would you like a glass of water?"

"Y…yes, please."

Mr. Rossman picked up the telephone receiver and pressed a button. He spoke to someone. Then he hung up and looked at Anacleto.

"If this Kaufmann boy duped you, then, all you have to do is explain that."

"I don't know if h…he dupe…duped me."

One of the secretaries brought a glass of water into the room. Mr. Rossman nodded to Anacleto. She held out the glass. He took it and sipped. She slipped out of the room.

"As I said, this is a discussion. Later in the week, we will hold a formal hearing. We will be deciding who is at fault for this…indiscretion and breach of school rules and…ethics—Kaufmann, you, Mr. Randazzo, all of you…"

Mr. Randazzo…?

"Well, would you like to say anything?"

"I don't know what t…to s…say."

"Very well. You may leave."

As Anacleto walked out, he thought that he should return and tell the principal that, yes, he had been duped…that he had never had any idea that the sculpture was anything more than a spiral-shaped column.

He stopped at the door. "May I say one thing?"

"Of course. Come back in. Sit down."

Anacleto stood behind the chair. He looked Mr. Rossman in the eye. "I have a question. What is wr…wrong about mak…ing a sculpture that is in the shape of a penis?"

Mr. Rossman's expression began to change from one of interest and sympathy to… something else, but, then, as if he had flipped a switch, it returned to what it had been.

"I think you know."

"No, sir. I go to muse…ums a lot. There are pl…plenty of nudes—"

"That's obviously different."

"Why?"

"Those are works of art."

"What Rudy and I made…I didn't know he had that in mind, but, what we made—"

"Is not art."

"Is n…not professional, and…may…be it's not even good, but it is art."

"It's pornography and it's an insult to Negro children."

"I am sor…ry, but I dis…agree. How could a de…piction of a male body p…part and a message about free…dom be considered por—"

"I'm not going to argue with you, young man. You may leave."

***

Mr. Randazzo told Anacleto that the right thing would be for them to avoid each other until after the hearing. Rudy was nowhere to be found in school. When Anacleto got home, he called Rudy's house. His mother answered the phone.

"Is Rudy th…there? This is Clete."

"Who?"

"Clete. I'm Rudy's friend."

"Friend? Wait."

She called Rudy. She must have dropped the phone because he heard a clunking sound. Then the line went dead. He dialed again. It rang and rang. He waited five minutes. Then he dialed again. He let it ring five, six, seven, times. He waited. Then he dialed again and let it ring a dozen rings. Then he waited an hour before dialing Rudy's house again.

This time, Rudy answered the phone.

"I need to talk to you, Rudy," Anacleto said. "I want, need to c…come to your h…house.”

Even though Anacleto had never been to the building where Rudy lived, he knew where it was. When he entered the apartment, he smelled garlic and…garbage. Rudy’s father, dressed in a tee shirt and boxer shorts, was asleep on a couch in the living room. His mother, who had silently answered the door and then left Anacleto standing in the small, dim foyer, had disappeared. Rudy, dressed in a bathrobe, stepped from the darkness of a narrow hallway. Anacleto walked to him.

Rudy’s room was large and messy, crowded with furniture, books, papers, sketches, canvasses, tubes of paints, and wood shavings. He removed a pile of books from a scratched, worn wooden chair. Then he sat cross-legged on the floor. Anacleto remained standing.

“Has the pr…principal spoken to you?” Anacleto asked.

Sullen, sunken-eyed, drained, Rudy shook his head no. Anacleto told him about his conversation with Mr. Rossman.

“That fascist pig!”

“We’re all in tr…trouble,” Anacleto said.

“I’m not. They cannot harm me in any meaningful way.”

“What do you m…mean?”

“I don’t care if they expel me…Graduation means nothing to me…I am beyond that.” Although his voice was weak, he spoke with conviction.

“What about me?”

“What are they going to do to you? You’re an honor student,” Rudy said.

“They could still—”

“No. They cannot. If you want, I’ll tell them that you were not in on my plans.”

“I wasn’t. You know that.”

“Do you mean you never knew what we were creating?” he asked, incredulous.

“I m…must be dense, but I nev…er did.”

“You’re not dense. You are too trusting. Let this be a lesson…always think ahead. Expect people to screw you over…If you do that, you’ll always be ready.”

“That’s a ter…rible way to live,” Anacleto said sadly.

“But that, my innocent friend, is the world in which we find ourselves…racism, militarism, corruption, persecution of gay people, fascism—”

“Okay. Stop. What are we go…ing to do?”

“You do nothing. I will exonerate you.”

“Rudy, if they expel you from school, you won’t be ever able to go to college, and you'll be drafted."

"I don't think I would pass the physical…or should I say...the mental?"

"Well, maybe."

"My old washed-out mom and my gaseous dad have spent their vast fortune supporting a Freudian analyst who politely asks me how many times a week I masturbate."

"I don't know. The Army is pr…pretty desperate."

"Whatever…It might be interesting to be in the lion's den," Rudy said. Then he stood up and approached Anacleto. "You don't need to step back from me, you know."

"I didn't. I was st…startled."

"Yes. I am nuts, just like Van Gogh; except for his psychosis, he was not much of an artist. His mental illness was his greatest gift."

"You *are* original. No one else sees things quite the w…way you do."

"But only you appreciate me," Rudy said, smiling.

"Tell me one thing…"

Rudy waited, his wan, pale face expressionless.

"If I had not come here to talk…to…y…you, would you have done any…th…thing to help me?"

"No one helps anyone else...You, of all people, should know that."

THE MANIFESTO

The next day, at school, Mr. Randazzo told Anacleto that Rudy had gone to Mr. Rossman's office at 8 a.m. and handed to him a ten-page explanation of the events leading up to the showing of the sculpture. Then he had walked out, and sat on a bench in the outer office. Mr. Randazzo knew this because Mr. Rossman, his face swollen and red and enflamed with anger, had barged into Mr. Randazzo's classroom during his first period class, sputtering and stammering and flapping his arms and waving the letter in the air. Mr. Randazzo had pushed Mr. Rossman out of the classroom and into the hallway, shutting the door behind them. The students, shocked by the bizarre exhibition that they had witnessed, had remained frozen in their seats for a few seconds before bursting into shouts, howls, and catcalls.

Mr. Rossman had then thrust the letter into Mr. Randazzo's hands. In florid, incendiary language, Rudy had vilified everyone from the principal and the rest of the school administration to the teachers, with the exception of Mr. Randazzo, all of the students, with the exception of Anacleto, the secretaries, the custodial staff, the kitchen staff, even the beat cop. He didn't stop there. His blistering attacks went all the way up the chain of command to the New York City Board of Education, the City Council, the New York State Legislature, the Congress, the Supreme Court, and the White House.

In the letter, he took full and sole responsibility for *Black Manhood Unchained*. He referred to himself as a "lone voice crying out for justice and peace in the deadening, restrictive desert of fascistic Twentieth Century America!!!!" He claimed to be an "artist-prophet who will usher in a new age during which black men and boys who have been beaten and shackled and proud black women and girls who have been repeatedly raped by white society will join with enlightened young white men and women to create a color-blind community that is not afraid to copulate in public…"

In his conclusion, he stated that "Some day, every town and city will have public squares and secular cathedrals in which the multi-hued next generation, the progeny of white women impregnated by proud black men and regal black women willingly carrying babies fathered by their white lovers will stand in awe and gratitude as they admire reproductions of *Black Manhood Unchained*. Those replicas, grand and black and towering, will stand on the fetid ruins of shattered churches and synagogues, with their defeated crosses and crucifixes and Stars of David, symbols of the old, vanquished civilization that gave birth so much war, bloodshed, and catastrophic failure."

He had signed the communiqué *Rudolph Van Gogh*.

Mr. Rossman had asked Mr. Randazzo to wait in the outer office with Rudy, saying that all of his classes would be covered until the situation could be resolved. Then Mr. Rossman had called the district superintendent, asking him to come to the school. He and Mr. Rossman had conferred for an hour while Rudy, much to the dismay of the secretaries in the outer office, loudly recited Alan Ginsberg's *Howl.* When the two men had emerged from Mr. Rossman's office, they had asked Rudy to sign an edited version of his letter. After reading the letter, Rudy had bitten off a large corner of the paper and shoved it into his mouth, at which point he began to sloppily and noisily chew it. The two men had retreated to Mr. Rossman's office again, where they talked for another twenty minutes. They had approached Rudy again. At his feet lay sodden clumps of the letter that he had chewed but decided not to swallow. They had handed his original letter to him and asked him to sign it again, this time using his legal name, Rudolph Kaufmann.

According to Mr. Randazzo, Rudy had replied, "I will, if you will let your wife use her legal name when she signs papers."

"What do you mean, Rudy?" Mr. Rossman had asked in a tired, quiet, conciliatory voice.

"What is her name?"

"Why, it's Mrs. Rossman."

"Do you call her 'Mrs. Rossman'?"

"No. Of course, not. I call her Margaret."

"Was her name Margaret Rossman before she married you?"

"No. It was Margaret Shanley."

"Would you allow her to sign 'Margaret Shanley'?"

"She would not want to. We are married. Her name is Rossman now. It has been for 40 years."

The two men had smiled at each other and at Rudy, thinking that his frenzied mental state had rendered him simple minded.

"Ah. Such is the nature of bondage in twentieth century America," Rudy concluded triumphantly.

Eventually, they had to settle for Rudy signing the letter *Rudolph Van Gogh* again. They had asked the two secretaries to witness the fact that Rudolph Van Gogh was, indeed, Rudolph Kaufmann.

Mr. Randazzo shook his head sadly and said, "That's that. It's sad. When he called me on the phone at home the night before the Expo, I knew he was delusional, and I tried to calm him, but I...I couldn't. It's over."

"Now I have to think about what I'm going to say when I g...go into Mr. Rossman's office," Anacleto said.

"What's there to say, Clete?"

"I don't know."

Anacleto walked to the office, and asked to speak with Mr. Rossman.

What should I say? What must I say? Rudy's out, but that doesn't matter to him...but he should be allowed—

"Mr. Roosevelt..." The secretary couldn't help smiling when she called his name. She gestured toward Mr. Rossman's office.

"Come in, Clete. Please sit. Good, good."

"Mr. Rossman, I—"

"I know why you're here. It's all settled. Rudy Kaufmann has signed a full confession, and you have been exonerated."

"Exonerated?"

"Cleared of guilt."

"Excuse me, Mr. Rossman. I know wh...what the word means. I...I j...just don't see how it...applies in this situation."

"How?"

"Yes."

"Are you trying to be funny?"

"Excuse me, Mr. Rossman. I am n...not trying to be...funny or rude."

"Then you are being dense. I would think that you, a student with such good grades, would understand and appreciate the fact that a major...breach of behavior occurred. The good news is that it is off you."

Anacleto coldly asked, "Wh...what is going to hap...pen to Rudy?"

"There will be a formal hearing at the superintendent's office. For now, he is suspended from school."

"Will he grad...graduate?"

"It depends on the hearing."

"You will f...find him guilty, won't you?"

Mr. Rossman's face was beginning to betray his annoyance with the conversation.

"Listen: he said the sculpture was his idea...that you were not aware of the theme or the...er...political message that he broadcast, not to mention the salacious nature of the project."

"I understand, and th...that's true."

"So?" Now he looked at his wristwatch.

"My question is...what is so bad about what he did?"

"Listen. You are no longer involved in this, and I have other appointments." He turned to the calendar on his desk.

Anacleto stood up and walked to the door. Then he stopped.

Keep your mouth shut...just walk out...

He turned back to Mr. Rossman, who had picked up the telephone receiver. His finger was poised, ready to dial, when he realized that Anacleto was standing in the doorway, looking at him.

"Yes, Clete."

"Mr. Rossman, when is Rudy's hearing?"

***

"You asked him *what*? Why?" Mr. Randazzo's eyes bulged as he waited for Anacleto's answer.

"It…it's wrong, Mr. Randazzo. He is who he is…I mean—"

"I'm bothered by censorship too, but this is a school, and there are rules."

"What rule says a student c…can't draw or sculpt the human body?"

"None, I guess, but you guys are only seventeen."

"Would you be in trouble if you showed us…Fragonard's or Goya's nudes or *The Kiss* by Rodin?"

"No, of course not."

"What about political art? What about…*Guernica*?"

Mr. Randazzo looked troubled. "No," he replied softly. "But it's not the same."

"Why?"

"Because Rudy did what he did to provoke…to cause a problem."

"What did Picasso have in mind with *Guernica*?"

"Picasso had earned the right by then," Mr. Randazzo explained.

"Isn't that…excuse me…isn't what you just s…said hypocritical?"

"I…don't know."

"Remember, early in the year, when Rudy asked Vinnie if he appreciated the finger paintings that his little brother does? Re…member what you s…said?"

"I asked if we should ignore work that looks like it's easy to do or from left field or from an unestablished artist."

Mr. Randazzo shook his head in resignation and in anticipation of what lay ahead.

***

The hearing was scheduled for four p.m. the next day. Mr. Randazzo had called the superintendent's office, indicating that he and Anacleto wanted to be heard.

THE HEARING

The next day, in school, a few people tried to convince Anacleto to not go to the hearing.

"Let that freak get what he deserves."

"Why are you helping that radical hippie?"

Some were hoping that Anacleto could help him.

"This is about free speech, man."

"He's nuts, but we gotta protect the First Amendment."

Anacleto could barely concentrate in any of his classes. He had not told his mother about the situation. He hoped she'd never find out about it.

He met Mr. Randazzo in his classroom at the end of the day. Since they had time, Mr. Randazzo asked Anacleto to wait while he finished marking some papers.

After about ten minutes, Mr. Randazzo said, "I can't do this…mark papers, I mean. I can't concentrate. Would you like to get a drink…of coffee or a soda?"

They drove in Mr. Randazzo's car to the building which housed the district superintendent's office. He parked and they walked to a nearby luncheonette.

"So, Clete, what do you plan on saying?"

"I've thought about it…a l…lot. I th…think it comes down to…what is art and are students allowed to create art…as they would…if they were adults?"

"So, to you, it's not a freedom of speech issue?" He sipped his coffee.

"That's part of it, but I th…think it's more about what is art. I'm going to tr…try to make that point."

"Okay. That's good. I plan on talking more about rights."

"Can you get in trouble, Mr. R…Randazzo?"

"No. If I wanted to become a principal, this would give me a black eye, but that's not what I want."

"How long h…have you been a t…teach…teacher?"

"Twenty-five long, hard years." He pretended to strangle himself.

"You do like it, don't you?"

"Yes. I do…most of the time."

"That's good."

"What do you like, Clete?"

"I read…a lot. I…I guess that's it."

"Do you have a girlfriend, Clete?"

"No."

"Women…the subject of so much art…so much beauty…faces, eyes, bodies—"

"I don't th…think I'll ever get mar…ried."

"Every young man says that. When some woman wants you, she will convince you that marrying her is all you've ever wanted to do."

"Is that what hap…" He stopped.

"Don't be afraid to ask. No. That's not what happened. For two years, I chased the woman who I wanted to be my wife. Finally, she married me." He sipped his coffee, and then he put his cup down and stared into it. "Marriage is complicated. Relationships are complicated. Well, five years later, it ended. I shouldn't have pushed so hard."

"Oh. That's too bad."

"That was years ago. I've been a bachelor ever since." He looked at his watch, and said that it was time to go.

They walked the half block to the superintendent's office and took an elevator to the third floor. Sitting there, in a waiting room, were Mr. Rossman, Mr. Collins, one of the assistant principals, and the two secretaries from the school office. They all nodded at Mr. Randazzo. He nodded back. They ignored Anacleto.

At exactly four, the superintendent, Mr. Grissom, opened a door and motioned for all of them to enter his office. They sat at a large conference table. No one spoke. After a few minutes, Mr. Grissom asked his secretary to call Rudy's house. She opened a folder, found the phone number, and dialed. Speaking softly, she explained who she was. She listened and then she hung up.

"That was Mrs. Kaufmann. She says he refuses to attend the meeting."

Mr. Grissom, visibly annoyed, asked her to dial the number again. Then he put the phone to his ear.

"Mrs. Kaufmann, this is Mr. Grissom. I'm the high school district superintendent. We sent you a letter...Yes. What?" He listened. His face turned crimson. He hung up. "Make a note of this, Mrs. Snyderman: Mrs. Kaufmann, Rudolph Kaufmann's mother, says that her son, Rudolph, refuses to attend this, quote, *kangaroo court*."

Anacleto shifted nervously in his seat.

"That is that. Rudolph Kaufmann is suspended indefinitely. Period."

He stood up, along with Mrs. Snyderman. Mr. Rossman and his group also stood. Mr. Randazzo and Anacleto looked at each other.

"Mr. Grissom, sir," Mr. Randazzo nervously began. "We would still like to be heard."

"Why, Mr. Randazzo? It is a fait accompli."

"But, how could it be? The fact that Rudy isn't here does not make him guilty of the charges, does it?"

"He's had his chance."

"But, we have not."

Mr. Grissom looked concerned.

"I don't see—"

"May I speak, please?" Mr. Randazzo asked.

"Yes. What?"

"Rudy is innocent of the charges until he's proven guilty—"

"I'm sorry. We don't have to sit and be lectured to, Mr. Randazzo."

"I'm not lecturing. I am an art teacher. I recognize art. Rudy was taking part in the school-sponsored Expo. His project had been approved by me."

"You should not have done so."

"I did not recognize the…implications of his theme, but—"

"But, that is the point. He created a…monstrosity…an embarrassing…thing with blatant sexual and radically political symbolism."

"But—"

"No, Mr. Randazzo. You have just confirmed our position. His project and his unacceptable behavior are all we need."

Everyone was silent. The meeting was over.

"M…may I speak?" Anacleto couldn't believe those words were coming from his mouth. He felt dizzy and unable to focus. He was chilled and hot at the same time.

"Who are you?"

"I am Ana…cleto. Anacleto Roosevelt."

"Oh, yes. How could I forget that name?" He smiled. "No offense meant."

"I'm…not offended. I'm com…comfor…ta…ta…ble w…with who I am."

Why did I say that? It's not true. What am I going to say now?

Mr. Rossman spoke: "Mr. Kaufmann is not here. There is no point in continuing this hearing. His failure to appear means he has defaulted."

Mr. Randazzo said, "I do not believe someone who is the subject of a hearing has to be present. He just has to be given the chance to be present."

"What, Mr. Randazzo, do you propose we do?" Mr. Grissom asked.

"I think the fair…thing…would be for you to proceed with the hearing…as you would, if Rudy were here."

"I don't think there is anything else to say. The case is closed. Mr. Kaufmann doesn't care to speak, and none of us care."

"I care, Mr. Grissom," Mr. Randazzo said. "And, there are plenty of people at the school and in the papers who care."

"What do you mean, 'the papers'?"

"Newspapers, radio, television. This story has gotten out. I've been called. I told a reporter that I would let him know the results of this meeting."

"No reporters called me, Mr. Randazzo." Mr. Grissom was clearly agitated.

"Oh. Shall I give him your number?"

"No. Please do not do that."

At this point, Mr. Grissom and Mr. Rossman conferred. They whispered, holding their hands to the sides of their mouths. After a minute or so, they shrugged their shoulders.

"In the interest of fairness, we will hold the hearing in the matter of Rudolph Kaufmann." Mr. Grissom nodded to Mrs. Snyderman. She turned on a tape recorder. Then she read from a file, giving a summary of the charges against Rudy, followed by a reading of the New York City Board of Education student rules that Rudy had violated. She then read from a list of minimum and maximum punishments for the offenses. Then she read Rudy's lacerating, rambling, disjointed, inflammatory description of the events leading up to the creation of the sculpture and his placing of the sign on the fence and the rest of his manifesto.

"Are there any interested parties who wish to speak?" Mr. Grissom asked.

Mr. Randazzo stood, introduced himself, and made a nervous, impassioned argument that Rudy was protected by the First Amendment when he created his work of art and when he entitled it *Black Manhood Unchained.* Mr. Randazzo looked a bit uncomfortable saying the name. Anacleto saw that all of the others in the room looked as if they were about to jump out of their skin.

Then there was silence. Mr. Randazzo looked at Anacleto, who picked up a pencil from the table. He stared at it. The inscription read NYC Bd. of Education. He stood up.

"I'm Ana…Anacleto Roosevelt. I'm a s…senior and I was Rudy Kaufmann's part…ner in the art pr…project." he explained his part in the creation of the tower. That's what he called it—*the tower*. "Uh…I guess I w…want to say…I mean ask…Did Rudy violate rules? Was the t…tower a work of art? What *is* art? Did Rudy and I h…have to restrict our in…in…inter… pretation of what is art because we are not legally adults? Uh…um…I mean…"

He had lost his train of thought. He closed his eyes and concentrated.

The sooner I say it, the sooner I can sit down again.

"Is the fact that we are stu…students the issue? If a teacher had cre…created the same work…type of sculpture, would the teacher be in tr…trouble? Are stu…students in New York City schools not allowed to be cre…creative?"

He looked at Mr. Grissom…at Mr. Rossman…at Mrs. Snyderman as she copied notes in shorthand. He knew that he was speaking in public more than he ever had at any time in his life. He was chilled and his head hurt. He wanted it to be done.

"What if he had not called it…uh…*Black Manhood Unchained*? What if the han…gers had been white and he had called it…*White Manhood Unchained*? What if the project had been a n…nude, in the tradition of so much of the great art of the world? Would he be pers…persecu …ted for that?"

"Hold on. He is not being persecuted," Mr. Grissom thundered.

"S…sorry…bad choice…poor choice of words…" He looked at Mr. Randazzo. "I should be more careful…a reporter, maybe that same one, called me today. I want to make sure I g…give him the right information."

He looked at the two scowling men. Their expressions had turned even more sour at the mention of the reporter.

"I think the tower is a work of art. Rudy created it for the school Expo…He was al… lowed. He's an American citizen. The Consti…sti…stitution protects his freedoms. He was address…ing the topic of slavery…that was legal only a little more than a hundred y…years ago in America. He was talking about the ster…e…otypes that so many people still be…believe are true…about black people…black men…He was cr…creating art. It was not…it is not about sex. It's not pornog…pornography. It's…anatomy and symbolism…it's…uh…it's about freedom…"

He was drenched. The words gushed from his mouth as fast as the sweat streamed down his face, arms, chest. But he was becoming confused.

What do I say now? Did I say it already? What did I forget?

"One more thing…this is a life and d…death decision…I mean the one you are go…ing to make. If you suspend him, if Rudy does not grad…graduate, then he cannot go on to college. He's a smart…a brilliant person. He's also a sore thumb. He…sticks out. If he does not go to college, he will be…draft…drafted. He would nev...never survive the Army. He would be tormen…ted. He would be in danger before he could make it…to Vietnam."

He stood there…no words were left. He sat. Then he stood again.

"Th…thank you." Then he sank into his seat.

The room was silent except for the whirring of the tape recorder. Then Mr. Grissom spoke: "Thank you. We have all of your comments on tape and in notes. We will consider what you and what Mr. Randazzo have said. Thank you. This meeting is adjourned."

They all stood up, and walked out of the room.

Mr. Randazzo and Anacleto sat for another minute before getting up to leave. As they waited for the elevator, Anacleto looked at his hand. It was bloody. He was still holding the pencil that he had taken from the table. At some point while he was speaking, he had snapped it in half and thrust one jagged end into his palm.

***

The next morning, Mr. Randazzo called Anacleto out of his homeroom class.

"They found against Rudy; he's been suspended for the rest of the term. He's to be home-schooled."

"Oh. I guess they…they did…didn't care about what we said." Anacleto shook his head sadly. "Did you sp…speak to that report…er last night?"

"I meant to tell you, Clete: I made that up."

"Oh. So did I."

They both smiled grimly.

"Listen, Clete…It's over now...the school's tearing down the sculpture today. You did a good thing, but...it's over now…don't dwell on it. If Rudy's parents want to take this to a real court, they can. They could call you as a witness, but that's up to them. I don't know whether Rudy was right or wrong. Certainly, what he did upset a lot of people. Don't let this define your life."

"I un…understand."

"You did a good thing. I did the right thing. If a teacher doesn't defend his students and speak up for what's right, then what?"

"But—"

"No buts, Clete. I don't know if I can stay in this school. I'll finish out the year, but…I can get a job teaching in Italy anytime I want it. Maybe this is the time."

"That would be nice."

"Sure…wine, cathedrals, museums."

Anacleto envied his ability to run away.

***

By the end of the day, everyone in the school had heard about the hearing. More people seemed to be on Rudy's side than against him. Placards and signs began appearing in the hallways. One of the black students shouted "Black Power" as he changed classes. That led to a few arguments in the halls. Copies of Rudy's manifesto had gotten out and were being circulated. Students called it *Rudy's Declaration*. Some students who knew that Anacleto was a good writer thought that he had written it.

"Man, you're a hero," Darryl Johnson, an all-star athlete who made the Honor Roll each term, informed him. "You're a righteous white boy."

Anacleto smiled and told him that he had nothing to do with what Rudy had written.

"But, you agree with it…right?"

"I guess. I th…think he had the right to express his ideas."

Darryl smiled. As far as he was concerned, Anacleto was up there with James Chaney, Andrew Goodman, and Michael Schwerner…except that they were dead and Anacleto was a living hero.

Boys and girls who had never noticed Anacleto before this situation wanted to talk to him. He was congratulated and had his hand shaken more in that one afternoon than in his entire life.

He walked home that day, accompanied part of the way by a few students who wanted to hear the entire story of the tower, of the meeting with Mr. Rossman, and the hearing at the superintendent's office.

"You know, Rudy won't be graduating," he told them.

"That sucks, but he's a casualty of war. This fight's not over," one boy declared.

"That's right. We'll have a meeting tomorrow…at lunch. We'll plan our next step," another one promised.

Anacleto smiled weakly.

He called Rudy's house when he got home. No one answered. Each time he called during the next few days, Rudy's mother answered the phone and said that her son was not available.

At school, even though the congratulations stopped and the Free Rudy Movement had petered out, Anacleto was still a celebrity.

COMING UP FOR AIR

It was a tropically hot, oppressive, humid June. Attendance at school was low because many of the seniors were at the beach. As Anacleto sat in class, sweltering, he reminded himself that every misdeed results in a punishment. It had happened to him over and over again. Each of his missteps had led to an unpleasant consequence.

"Come on—cut with us tomorrow. No one's going to find out and, if they do, what's going to happen? You'll still graduate—with all sorts of honors, Clete," Albie, with whom he had become more friendly, assured him.

Even as he dredged up unsettling memories of previous poor choices, he said that he would join them. The next day, Albie, along with Bruce and Vinnie from the art club, and Anacleto went to Coney Island.

The sun was blisteringly strong and the breeze coming off the water was feeble. The ocean, a deep blue-green, was inviting. Anacleto swam...far out from the shore. Then, stopping, he allowed his legs to drop. He brought them together, took a deep breath, and placed his arms at his sides. Slowly, his eyes closed, his body immobile, he descended. The ocean absorbed him, welcoming him to its cold heart. The absolute silence highlighted the regular, now mild, buzzing in his brain, the symptom of his affliction that he had learned to ignore most of the time in the noisy, dry world above.

Then he began to feel a tightening in his chest and throat. Ignoring it, he allowed his body to continue to sink. When the tight burning in his lungs and throat became too painful to bear, he forced his arms to reach up and pull down and his legs to kick. He propelled himself up, gratefully returning to the world and life that had always been such a disappointment. Then, with smooth, even strokes, he swam back to shore and returned to his blanket.

Anacleto spotted the police officer first. His companions were sitting on their blankets, intently looking at a woman in a pink bikini who was trying to get up the nerve to plunge into the surf. Anacleto was standing, looking in the opposite direction, drying himself. The dark figure stood at the railing of the boardwalk, scanning the beach. It did not register at first that he was looking for them—well, not them exactly, but for boys and girls who should have been in school. Then he walked heavily down the wooden stairs and moved along the sand, toward them.

"Oh, uh oh...th...there's a c...cop com...ing this way," Anacleto croaked. The others turned, and saw him—a large, muscular, glowering police officer who looked like he wished he had been assigned to any other duty that did not involve slogging over hot sand in full uniform and shoes. The other boys hurriedly grabbed their clothes and blankets and ran off.

"Good thing you didn't run," the police officer wheezed as he grasped Anacleto's arm.

Anacleto gathered his belongings and walked with the police officer to the boardwalk, where he wrote down Anacleto's name and address. He asked which high school he attended. Then he said that he needed to know the names of the boys who had run away.

"I…just met them."

The police officer smiled, a hard, non-judgmental, but disbelieving smile. Anacleto knew enough to remain silent.

He who talks first loses.

"Son, you're full of shit. What are their names? Do they go to the same school as you?"

"I d...don't know, officer. S...sorry."

"I'm calling your school. They'll be expecting you."

He took the subway directly to his school. Where he belonged.

***

"It's June, and you're gonna graduate and go to college."

Anacleto's mother beamed. He looked at her wrinkled skin and tired eyes. She looked much older than forty-seven.

That's what loneliness and having a crappy life does to you.

He wondered what she would do when all of her sons were out of the house. George and Ronnie were still in Vietnam. Lucia hoped for a phone call or a letter informing her that they would both be home soon. Anacleto thought it strange that he felt closer to them now than he ever had when they shared the same roof. He wondered whether that would change again once they were back home. *Would* they come home?

Frank checked the mail every day, hoping he would not find a letter from Selective Service. James, a teacher, had a deferment. Anacleto would be safe from the draft as long as he was in college. He wondered whether he was safe from life.

He had stopped working at the body shop. Enough was enough. He responded to an ad for a summer job that he had seen in *The Post*. It involved picking up and delivering blueprints for a company on Fifth Avenue and Forty-Second Street. A job that did not involve smelling gasoline or paint. When he had gone for an interview one day after school, the owner of the business, Mr. Blumenthal, a tall, thin, white-haired gentleman dressed in a blue suit and the whitest white shirt that Anacleto had ever seen, invited him into his office.

"We take high-resolution photographs of architectural renderings, important documents, all sorts of business papers—all of them large-sized. You see those cameras mounted on the ceiling there? They are state-of-the-art."

"They're very...impressive," he responded.

"Impressive? Yes, they are. We take...actually, Mel—that's Mel—he takes most of the pictures...We take them for big concerns throughout the city. The blueprints, renderings, etcetera are laid out on that giant table—under the camera. Mel is a craftsman. He's the heart of this business. We develop the pictures right there—back there in the darkroom. Then, when they're ready, we roll them and place them in cardboard tubes—like those. Then the messengers take them to the people who ordered the reproductions. We keep copies in case they need more pictures some other time."

"I see."

"Your job is to take the tubes to offices all over the city or to bring tubes with other pictures back to this office. Most of our clients are in midtown, so you can walk, but sometimes you'll have to go by subway or bus or taxi. We pay the fare, of course. Speed is important. Our clients don't like to wait."

"Right."

"This is a very important job. You can't delay or go to the wrong place. Our clients are architects and builders and other important people. Do you understand?"

"Yes. I w...want the job."

"You'll be substituting for the regular messengers; each one gets a one-week paid vacation. We also generally have more business in the summer, so we need the extra workers."

"Okay."

"I hired another college boy. You'll meet him." Then he looked at a clock on a wall of his office. "You work from eight-thirty till five—you get a half hour for lunch. That's forty hours a week—that's fifty dollars a week, except for what we hold out for Uncle Sam. Sound good?"

"Yes, sir."

"See you in the summer."

THE FORTY-FIVE MINUTE RUN

From his family, only Lucia attended Anacleto's graduation ceremony. Even though he was happy to be graduating, the ceremony itself meant very little to him. It was only high school—not that much of an accomplishment. He was surprised that Frank had not bothered to go to his college graduation the month before, but, then, neither had James the year before that.

"You received so many honors, so many, what are they?…accommodations?"

"They're commendations, Mom."

She smiled goofily.

He congratulated Anne and Francine and her father. Anne looked like she was about to be sick. It was hot in the theater that had been used for the ceremony; the air conditioning system had broken down that morning.

***

A few days later, Anacleto started his new job.

Mr. Blumenthal, wearing another (or, maybe the same) dazzling white shirt, asked him to wait on a bench to which he pointed. Four older white men and a black boy about his age joined him a few minutes later.

"Hi. You ever work here before?" the boy asked.

"No. You?"

"No. I'm Todd. So what do we do?"

"I'm Clete. I guess we wait until we have to deliver a print. Where are you from?"

"The Bronx—Tremont. You?"

"Brooklyn…Bensonhurst."

"You finish high school? I just graduated," Todd said.

"Yes…I graduated."

"I'm glad I got this job…actually, any job." He smiled when he said that.

"Tough getting p…people to hire you, huh?"

"What do you think?"

"That st..stinks. I'm starting Brooklyn College in September. You?"

"I'll be going to Fordham."

"Nice."

They looked around. Several men were working on the camera that was mounted on the ceiling. Two others were examining a blueprint that was laid out on the large table beneath. Mr. Blumenthal was in his glass-fronted office talking to a secretary.

The four men who sat on the bench were the regulars. They sat with their eyes closed. Then, one by one, they were called and given tubes to deliver. Todd and Anacleto waited. One of the regulars, a red head with a florid face, returned.

Then a short, thin man, who introduced himself as Jose, called Anacleto. "Clete. That's your name, right?"

He shook his head.

"Okay, here's your first run. Deliver this to the address on the tube. It's on Madison Avenue. You can walk. It goes to this office." He pointed to the label. "Make sure whoever you give it to signs this receipt."

Anacleto left the office, took the elevator down to the lobby, and walked out to the bright, hot, sidewalk. Although he knew Manhattan pretty well and had studied a street map the night before, he was a little nervous about walking in the wrong direction and taking too long. He delivered the tube, remembered to ask for a signature, and was back in the office in twenty minutes. Jose smiled at him. Todd was not there. Anacleto sat and waited. The red faced messenger scooted down the bench to Anacleto.

"That was a forty-five minute run."

"Wh...what?"

"I said it was a fuckin' forty-five minute run. You was back in less than a half hour."

"I...don't understand."

"It's like this: you go out...you take your time. Maybe you stop for a soda or a coffee or a candy bar. Maybe you look at the girls or you go into a store. You don't break your fuckin' ass rushing back. Get it?"

"Oh... get it. Sorry."

"Remember...we been doin' this for years...you don't wanna make our job harder when you two college boys leave us, do you?"

"No, sir."

The man moved back to his regular spot on the bench.

Anacleto was called a few minutes later, and told to pick up a blueprint from an office that was two blocks away. He walked slowly. Then he saw a bookstore. Browsing the shelves, he spotted an anthology of Nathaniel Hawthorne stories. Book in hand, he moved on to his destination.

When he returned to the office, thirty minutes after he had left, the regulars on the bench smiled at him. He nodded back at them and started reading the book.

He made sure to add a few minutes to each run by stopping for coffee or a soda, wandering through stores and art galleries, or strolling through Bryant Park, which was nearby.

The office was across the street from the main branch of the New York Public Library. One day, during lunch, he ascended the grand steps, past those stone lions, and entered. He sat at a table and skimmed through that day's issue of *The New York Times*. He felt at peace with his life.

That summer, he traveled throughout Manhattan, occasionally to offices in Brooklyn or Queens. The places that he visited were sleek, upscale—mostly architectural firms and commercial construction companies. The receptionists and secretaries were all smartly dressed. He enjoyed the freedom and was surprised by the degree of gratitude and respect accorded to him by the people he served.

"You have our prints! Great! Thanks a lot, young man."

Occasionally, he would receive a tip, usually a quarter or fifty cents; once he was given a dollar.

Most nights, when Anacleto got home, he showered, had a quick bite, and watched television or read. On weekends, he went out with people with whom he had become friends during his last year of high school. One night, he went with Dominic and his girlfriend, Danielle, and a friend of hers, Maxine, to Palisades Park, in New Jersey. After going on some rides and eating ice cream, Dominic drove to a park and stopped the car in a rest area. He and Danielle kissed and groped. Anacleto and Maxine sat in embarrassed silence for a while; then they exited the car.

They walked for a bit. Then they sat on a bench. He moved close and put one arm around her shoulder. When he kissed her, she held back; then she kissed him quickly and moved away.

They sat for a while longer, forcing themselves to talk. He asked whether she wanted to go back to the car. As they approached it, they heard moaning, so they waited a short distance away in uncomfortable silence for what seemed hours.

He didn't see Maxine again.

This September, he assured himself, he would be in college, surrounded by enlightened girls, one of whom would be right for him.

Late one afternoon, Mr. Blumenthal asked Anacleto to deliver a print to an office in Park Slope. He said that, since it was so late and since Anacleto lived in Brooklyn anyway, he shouldn't return to the office after he had dropped off the print.

After making the delivery, Anacleto walked the few blocks to Prospect Park. As he strolled in the shade of the cool, leafy canopy, he stopped in his tracks. A few feet away from where he was standing, sitting on a plaid blanket on the grass…was his father. It couldn't be, of course, but the man looked so much as he remembered his father looking, dead for so many years, that Anacleto couldn't breathe. He slowly circled the blanket, looking around, pretending to be searching for someone, and peering at the man from every angle. Then the man turned to Anacleto and frowned. Embarrassed, Anacleto averted his eyes and walked away.

That same afternoon, he met Rochelle. She stood next to him, looking at the sea lions in their pool. With each dive and splash, she laughed, holding her hands to her mouth. Then she smiled at Anacleto and said, "They're so funny."

He smiled back, desperately searching for an intelligent reply. Finally, he just grinned. She said that she was from a small town near Omaha, taking summer classes at NYU. They bought Italian ices and sat on a bench in the shade.

"You seem to be en…enjoying yours…I guess you can't get ices in Om…Omaha," he said.

She laughed, spraying bits of lemon ice on his shirt.

"I'm so sorry about that," she apologized.

"It's okay. It'll blend in with the p...pattern."

They both laughed. He didn't know why, but it all seemed so funny.

"I'm not always this silly, you know," she said.

"I'm sure you're a good student. Going to NYU."

"I don't know. You must be smart too—going to a city college. I hear they're tough."

"I…I'm not…I mean I always do well in school," he explained.

"I'm holding my own," she said.

"What are you majoring in?" he asked.

"I'm taking a business degree. I want to work for one of the big department stores."

"Oh, that's nice," he offered.

"What do you plan on doing?" she asked.

"I…haven't really thought about it. I guess I don't know."

"That's okay," she offered. "You have time."

They talked about the usual things—families, music, jobs, and then she began telling him about her boyfriend. He swallowed hard and pretended that he was interested. He hardly heard her. After a while, he stood up, looked at his watch, and said that he needed to meet someone. He smiled, and walked to the subway.

ANNE

One afternoon, as he walked from the train, he began dreading the thought of going into the furnace that was his house. His mother had talked, during the scorching heat of the previous three summers, about buying a window air conditioner for the kitchen, but she had never gone further than to price one.

"How could we afford to spend that much? Fans work just fine," she told her sons as they slumped at the table, drenched, sticking to the vinyl seats of the old kitchen chairs. She would serve cold chicken and fruit salad or just sandwiches for dinner on hot nights. "Who wants to go near a hot oven tonight?" she would ask.

Anacleto had bought a unit for the window in his room. Frank, who had moved to James's old room months earlier, slept in his old bed in Anacleto's room on the hottest nights.

Anacleto walked into his house and told his mother that he was going to the beach.

"Now? I'm going to make dinner soon."

"That's okay. I'll eat something there."

"What? No. Don't go. It's late. I'm afraid…"

He assured her that going to the beach in the late afternoon was just as safe as going earlier in the day and that, no, he did not want to bring a ham and cheese sandwich.

When the train pulled into the last stop, Stillwell Avenue, and he walked onto the platform, he breathed in the cool, tangy air. He could smell hot dogs and…people.

The beach was still somewhat crowded, although there were many smooth, rectangular blanket spots marking places where people had camped and then departed. He shuffled through the warm sand until he was near the water's edge. It was high tide; the waves were breaking so far onto the beach that they were almost at the wooden lifeguard towers. One young couple screamed and then laughed as a splash of chilly water reached their blanket and shocked them awake from their naps.

Anacleto placed his blanket far from the high water mark; he stripped down to his bathing suit and placed his sneakers and clothes on the blanket. Then he folded the blanket in half and covered his clothing.

Just a few yards away, the turbulent late afternoon waves broke with a roar. He walked to the water's edge, enjoying the cool, wet breeze, and stood there, allowing the surf to splash against his legs and feet. The water was chilly. It refreshed him after his day of city heat and humidity. He shivered with pleasure.

After a few waves, his feet had sunk a couple of inches into the creamy mud, almost disappearing.

Would I sink and disappear completely if I stood in this spot all afternoon? All night?

He ran in, jumping over the little waves, and then he dove into a monster that came hurtling toward shore. It spun him around so that when he stood up in water that reached his chest, he was facing the beach. He licked his lips and spit out the salty water; the next big wave washed over him. He stood up, sputtering, and then he dove in again and swam. He had always enjoyed swimming. When he was a baby, his father had carried him into the ocean and dropped him in the water; he assumed that he would have to fish the child out immediately, as he had needed to do with his other sons, but Anacleto wiggled his hips and legs and swam like a tadpole. His father used to laugh, saying that his youngest one could have swum to Italy right then and there.

Back on his blanket, his eyes closed, bathed in the weak rays of the afternoon sun, Anacleto listened: people talking and laughing, the surf, bells, a whistle*...the bench at work, the gun, my mother, the empty basement. "It's me...Santo. Shhhh...They're gonna get you, Cleto. Watch your money. No,...your life. Your family."*

He pulled himself awake.

"Hi, Clete."

Her face was right over his, blocking the sunlight. The ends of her dark hair tickled his nose. He blinked, cleared his throat.

"Wake up, boy."

His head hurt. She straightened up, pulling her face away and grinning at him. He sat up and rubbed his eyes.

"Oh, hi, Anne. I g…guess I fell asleep."

"I would say…yes. You were out cold."

He felt confused, stupid. He was sure his breath was stale.

"Wh…what are you doing here?" he asked.

"What do you think I'm doing? I came to the beach…with Janice and Maria. I didn't have any work today."

"Oh, sure. I m…meant what are you d…doing *here*?"

"Oh, we were going home, and I saw you. So…here I am."

He couldn't think of a thing to say.

"Are you alone? When are you going home?"

"Yes. I…I don't know. I mean, I'm alone. I guess I'll go home in a little while." He thought that everything he said sounded brainless.

"Okay. I'll stay with you. I didn't really want to go home yet."

Anne waved at two girls who were waiting, impatiently, a few yards away. Then she slipped out of her sandals. He watched her remove her white cotton blouse and cut-away blue jeans, revealing a pink and blue two-piece bathing suit.

"So? Are you going to make room for me?" she asked, pretending to be annoyed.

He moved aside, feeling awake and very panicky. As he swished his tongue around in his mouth, he looked at Anne. She was combing her hair and smiling at a bald-headed baby waddling past them, followed by its father. The baby's diaper was obviously full. Anne laughed and then she smiled at Anacleto, gesturing with her eyes for him to look at the baby.

"He's cute," was all that he could think of saying.

"Sure. But look at that load."

They laughed.

"Babies are great. I want to have a bunch," she said.

"Sure. They're c…cute."

Then she said, "But I don't want any babies now."

"Oh,…oh. Of course. I k…know."

Then she laughed again. "You take everything so seriously. I was joking."

"Oh...I guess I do t…take everything…" His voice trailed off as Anne lay down next to him.

He was still sitting up, bracing himself with his palms down on the blanket. Anne closed her eyes. He had never noticed her freckles before. Small and light, mostly on the tip of her petite nose and on the high, rounded parts of her cheeks; they were brownish-red highlights that blended into the smooth tanned skin of her face. She looked fuller and more shapely than he thought she would in a swimsuit. She always looked so skinny, starved almost. She wore loose fitting clothing all the time. Maybe that's why she always looked so slim. Either that or she had filled out a lot recently and he had not noticed.

Her hair, a rich, raven-black mass, was spread out like an exotic, dark growth beneath her head. He lay down next to her. He closed his eyes and lay there, perfectly still. Then he gently scratched his leg and moved his hand back so that it touched her hand. She did not move it away.

They talked for a while—people they both knew, his job, her jobs—she worked a few hours a week booking and confirming appointments at a chiropractor's office in the neighborhood and she helped her mother with her Avon orders. She had not managed to find a job in Manhattan for the summer.

She turned to look at him. "It looks like you've been working out a lot."

She squeezed one of his biceps.

"Y…yes. I've been working h…hard at it for a while now."

"You know, I've never seen you in a bathing suit," she said.

"I've n…never seen you in one," he replied, thinking that he had pictured her naked… plenty of times as he lay in bed. "You look nice…very nice."

"Thanks."

"How's your mom?" he asked.

"My mother? She's good."

"I like your mom."

"I know. I've seen you looking at her," she said laughingly.

"No…I…no. She's…just nice."

"Clete, she's beautiful. I know that. And…she has a nice bosom."

"I don't— "

"Yes you do. Everybody does. She's quite a looker. I don't mind if you look. I hate it, though, when I see men and some of the boys in the neighborhood…they don't just look at her. They lick their lips and make gestures. Disgusting!"

"I…never—"

"I know. You're a good guy."

At this, she put her hand on his. His temperature shot up instantly as an electrifying warmth coursed through his body.

She continued to talk. Anacleto was speechless.

"You were Santo's only friend," she sighed.

"He was…he is my only real f…friend."

"I think about him every day," she sighed.

He waited. She waited for him.

"Clete…Was he in as deep, as bad as I think?"

"I don't know. It was…bad."

She released his hand and turned on her side so that she was facing him.

"My father loves…loved him, you know."

"I've never seen your father looking any way except ang…angry."

"Oh, he's mad a lot…but, deep inside, he loves us, especially my mom. If I tell you a secret, do you promise not to tell?"

"Of course."

She knows about his other family.

"You know, he has crazy hours. He comes in the afternoon and leaves again late at night."

Anacleto thought of telling her that he had been keeping track of her father's comings and goings for years. And now, they both knew where he went.

"That's because he travels so much…doing sales."

He was glad he had kept his mouth shut.

"Well, every night, about ten o'clock, they go in the bedroom and close the door."

When he didn't respond, she exclaimed, "Every night! Don't you see…every night! After all these years."

"Oh. Well, you said he loves her."

They lay in silence for a few minutes.

Then she asked, "Do you think you could try to find out about Santo? I mean, you must know people who know him."

"I've looked...for him. You know...I've asked people, but, sure, I'll make some phone calls and I'll look some more. Maybe he's b…back from wherever he went," he said. Then he looked at her; he saw the desperation in her eyes. "I will…I will try to find out what happened to him."

She leaned over him and kissed his cheek. He was enveloped, for one hot instant, in the curtain of her fragrant, sumptuous hair. He breathed in her scent—sweet, musky, salty. Then she sat up and said that she was hungry.

They got dressed, shook out and folded the blanket, and walked over the now cool sand. When they reached the boardwalk, he put on his sneakers and she slipped into her sandals. They were both wary of splinters.

"What do you want to eat?" He liked the thought of paying for her food…for anything else she wanted. He smiled, thinking how upset his mother would be if she knew.

They ate pizza—not as good as what we were used to, but they were both too hungry to care. They walked the boardwalk. He tried target shooting, and won a plush kitten, which he gave to her.

Then they strolled to the train. Even though it was a short trip, the sun, the water, the rocking of the subway car lulled them both to sleep. He awakened just as the doors closed and the train pulled out of their stop. He sat up, awakening Anne, whose head was on his shoulder. Then he grabbed her hand and stood up. She pulled him back to his seat. They got off at the next stop and took the stairs down to the sidewalk, deciding to walk home instead of taking another train back to their station. They crossed the busy street. The dying rays of the late afternoon sun, as they passed through the spaces between the tracks and railroad ties in the elevated platform above, created a ladder-like pattern on the street. One of Anne's sandals slipped off as it caught on the edge of one of the old trolley tracks that had been mostly covered with asphalt years before. She deftly bent down, picked it up, and put it back on without losing a step.

"Can I tell you something else? Even more of a secret?" Her eyes were wide, sad, moist.

"Of course. You can trust me," he told her, hoping she would believe him.

"You know what I said before…about them doing it every night?"

He shook his head.

"Well, my mom's not really happy. She told me the other day that, if he ever stopped giving her money, we would move and not tell him where we went."

"Why would he stop giving her money?"

"I don't know. She says things sometimes. I didn't understand. She wouldn't explain. She sort of told me to forget about it."

By the time they reached home, it was dark. Before she went into her house, they kissed lightly and sweetly. Then he sat on his stoop, thinking. He tried to picture her father's other family. He thought of *his* father, entombed in the earth for so many years. He pictured his mother alone in bed every night and Anne's mother in her solitary bed. Then he thought of how he and Anne had kissed.

As he unlocked the door to his house, he marveled at how quickly life can change.

***

They took walks every evening. They went to the beach. Once or twice they dozed off, awakening to find themselves completely alone except for the squawking seagulls. They waited for the fishing boats to return to their berths in Sheepshead Bay: Blue Thunder, Atlantic II, Victorious. The rough-looking crew members would scale and fillet blues, snappers, flounder for customers right on the boats. Then they would wash down the decks with salt water pumped from the bay, jetting out of large, orange hoses.

One day, they went horseback riding on a trail along the side of the Belt Parkway. Another time, they visited the aquarium in Coney Island. Anne loved the penguins. One Saturday, they rode their bicycles for miles, ending up at Prospect Park. When they kissed good night, after having been together from early morning until dark, Anacleto felt bereft, as if he would never see her again.

TOUCHING HER HEART

One Friday night, worn out from his deliveries in the city, Anacleto drifted off to sleep on Anne's bed. Francine always left them alone as long as the door to Anne's room stayed open. Anacleto was awakened by the sound of Mr. Faricola slamming the house door as he left for the night.

"Why didn't you w…wake…me?" He was groggy.

"You weren't out that long. You're cute when you sleep…like a baby."

They both heard the sound of her father's car starting and pulling out of its spot.

***

They went to outdoor concerts and saw lots of movies. They enjoyed *M*A*S*H*, but the people in the theater in the Village where they saw it fascinated Anne so much that, on the subway ride home, she couldn't stop talking about what had been going on around them.

"I can't believe that girl actually pulled down her top and breast fed her baby right in the theater. And that guy with the long, long dreadlocks."

They loved *Woodstock*...Anacleto wished they had been there.

They went to the Thalia in upper Manhattan to see an older film, *Bonnie and Clyde*. Anacleto was pulled so deeply into the story that the violent ending kicked him in the guts. When they got back to Anne's house and went to her room, he sat there, remembering the lovers' bodies shaking and thrashing as those machine gun bullets ripped into them. They were dead. Why did the police keep on shooting? He could not wipe the bloody image from his brain.

***

Anacleto did not think he knew how to push Anne, so he didn't try. They took comfort in the uncomplicated trust in which they held each other, but he wanted more. At the same time, he felt guilty about his base desires.

He liked spending money on her. If he saw her eyeing a blouse or a pair of shoes in a store window, he would drag her in, despite her protests that she had only been window shopping. It pleased him to buy things for her. She gave most of her the money she earned to her mother.

"My mom doesn't ask, but she never has enough to run the house. Besides, I don't need it."

He took out his wallet, displayed the fifty dollars that he had, and gave her half. Surprised, she pushed the money back to him.

"It's ours. Whatever I h…have, you have."

"No, Clete. That's not right. We're not a married couple…or even engaged."

As far as he was concerned, she was his and he was hers…he felt they were closer than most married couples. He couldn't imagine being with another girl. He couldn't imagine another girl being interested in him. He didn't understand why Anne was interested in him.

"Take the money. I hate to think of you walking around with nothing. In case you need to b…buy something, when I'm not around."

"No. It's not right. But you're sweet and I love you."

He felt instantly warm. "You know, you are beautiful," he said, blushing.

"Well, I do love you. And you are wonderful. But, one thing—don't lie to me."

"When? I never—"

"You just did—you know I'm not beautiful—Maybe sometimes I look pretty." She gave him a hard look.

"You are beautiful."

"No. When I fix my hair and put on make-up, I'm okay, but I'm not beautiful. I don't care. It's just—"

"What?"

"You shouldn't lie to me or to yourself. You can find lots of prettier girls."

"I'm not—"

"I know. I trust you, but we have to be honest," she said.

"I know."

He wanted to assure her that he would never lie to her and that they would always be together. He knew it...it had to be.

"It's just, who knows what will happen?" she asked.

"I know you can trust me. If we ever…if we're ever not together, it won't be…because I don't l…love you," he assured her.

"You don't know that. Men always promise. You don't have to do that and you don't have to settle."

"Settle? I'm not. I—"

"Don't get me wrong…I don't have an inferiority complex…I could have another boyfriend…easily…Guys come onto me all the time, but I want you. I think you're perfect."

"Wow! I w…want *you*. Please take the money. I'll give you half of what I h…have every week. If you don't spend it, and we're together years in the f…future, we'll have a nice…uh—"

"Nest egg?"

"Right."

He pushed the money into her jeans pocket.

"Maybe you'll l…lay some eggs," he teased.

"Well...if you play your cards right, you'll be laying me." She laughed as she said that.

"Don't even t…talk about…that." His head began to spin and his mouth went dry.

"Why not?"

He spoke before he thought: "Well, I think about it...hav…ing sex…making love to you all the time. When you talk about it, I get, you know. But I know..."

She looked serious. Then she smiled again and said, "Take this the right way: I'm not ready and you're not ready. If I could look into the future and see you next to me the way you are now,…I'd—" Then she blushed.

"I understand. You're worth w…waiting for. Just…it's so…"

He stopped talking and held her tightly.

She playfully pushed him away. Then she kissed him lightly on the lips. He reached out and tickled her abdomen and neck and her abdomen again; as she laughed and squirmed and moved her arms up and down to cover herself, he threw her down on her bed. Then he lay next to her and held her. She kissed his lips and forehead and nose. Then they held each other. He breathed in her scent. He wanted to be able to remember it later on, when he would be alone in his bed.

Just then, they heard her father come into the house and call to Francine. Anacleto jumped, but Anne reassured him that it was all right. He always felt nervous when Mr. Faricola was there. He never said or did anything to make Anacleto feel that way, but he was sure that Mr. Faricola did not want to get to know him.

Maybe he knows me well enough. The night he watched Santo and me from his parked car.

He held Anne close to him and listened as Mr. Faricola began roaring about something. Anne froze. She stood up and adjusted her hair.

"Stay here." With that, she walked from her bedroom.

Anacleto stood at the open bedroom door, and listened.

Mr. Faricola was yelling about Santo. Anne and her mother were telling him to calm himself.

"That son-of-a-bitch! When I see him, I'm gonna ring his fuckin' neck! That good for nothing bas…piece of shit!"

Then Francine was crying. Anne was talking to her father so quietly that Anacleto couldn't make out what she said.

Should I go? We were just holding each other, kissing and caressing Now, he's here and there's a problem. I should go. Maybe that would be best for them. Who needs a stranger in the middle of this?

Anne returned to her room. Her eyes were red. "I need you to…please talk to my father."

"What? About what?"

"About Santo. He just heard that Santo had been…selling hard drugs. Dad says he spoke to Mr. Caspari, and he has a friend who's a cop who said that Santo was selling…you know… heroin…somewhere."

Anacleto felt sick thinking about the drugs, the people Santo dealt with, and how his money was helping Santo. Before Santo disappeared, Anacleto had thought about calling the police…telling them that his friend was over his head…forced into that…life. Maybe…they would have warned him…arrested the others. But, in his neighborhood, you called the police only when there was an emergency. And Anacleto knew Santo wouldn't have been frightened by anything a cop would tell him. He might have figured out that Anacleto had called the police. He had not been afraid of Santo hurting him. He just didn't want to hurt Santo.

"I don't know, Anne. Maybe I sh…should just go—"

"No. I need you. Please."

He walked into the kitchen. Leo Faricola sat, staring at the table top. He didn't raise his head. Francine stood nervously behind him. She glanced at Anacleto; then she walked out of the room.

"Mr. Faricola."

"Yeah?"

"I c…could…couldn't h…help hearing—"

"He's dealing drugs. He's selling shit to kids. You know."

"I…I d…don't—"

"I know. You know. This is over the line."

The kitchen was warm. Weak rays of late afternoon sunlight filtered in through the delicate window curtains. Dust motes floated in the air. Anacleto could not think of what to say next.

"You know," he said, accusingly, "…you're some piece of work." His angry eyes burned as he stared at Anacleto.

"I…don't know—"

"Yeah…you do. You know all about Santo. You been helping him. I don't know what else you do, but you know all about it and where he is."

"No. No. I d…don't."

"You're a liar," he concluded, and turned away.

As Anacleto walked back to Anne's room, shaken, he tried to picture where Santo was at that moment. What was he doing?

What am I doing?

"I think I should look for him, Anne."

"You said you've been looking. Where will you look this time?"

"I have looked. Maybe he's back. I have an idea, but I…I'm n…not sure."

"An idea? You know where he might be? How long have you known?" she asked.

"No. I don't know, it's just a place—"

"Why haven't you checked it?" And she began to cry.

"Please…listen to me. It's a place he used to go to…I have checked. I don't think he's there now. I have looked. I'll check again. At l…least it's a place to start."

"I'm so upset." And she cried harder, her shoulders shaking, strands of her long, black hair hanging down over her face.

"I know. I understand. I'm upset too."

"I think I better stay here. My mother needs me."

"Be careful. I wouldn't want y…you to get h…hurt."

"I know. He won't hurt me." Then she reached for Anacleto's left hand, and kissed it and put it on her blouse, on one of her breasts.

He knew he was touching her heart.

NO DIRECTION HOME

Anacleto waited until dark. He knew it was unlikely, but he hoped he would find Santo at his bench in the park. He had looked before, thinking that Santo might have returned. Instead, he had seen the two young men who had come to Santo that night, right after his knapsack had been stolen. He had asked people at school, but none of them had known where Santo was.

When he approached the maintenance shed and the bench, the same two men were there. Their dead eyes scanned him as he approached. The white man, the skinny blond, lit his friend's cigarette for him. He shifted a knapsack that looked like Santo's from one shoulder to the other.

"Have you g…guys seen the other guy…the…you know…"

The black man eyed Anacleto for a moment before replying.

"Who you mean?"

"S…Santo."

"Santo? You his friend?"

"I…know h…him," he nervously replied.

"We here now. You lookin' to buy?"

"No. I…um…I'm w…wait…waiting for—"

The blond, who had been glaring at Anacleto as his companion had been talking, snarled, "Get the fuck outta here—now!"

"But…wait…I j…just—"

"Don't you wait for him here. He ain't comin' back." The blond smiled at his friend.

"I don't want to both…bother you guys—"

"As I said—"

"No…listen…I don't mean to b…bother—"

"Boy, you be botherin' us already. My man, Stevie, he told you—your friend ain't coming back." The black man pushed Anacleto, who attempted to act unruffled.

"I just thought…maybe I'll wait for him…over…there." He walked to the wooden fence to wait.

"Shithead, I told you—Don't you wait here," the blond growled.

"I'll j…just wait out here. I won't be in y…your way."

Anacleto turned from them, ignoring the warning, and stood by the fence. He didn't expect Santo to appear, but he could not imagine where else to look for him. Maybe one of the people coming to buy from the two men would know where Santo was.

He heard the scrabbling of feet on the path before he saw Steve, the white man, lunge at him. He punched Anacleto's shoulder, knocking him to the ground. Anacleto curled up, bringing his knees to his chest and covering his head with his hands. Pain shot from the small of his back to his skull. Again…again.

He lay there, grimacing and shaking, praying that the kicking would stop. He saw a pair of black sneakers in front of him. He knew they belonged to the black man. Only Steve was kicking him.

One more kick. It stopped. He lay perfectly still.

"That's enough, Stevie. We don't want this shit layin' here all night."

"Leave me alone, Darren!"

Pain shot up and down Anacleto's spine. He turned and, as Steve's foot came at him again, Anacleto grabbed it and pulled back hard. Steve crashed to the ground. Anacleto forced himself up and, looking down at Steve and then at Darren, he held his fists up to his face. Then Steve was up, his face contorted with rage. Darren stood behind Anacleto. Steve motioned for Anacleto to come closer. He took a fast look at Darren, and then he approached Steve. He swung, but he was out of range. Before he could recover his balance, Steve caught Anacleto on the side of his face with a lightning-fast punch. Anacleto went down.

Then…

No!…Wet…warm…on my head, my hair, my face…No.

"Stevie, you be gross."

They both laughed.

Finally, it ended.

Steve put his face down to Anacleto, and said, "Listen, you piece of shit: we got a gun. You come here again, we put one between your eyes. Understand?"

Still covering his face, Anacleto nodded.

When the sound of their voices had receded, Anacleto slowly sat up, wiped his face with his hands, and leaned against the fence. Peering between his fingers, he saw them: they were dangling from trees, stretched and twisted, rough braided ropes encircling their necks. They were desperately digging into the spaces between their skin and the ropes, frantically attempting to loosen the tightening nooses. Blood spurted from their necks as they feverishly gouged their skin. They writhed in pain and panic as they gasped for air. Then one, then the other stopped moving. They swung slowly, their fingers trapped under the bloody strands of rope, their tongues limp, hanging from their mouths.

Big black birds landed on their shoulders and pecked out their eyes.

***

As he painfully limped home, with his head down, grateful for the relative emptiness of the dark streets, he agonized over the thought that someone might see, might smell him. He wondered what he was doing.

Why do I follow trouble? Why do I suffer this kind of humiliation? My life had been simple and safe. My house was safe. I need to rest...Was I so unhappy before? I can't remember.

***

Later that night, Frank told him that Anne was on the phone.

"Anacleto, I don't like girls who call boys—"

"It's nothing, Mom. Sh...she's my friend."

"Yeah. Some friend. You watch out."

He picked up the phone.

"Why didn't you come over? Did you find out anything about Santo?"

"I'm sorry. I...didn't."

"Why didn't you come to tell me?"

"I...don't know. I'm sorry."

"Come over now."

"I'm tired. I'm going to bed."

"Oh? It's only ten o'clock. Come over, please."

"No. Not tonight. I don't feel good. I need some time alone."

She was silent for a while.

"I don't understand."

He didn't care.

"Okay. See you tomorrow."

He didn't respond.

"Good night, Clete."

***

The next morning, he forced himself out of bed and went to work. He ached, but more than his sore, inflamed back and sides, he was consumed by a sense of dread. He did not know what to tell Anne about Santo. He was also angry. He wanted to hurt Steve; he daydreamed about hitting him on the back of his head with a baseball bat.

What's the point? People come together and seem to be happy, but for how long? All those love songs and slow dances and glittering words about lifelong happiness and commitment...two years later, one year later...they're just memories.

Riding the subway from work, he wanted to be with Anne, but he also wished he had never met her or Santo. When he got home, he quickly ducked into his house.

"Your girlfriend called—twice," Frank reported.

"I don't like that girl," his mother informed him for the fiftieth time that summer.

"I'll call her later. I need to take a shower."

He locked the bathroom door, undressed, and turned on the faucets. As he soaped himself and scrubbed, he thought of a girl he had seen on the subway. Coffee-colored skin, dark, curly hair, cut-away shorts that revealed a bit of her round buttocks. Her friend had called her Carmen.

"What the hell are you doing in there?"

"I'll b…be right out, Ma."

"You okay? I have your dinner ready."

"I'm okay, Ma…I'll be r…right out."

"She called again…just now."

"Okay, Ma."

He quickly rinsed and dried and got dressed.

"Now where are you going? You didn't eat."

He walked out.

Francine answered the door. She looked uncomfortable. And worried. Anne came to the door and let him into the apartment, past her glowering father, and to her room.

"Where have you been? Why didn't you call me? I was going crazy."

"I…I…I don't know."

"What do you mean you don't know?"

"I mean I was busy and I had to work late."

"What's the matter, Clete? You're a nervous wreck."

"It…it's j…just…"

She waited.

"I don't know."

"What happened last night?"

"Are you s…sure you want to know?"

She grasped his cold hands. Terrified, she asked again what had happened.

"I went to Santo's old s…spot. There were—"

"His spot?"

"Oh…I m…mean the p…p…place he used to go—"

"Where is it?"

"I told you last night…He used to go there. He wasn't there…not that I thought he would."

"What are you talking about? Tell me!" She was frantic now.

He told her about Santo's bench in the park near the maintenance shed. He told her about the men who had been there. He told her about the heroin. He did not tell her that one of them had beat him and what else he had done.

"You knew he was selling hard drugs, and you didn't stop him?" she accused.

"Did you try to convince him to stay in school?" he asked.

"You're right, but you…I guess you're right. He's such an idiot! My mom's a wreck. Dad says he's going to find him and beat him up."

"He hasn't worried about Santo for all this time, and now, he's…angry?"

"Quite a father, isn't he?"

"I'll find him," Anacleto promised.

"Why don't you hold me?"

He held her. He wanted to protect her.

"Where will you look?"

"I don't know. It's not as if I haven't tried."

"Then how will you find him?"

"I don't know. Let m…me think."

He sat on her bed. She sat next to him.

The knapsack. How did they get it? Did that girl steal it for them? A gun? Too dangerous. I don't need this. I'm so tired.

He looked at Anne. In the midst of chaos and heartache, she looked so pretty. She needed comfort. Despite his best attempts to suppress the feeling, he was suddenly feverishly hot and aroused.

She's not ready for…that…certainly not now. It's not right. We have to wait.

He had to get out…get away. Far away.

"L…look. I…w…want to go out and l…look for him…now."

"I'll go with you."

"No!" He had not meant to be so emphatic. Anne began to cry.

"I'll be back. Stay here."

He left. He walked quickly down the darkening sidewalk, turning around, checking behind him to make sure Anne was not following. He wanted to escape to...he did not know. Where does a person go, he wondered, when he wants to be free of the messy entanglements and tedious problems of his life?

After he had crossed a couple of shadowy streets, he slowed down. Without any destination in mind, Anacleto continued walking.

No direction home….ha.

RICKI

The usual static started up. It wasn't any worse than the regular annoying buzz, but as he walked, he began to feel dizzy, confused. Too many sounds. Gray sounds, black sounds. He wanted to go home, but he knew that Anne might see him, and he didn't want to be with her. So, he walked. He reached a corner which was, as he knew it would be on a warm summer night, crowded with young people. The girls were clothed in thin, breezy blouses or bathing suit tops over jeans, shorts, or tight pants. There were groups of boys, some pretending to ignore the girls, others approaching them and flirting. Two boys began singing to a couple of girls who were passing them: "Sugar, ah honey honey…You are my candy girl…And you've got me wanting you."

The girls stopped and listened. Then they smirked.

"I got what you need, baby," murmured a tall, well-built young man with long, black, slicked-back hair.

"I don't think you got anything that any girl even wants," one of the girls replied.

That exchange was followed by laughter and jeering from a group of boys who stood nearby.

"Ugly bitch!" the boy shouted at the girls.

"Hey, watch your mouth, Richie!" his companion admonished.

Anacleto was hungry, so he walked to the outside counter of the pizzeria that was the focal point of the hangout, and waited his turn. The owner and all of the workers at the pizzeria were related. They came straight from Italy and worked and worked. After a couple of years or so, the owner would give one or two of them who knew the business well and could speak English adequately a chance to manage a new pizzeria that he had opened in another part of Brooklyn or in Queens. There seemed to be an endless supply of cousins.

Anacleto ordered a slice of pizza, paid, and walked to a spot on the busy sidewalk a few feet away. He noticed two girls. One was short and slim, with lustrous blonde hair; the other was taller, with a full-sized figure and short brown hair. They talked and laughed and looked at the boys and giggled. A couple of boys who appeared to be their age approached them. The girls turned away.

"Hey, you wanna ride in my car? It's over there," a boy asked a few girls, all of whom laughed and declined.

What am I doing here? Where else should I be? I don't know where to look for Santo. I don't want to be with Anne and her crazy father right now. I don't want to go home and sit in my room.

He needed to talk to someone, anyone. Just talk. That was all he wanted. He smiled at a short, slightly plump girl with glasses.

"It's a b…beau…tiful n…night," he offered.

"Yeah. It is." Then she turned away and walked over to a group of friends.

The dark, cloud-covered sky hung low, but the overhead street lamps and the lights from the pizzeria illuminated the crowded corner.

A patrol car moved slowly along the curb. Two sets of eyes took in the scene. Then the car drove off. Then a car horn honked over and over again. Everyone turned to look; a convertible filled with boys crept along the street, near the curb. The driver blew his horn repeatedly. At first, Anacleto didn't understand what he saw. Two or three boys in the car were yelling, "Moon, moon!" as a boy crouching in the front passenger seat flashed his naked rear end. It wasn't until everyone around him began to laugh and point that Anacleto realized that he was seeing what he thought he was seeing. He wondered why anyone would want to do that.

The slim girl with the blonde hair who he had noticed earlier laughed, and then she smiled at him. She was wearing a thin, sleeveless white blouse, the bottom of which was tied in a knot at her waist, very short, dangerously tight black shorts, and sandals. A small black pocketbook was slung over a shoulder. She approached Anacleto. He took in a whiff of her delicately sweet perfume: like a flower garden.

"Oh, they're naughty boys," she said.

"Crazy," was all he could think of saying in reply as he took in her emerald-green eyes.

"That's why we come here."

"Huh?"

"I don't mean to see boys' asses, although his *is* cute."

"Oh."

Her full-figured friend walked over to them and said, "I've seen better."

"Screw you!" The thin one laughed.

"Screw you!"

They laughed and playfully pushed each other.

"What's your name?" the thin girl asked.

"It…it's…Clete," he mumbled.

"Cle? That can't be it. I'm Ricki, and this is Gloria. What's your name? Say it again. You're very shy, aren't you?" She smiled.

"Cl…Clete."

She smiled again. Gloria walked off.

"I've never seen you at sc…school," he said.

"No. I go to a dumb all-girl Catholic high school."

"Oh. Wh…what y…year are you—"

"I'm seventeen. I'll be a senior next term. How old are you?"

"Eighteen in November; I'll be starting college in September."

She smiled broadly. "You come here a lot?" she asked.

"No. I was sup…posed to be do…ing something, but—"

"You came to check out the girls?"

"No." he laughed. "I got hungry."

"We came here to get something too."

"Oh."

"It's not what you think," she said.

"I…was…wasn't thinking anything."

"Me and Gloria, we don't like this going out with different boys all the time," she explained.

"Oh."

"Yeah. We're tired of that crap. I keep trying to find the right man…" Then she smiled again and shrugged her shoulders.

They talked. Actually, she talked…about nothing. She named almost everybody on the corner and disclosed everything she knew about each of them. She lit a cigarette and inhaled, allowing the smoke to trail from her nose as she told Anacleto her entire life story: birth, brothers, sisters, her fat father, her skinny mother, what she had gotten for her birthday (earrings, the ones she was wearing), movies she had seen, none of which interested him. She told him about her summer job at a day camp.

"Do you have a car?" she asked.

"I…have…my driver's…No, I don't."

"You'll be eighteen, you said? You said November, right?"

"Y…yes."

"That's good. It's only three months away."

"Yes."

"You think you'll buy a car?"

"I've thought about it…not y…yet. I need to save m…money right now."

"That's ok. Tell me about you. Is your family crazy like mine?"

He told her about his family and about his father.

"That's too bad. That's sad. I wish my old man dropped dead."

"Why?"

"He's a freak."

He waited.

"I told you I have a crappy family," she explained.

"Right."

"Are you Irish?" she asked. "Your name sounds Irish."

"No. It…talian."

"Is Clete your real name?"

"It…it's An…an…a…cle…to."

"That's nice. I like it. Do you have a job?"

He told her about his job. He felt foolish revealing his life story to this…stranger, but she was pretty and he felt flattered by her attention.

"Do you have a girlfriend?"

"Y…yes."

"Then what are you doing here?"

"I…told you…I had to…I don't know."

"Things ain't so good?"

"It's c…com…compli—"

"Complicated? I bet she makes you stutter."

"No! In f…fact, I'm re…re…relaxed when I'm with her."

"Yeah, I'll bet you're relaxed. She bores you to death, right?"

"No."

"You're the loyal type," she decided.

Then what am I doing talking to you?

He began telling her what he thought was right and wrong until he realized that her eyes had begun to glaze over.

"I can't be…lieve how much I talked. I…I'm sorry," he said.

"No. It's good. You feel comfortable with me. That's nice."

"Yes. I do."

"I'm not as deep as you, but I have some ideas too," she said.

"Tell me."

"Really?"

"Sure…I want to hear your ideas," he assured her.

"Wow. Most of the time, when I meet boys, all they want to do is try to feel me up."

He understood why.

"I want to hear."

She talked a blue streak. She was most certainly not very deep, but she was funny. Her sparkling eyes danced when she spoke. She had the most expressive mouth and fullest lips he had ever seen. This girl, Ricki, had a way of talking that, despite the shallowness of her ideas, was delightful.

She looked around. Her friend had disappeared. In fact, everyone had begun a mad rush to the corner.

"Fight! Fight!" someone was yelling. Dozens of people were pushing each other for a better view.

"I don't wanna stay here anymore," she said.

"Oh. I think I'll g…go too."

"What?"

"I…should go," he told her.

"No. Don't go. But, let's get out of here. I don't like fights."

"I d…don't either."

They walked a short distance away from the corner. A cool sea breeze wafted over them from the Narrows, just a few blocks away. Anacleto began to feel nervous and uncomfortable, but he couldn't stop looking at her long, smooth legs, her shiny hair, her small, firm rear.

What am I doing? I have a girlfriend, a wonderful, intelligent friend who loves me…

"You're very nice, you know," she said.

"Uh…thank you."

"You're supposed to say something to me now."

"Oh. You know that…you…you're…pretty."

"I know, but a girl likes to hear that."

She smiled.

"You are v…very pret…ty."

"Thank you. You're a nice looking *man*."

"Oh. Thanks."

"You're different from most of the guys I meet."

"I…know I am. Very diff…different."

"I mean it in a good way. You're…not a phony, not a big shot. I like that."

"I don't s…say much."

"That's okay. What you say is real."

"That's me—real, but boring."

"You're not boring. I could get to like you…real fast."

"Oh. You're very likable too," was his nervous reply.

"Do you want to walk to the bay?" she asked.

"Now? I th…think I—"

"Come on. We'll look at the ships. It's cool there."

Then she spotted Gloria; she walked over to her. They talked for a few seconds. Then Ricki returned.

"What's your last name?"

"It's Roosevelt."

"Like the president?"

"Yes. It wasn't always Roosevelt. It used to…to be an It…Italian name."

"Mine's Shreiber. German. We're poor, but proud." She shook her head, laughed, and then she took out another cigarette, handing Anacleto a pack of matches. She shook the pack and propelled a cigarette to the top, offering it to him. He took it and lit her cigarette and his.

What the hell…

"Okay, let's go."

They walked the few blocks to the promenade, stopping at the green wrought iron fence that overlooked the bay. On the top edge of the railing, in black marker, someone had written *Joey is the best he does me every nite*

He tried to cover it with his arm.

"Do you think Joey is the best?" She grinned at him.

"I th…think Joey wrote that," he replied.

Ricki laughed. "You're funny…cute and funny."

She talked and talked about how much she loved going to the beach.

"I look great in a bikini." She posed.

"You look good n…now."

"Well, anyway. I can't stand these boys and I don't want to wait for dates."

"Oh. I…I."

"I'm past that."

"I know."

"I can't stand this bullshit of meeting boys and going out with them…and they're all self-centered babies."

"I know…I mean…I underst…stand."

"All they want is to get in my pants."

"They're v…very nice pants."

"Ha. Well, it's not the pants they want. I can't stand it."

"I know. I was jok…ing."

"I'm not afraid of doing it, but not with just any slob, you know. You know?" She held his eyes with hers.

"Of course. Sure. I th…think it should mean some…thing," he said, the familiar heat rising in him again.

"When I have a steady boyfriend, when I'm sure I'm in love with him and I know I can trust him, then…I'll…be ready."

"That sounds right," he nervously agreed.

"I haven't been sitting in my room waiting, you know. I've had lots of dates, but I can't stand it when a guy—just some guy thinks he has the right to put his hands all over me."

"I…That's terrible."

"You would never do that, right?"

"I never have," he replied.

"Now, kissing's something else. If I like a boy, I don't mind making out. I've made out a lot. I started with my cousin Tommy. I was twelve. He was sixteen. He was like…my first boyfriend, sort of. We made out in the basement of my house hundreds of times. He wanted to do it with me, but I told him no. Like I said, I think a girl should wait for a steady boyfriend. You know?"

He understood the rules. He and Anne had rules too. They had both known them from the beginning without ever needing to say anything.

They looked at the smooth, dark water. She rummaged through her pocketbook and pulled out her cigarettes. She lit one and held another out one to him. He told her he didn't want it. She smoked and they looked at and listened to the water washing the rocks below them.

What the hell am I doing? This isn't right.

"Let's w…walk," he said.

"No." She put her arms around him.

"I think I should g…go home."

"No. We're getting to know each other."

"But I have a g…girlfriend."

"But she's not as pretty as me."

"No, but that's n…not so…important."

"Now, that is different. I've never heard any boy or man say that."

"I am different, but not al…ways in a g…good way."

"I like you, Clete. Do you like me?"

"I…sure, but—"

"No buts. Just stay here with me."

Far out, near the horizon, lights appeared. Dim at first, they grew larger after a minute or so. A freighter or a cruise ship coming into the harbor. Passengers or cargo from…who knew where. Other places, other ideas, other people…lonely people.

He looked at Ricki. "Listen…I th…think we—"

"No. Stay here."

A sudden breeze sprung up. She shivered. She moved closer to him. He felt the warmth of her body…her animal heat. It shot through him. He touched her hand. She grasped it and then she squeezed between his body and the railing. She leaned her face on his chest and put her hands on his waist. He stroked her hair. She purred and looked up at him. He got lost looking into her green green eyes. Her perfume was flowery sweet.

She put her warm hands to the sides of his face and drew him down to her. They kissed. She was more aggressive than he expected. She was…ferocious. He felt his tongue being drawn into her mouth.

Anne kissed the way he did: lips, tongue tips, wet, slow, deep. They breathed each other in. They exchanged a promise with each kiss.

Ricki drew his tongue in deeper. That's all it was: his tongue in her mouth. No warmth. He slowed her down and took control. She seemed to like that. A few minutes later, he gently pushed her away.

"Wow. I n…need a br…breath…er."

"You kiss nice," she replied.

"Let's walk."

"What's the matter? You don't like it?"

"No...I mean yes. It's n…not that. Let's w…walk."

They walked. She held his hand. As they passed the trail that led to where Santo had dealt drugs, Anacleto felt guilty. He didn't know where to look for him, but he knew that he should be trying.

What am I doing? She wants a boyfriend. I already have a girlfriend…with a brother who's trouble…who's my friend, my first friend…who's...missing or worse. How can I do this to Anne? But, she won't know. I'll just kiss Ricki for a while more. Then I'll take her back to that corner or I'll walk her home.

Then he decided that he didn't want to be with Anne. At least, not now. If only the situation with Santo didn't interfere with their lives. If it were only Anne and him. Santo was the problem. But he was Anacleto's friend.

And I am his. His only friend.

They came to a dim, deserted, grassy spot. They stopped walking. Ricki moved closer to him. He wrapped his arms around her. She looked up at him. He kissed her; she responded by kissing him harder, deeper, moving her arms over his back. She pressed against him, almost pushing him over. He held her close, breathing in her sweet scent. Her hands moved up and down his back. Aroused, he tentatively touched her buttocks. She didn't object, so he squeezed and held tight and pulled her even closer. They pushed their tongues deeply into each other's mouths. He kissed her cheeks, her neck, the top of her chest. She threw her head back. He pushed her to the dewy grass and straddled her, pressing and grinding against her. He was incredibly aroused; he was hot and feverish with desire. He tried to fight the surging, escalating, hot energy that, even then, in the midst of his fevered excitement, he knew would lead to regret.

She held his body tightly against hers. Her hands roamed over his back. She kissed his neck; she breathed hotly into his ear. She was powerful. With one push, she rolled them both over. Now she was on top, grinding against him as they kissed. He felt that he would burst…he thought ahead to how he would feel if they didn't stop.

No, no.

"R…Ricki…I…think—"

"Shh. You think too much." She kissed and pressed her warm body against his. He pushed her off, and lay next to her. She climbed atop him again, kissing him, pressing hotly against him.

This is wrong, but it feels…

He was burning with an overwhelming, feverish animal need to return her kisses and push against her, but he also wished she would stop, leave him alone, save him from doing what he knew was wrong.

"We can't do it—not yet…we have to be going steady for a while," she breathed into his ear, and then she licked it.

"I…know," he whimpered.

They kissed and caressed each other. Ricki continued grinding her body against his. He was dazed…not quite head-fogged, but definitely disoriented. When he opened his eyes for a few seconds and looked around, he wasn't sure he knew where he was. He didn't care. At that moment, the all-encompassing blistering, electric pleasure that he was experiencing became all that there was of existence.

He closed his eyes again and rolled the two of them over so that he was on top of Ricki, grinding, pushing against her, his groin pressing against hers. She clasped him tightly with her arms and wrapped her legs around him.

Then he became rigid. Suddenly…it was there…that sizzling, powerful throb, that searing surge of supercharged energy…what he simultaneously desired, needed…and feared. He pushed against her…ground into her with animal-like force, kissing her…then, he shuddered with painful, dark, guilty pleasure.

Now I've done it…too far…too late. I'll be punished.

In a flash, he rolled off and away from her, panicky that she would feel the wetness through his pants. He was suddenly ashamed.

"What's the matter, Clete?"

"Noth…ing. I th…thought I h…heard s…s…someone."

"So what. Come back here."

That was the last thing in the world he wanted.

***

He walked her home. She lived in a small house, more like a converted bungalow with a front porch, in Bay Ridge. The house needed to be painted, the wooden steps were splintered and broken.

They sat on a rusty aluminum glider on the porch, and talked.

"I wish I went to a regular high school. Catholic school is so stupid."

"The uni…forms are c…cute, especially when the girls roll up…the bottoms of those pleat…ed skirts."

"I roll mine high. You're not surprised, right? I can't wait for school to start. I want my friends to see you," she bubbled.

He smiled weakly.

"What time are you coming over tomorrow?" she asked.

"T…tomor…row? Listen. I…don't—"

"What? Don't tell me you're busy. I don't think so—"

"No. I mean…I'll b…be work…ing late t…tomor…row."

"How late?"

"Uh…nine."

"That's okay…I'll wait for you," she said.

"Uh…That's too l…late. I get up early."

"Where's the office?"

"Midtown."

"Okay. Call me tonight when you get home. We'll talk about tomorrow."

"Tonight? I…c…can't. I…We...don't have a phone."

"Bullshit!"

"No…my mom did…didn't pay the bill." He was ashamed even as he lied to her.

"Oh. I know all about that. My pitiful mother doesn't even have food in the house most of the time." Her face lost its radiance and grew dark. "I can't stand my life…my family. I can't wait to get away."

"Oh."

"I'm not waiting around. I wish I could move out tomorrow…tonight…right now." She looked at him sadly.

What do you expect me to do?

"Oh. How c…come you're in Cath—"

"Catholic school. It's paid for…not by my parents, believe me."

"Oh."

"Call me tomorrow…anytime…from a phone booth."

She wrote her phone number and name on a wrinkled scrap of paper that she dug out from the bottom of her pocketbook. Then she held his face and kissed him hungrily and deeply. Surprisingly, he came to life again. He returned her kisses.

She stood up. As she took her key from her pocketbook, she bent toward him and repeated, “Call me tomorrow.”

He stood and waited behind her as she unlocked and opened the door. She turned to him again. Before she kissed him goodnight, her eyes turned steely.

“Listen, Clete. You better call me.”

He felt like a fraud.

“I’m your girl. You’re my boyfriend. I’m good for you.”

He struggled for the right words.

Then, staring him straight in the eyes, she said, “I made you come.”

Then she walked into her house and closed the door behind her.

HIS WEAK AND FICKLE SOUL

The next day, during his lunch break, Anacleto walked to a phone booth in the lobby of the building. He sat, staring at the phone, weighing his options. Ricki seemed to be incapable of participating in an intelligent conversation, although it was a treat just to watch and listen to her talk. Of course, she was adventurous. She was ready—no eager—to transport him to astonishing levels of sensual delight that he had only dreamed about before last night. And, if he was with her, he could forget about Santo. She certainly was pretty. Of course, she expected him to commit himself to her.

But he was already committed to Anne. Anne. It would break her heart. He had promised.

But she would never do with him what Ricki had done—at least not now. He would never push her and she would never do it. They had reached the outer limits of their lovemaking...at least for this period in their lives. It was clear that his tentative explorations of Anne's body in the heat of passionate kissing was as far as he could go. She seemed to like it, but he knew there were limits. She would never touch him as Ricki had...at least not now. That had been fine with him...until last night.

But, when he had traveled home from Ricki's house by bus, he had felt empty and cold. When he crawled into bed after having been with Anne, his heart was always full and his body warm.

However, just thinking about Ricki aroused him. The boys in his neighborhood called a girl like that a whore. They pronounced it *who-er*. He didn't feel that way. He felt there was nothing wrong with her knowing what she wanted and knowing what felt good. But, had she done with other boys what she had done with him?

This is so wrong. But she is so ripe.

Anne would be brokenhearted if she knew. He understood that it was just lust, not love.

Did you ever have to make up your mind?

He had already crossed the Rubicon. Why regret it?

Funny...it was the same place...the same park...where Santo had been...

He trembled, cursing himself, as he dialed Ricki's number.

***

He went to Ricki's house directly from work that day. He had told her, over the phone, that his schedule had changed, so he would be able to meet her at six.

They played miniature golf and had a bite to eat. She wore a short summery yellow and blue dress and the same sandals and earrings that she had worn the night before. A small yellow pocketbook was slung over one shoulder. Her lovely hair and incredible eyes were intoxicating.

She was playful and happy. She kissed him each time one of them sank a ball.

She took out a cigarette. He took a pack of matches from his pocket and lit it for her, declining the one that she offered.

"What t…time do you h…have to be home?"

"My parents don't care. My father drinks beer and falls asleep watching TV and my mom goes out almost every night."

"Where does sh…she g…go?"

"My old man don't ask and I don't ask. It's not a marriage made in heaven."

"Oh. That's t…too b…bad."

"No, it's not. I don't care."

"I still don't un…derstand about Catholic school."

"It's cause I got kicked out of my other school in the sixth grade and my Uncle Chris, he pays my tuition."

"Whose br…brother is he?"

"He's not really my uncle. He's a…kind of…distant cousin."

"That's generous. Why didn't you go to another public school?"

"My mom and Chris said I needed discipline." She laughed. "And he pays for a lot of things for my family."

"What about your dad?"

"He's just a lush. He don't care about nothing."

"Oh."

She reached up, put her hands on his shoulders, and kissed him.

"Let's get out of here," she said.

"Where…where d…do you…"

Clasping both of her hands at the back of his neck, she put her mouth to his ear and hotly whispered, "Leave it to me."

They traveled by bus to an apartment building, and Ricki opened the lobby door.

"What are w…we doing here?"

"My sister lives here. She's divorced."

"Is she home?"

"We'll find out."

They took the elevator to the third floor, and Ricki knocked on the door of her sister's apartment. After a few seconds, the door opened.

Joan looked the way Anacleto imagined Ricki would in a few years. She was pretty in a hard, heavily made-up way. Her lovely blue eyes held him; they took his breath away. Their iridescent sparkle illuminated her face. She wore a thin white blouse, her lacy white brassiere clearly visible through the sheer material. Her mane of rich, honey-blonde hair hung down to the small of her back.

She was twenty-six, the oldest of Ricki's four siblings. They sat on a large white leather couch. Anacleto stared, mesmerized, as Joan's black miniskirt rode up her bare, tanned legs to a breathtakingly perilous height. A pair of black very high heels lay on the carpet between the couch and the coffee table.

"I… have four br…broth…brothers," Anacleto answered in response to Joan's question. "I'm a little ner…nervous."

Joan laughed. She was intelligent. It was clear that Ricki adored her. The sisters talked and exchanged private jokes. Anacleto was uncomfortable at first, but, after a while, he relaxed. He listened. He wished he had that kind of relationship with his brothers. Then Anne popped into his brain. He looked at a painting on a wall—an abstract nude.

Each time Joan moved or re-crossed her legs, his eyes were drawn to the hem of her skirt. They talked a while longer. Then he asked where the bathroom was.

When he emerged, Ricki was sitting on the couch, alone, smoking a cigarette. Joan smiled at Anacleto as she walked out the door.

"Where d…did she go?"

"She has a date. She has lots of dates. Her husband, Carl—I mean her ex—is such a bastard. They were married only a year, and he was cheating on her the whole time."

"Wow. That's a shame."

"And she had such a nice wedding. Two hundred guests, a seven-piece band. She kept both rings. Big rocks. He had money. The bastard!"

"You two are cl…close."

Ricki smiled. Then she kicked off her sandals and stood up.

"I'm close to my other sister, Trish—she's eighteen. I'm kinda close to my two brothers. Frankie, he's your age."

"I have a br…brother Frankie too."

She had walked to the small kitchen. He heard the refrigerator door open, followed by a rattling sound. Then the door closed. She returned to the couch with two cans of Bud.

"I know. You told me."

She opened both cans and handed one to Anacleto. He took his first sip of beer. It slaked his thirst, but it did nothing to clear his avalanching head fog. In fact, after a few sips, he felt a bit dizzy. Unsure as to where to put the can, he held it on his lap.

"Tell me. What about your other brother?"

She took a long, loud gulp from the can of beer.

"Eddie? He's twenty-one. He's okay."

She finished drinking in three long slurps. Then she stood up, walked to the kitchen, and returned with two more beers. She left one can on the coffee table in front of him and opened the other one.

"S…so, you're the baby," he said.

"I told you that."

She sat, took another long gulp, and then moved closer to Anacleto, leaning her head on his chest. He stroked her hair. She placed her beer on the coffee table; then she put his there too. He was glad to be rid of it.

Ricki looked up at him and said, "I want a big wedding too."

He laughed, but he stopped when he saw that she was serious.

"You're only sev—"

"Don't give me that 'You're only seventeen' bullshit. I'm the most responsible one in my family."

"I di…didn't mean to say that you're—"

"I can take care of myself. I have for years. I'm moving out of my disgusting house as soon as I finish high school and get a job."

"Okay. S…sorry."

"Am I your girl?"

"Are y…you?" He smiled, hoping she would laugh.

"Don't be cute. I really like you. I could fall for you…easy."

Suddenly, he was hot, but he also felt faint and sick to his stomach. He pushed her away and put his head down, covering his face with his hands. Then he looked at Ricki through his finger lenses. He didn't like what he saw.

"What are you doing? You look like a retard."

Flustered, he put his hands down. He stood up. Then he sat again.

"It…it's a nice apar…apart…ment."

"Yeah."

"I…I'm n…n…ner…vous."

"I can see that. Why are you nervous?"

He smiled weakly. He wasn't just nervous. He was terrified. He wanted to leave. She took his hands in hers and examined them.

"They're cold, but they're strong. This one is smaller, but it's strong too. You have a lot of muscles."

"Le…let's go, Ricki."

She placed his hands in her armpits and held her arms against them; her warmth was astonishing.

"You're really sweet and cute. You know?" she said, smiling brightly.

"You're very pretty, but I don't know—"

"There's nothing you have to know except that you're the guy for me. You'll never regret it. I will love you and make you very happy."

"I…have…a girlfriend."

"Then, what are you doing here?" Her voice was sharp and her icy stare sliced into his rattled, foggy brain. She moved away from him. His hands felt icy cold again.

"I…like you too. I need to think," he replied.

"No. Thinking will leave you in a corner...by yourself."

He listened. He pictured Anne sitting next to Ricki, waiting for her turn to speak. But, he wondered, was she waiting? Was she sitting in her house with her crazy father, looking at the telephone, or was she relieved that he wasn't there? He knew he had no reason to think that. He was projecting.

"Let me tell you something," she said, holding his hands again and looking at him sweetly: "You know what you want. You want me, just like I want you. I make you hot…You make me hot, but…it's more than that for me. I really do like you more than any other guy I've ever known. I'm very…sensitive to my feelings and I know how I feel about you."

"I'm sure you're right, but—"

"After last night, I know you're my guy. Believe me, you won't regret it—ever, for one second."

Then she moved close and pushed her body against his and kissed him with such hot passion that he thought his head would explode. Then she kissed his forehead and caressed his face.

"We have the apartment to ourselves. My sister's not going to be home for…I don't know. Maybe all night. Besides, she won't care if we fool around. Not all the way…not yet."

"I…need some air," he said, starting to stand up.

Ignoring his plea, she pulled him down. He complied. She slowly and carefully unbuttoned his shirt and, reaching under it, began massaging his shoulders and chest. More than feeling good, her touch put him at ease and relaxed him. He put his hands on her hips and held her tight as she rubbed his chest.

"You're strong," she purred.

No. This is wrong…

He stood up abruptly. "I need some air."

She stood up and led him across the living room to a sliding door; she opened it and they walked out to the balcony. The breeze from the ocean, a few miles away, refreshed him. The streets below were quiet. Where were the people? Were they home, where they belonged? How many husbands and wives were out right now, apart from each other? He didn't want to be that kind of person. He didn't want to hurt anyone. In the distance, he saw the elevated line that he had been on so many times. This was not one of the apartment buildings that he used to look at from the train and wonder about, but he wondered now…were people who lived in this place afraid, vulnerable?

We're all vulnerable…

Ricki pulled his face down to hers. She kissed him sweetly.

"I have to be able to trust you. Can I trust you?" she asked.

"Sure, but I th…think we should go."

"Your hands are still cold."

She began walking back into the apartment. At the terrace doorway, she stopped, turned around, and smiled seductively at him. He waited. He knew this was the moment. He quickly weighed his choices. He knew what he should do, but he felt weak. He followed her in. They sat on the couch and held each other. They kissed, they touched. She was gentler, more loving than she had been the night before. He became more aggressive. The more he pressed against her, the more submissive she seemed to become. His hands wandered over her body. He cupped her breasts in his hands. She kissed him harder, deeper, more intensely. He was amazed and energized by her smoldering ferocity. She moved back a bit and unbuttoned and slipped out of the top of her dress, letting it fall to her waist. Weak. He felt so weak. He knew he was being manipulated, but he was powerless to resist. He kissed her—hot, intensely hot. His hands roamed over her bare shoulders and back. She pushed him down on the couch and lay on top of him. They held each other tightly, kissing, tasting. He held her face in his hands. She ran her fingers through his short, curly hair. Reaching behind her, he tried to unclasp her bra. He was warm, very warm. His fingers could not figure out the clasp. She laughed, sat up on him, and swiftly, joyfully undid it. She let it fall to the floor.

He stared at the first pair of breasts he had ever seen. They were larger than he had expected them to be…rounded and firm. Creamy white and pink and darker pink. He held her over him, kissing, tasting. Then she sat up, moved off him, pulled him into a sitting position; she helped him out of his open shirt. Then she pushed him down and pressed her body against his. They kissed deeply. Heat radiated from her firm breasts to his bare chest. They were both warm, their skin slippery with perspiration. Then she gently pushed him away and held him with her incredible green eyes.

"Can I trust you?"

"I…I don't—"

"You're gonna be here?"

I am here. I should be home alone or with Anne. Is she waiting for me? Who am I? I was a good person. The corruption is infecting me. Why do I hold myself back?

"Well?" She was impatient.

"I'm h…here, aren't I?"

"Promise!"

By now, he was cooling, losing interest.

"I th…think I…we…sh—"

"Listen. I can get any boy my age, but I want a man...I want you."

"I'm not a man. If I was—"

"You're a man and I know how to be a woman. I can be very good for you—"

"You are…I th—"

"No more thinking! Do you think about everything you do?"

"No…I just think—"

"There you go! Do you think every time you before do anything?"

He was stunned, helpless.

"Don't be so damned afraid! And don't waste my time!"

He stood up. She stood in front of him, blocking him, the top of her little dress hanging from her waist, her breasts pointing at him accusingly.

Almost fully naked.

"I…th…I mean…we…should go."

"No! Stay. Please," she pleaded.

"But—"

"Don't you like me?" she asked sadly.

"Sure. You're n…nice and so pretty. I really do like you. I'm confused. I don't want to make a mis…take."

"Do you think I'm a mistake?"

"Oh, no. You're wonderful. You're more than I d…deserve. I mean, I'm not sure—"

"There's nothing to be unsure about. It's okay if I like you more than you like me," she explained.

"It's just…"

Then she softly murmured, "Hold me, please."

They sat again. They kissed, but he was nervous, overcome with guilt.

"You feel so good," she said as she ran her hands up and down his back. "You're so strong."

"This is...I just need to th…think."

"No more thinking," she whispered. Her warm breath in his ear aroused him to new heights of heated exhilaration. He kissed her deeply, hungrily.

Then, summoning his last reserves of courage, he stood up again.

Her eyes tightened and grew cold. She reached up and grabbed the front of his pants and unbuckled his belt. He knew what he had to do, but he did nothing…he watched her hands; he was apprehensive, but incredibly aroused. He knew he should stop her, but he was too weak to do so. She undid the top button of his jeans and pulled him back down to the couch. Then she reached in, past his undershorts. Her hand was warm.

The sensation of her touch was astonishing. He thought his heart would burst. She held him gently and then more firmly. She caressed...rubbed...stroked... squeezed…

He moaned. He was overwhelmed by the throbbing, pulsating, hot, excruciatingly joyful feeling that had taken control of him. His very being was centered *there*. His lifeblood was pooling *there*. A soft, warm magnet was drawing all that was *him* to a new, more exhilarating level of existence. His very essence, his heart, his soul, his very being were *there*.

She nestled her head against his chest. He wrapped his arms around her. She withdrew her hand. He whined. She sat up and unzipped his pants. Then she put her hand back in. She rubbed slowly and gently and then more quickly. They held and kissed each other in a long, fevered embrace.

Throbbing, pulsating, wonderful, guilty, overpowering…

"Soon," he whispered.

He was about to explode…cover the world…

Her hand was guiding his brain, his heart, his very existence.

"Oh…"

The release was so total that it hurt.

She waited a few seconds and then she extracted her hand, wiping it with a tissue from a box that was on the coffee table. She handed a couple of tissues to him.

She looked as composed as he felt flushed.

He stood up and, turning away from her, he shoved the wad of tissues into his underwear. Then he zipped up, closed his pants button, and buckled his belt.

***

They walked back to her house.

"I'm sor…ry. Don't feel g…guilty."

She stopped walking, and looked at him.

"What? I don't feel guilty. You know how I feel about you. I've never felt this way about a guy…You wouldn't believe how many guys…men want to go out with me."

He believed.

"I'm not sur…sur…pr…surprised. You're beau—"

"You shouldn't be nervous anymore. I'll take good care of you. You are what I want. I don't want any other man."

"Have you—"

"No...I told you. I've gone out with lots of boys and a couple of older men. One was my next-door neighbor before we moved here. He was thirty-six. Married."

"Oh."

"He just about tried to rape me."

"Did you call the p…po…police?"

Her smile was mocking.

"No. I guess y…you did…didn't."

"Look…I've been with a lot of guys, but I'm still a virgin. I want to save that for you…and soon."

That comment sent a sharp, hot electric shock to his overloaded brain.

This isn't what I want. But…what ***do*** *I want?*

They reached her door. They kissed, but he could not respond as she obviously hoped he would. She closed the door.

As he descended the front steps and walked to the sidewalk, he cursed his weak and fickle soul.

BAPTISM IN THE KITCHEN

He called Anne from work the next day.

"I'm sorry. I…I…know…I've b…been…I mean…I know…"

"Yes. I know too."

"I want y…you to know that I'm s…sor…sorry…"

He waited. She remained silent.

"It won't hap…pen again."

***

Anne was alone. She let him into the house.

He repeated what he had said to her over the phone earlier in the day.

Her face was blank.

"Do you want some juice?" she asked.

She filled a tall glass with apple juice. He sat at the kitchen table.

"I didn't find out anything about Santo," he told her.

She stood, with her back to the refrigerator door, the glass of juice in her hand.

"I know. I think he's dead."

"What? No, no. Don't say that. He can't be d...dead."

"My mom and dad went to the police station and filed a report."

"He's prob…ably—"

She approached him.

"I know you didn't look for him."

"I…"

The cold-wet instantly shocked him. The impact of the icy juice hitting the top of his head, pouring down his face and the back of his hair, trickling down to his neck and shoulders, and then running into his shirt confused and stunned him. He looked up at Anne. She held the empty glass above him, allowing the last drops to fall on his saturated hair. They were the final droplets of a shockingly sudden cold rain shower, a sticky, angry one. He didn't move as rivulets of juice made their way down his chest and to his pants, wetting the top of his undershorts. And then the last of the juice dripped further down...to his guilty spot.

"You're a bastard and she's a tramp!"

"Who?"

"I never thought you would do this, Clete. I trusted you!" Her face was twisted in anger. Tears rolled down her face.

He lied. He had the truth ready, on his tongue, but he swallowed it.

"I didn't do…Do what? What? I…I…did…did—"

"You did. Jenny saw you—at the hangout…on 86th."

She hit him on his shoulders…She pushed the back of his head. He did not try to stop her.

I deserve this...maybe if she hits the spots Ricki touched last night...

"Oh… I…was…there…and—"

"And? I'm so hurt. I thought I could trust you." She moved to the sink and, leaning over it, she sobbed. "I promised myself I wouldn't get mad or curse at you because I do love you."

He remained silent. The juice was cold. His undershorts and jeans were sticking to him as a wet, cold, gummy reminder of his betrayal. He squirmed.

"So?" She rubbed her face with her hands.

"I w…walked w…with a g…girl."

"You went to the bay, and you..."

"No! I d…did n…not."

"You laid her."

"No...that's not...I didn't."

"Liar!"

"I k…kissed her. That's—"

"Liar! Jenny knows her…Ricki something or other—"

"I…don't—"

"I don't either, Clete."

"I did…didn't ... "

"What else did you do?"

"I, er..."

"What else did *she* do?"

Anacleto looked down.

She glared at him.

Now she hates me. This is what I deserve.

"I'm sor…ry, but I didn't...I don't know what happened…"

As he said that, he knew that by holding back the full truth he was lying and that he would be punished for it over and over. More than being with another girl, worse than the kissing and touching and ejaculating, worse than anything else was lying to Anne. He was descending into the depths of hell.

"You're not who you think you are, Clete. You think you're a nice guy. WELL, YOU'RE NOT!"

He shivered and his head began to hurt. He was dizzy.

"You're not almost a man. You're a child. I know what happened."

I'm weak and insecure. She should know that.

"You haven't figured out yet that some things are worth fighting for. That you can make decisions and stick to them!"

"I…don't know—"

"That's it, exactly! You don't know. You had me. All you had to do was to be loyal. I trusted you. I would have been ready to let you…for us…to have…sex… sometime…maybe soon; maybe sooner than I said…you just had to give me time. I trusted you."

No…No.

He spoke slowly and deliberately. "That wasn't it…I didn't pl…plan…I was happy with what we had. Very happy."

"Then it's more of a shame that you let a little tramp do you because…now, you can never have me."

He put his head down.

I am Anacleto. This is real. I'm a disgusting fool.

"Oh, Clete…you don't have to do that. Pick your head up. Go to the bathroom and wash yourself off."

He washed up in the bathroom. He did not look at his reflection in the mirror.

THE UNDERSTANDING

He was surprised at just how adaptable he was. Within a few days, he had learned to accept the end of his relationship with Anne. A few days after that, she stopped him on his way to work.

"Let's go out to dinner tonight," she suggested.

His week-long headache disappeared in an instant as he walked briskly to the subway.

He went straight to Anne's house after work. She invited him in and said she'd be ready in a few minutes. He waited in the kitchen. Francine came in. They greeted each other warmly. She smiled. He smiled back. Gradually, as they looked at each other, their faces fell.

"He's gone. My boy—"

"You don't know that. He…he's prob…probably just—"

"No. He's never stayed away for more than a day or two. It's close to a year now."

Her eyes were red. She sobbed. He wondered what Anne had told her about his mistake...his infidelity.

"He's probably sc…scared to come home. He didn't mean to st…stay away so long, but now—"

"Santo's not scared of anything. You know that," she replied.

"His father—"

"Santo isn't afraid of him either."

Anne walked into the kitchen. She bent down and hugged her mother and kissed her cheek.

"We won't be gone long. "Do you want us to bring you anything, Mom?"

"No. Your father will be here soon. He's bringing something home for us to eat."

As they walked, he took Anne's hand. It lay, unmoving, in his. She withdrew it and scratched her nose. Then she shifted her pocketbook to that shoulder so that she could hold the strap with that hand. She said that the police had told her parents they could file a missing person report. Finding missing adults, they had said, was difficult because, most of the time, missing people didn't want to be found.

They sat in a local Chinese restaurant, sipping soup and exchanging small talk. Then Anne told him what he had seen for himself: Francine had become alternately frantic and utterly depressed. She put her spoon down, and sighed. He had lost his appetite too.

Walking home along the dark, quiet sidewalk, Anacleto recollected all of the places that he and Anne had gone during the short time that they had been close: restaurants, amusement parks, the beach, the Village, Chinatown. He had hoped that, one day, they might travel to other places, other countries, other worlds.

At her house, Anne stopped him at the door.

"I wanted to tell you so much, but I can't," she said, and then she sighed.

"It's o…kay. We h…have t…time."

"No."

She said the word quietly, but it hit him with the force of a bullet. It ricocheted in his skull.

"I wanted to…straighten this out before we both started college."

"It's okay. Anything you want to—"

"I wanted to say that you're a good guy….and you don't have to worry about me."

"I'm not good…I was, but I did a terrible thing."

"You did what made you happy."

"It was stu…stupid and I regret it. Can we go back to where we were? I'll wait."

She smiled. He moved to kiss her. She pulled back.

"That's not for you. We're friends now. We'll always be friends, but we don't kiss good-night."

"Anne, I'll wait. I…deserve pun…pun…punishment."

"It's not punishment, Clete. I'm not even angry with you. You knocked me for a loop. I wish I hadn't found out, but I did. My whole sense, my trust, my…I don't know how to say it…"

"I un…derstand."

"Maybe you do. Look—I didn't give you what you wanted—"

"No! It's n…not that. Y…you…uh." His voice trailed off. He didn't know what to say.

"Why did you do it?"

"I'm not nor…normal. You know that. I don't…know…h…h…how to live."

"That's not it," she said, sure of herself. "You're a smart guy…you're more confident now than you've ever been."

"I guess. I'm broken up a…bout..."

He told her that her that he was angry at Santo. He admitted that he had wanted to be alone and that he had not looked for Santo. Where would he look? Did Santo deserve this much devotion?

"Do I?" she asked.

"Yes!" he answered instantly.

"Well, you blew it. And to think, I trusted you."

"I'll wait. Just l…let th…things stay the way they are…I'll wait."

"And go sneaking off with Little Miss Wiggly Ass while you're waiting?"

"N…never. I haven't called her. I won't see her. I didn't even tell her…where… I… l…live."

"You mean you lied to her too?"

"It…it's not like that…"

He tried to explain how she came onto him like a tigress, but Anne sneered. He told her that his judgment had taken a back seat to his hormones.

"What about your sense of right and wrong and your feelings for me?"

"It was s…so quick."

"Did you lay her?"

"No! I sw…swear. Nothing like that. I want us to m…make l…love some… some… day—"

"Well, that's never going to happen."

"Just…wait…I want you and m…me to b…be—"

"We're just friends, Clete. Don't wait for me. Friends go out with other people."

She closed the door.

And he learned to live with their situation during those final days of the summer of 1970.

SANTO'S SUBWAY STORY

When Anacleto left his summer job in late August, Mr. Blumenthal said he hoped that he would be back the following summer. He quickly fell into the routine of classes, studying, and part-time work at the college library. He started out as a stacker, but after his first two weeks, he was trained as a research assistant, and received a raise.

"Most of the students who work here don't want to put in more than a few hours a week, and they end up being undependable," Mr. Stanhope, his supervisor, said. "I hope you don't disappoint me, Clete,"

Anacleto assured him that he loved books and libraries. Mr. Stanhope raised a skeptical eyebrow at that.

He celebrated his eighteenth birthday with James and Frank. They took him to a club in Manhattan, where he had his first legal drink. His only other one had been with Ricki. His brothers were more excited about it than he was, but he was pleased that they had thought about him.

"What's the matter? Can't you ever let loose?" they asked him teasingly.

"I am letting loose," he replied, guzzling his beer, attempting to enjoy it.

As he and Frank approached their house, they saw two figures walking hand-in-hand. Anacleto turned his head and looked down, pretending he hadn't seen.

***

One Friday afternoon in early December, Santo called. At first, Anacleto didn't recognize his voice.

"Is it really you?"

"Yeah. I need you. I called your house another time." Santo sounded weak, desperate. Then Anacleto remembered the mysterious phone call a few months back…the voice had sounded as if it was underwater… drowning.

"I just got home from work," Anacleto told him.

"You gotta meet me."

"Where? What happened?"

"Meet me at the bus terminal," he said.

"Why? Come home. Your mom and Anne think you're dead."

"No. You gotta meet me…and bring money—a hundred should be enough."

"I don't understand. Why can't—"

"Please, Clete. No questions."

"Are you at the terminal now?"

"No."

"At least tell me where you are."

"Not now, Clete. I need you to meet me. I don't have any money."

"Where are you?"

Santo sighed. Then he said that he was in a county jail in upstate New York. He was due to be released that afternoon. Anacleto tried to hide his anxiety and surprise by asking, "Don't they give you money?"

"They're givin' me a bus ticket to the city and ten dollars."

"So, can't you take the subway home?"

"You gotta meet me at Port Authority—with money."

"I don't understand."

"I can't talk now. Meet me there."

"When?"

"I'll be there about nine."

He told Anacleto where to wait for him.

"Okay," Anacleto replied, confused and wishing he hadn't answered the phone.

"Bring the money."

"Okay, Santo, but…"

He waited.

"Never mind, Santo. I'll bring it."

He took a hundred dollars from the coffee can. He put fifty into each of his two front pockets. When his mother arrived home from work, he told her he was going out for the evening and that he didn't want any dinner. Her sad, beaten-down expression was heart-rending. He really did want to stay with her. No…he didn't want to stay with her, but he felt her loneliness. He hugged and kissed her, and then he walked to the door.

It was too early to leave, but the last thing he wanted at that moment was for his mother to start questioning him. He walked out and started toward Anne's house. Then he stopped. Then he started down her alleyway.

He won't want her there…Maybe she shouldn't see him, but I'll have to tell her that I spoke to him…No…not now.

He wasn't ready to tell her.

***

He arrived at the Port Authority Bus Terminal at eight. He had a hamburger and a Coke and bought a newspaper. Then he sat on a bench near the bay where passengers from the bus that Santo was supposed to be on would disembark.

He glanced at a tall, very pretty, heavily made-up woman in a short skirt who smiled at him and then mouthed, "How are you?" He knew she was too good to be true or too good to be free. Besides, he didn't have the heart to talk to members of the opposite sex these days. He turned back to his reading. He peeked at her over the top of his paper a few times. Then he saw her smile at a much older man. After talking for a few seconds, they walked off together.

Time passed very slowly. He tried to imagine what Santo would tell him and how he would look. He hadn't seen him in more than a year. Would Santo contact his mother? Would he disappear again? That would be best—unless he was ready to be a normal person and a friend and a brother and a son again. Had Santo ever been normal?

Have I ever been normal?

The bus was on time. Anacleto looked at the people as they disembarked, searching for Santo. After a while, it seemed as if no others were coming through the door. He wondered whether Santo had missed the bus. The last passengers walked past him. Anacleto felt sick to his stomach. He wanted to go home. He wasn't sure he wanted to see Santo again, but he couldn't leave. And then he saw him, but it wasn't really him. The tall, thin man walking toward Anacleto couldn't be Santo.

"Hi, Clete. How you doin'?"

"Santo…you look…different."

"Yeah. I was sick and I lost some weight."

"I'll say…Looks like you lost a lot of weight."

Santo's skin was ghostly pale and he needed a shave. He lit a cigarette and took a long drag.

He looked at Anacleto. "You're looking good. You put on some muscle."

Then he took Anacleto's hands in his and looked at them, turning them over. Anacleto wondered whether Santo was remembering the first time he had examined them…when he had held Anacleto captive against a parked car. How many years before?

"You look good," he repeated.

"Do y…you want something to…eat?" Anacleto asked.

"Yeah. I can eat."

While he watched Santo hungrily devour two hamburgers and guzzle two cardboard cups of black coffee, Anacleto told him about school and his job at the library and the fiasco involving the sculpture. Santo did not seem to be paying attention, so Anacleto stopped talking. Santo's hair was short and stiff, his face was lined, and his eyes were bloodshot.

It was hot in the bus terminal. Santo's face was covered with perspiration.

"Do y…you want to go out? It's nice outside."

"No."

"You look like you're dying of the heat," he ventured.

"Yeah. I'm dyin' all right."

"What happened, Santo?"

"I can't tell you now. Did you bring the money?"

"I told you I'd bring it, but what's it f…for?"

"It's a long story, Clete."

"I've got time."

"No. Not now."

"When?"

"I don't know. Do you have it? Give it to me."

"No. I think I deserve some answers. Do you have any idea what you've done to your m...mother? To Anne?"

Santo's look was cold, dead.

"You don't give a damn about them, do you?"

Suddenly, Santo looked panicky. "Did you tell them I called you?"

"No."

"Are you going to?" he asked.

"No."

"Good. I don't wanna be bothered," he said in a weak, throaty voice.

"That's not right. They think you're dead."

"I am dead. You're looking' at a fuckin' ghost."

"I d...don't understand."

"Look, Clete…you're still my only friend. You *are* my friend, right?"

"I don't know. I don't know."

"You came here. I'm…you know, grateful. You're my friend."

Anacleto searched Santo's eyes…they were empty…maybe he *was* dead.

"What happened, Santo? You owe me that much."

"You wanna know who fuckin' owes? It's you…you owe me."

"What are you talking about?"

"Not here. Not now."

Anacleto waited. He had what Santo wanted. Suddenly, Anacleto's need to know became more important to him than his desire to help Santo or to be rid of him.

"Are you gonna give me the money?"

"No. Not until you tell me what happened and where you're going."

"You're a selfish little prick."

"No...I'm not. I'm trying to look out for you."

"I don't need help from you or anybody."

Anacleto remained silent.

"You gonna give me the money?"

"Not until you tell me what happened and where you're going…and what you mean by how I owe you."

Santo shook his head in disgust. "Okay. Wait here a minute."

Santo went to a pay phone. He made three or four phone calls. The final one lasted for a few minutes. Santo appeared to be pleading with whoever was on the other end of the line. Then he hung up and returned to the table.

"Okay. We're takin' a trip to Queens. We'll talk on the train."

***

The subway car was crowded, so Santo motioned for Anacleto to follow him to the platform between the cars. It was noisy and windy there, but they were alone. That was what Santo wanted. They swayed with the motion of the train and held onto the grimy chains between the cars. After a few minutes, Santo looked at Anacleto.

"Remember those two guys who came to me that night in the park after that bitch stole my stash? The colored guy and the blond haired guy?" Santo talked close to Anacleto's ear so that he could hear him above the screeching and rattling of the subway car.

Anacleto remembered them better than Santo could possibly know.

"About a week after that, after you gave me the money and I got set up again, they came back. They were regulars."

Santo lit a match, cupped it and brought it to the cigarette that was in his mouth. The rushing, swirling wind blew it out. He tried two more times before he was successful.

"Well, like I said, about a week later, they came back and they took my stash and my money and beat the crap out of me." He looked ashamed. "They had a fucking gun, the bastards. Steve—he's the white guy—he held it to my head and Darren, the other guy, he took everything. They told me I was through. I figured I would leave and come back with a baseball bat and break their fuckin' heads, but they punched and kicked the shit out of me some more." Santo closed his eyes and took a long drag. He looked through the window into one subway car and then into the other one. His eyes, in the dim light of the subway car platform, looked deep and dark and sad.

"How's my mom and Anne?"

"They're okay. Unhappy, but okay. You know you have a br…brother? Peter. A real cute kid."

"Yeah? He probably got my mom's good looks."

"He's a cute kid."

"Yeah. Don't you tell them about me. If I can see them,…I will."

He lit a new cigarette from the stub of the old one.

"You wanna hear more?" Santo asked.

"I want to hear everything."

Santo moved to the outer edge of the platform and spit into the whirlwind of the subway tunnel. Then he returned.

"Okay. After they beat me up and took everything, they dragged me to a car, a blue Mustang, and put me in the fuckin' trunk. I was going in and out, but I was clear enough to think that they were gonna put a bullet in me."

He took a monumental drag on his cigarette. As he exhaled, he broke into a coughing spasm that lasted for almost a full minute. Anacleto tried to pat his shoulder, but Santo waved away his hand.

When Santo had caught his breath, he continued: "I gotta say this—you shouldn't be makin' me tell you."

"Why not?"

"I shouldn't have to beg for the money."

"You're not beg…ging. You're telling me so th…that I understand where my money's going."

"If I felt better, I'd just beat the living shit out of you and take the cash."

"Santo," Anacleto laughed, "Maybe in a week or two, but, right now, I've got ten pounds on you and…I've been working out."

"Yeah. You look good. You lay my sister yet?"

"No. I'm not even talking to her these days."

"How come?"

"It's personal, but I'll tell you. Finish your story first."

"You're full of surprises, Clete."

"Life's full of surprises."

"Ain't that the fuckin' truth?" Santo smiled bitterly. "Okay, so they drive for a while. I don't know how long 'cause I'm kinda groggy. They stop and they pull me out and throw me into some empty lot in some crappy neighborhood and they pound away on me again. Actually, it's all Steve." Santo's face twisted in a grimace of anger and remembered pain. "I am gonna kill that piece of shit."

"You're not going to kill Steve, Santo."

"Oh, yeah? Why not?"

"Number one, you're too sick. Number two, you won't find him. Number three, you'll end up in jail again."

"Yeah? Numbers one, two, three—you're wrong, wrong, wrong."

"Number four, Santo, I know more about you than you'll ever know. You're not going to kill Steve."

Anacleto almost told him that he would kill his father one day, but he knew that was a head fog illusion from when he was twelve years old. *Stupid*, he thought.

Santo sulked for a while. Then he resumed: "They leave me there, on the ground, with garbage and dog shit all over the place. Then they start to argue about what to do with me. I hear Steve say something about how they had to get me outta the picture, but Darren is kind of...you know, reluctant. Then Steve goes back to the car...I figure to get the gun...and I'm alone with Darren. I'm still layin' there. I have just enough strength to kick him in the shins. He goes down, and I get the fuck outta there. I know I can't hide out in that crappy neighborhood. I run before Darren or Steve catches up with me or somebody else spots me and decides to cut me to pieces.

"I see a kid on a bike. I take it from him and I pedal. I didn't know where I was or how to get home, but I keep moving. Finally, I got to a better neighborhood —it was the middle of the night. I slept in a park."

He closed his eyes for a few seconds; then he started to light another cigarette from the old one.

"Stop, Santo. You're making yourself sick."

"This? This ain't nothing." He smiled. "Let me cut to the chase: I got back to our neighborhood in the morning. I went straight to…one of the guys I bought from. I musta looked like a dead man because when I pounded on the door of his club…you know, one of those social clubs…I ain't sayin' which one…and this guy answers it, he turns white. I'm thinking they feel bad for me. Well, the big man, he comes into the room and he lets me wash up and he gives me some clean clothes. I had coffee and something to eat. Then I told him the story. You see, I lost five hundred dollars of his product and all the cash I had."

"What did he say?"

"That was the funny part. He acted like the money and the heroin was no big deal…like all he cared about was me. He says he's gonna get them for me. He tells me to go home and take a couple of days off. He's gonna get word to me. That was suspicious too because he never called me. I always had to go to the club."

"Oh. You thought—"

"Yeah. I leave, but I don't go home. I know there's a way up to the roof of the apartment house across the street, so I go into the building and up to the roof, and I hang out up there. It's empty, so I stake myself out. A couple of hours pass, and it's late afternoon, and who do you think I see pull up to the club?"

"Steve and Darren in the blue Mustang."

"Right. Now, I think...I'm gonna find out who's shitting who. Well, they come out fifteen minutes later and get back in the car and drive off. Nobody follows them. I go to the park that night, and it's business as usual. They don't see me...but the two bastards are there, selling my product from my spot. Look, the next stop is where I'm gettin' off."

"Okay, Santo, but I'm going with you."

"No. When I get off, you get off and you take another train home."

"Then, you're not getting the money."

He scowled. "Okay, I'll finish the story on the station. Then you go home."

They reentered the subway car and, when the train stopped, they walked out to the station platform. They sat on a bench, and Santo continued.

"I couldn't go home—in case they were looking for me. I couldn't go into the park. They had that fuckin' gun."

"You should have come to me."

"And what were you gonna do? You were a pussy in those days." He smiled. "Besides, this wasn't dealing H. This was for dealing in blood."

"I would have helped you, Santo."

"I didn't want you to."

Anacleto wasn't sure he really would have.

"Anyway, I knew a guy. He used to buy a lot from me. I gave him credit all the time. He owed me, so I hung out by his house until he got home. He let me stay there that night and the next day. Then I went back to the park that night and...same as before: those two cocksuckers are doin' business."

"So, you knew your suppliers weren't g...going to do anything to them."

"Not just that, stupid, but they were in it together...Get it?"

"Why?"

"You sure you wanna know?"

"Yes."

"It's partly your fault. That girl...the one that was gonna go down on me that night...the night you were there spying on me?"

"I know," Anacleto sadly replied, his stomach turning as he remembered.

"Well, when she stole my knapsack with my stash and most of my money, it ended up with Steve and Darren, and they showed my associate that I'm not doin' my job right."

"I'm sorry, Santo."

"Don't sweat it now. There's more."

They were both silent a few seconds.

"There was something else in the bag, Clete."

"What?"

"The gun."

"What gun? Oh, you mean—"

"Yeah. I had the other gun. Remember when Albie's father dropped the cartridge box? Remember, me and Albie picked it up? Well, everybody was so hot to see the gun go off that I had a few seconds to put one of the other ones in my pocket…and a handful of bullets."

"You had it the whole time."

"Yeah."

"Didn't you understand how much trouble I was in?"

"Are you kidding? Do you think being in trouble with your fuckin' mother—no disrespect—is the same thing as dealin' drugs and having to watch my back?"

"But…you weren't selling drugs or dealing with connected people when you stole the gun."

"No, but…you know my stinkin' life…I knew it was gonna come to that or some other kind of shit sooner or later."

"You don't feel any guilt, do you?"

"I never have and I never will. Like I told you, life is a game—you gotta play to win. Now, what about the money?"

"No."

"Whadda you mean 'no'?"

"You have to tell me the rest—jail, how come you're so sick, where you're going—"

"I'll tell you about jail, but that's it...I knew I hadda get away, so I hung out in the East Village. I knew a place where I could score some H on credit and sell it. It worked out for a while. I met this girl, and we were sorta livin' together, but she had a bad habit and…" Now Santo began to rub his face with his hands. "I'm so fuckin' tired," he said.

"What happened?"

"I partied with her once or twice," he replied dryly.

"You mean…you took…you used—"

"Yeah. It was great…for a while."

Anacleto shook his head. He felt the weight of Santo's life.

"Then…It's the devil, Clete. I got…hooked." He looked sad.

"And you got arrested."

"No. Not in the city. Charlene—that was her name—Charlene had some friends in Poughkeepsie. So we went there one weekend. We had a big party, but there was a fight and the cops came and they found lots of shit and we all got hauled off to jail."

"That's when you should have called me."

"I did. Then I hung up, but it was the best thing. I don't mean that jail was good, but it fuckin' saved my life."

"I wondered if that was you back then. You know, your mom went to the police. She filed a report about you. They should have come across your name because of the arrest."

"What can I tell ya?"

"What did they do? I mean you went to jail."

"The judge sentenced me to six months in jail and a program. Jail sucks. It was worse than you can think. I don't mean rough, like in the movies, but nothing good—crappy food, lumpy bed, stinkin' toilets, no girls, and lots of rules."

"But, your…ad…diction…your habit?"

"Yeah. That was bad…The first week after I got arrested...I just wanted to fuckin' die…It hurt so much. They gave me some medicine to relax me and ease the pain, but it was strictly cold turkey. I don't wanna remember the pain. It was so bad I wanted to croak."

"But, you're healthy now."

"I don't eat so good."

"You did pretty well with those hamburgers."

"Yeah, but I'm having cramps now and I'll probably crap my brains out later."

"Are you over it?"

"You mean the junk?"

"Yes."

"I still think about it, but it's poison and I scarred my arms pretty bad."

"Is that why you're wearing long sleeves?"

"Yeah. I'm mostly healed. I don't have any other clothes anyway."

"Where are you going now?"

"There's this girl—where I'm going—a girl I know. She lives around here. She'll put me up for a couple of days."

"Does she do drugs?"

"No. Never. I had to swear to her I don't no more before she would let me go there."

"And then what?"

"Then I'll make my move."

"What move is that?"

"I haven't figured that out yet. Can I have the money?"

"I only have fifty."

"How come?"

"I'm not a bank, Santo. You should be grateful for this."

"You got me into this. That girl—the one that stole my stash—she never would have got the drop on me except for you being there."

"Do you think she was with Steve and Darren?"

"I guess so. Otherwise, how is it they got the gun and the backpack?"

"Here's what I'll do: take the fifty. When you need more money, call me."

"You gonna tell anybody you seen me?"

"Not if you don't want me to."

"You know I don't. What happened with you and my sister?"

Now Anacleto was the reluctant storyteller.

"We went out for a while. It was great. She's…special. So special that I didn't push her. She wasn't ready and I was…content, so I didn't push her. Do you understand?"

"If she was any other girl, I'd call you a jerk, but she's my sister, so I'm glad."

"Anyway, I…sc…screwed up."

Santo waited. Then he grinned and said, "One good turn…Finish."

"I met a girl. I was supposed to be looking for you. I didn't know where to look, so I hung out and I met this girl….and Anne found out."

"You bang her?"

"No."

"So what's the big deal?"

"The big deal is I cheated. And I was dishonest with Anne."

"If you didn't lay her, it's not cheating. And if you laid her and Anne didn't find out, that's not cheating. It's only cheating if you do the deed and get caught."

"Well, I sort of lost my head with this girl. I almost ch…chose her over Anne. Then, when I went to Anne a couple of days later,…she dumped me."

"So…make it up to her. Promise her anything."

"You don't understand, Santo. I thought of her as l…like—"

"Who? Anne?"

"Yes."

"You thought of her as what?"

"Never mind.

"Screw you…'Never mind.' I spilled my guts out to you. Now you talk."

Santo had the toughest, scariest smile Anacleto had ever seen. It was a smile of… confidence and it was more effective than a threat.

Anacleto reluctantly continued: "I thought of us…Anne and me…as sort of…as we'd be together for life, and I wasn't on the level with her."

"Boy, are you a sap! Here's what you do: you go to her and you tell her that guys do that. But you learned your lesson, and it'll never happen again and she's the only girl for you."

"It's too late…too much w…water under the bridge."

"It's too late if you give up."

"I d…don't know."

"You're so negative! Guys like you, in jail…they don't make it. You gotta be positive."

"I guess—"

"No guessing…I'm right. Remember when I taught you to play ball?"

Anacleto shook his head.

"Life's like a game and you gotta always try to win."

"I know."

"If you think like a loser, you'll be a loser."

"There might be another complication."

Santo snorted, shook his head in disgust and mimicked him: "Com-pli-ca-tion."

"There is."

"Yeah? Well only a loser sees a complication. A fuckin' winner sees a challenge."

"I g…guess."

"Well?"

"I've seen her out with other guys."

"So? Are they layin' her?"

Hot, jagged pains shot through Anacleto's head and he felt his gut twist into a burning, sour knot.

"I…don't know. I doubt it. She wasn't ready with me and we were…"

Santo loudly cleared his throat and sent a gob of spit to the platform. Then he lit another cigarette.

"Listen: think about what I said about being a winner. We'll talk again in a couple of days. Where's the money?"

Anacleto pulled fifty dollars from one of his pants pockets and held it out to Santo.

"Call me," Anacleto said. If my mother answers the phone, say you're…I don't know…Vinnie. She won't recognize your voice anyway."

Santo shoved the neatly folded bills into his pocket. Then he turned and slowly shuffled away.

As Santo walked along the subway platform to the staircase that led to the street, he looked like one of the many tired, lost souls who you see, but don't really see.

A SAD WORLD

Anacleto looked out the window. Anne was pushing Peter in his stroller. He went out.

"Hi."

"Hi, Clete. How are you?"

"All right, I guess."

They walked and talked for a while. Anacleto played with Peter. He felt a special connection with the boy.

"I'm going in the house. Do you want to come in?"

Anne put Peter in his crib. Anacleto sat at the kitchen table.

"Do you want a drink?"

"Are you going to pour it on my head?"

She laughed. He smiled. They talked about school. She was attending Hunter College in Manhattan.

"Have you spoken to Rudy?" she asked.

"No. I don't think he's there. I don't know what happened to him."

"Another one missing in action," she said. "Oh, my gosh. I didn't mean—"

"It's okay. In fact, Georgie wrote and said that he'll be rotated back to the States s...soon."

"What about Ronnie?" she asked.

"He still has a year to go on his hitch."

"You worry about them, don't you?"

"Sure, but I try not to think about it. What good does worrying do? My mother is a nervous wreck all the time."

"Of course. I understand. My mom is…you know…"

"What a…sad world. Nothing ever changes. War, bl…bloodshed, misery…"

"I know. People make their own problems. Take Rudy—he didn't have to put up that sign, right?" she asked.

"I guess, but, maybe it was the right thing to do."

"Do you think so?"

"I don't know. I never knew. It was a…surprise. He used me."

"So?"

"That's between Rudy and me. That has no…noth…nothing to do with whether it was right or wrong to make the sculpture."

"It was gross—a big, black penis."

"Would it have been bet…ter if it had been a white penis?"

"No, but it's worse because there's already so much animosity between white and black people in this country," she said.

"Rudy was trying to cre…create art with that idea—"

"Maybe, if he had stuck to one theme—sex or racism, but not both," she decided.

"It wasn't sex. It was a tower, a sculp…ture that looked like a body part. It was a symbol," he explained.

"I know the symbolism—black males as dangerous, predatory, sexual creatures, the idea of slave owners raping black women…black manhood as a dual-edged—"

"Okay. We've both read the same b…books. So, what's so bad about making art about it?" he asked.

"You were kids, not adults," she said.

"I'm not a kid now. I'm eighteen, and so are you. I've had to take care of myself and my mother and I don't depend on anyone for anything…including money. I had to file for Se…lec… tive Ser…vice. I could be in Vietnam next year."

"God forbid, Clete. No!"

"It could happen."

"You're going to college. You have a deferment."

"What if I drop out or if more bodies are needed and they change the deferment rules?"

"Oh, God, no. I…I couldn't bear the thought of...I mean…"

They looked at each other. The room was so silent they could hear Peter's slow, steady breathing from two rooms away.

"I forgive you, Clete. Actually, I forgave you long ago."

"Oh. I'm so sorry. I was so stupid."

"I was stupid too. I've missed you so much," she said.

He took her hands and closed his eyes for a second. When he opened them, she was still there.

"I told you I would wait," he said.

He stood up and pulled her close. They wrapped their arms around each other.

"I know. It was stupid. Everyone's allowed a mistake," she said. "I have missed you so much."

"I've thought about you every day," he whispered.

She clung to him.

Back where we were.

They kissed with more heat than ever before. He sat down and pulled Anne onto his lap. They held each other and kissed for a long time.

"Where's your mom?"

"She's out shopping with my father."

"When are th…they coming back?"

"I guess not for a while, but that doesn't matter. My mom will be so happy to see us together that she wouldn't care if we were screwing."

They kissed deeply and clung to each other. Inflamed, he grasped her breasts. She stiffened for a second, and then relaxed. He pushed her off him, led her to her room, and closed the door. Still holding her hand, he sat on her bed and then he lay down, pulling her on top of him. They held each other tightly and kissed. He pressed his body against hers, holding her rear in his hands.

"Clete, wait. This is too soon. I think we should wait."

"I have waited."

"I know. I know you have," she replied, sounding nervous and trapped.

He released her. They sat, side by side on her bed.

"Then, why have you gone out with other guys?" He was angry.

"I…guess I wanted to get even," she answered quietly.

"Get even. You're probably w…way ahead of me now!" he snarled.

"What do you mean?"

"You know. I never did…you know…with her. I haven't even spoken to her."

She remained silent.

He pushed Anne down and straddled her, kissing her hard, his hands wandering over her body, roughly taking back what was his.

"Clete, no." She squirmed and pushed him off. "What are you doing?"

"I…need…you."

"I…need you too, but wait. I'm not ready," she gently explained.

"You mean you're n…not ready f…for me."

"What?"

"Do you think other g…guys would wait for th…this much time?"

She sat perfectly still, her face a frozen mask. As she cooled, so did he.

He stood up.

"Well?" he asked.

"Clete, listen to me. I don't know what you think, and I don't want to know. I think you should either relax or go home."

"I'll go. I waited be...because I thought you were worth waiting f…for and because I screwed up—"

"I'm glad you—"

"But, I'm not going to be a fool…If you don't want me, if you want guys who want to screw you and never see you again, then,…that's not worth wait…w... waiting for—"

"What?"

"I've seen you with guys—"

"And?"

"I'm not asking. I don't want to know. Don't tell me—"

"Tell you what?"

"Who you've…had sex with…I just want to move on."

"Get out! Get out!"

Then she stood up and pushed him out…out of her room and through the house and out the door.

After the door slammed, he stood, staring at the diamond-shaped window in the door, but she was gone.

WHO KNOWS WHAT THE FUTURE WILL BRING?

He lay on his bed, staring at the ceiling, hoping that if he focused on one crack, the pounding in his head would stop. Then he picked up the telephone receiver and dialed. A woman answered the phone.

"Hello." He tried to compose myself.

"Hello. This is Clete. Is Ricki there?" He squeezed his eyes shut.

Let her be there...

"Hold on."

"Hello?"

"Hi. It's Cl…Clete…How are you?"

Silence.

"I know I sh…should have called you. How are you? How…how's school?" he asked.

"It's okay. How are you?"

"I started college and I'm working about twenty hours a w…week at the school library."

"How's your cold fish girlfriend?"

"Oh, we haven't s…seen each oth…other for a while—"

"How long?"

"Oh. A while."

"So why did you wait so long to call me? Why did you disappear?"

"I…I wasn't ready…I needed to cl…clear my head."

"Too bad."

I knew it...

"H…how come? Am I too l…late?"

"I have a boyfriend."

"Oh…I hope…he's good…for you."

"He's…good."

"Well,…th…that's the st…story of my life…too late."

"Too bad. I really liked you. I still think about you sometimes."

"I want you to know you meant a l…lot to me…You were—"

"It's okay, Clete. I gave you a hand job. You don't have to be so grateful."

"No. I sw…swear, I wanted to call y…you to talk to you. It was m…more than the s…sex."

They talked for a while longer. She wasn't in a rush to hang up. After a while, the pounding stopped, his headache began to clear, and he was able to laugh. She laughed too.

This is good. She's funny. It's not just about sex.

"You know, Clete, I wish I was going out with you, and not Charlie. I like you so much better."

"So, tell Charlie to take a hike."

"I can't. I'm not sure I want to…I'll have to think about it."

They talked a bit more before she said she had to go. He promised he would call again.

What a pathetic mess.

***

He called Ricki again a few days later. She asked him to meet her.

"When?"

"Now. Can you come over?"

"Did you break up with…what's his name?"

"Charlie. No, but I'd like to see you."

He took a fast shower, changed his clothes, and ran to the bus stop. Ten minutes later, he was sitting on the bus, next to an open window, with a cool, refreshing breeze lifting his spirits. Once again, he wondered what he was doing and why he could never seem to make a decision that did not seem wrong or contrary to his best interests.

She has a boyfriend…What am I thinking?

His brain swam with its usual jumble of thoughts…he almost missed the stop. He got off and walked to Ricki's house and rang the bell. She came to the door.

"Let's go. I don't want to take a chance," she said, scanning the street.

They walked quickly, ducking down a side street, Ricki nervously looking around. Then they turned onto another street. She slowed down. They walked at a more leisurely pace now.

"I don't want to take a chance of meeting him, you know."

"I un…derstand."

She seemed to have developed even more of a sumptuous figure than she had before. Maybe because of her makeup, she looked older than Anne. Her bright, shimmering hair was lovely and her remarkable green eyes, sparkling like the surface of a sunny tropical lagoon, were mesmerizing.

"You look nice, Ricki."

"Thank you. You too."

"Where sh…should we go?"

"You tell me," she said.

"I don't know. Do y…you want some…thing to eat?"

"No. Not now. We could just talk."

"Sure. I wish there was some place where we could be alone."

"I know, but,…I don't know."

"I under…stand," he conceded.

"No. You don't. I wish—"

"What?"

"I wish you hadn't disappeared."

"Me too. I…made the wrong choice."

"I wanted you to call me. You never gave me your number. I looked it up in the phone book. I almost called…lots of times, but I remembered you said it was disconnected. Anyway, I got the message…you didn't want me."

"I…One of my problems is…I don't always know what I want or what's best for me."

"Don't beat yourself up," she said. Then she placed one of her warm hands on his face.

"Can we…go to your sis…ter's apartment?" he asked.

"No. She moved to Manhattan." She looked sad.

"That's not so far…I mean for you to see her."

"I guess, but it's not that close either. I miss her."

"That's too bad. I know you're unhappy at home."

"That's for damned sure. How are you?" she asked.

"I'm…okay. I'm glad to see you," he repeated.

"In case you're wondering, I'm still turned on by you, Clete, but I don't want to…you know…make a change...unless I'm sure. You know?"

"I understand. I screwed up once. You need to know I'll be here."

"Yes. I thought about you…so many times, but I figured you were with your girlfriend."

"I've thought...about you a lot."

"I don't know what to do. You have to give me time. If you want me, you're gonna have to convince me. You see, I'm more…centered now, and I have a boyfriend."

"I know…Charlie."

"Yeah. But I really do like you a lot, Clete. I just don't feel for Charlie what I felt for you… I…Never mind."

"What?"

"No. Never mind."

They walked to a little Italian place nearby. They weren't hungry, so she had a soda. He had coffee. Then Ricki said that she had to get home. Charlie was going to pick her up.

"What did you start to say before?" he asked. He tried to hide his nervousness.

"If I could look into your heart, Clete, and I knew you wanted me…really wanted me, I'd tell Charlie to … you know."

He knew, but he couldn't say the words that would keep Ricki by his side. He wanted to, but he couldn't.

A block from her house, she kissed his cheek, asked him to call her in a week, and ran off down the street.

He avoided passing her house on his way to the bus. The last thing he wanted to do was to see Charlie.

***

When he called Ricki a week later, she said that she had tried hinting to Charlie that she wasn't happy. He had become panic-stricken. Then he blew up at her. She ended up reassuring him that he had nothing to worry about.

"Give me more time, Clete. Call me in another week. We'll go out…on a real date this time. I can't do that to him…not yet. Before I do, I have to know…I can't put him down unless I know you're gonna be here for me. I mean, you had your chance. Not that I hold it against you, but you didn't even call. He's here…I mean he's not here now—but he's always there for me."

"I understand," he replied softly.

"I need to…see you…know what…you have in mind…what you plan to do."

"Sort of like a tryout so I can m…move up to the Majors?"

"That's a game. This is life. I need a boyfriend who's gonna take me away from my shitty life," she replied after a few seconds.

"Isn't it all a game?" he asked.

"I don't think of it that way. I want what I want. It's dead serious to me."

Why do I do this? I have to wait for Anne. I love her, not Ricki.

He called Ricki a week later. She was still undecided. He was actually relieved. He told her that he had started seeing Anne again. That didn't seem to upset her. She asked him to keep in touch.

"Who knows what the future will bring?" she said.

KEEPING SILENT WATCH

One cold January afternoon, when Anacleto arrived home from school, he ran into Francine as she was leaving her house. She told him she was on her way to the grocery store. He asked her how Peter was doing.

"Oh, he's fine. You should come in and see him. Why don't you go now? Anne's watching him."

"Okay. Maybe I will. Later."

He went into his house and tried to work on a term paper. His mind began to wander.

What's the use of thinking about her, of remembering?

He wondered why he was remembering…what was he remembering? He thought about the hours they had spent in her room, sharing secrets, holding and kissing each other, laughing and whispering. A few times, they had both dozed off. Upon awakening, he had found himself entangled in the fragrant web of her silky black hair. She laughed as she lifted her head and carefully pulled herself loose. He had wanted to remain enveloped in that soft sweet-scented jungle forever.

***

The next day, he stood in the foyer of his house skimming through the mail that had been pushed through the slot in the door. Then he opened the door and looked out, just catching a glimpse of Anne and a man disappearing into the alleyway that led to her door. Anacleto's stomach dropped; he moved back into the foyer of his house. Then he emerged again and stood on the stoop. The sound of her door closing thundered in his head. He waited. His heart pounded in his chest. He walked to the alley and looked at the door. Then he walked back to the sidewalk; he saw a blue Mustang parked a few houses down the street.

Francine's home. He won't stay long. Was it Steve? It looked like him. Can't be…But it's a Mustang, and it's blue. That bastard! How would she know him?

He couldn't stand on the sidewalk. He couldn't go back into his house. He couldn't go to work.

He went into his house and took the key to his mother's car. How many blue Mustangs could there be? When he looked again, the car was still there. He walked down the driveway, opened the garage doors, started his mother's car, and backed it out. He scraped the rear bumper against part of the backyard fence that bordered the alleyway. He put the car into drive, moved forward a few inches, turned the wheel, and backed out of the driveway into the street. Then he backed up a few yards and double parked across the street from Anne's house. A few minutes later, when a nearby car pulled out of its spot, he parked.

He waited.

After a while, Albie came by and began talking to him. Anacleto fidgeted and kept glancing at the door to Anne's apartment.

"What's the matter, Clete? Something bothering you?"

"No…noth…nothing. I have…to…have to…wait for…somebody."

"Who?" he asked.

Anacleto didn't answer. Finally, Albie left.

But Anne and…it had to be Steve…had been in there for twenty minutes. He couldn't stand it any longer. Agitated, cold, his heart racing, his head splitting, he exited the car and walked quickly to Anne's door. He knocked. He rang the bell. He knocked again. No one came. He pounded on the door. The blood being pumped from his heart was surging through his brain, splitting his skull wide open.

Please, please answer the door… Anne…Oh…

The doorknob turned. Anne stood there glaring at him. Her hair was undone and she was wearing a long tee shirt...no bra and probably nothing else underneath.

"What do you want?"

"I…I…thought…I w…would l…like to see…Peter." His throat was so dry he almost choked. "It's been so long since I've seen him—"

"Why are you here?"

"I…didn't—"

"He's not here, Clete. My dad and mom took him out."

"Oh…Anne. I w…want to c…come in…just for a min…ute—"

"No. Are you crazy?"

"I'm not the one who's cr…crazy. I…Please let me come in—"

"No. Leave me alone."

He heard water running in the nearby kitchen sink. Anne looked stricken.

"Go!" she screeched before closing the door.

He stood, paralyzed. Then he walked back to his house. He lay on his bed, staring at the ceiling, his head a massive, gaping wound. He closed his eyes, praying for sleep.

Now what? Why did I do that? It hurts…it hurts so much…

He went to work, leaving his mother's car where he had parked it, across the street from where Anne lived, keeping silent watch.

SANTO'S PLAN

About two weeks later, Santo called.

"What's the matter, Santo?"

"Nothin'. How you doin'?"

"I'm feeling like sh…shit."

"You sick?" Santo asked.

"No. Sorry. I have a lot on my mind."

"I wanna meet you in the city—today."

"I don't know. I have…a tight schedule."

"Clete, I really need to talk to you. I need your help. And I need money."

"Are you—"

"No. I'm clean. I'm feeling good, but I need to see you. Huh?"

"And…you won't come to see your mom or Anne, right?"

"Not yet. I promise…as soon as I…take care of business, I will."

Anacleto arranged to meet Santo at a bar in the Village at seven after his shift at the library was over. He felt like a ghoul, talking to Santo and not telling Anne and Francine that he was alive and, according to him, well. He had to at least give them a hint, throw them a lifeline. He walked to their house and rang the bell. Francine answered the door.

"Hi. Anne's not home. Do you want to come in? See Peter?"

"No, thanks. I can't stay. It's…I…"

She waited.

"It's...Do me a favor. Please tell Anne that I'm sorry."

Then he left.

***

Anacleto sat in the bar sipping a beer. After an hour, he was ready to leave. Then Santo appeared. He had gained a couple of pounds and looked more like his old self. He greeted Anacleto with a grappling, warm hug. He ordered a beer.

"I guess I'm paying," Anacleto said.

"Yeah. And you gotta give me the rest of the money. But, I'll be okay soon. I'm starting a real job next week."

"That's great! Doing what?"

"Construction. This girl I live with, Roseanne, in Queens, her father owns a construction company, and he's givin' me a job."

"Great. What about the draft?"

"Dunno. Never registered."

"That's not good."

"Clete, don't worry about me."

"I do. Ok. Santo, I want to ask you something. This guy, Steve, he was a…junkie, right? I mean, I s…saw him that time with you and he looked bad. Did he always look that way?"

"Why you askin'?"

"Oh. I ran into him again. He didn't l…look…He looked like he was okay. Clean. Neat. Together. I just wondered."

"Funny you should ask. I been doin' some inquiring. I still know a lot of people."

Anacleto shook his head.

"Well, I found out where Steve is. He set up in a new spot…with lots of product. He don't have a habit. He smokes a lot of pot and he drinks a lot, but he ain't a junkie."

"So, why was he so desperate when he c…came to you that night…the night when the girl stole your knapsack?"

"He was using a little then, but he was faking how bad he was so he could buy a lot of H. He was sellin' it for a couple of dollars more to kids around the schools…kids who, I guess, didn't know other dealers or couldn't get out at night 'cause they were young. You see, I had the official spot in the neighborhood, and he couldn't move in, so he earned a few bucks that way…buying a lot from me, like he was hooked, and then sellin' it."

"So, he wasn't —?"

"Naw. Just like I said…it was just to get me to sell him a lot without me getting suspicious."

"Do you th…think he knew the girl who stole your knapsack?"

"I don't know. She musta gave everything in the bag to him or shared it with him. Then, when he sold whatever he had, he went to…the man, the son of a bitch who was supposed to be so good to me—supplying me and protecting me."

"What's his name? How do you know him?"

"Better you don't know. You might mention his name some time, and then your mama won't see you no more."

"How d…do you know him?"

"My friggin' father. He knows all these people. I go to this man back then. I tell him my name. He asks me if I'm Leo's son. He thinks my father's okay with me dealing."

"Your father does know."

"So what? Anyway, he goes to the man—"

"You mean Steve?"

"Yeah. Who else, retard?" Santo smiled affectionately when he said that. "Steve goes to the man and he tells him that I been sellin' at a higher price. He tells him that I got all the money that I owe, but I been holdin' out. He tells him—Steve tells him that he can make it right. He says he can take care of me and take over the spot in the park and bring in the money I owe and lots more money. He just wants to get approval first."

Anacleto understood, with sickening clarity, that he really had been the cause of this misery. If he hadn't been there, the girl wouldn't have been able to steal Santo's stash of drugs. Of course, if Santo hadn't been selling drugs to get money to move his mother out…

"You're not drinking," Santo observed.

"I d…don't drink much."

"You don't drink much…you don't get laid...Do you jerk off at least?"

"Every day," Anacleto replied brightly, hoping to appear happy and carefree.

Then Anacleto spotted a small table near the back of the bar, laden with meat and piles of bread.

"Do you think the food's free?" Anacleto asked.

"Only one way to find out," Santo said, as he slid from his barstool, beer stein in hand, and headed for the food. Anacleto followed. They made heaping corned beef on rye sandwiches and brought them to a table.

"This is good," Santo exclaimed.

They ate and drank. Santo walked to the bar and ordered two more beers, even though Anacleto hadn't finished his first one. Santo sat, chewing, and slurping his beer, and talking up a storm.

"Yeah…Roseanne's great. Not just a good lay, but she's smart. She has a good job in her father's business. And now,…I told you about the job for me, right?"

"Yes. I'm happy for you. Next time, *you* can take *me* out."

"How's my ma and Anne and…geez—I forget his name…"

"Peter."

"Right. Pete. Little Petey."

Santo looked at Anacleto, anxious to hear about his family.

"They're fine. The little guy's so cute and so f…funny. But…uh…Anne—"

"What? What's the matter, Clete?"

"Oh…she's unhappy and so's your mom…about you, I mean."

"I know. I don't think about them a lot, do I?"

"No, you don't."

"I…can't talk to my ma. I can't explain things to her."

"What's to explain? You got in tr…trouble. She won't be surprised. Now you're home. Believe me, just hearing your v…voice or, better than that, seeing you will be a gift."

Santo sipped his beer, and then closed his eyes in thought. He looked calm and relaxed. Anacleto felt he shouldn't judge him. At least he was honest about what he wanted and didn't want. He lived his life as he thought he should. He acted, and did not look back. His world was his. His choices were his.

"Okay, but I can't do it—not now. Soon."

"But you have to really call them. You can't just promise."

"I will. I just gotta take care of something, and I need your help."

The angry tightness in Santo's eyes told Anacleto all that he needed to know.

"It's a…bout Steve, right?"

"Yeah." His face lit up with a grim smile of great satisfaction.

***

The next morning, Anne called. "My mom said you came looking for me."

"Oh. I…I—"

"You what?"

I saw Santo. He's fine. Well, he's not fine, but he's okay. He's alive.

"I guess I just wanted to apologize for banging on y…your door that time."

"Oh…Forget it."

"I guess I was…interrupting—"

"No! I was just going to take a shower. You weren't interrupting."

The lie hurt more than the truth.

"Anyway…sorry."

"It's okay."

Neither of them said anything for a few seconds.

"How are you doing in school?" she asked.

"Well. How about for you?"

"My grades are okay, but I just don't have my heart in it."

He wondered *where* her heart was.

THE COURTYARD

A few nights later, he met Santo again. He was sure it was the wrong thing to do. But, as his first friend, the one who wrenched him out of the darkness years before, Santo had a soulful hold on him, one that defied rational explanation. That is why Anacleto was there. What Santo wanted Anacleto to do violated every principle of survival that he had developed over the years.

"Santo," he had said over the phone, "I…th…think this is a bad idea."

"No. It's a good idea."

"You can get h…hurt or end up in jail."

"A man's gotta do what a man's gotta do."

And so, they met at a subway station on Nostrand Avenue in Flatbush and walked to a sporting goods store where Santo picked out a baseball bat, a Louisville Slugger. Santo smiled as he looked at the logo. Anacleto paid for it.

Then they stopped at a coffee shop. Santo ate a hamburger. Anacleto had coffee, wiping his sweaty hands over and over again on paper napkins so that he could grasp his cup.

As they walked to their destination, Anacleto felt that if he didn't try one more time, he would burst: "Santo, stop. I…look at me. Why d…do y…you have to do…this?"

"Man, you're a nervous wreck. And stop wiping your hands on your pants. Stay cool, Clete. Hey, that's your new name: Cool Hand Clete."

"It's not funny. I don't get it, Santo. You're out of jail," he whispered. "You h…have a girlfriend. You're starting a job. Why must you d…do this?"

"A man's gotta do what a man's gotta fuckin' do," he repeated firmly. "And you don't have to be here. I asked you, but you coulda said no."

"I wouldn't l…let you come alone."

"That's my man. You know, Clete, when you stand straight and you don't cover your face—"

"I don't do that anymore."

"Yeah. But you used to. Anyways, you're big and tall and strong. You're a match for any guy, but—"

"But what?"

"You don't got it here," Santo said as he tapped Anacleto's chest.

"I'm not scared so m…much as sick at the thought that you're going to ruin y…your life," Anacleto replied.

"That's what I mean, Clete. Heart. You don't have heart. If you had heart, you'd say, 'Man, I can't live knowing that cock-sucker didn't get what's comin' to him.' You don't love yourself enough. That's your problem. That's always been your problem. That, and the fact that you're always lookin' for the safe thing to do."

He looked at Anacleto long and hard.

"So, what's it gonna be? I don't care," he said. "I'll go in there and break his arms with or without you. And…I'll tell you something else: I don't fuckin' care if I die. I just got to hurt him. So…don't tell me about ruining my life."

"I don't want to argue with you."

"Come on—there's a 'but' there. Spit it out," Santo challenged.

"There is; you're not afraid. Y…you think that every…thing in life is a challenge and it's just not worth living if you're afraid, if you don't meet that challenge…head-on. Right?"

"That's one way of lookin' at it," Santo agreed.

"But…what about the people who love you and depend on you? Sh…shouldn't you think about them?"

Santo reflected. Then he answered: "I do. I do, but *I* gotta come first. I ain't no good to no one if I don't take care of myself first."

"Okay. I understand, but…one more thing: haven't you found out that your way leads to …disaster?"

"What do you mean 'disaster'?"

"You know…I don't want to sound negative or afraid or anything that you th…think is so bad, but—"

"Come on, tell me. What?"

"I mean, you've had trouble—heroin, getting beaten up, jail. I know, life can suck, even if you try to walk the straight and narrow, but don't you th…think you've been…tempting fate?"

"Okay, listen. I like you. I even love you like a brother, but…enough is enough. I'll answer you one more time because…because…I don't know why, but I'll answer you."

Santo lit a cigarette and thought for a few seconds.

"It's like this: I don't ever want to hide or duck out of sight or get stepped on. If those things happen to me, then I know I have to…to come back and hurt whoever did dirty to me. It's part of me…It's how I breathe. I live in a dirty, crappy world. You do too…you just think it's gonna get better…As far as the bad stuff that happened to me…" He reflected again, picked some lint from his pants, then he looked directly into Anacleto's eyes in an attempt to reach a place inside of him. "It's just stuff. Whether I live a long, happy life or I die today or if…I get sent back to jail or I…I get hit by a bus and become a pissing-and-shitting-in-my-pants gimp, this is what I have to do. I can't go away and sleep. That's it. All my life, I been out there…I don't put my head down."

As I've been doing my whole disgusting life…

Santo patted Anacleto's shoulder and began walking. Anacleto followed. After a few blocks, they reached a derelict apartment house on a street that had clearly seen better days. The blue Mustang was parked in front.

"Now, this is the place. It's abandoned, but the door ain't locked...somebody broke the lock. You go through the lobby to the back. Just look around. Then you come back. You don't think he'll remember you, do you?" Santo asked.

"It's possible. I told you—I saw him again."

"All right. Whatever. I'll wait here."

Anacleto trembled as he opened the rusted iron and glass door and entered the garbage-strewn lobby of the building. It stank of beer and urine. No illumination came from the fixtures, but he could make out faint light from the courtyard through another iron and glass door at the rear of the lobby. Several panes of glass were missing from that door.

Feeling as if he was walking to his death, expecting with every step he took that he might be jumped, he made his way to the rear door and out to the steps that led to the courtyard. In the shadows, a distance to his right, sitting on folding chairs under a tree, were two figures. They were engaged in a whispered conversation. Neither one moved as Anacleto emerged from the building lobby, but he knew they were looking at him. He looked around; then he started back into the building.

"Hey!" one of them called. "Who you lookin' for?"

"No…nobody. I thought…there was another building b…back here." He slipped back into the lobby and walked gingerly through it, out the front door, and back to the sidewalk. Santo was nowhere in sight. Anacleto walked down the street toward the corner. Santo came up from behind. Anacleto almost jumped out of his skin.

"So? Tell me."

Anacleto's mouth was dry and he was shaking. He breathed deeply and spoke deliberately, looking at Santo, hoping that he would not sense his fear: "You w…walk out the b…back door…To the right, about thirty feet, there's a tree. Two guys were sit…ting under it. I th…think I r…recognized Steve. I'm not sure. It was dark...just moonlight."

"Okay. Calm down, man. Was anybody else there?"

"No. Just two guys."

"Good. Your part is over. Thanks. Go home."

"No. I want t…to w…wait for y…you."

"Suit yourself. Stay here. I'll be back in five." He smiled. "Or I won't."

Santo, baseball bat in hand, walked to the building, looked in through the glass of the lobby door. Then he entered.

Anacleto walked back to the building. He could see Santo standing in the lobby in front of the rear door, looking out to the courtyard. He saw Santo place the baseball bat against a wall in the lobby, next to the jamb of the door that led out to the courtyard. Then Santo opened the door and walked out.

Anacleto slipped into the lobby and, breathlessly, his heart thumping loudly in his chest, he walked to the rear door. Standing to one side, in the darkness, he looked out. Santo stood right outside the door on a rectangular concrete slab, his hands on his hips, silently looking at the two figures.

"Steve…that you?" he asked in a hard, cold voice.

"Yeah? Is that…Santo?"

"Yeah. It's me."

"Man, where you been?" Steve moved a few feet toward Santo. Anacleto could see him clearly now. The other figure moved to Steve's side. It was Darren.

"Oh, I been away. You know, Steve."

"Yeah. I guess I heard. What you want?"

"I'm not here to buy, Steve. I wanna talk to you."

"Don't talk so loud. Come over here," Steve replied.

"Naw. I think I better stand here."

"Man, you afraid of me?"

"Naw, Steve. I'm not. I just don't wanna have to fight two guys again. In fact, I don't wanna fight. I got a proposition for you."

"You ain't got shit," Steve challenged.

Anacleto could see Darren whispering to Steve. Steve didn't reply.

"You changed, Santo. Used to be, nothing scared you."

"I told you, I ain't afraid. I just don't like the odds. Especially, you think I'm here to get you...I ain't."

"Well, then, come on down, my man."

"No. I'll just talk from here."

Darren walked a few feet away from Steve, past the tree, and disappeared into a pitch black corner of the weedy courtyard.

Anacleto was beginning to regret having walked back into the building. He knew that someone was going to get hurt. What would happen if it was Santo? Would he drag Santo away or would he run? What if someone called the police?

"You can't stand there all night and I can't leave my…place of business. Be a man. Come on over," Steve offered again.

"Gee. 'Be a man.' And that's comin' from a sniveling punk who couldn't face me alone. He hadda have his bodyguard with him. Oh, and he hadda have a gun."

"Keep your voice down. And…I don't remember no gun, Santo."

"There's a lot you don't remember. Where's Darren? He hiding in the shadows?"

"No," Steve stage-whispered, "…he got a problem. He ain't good for nothin' these days. Right, Darren?" Steve looked to the shadowy corner. "You see what I mean? He's out…out cold in the weeds back there. Same shit every night. You know these colored guys. Never there for you. He ain't a real man. You a real man, Santo?" Steve taunted.

"More than you'll ever be, Steve."

It was clear that Steve wasn't leaving his spot near the tree. Santo knew that he had to remain near the doorway to the lobby, and the baseball bat. Anacleto held his breath. He thought about picking up the bat and holding it for Santo in case Steve and Darren, who he was sure hadn't passed out, rushed Santo; but he didn't want to be a part of this frightening situation.

What the hell am I doing here?

Then he heard the front door of the lobby open. It was Darren. Anacleto moved away from the door, into a dark corner of the lobby. Darren gently closed the door and then he inched toward the rear door and looked out. He waited. Anacleto held his breath, frozen with fear, praying that Darren would not realize he was there, would not peer into the dark, gloomy corner just a few feet away.

"Man, Santo, this is stupid. I don't wanna hurt you and you say you don't wanna hurt me. Come on down here," Steve challenged.

"Naw. I'll stay here until you get tired of waiting. I'll scare off all your business tonight."

"You don't wanna do that," Steve warned.

"Don't matter. You don't seem to be doin' so good."

"It's early. You know how it goes."

"Yeah. I guess I do," Santo replied.

Then Darren moved closer to the door. He stood quietly, studying Santo's back.

"Okay, Santo, I'll come over to you," Steve announced, and approached him.

Anacleto's chest constricted as he saw Darren pull a folding knife from his pocket, open it, and grip the door handle.

"You're not packing that piece, are you, Steve?"

"No. Why would I? We're just gonna talk, right?"

Darren slowly turned the door handle. Then he spotted the baseball bat. He released the handle, closed the knife, and placed it in his pocket. He reached for the bat. Anacleto took two quick steps forward, and kicked it away. It went skittering along the floor of the murky lobby. Startled, Darren froze and stared at Anacleto for a second. Anacleto could see, out of the corner of his eye, Santo turn his head toward the sound. At the same moment, Steve swung at Santo's face, and missed. Darren took the knife from his pocket again, opened it, and pulled the door open, calling out, "Back here!"

Santo swung at Steve, missed, and then he turned sideways so that he could see the two of them. They circled Santo, slowly, wolf-like, Steve prepared to punch and kick, Darren was ready to cut. Santo stood his ground, his arms up, his large fists protecting his face.

As if at a signal, Steve swung at Santo's face and Darren lunged at him with the knife. Santo blocked Steve's blow, but Darren slashed at his back. The knife ripped into the back of Santo's leather jacket. Steve massaged one of his hands with the other one while Darren prepared to hack at Santo again.

"Kill him! Kill him!" Steve roared.

Anacleto was horrified, sickened, paralyzed with fright. He concentrated, tried to control his fear…to keep the sense of otherworldliness from transporting him from where he was. He dropped to his knees and felt along the dark floor of the lobby, searching for the bat. Finally, he grasped it and ran back to the rear door. He looked out: a few feet away, Santo and Darren were locked tightly together face to face. Santo held the other man's arms, but Darren still managed to repeatedly slash at Santo's back. Steve punched Santo's head.

Anacleto slammed the bat down on the rear door. Wood splintered from the bat and glass exploded from the door, raining on the three men in the courtyard, startling them for an instant. Engulfed by a powerful, blistering rage, Anacleto threw open the broken door, took a hurried blind step, stumbled forward, and clubbed Darren on his shoulders. He fell to the ground, the knife clattering to the concrete pad. Steve jumped to the side to avoid colliding with Darren as he collapsed. Then he bent down to retrieve the knife. Santo swung at Steve, clipping him on the side of his head. Steve dropped to one knee, put a hand to his head; then he stood up, a little unsteadily, and waved the knife at Santo.

Santo looked at the knife. Anacleto moved toward them. In the dim moonlight, Anacleto saw that the back of Santo's jacket was a mass of blood-splattered ribbons.

"Hey, this ain't fair. There's two of you," Steve complained, holding his head.

"I don't need him," Santo snarled.

Anacleto held out the splintered bat. Santo grabbed it and swung hard at Steve, missing him. Steve retreated to the tree in the dark recesses of the courtyard.

Santo followed slowly, limping, holding the bat on one shoulder. Steve bent down behind the tree. Santo waited, just a few feet from Steve.

"You going for that gun now, Steve?"

Steve stood up. The gun...one of the pistols that Anacleto had taken from the attic and shown to Santo, was in Steve's hand.

"I seen that kind of gun go off, Steve. It holds one bullet, right? And there ain't no guarantee you're gonna hit me. That is, if it fires and it don't blow up in your hand."

"I sure scared you with it the last time. Didn't I, Santo?" Steve taunted.

"Yeah. Well, I was a little surprised that two guys couldn't take me without a gun, even if it is a shitty little starter pistol. Besides, you held it to my head. Not much chance of you missin' from that distance."

"What the fuck you doin' here, Santo. I won. You lost. Go on home," Steve whined, holding his head again.

Anacleto heard a scrambling sound behind him. Darren stood up, wobbled a bit, and stumbled into the lobby.

"I guess your buddy's goin' home. You're alone, Steve," he warned.

"I got the gun. Maybe I'll shoot your friend. You don't want that to happen, do you?"

"Shoot him, you piece of crap. Then I'll bash your skull in."

"You hear that?" Steve said to Anacleto. "He don't care if I shoot you. Say, I know you," he laughed. "I pissed on you, didn't I?"

Anacleto wished he had been holding the bat at that moment: he would have crushed Steve's long, thin blond head, and to hell with the gun. He walked to Santo's side. He hoped that his eyes revealed the hatred and disgust that he felt for Steve at that moment.

"Oh, so you're a pisser, Steve?" Santo laughed out loud. "Say…I got an idea. I'll drop the bat. You put down the pea shooter, and we fight it out…man to mouse."

"Now that's a pisser, Santo. That's funny. No. I think I'll just aim for your ugly face and fuck you up!"

"You're a little girl cocksucker, Steve."

"Well…you know, Santo…I wasn't gonna tell you this, but *I* ain't a cocksucker. You know who is? Your sister, Anne. She did me plenty of times—"

"You're a fuckin' liar! You don't even know my sister."

"I know her. I laid her in your house…in her pink bedroom…with the…let's see—blue linoleum floor and the baby doll collection on a shelf under the window. When I was plowing into her, I used to laugh at the daintiness of it all."

Santo swung the bat, but Steve hit the ground and the bat slammed into the tree, bouncing out of Santo's hand. Steve straightened up, grabbed Santo, and, ramming the gun against his right temple, fired.

There was the same sharp crack as when Mr. Caspari had fired the other gun in his backyard. The same acrid smoke. But this time, in the darkness of the little courtyard, there was a bright flash and Anacleto felt a shower of sparks hit his face. There were loud, sharp screeches as both Santo and Steve screamed in pain; Santo fell and Steve flew back, slamming into the tree. Santo put his hands to his head and jerked spasmodically, writhing in agony. Anacleto was frozen. He wanted to go to Santo, but he was rooted to his spot, unable to move, as in a dream.

No...He's dead! Mother of God, please don't let him be dead!

Then he forced himself to move forward. He knelt by Santo's side. Pulling Santo's hands away, Anacleto touched the side of his head. He felt blood. He took a closer look. In the dim light, he saw that the wound was black and bloody and raw.

Steve was thrashing about on the ground, holding one hand with the other, moaning, "Oh. Oh…shit! I…My fuckin' hand!"

The shattered gun lay on the weedy ground between Santo and Steve. Santo was conscious, grimacing in pain and moaning. He pushed Anacleto's hand away and held both of his hands against his wound.

"Get up, Santo. Let's go home. Or...I'll t-take you to a hos...hospital." As he said this, he attempted to lift Santo to his feet.

Steve painfully stood up. He held his bloody hands together. Then he bent down and picked up the knapsack with his uninjured hand and threw it over his shoulder.

"Clete, get it. He can't…hurt you," Santo moaned.

Anacleto grabbed the knapsack and pulled. Steve held onto it with his uninjured hand. Anacleto pulled with his left hand and swung at Steve with his right, missing him. Steve managed to kick Anacleto in the shins. He fell. Steve began walking, uncertainly, to the rear lobby door. Anacleto stood up and limped after him. At the door, Anacleto grabbed the knapsack from Steve and pulled. Steve turned toward Anacleto and held the knapsack tightly. Then he kicked Anacleto again, connecting with his knee. The pain instantly infuriated Anacleto. As Steve turned back, Anacleto pushed him into the door. Steve's head crashed through one of the remaining panes of glass. Anacleto hoped the shards had cut his face to shreds.

Steve pulled his head out and, wobbling on unsteady legs, he reached for the handle of the door and stumbled into the lobby, pulling the door closed behind him.

Then he turned, looking at Anacleto through the damaged door, and rummaged through the knapsack. Anacleto pushed the door open, punched Steve square on his nose, and tried to grab the knapsack again. Blood streaming from his nose, Steve lunged at Anacleto, pushing the knapsack into his face, causing Anacleto to lose his balance. Anacleto held onto the knapsack and pulled Steve down with him. They both hit the tiled floor of the lobby—hard. After an agonizingly painful minute, Anacleto pushed Steve off him and managed to stand. Steve moaned and turned over so that he lay on his back. His face was a ragged, bloody mess.

Anacleto slowly straightened his sore back. He looked down at Steve and then he kicked him—only once—between his legs. Steve moaned again. Then Anacleto picked up the knapsack and walked back to the courtyard. He grabbed the baseball bat and helped Santo to his feet. He was shaky, so Anacleto sat him on one of the lawn chairs that was near the tree.

"We better go…before the police come."

Santo shook his head in confusion. The gunshot so close to his ears had affected his hearing. Anacleto helped Santo up and walked him to the building, through the lobby, and out to the sidewalk, where a small group of people had gathered. One man warned them to stay away. Anacleto felt ashamed and guilty. The people deserved to live in a safe neighborhood.

When Anacleto and Santo reached the corner, they heard police sirens. Anacleto froze. Santo stood straighter and pushed Anacleto from him.

"I better walk…walk on my own. Too…suspicious."

He took the bat and dropped it down a storm sewer. He pulled off the bloody jacket and threw it down the sewer too. The back of his shirt was a wet, bloody mess. Anacleto took off his jacket and helped Santo squeeze into it.

At the subway station, Anacleto left Santo on a bench, holding his hands to his throbbing temple. He bought a baseball cap from a news stand on the platform and put it on Santo's head at an angle so that it covered most of his wound. Anacleto wanted Santo to come home with him, but he insisted on going back to Queens. They entered a subway car; once the train started moving, Santo fell asleep against Anacleto's shoulder.

The backpack that Anacleto had hurriedly grabbed from Steve's side was partially unzipped. When he looked inside, he saw plastic bags of what he assumed was heroin, a wad of cash, a few bullets, candy wrappers, and a long-bladed hunting knife. That's what Steve had been looking for before Anacleto had punched him on his nose. No one was sitting near them. Slowly and carefully, Anacleto took out the bags of heroin, and shoved them into his pants pockets. He looked at the knife lying at the bottom of the bag—sharp and deadly. He didn't want to touch it. He didn't want to leave it in the bag, but he couldn't take it out while they were on the train. He zipped the bag closed.

Santo awakened long enough to tell Anacleto they had to change trains and which stop in Queens was his. When they arrived at Santo's station, Anacleto had to help him to stand and to walk out to the street. He followed Santo's directions, and brought him to Roseanne's apartment. Santo couldn't find his key, so Anacleto rang the bell. Roseanne, tall and slim, with red hair and vivid blue eyes, came to the door. They helped Santo to the couch in her living room. She washed his head wound first. It was red and raw, with burned, blackened flesh on its perimeter, but it did not appear to be deep. She applied antiseptic and bandaged it.

The knife injuries to his back were superficial. Santo's grip on Darren's arm had been powerful enough to prevent the slashes from penetrating his skin deeply.

Santo refused to go to a hospital. He couldn't take the chance.

"He swore to me nobody was going to get hurt," Roseanne said, looking devastated.

Anacleto looked down.

She assured Anacleto that she would take care of him. He took his jacket and left, telling Santo he would call him the next day.

On the train ride home, people stared at Anacleto. He pushed the bags of drugs deeper into his pockets. When a police officer entered the subway car from an adjacent one, Anacleto quickly picked up a copy of the *Post* that was lying on the seat next to him and held it up, pretending to read. At that point, the enormity of what had occurred hit him. He began to lose control. His head, which had been pounding away all evening, was being ravaged by excruciatingly painful surges of sharp, biting sparks of electricity. He felt that he was about to rise up and float above the chaos that was his life. He had clubbed Darren, but he had staggered away. Steve had shot Santo in the head and the pistol had exploded, wounding Santo and injuring Steve's hand. He had pushed Steve's head through the glass of the lobby door and punched him and then…the only thing that had felt good—he had kicked him in the balls. He hoped that would change Steve's life.

But, what if Steve was dead? At that point, as long as he wasn't implicated, Anacleto didn't care.

How can I not care? He might be dead. I might have killed somebody…

They'd put him away for twenty years for possession of the heroin in his pocket. The bat was in a sewer. It had Santo's fingerprints, as well as Anacleto's. Santo's jacket too. The gun. It was shattered. Could the police recover prints from that? Anacleto worried that he may have handled it years before…he couldn't be sure. He knew it hadn't been the one that Mr. Caspari had fired. He had grabbed that one from Mr. Caspari and put it in the cheese box. He remembered that his mother had broken up and disposed of two guns; but he may have touched the one that Steve had fired when he and Santo had been examining the guns in his room years before.

The knife...the one in the bag. he had forgotten to take it out. It was in Roseanne's apartment...with Santo.

Oh, God. Please let me get home.

In the midst of his panic, he understood that, if there had ever been a time when he had to maintain control, this was it. With great effort, he concentrated on a news article about a house fire in the Bronx. He thought about how his father would have raised a finger and animatedly read the story to his boys at the dinner table. He and his brothers would have listened and their mother would have struggled to comprehend the deeper, existential aspects of the tragedy.

When Anacleto finally dared to glance up from behind the paper, the police officer was passing through the door at the end of the subway car to the next one.

He endured the rest of the ride home.

***

He walked stealthily into his house and made his way to the bathroom, where he opened the bags of heroin and dumped the contents into the toilet bowl, flushing three times. Then he pushed the empty plastic bags deep into the small garbage pail, making a mental note to empty it into one of the big outside garbage cans in the morning.

He urinated, suddenly realizing that he hadn't used a toilet for at least eight hours. He flushed again and washed his hands. He cupped his hands and, repeatedly filling them with water, he drank long and hard. Then he looked at himself in the medicine cabinet mirror. Who was that? The tired, haggard face that looked back at him was speckled with blood and bits of metal and minute fragments of...bloody flesh. As he washed, he wondered, were they from Santo's head or from Steve's hand...or both?

PART OF HIS PENANCE

When his alarm clock awakened him the next morning, Anacleto lay in bed, trying to convince himself that the events of the night before had not really occurred. He went to the bathroom and rummaged through the garbage pail. The empty heroin bags were there.

He felt sick. He leaned over the toilet bowl, retching, the taste of bile filling his mouth.

This is part of my penance...just a part...more to come...punishment for venturing where I don't belong.

His mother told him that she had gotten a phone call the night before. He waited to hear, dreading what she had to say.

"It's your brother—"

"Who? Which one? What happened?" he asked, certain that the news would be more than he could bear. She always did that: said "Your brother," as if he had only one.

"It's George. He called me from…Virginia. He's home." His mother smiled her silly, happy smile.

He hugged and kissed her. "That's great, Mom. When's he coming home?"

"He don't know. He says not for a while. He says we should visit him."

"When?"

"Soon. He didn't know when, but he says he's not going back there. Thank God."

"That's wonderful," Anacleto said, hugging and kissing his mother again. She looked at him; he felt that she was attempting to penetrate his mind, almost as if she knew where he had been, what he had done.

"What about Ronnie? Have you heard from him?"

"No. Not since that last letter."

"I'm sure he's okay too, Mom."

"Sure. He'll be fine," she responded, smiling weakly.

***

At the school library, Anacleto skimmed through every morning newspaper, hoping he wouldn't find an article about a murder in Brooklyn. Actually, there had been a murder in Brooklyn. An old woman had run down her husband because, according to her, "He never treated me right in fifty-nine years."

He called Santo from the library.

Roseanne answered the phone. "He's okay, but his head hurts…bad."

"Do you think he needs a doctor?"

"No. It's not deep, and it's clean. The cuts on his back are…just cuts. I told him to get a tetanus shot, but he said no. I'm not going to fight with him. I think he'll be all right."

"I want to speak to him. Should I call him l…later, you think?"

"Sure. Call him later. You're a good friend. I know what happened last night. Even though he promised me he was just going to talk, he knew. He swore to me that it's all over."

"It is," Anacleto told her, trying to convince himself.

"Well, I'm glad you were there. You saved him."

He skimmed the afternoon papers. No story about a young blond man being found dead in the lobby of an abandoned apartment building in Brooklyn.

He rode home on the bus, convinced that the police would be waiting for him at his house. No one was there.

He called Santo again. He sounded upbeat.

"We got the fuckers. And I got their money. Now they're the ones in big trouble."

"They hurt you pretty badly," Anacleto pointed out.

"Not so bad. I walked away…with your help. You saved me," he declared.

"What do you th…think happened to…Steve?"

"Whaddaya mean?"

"I mean, he was down…"

"Yeah. I know. If you think you killed him or something, you didn't," Santo remarked without emotion.

"How do you know?"

"I looked at him on the way out. He was moving around on the floor. I guess you didn't see because you was supporting me."

"I know...he was moaning, but I was worried...I am worried."

"Don't be."

"Did you look in the knapsack?" Anacleto asked.

"Yeah. I told ya', there was lots of cash."

"You know what else was there."

"I know what wasn't there—no junk. I can't understand it."

"You didn't want to…sell it, did you?"

"I figured I would, but, that's okay. I'm better off not even seein' that shit."

"You know there was something else in the bag."

"Yeah. I got it."

"What are you going to do with it?" Anacleto asked.

"I'm keeping it."

"No, Santo. You shouldn't." He cursed himself for forgetting to take the knife from the bag.

"I'll keep it here. You're right, but I wanna make sure they ain't lookin' for me first."

"When are you going to see your mom and Anne and Peter?"

"Soon. I'll call them."

"I want to tell them I spoke with you. Call them today, Santo. Make them f…feel better."

"Okay. Soon. Maybe."

THE DISEMBODIED HAND

The next afternoon, even though he was sore, Anacleto decided to run. He put on a sweat suit and sneakers, and went out to the street, where he met Anne coming home from school.

"Oh, you're running. That's nice."

"Yeah. I try to…to run a few times a week."

"I have to tell you something," Anne said.

He hoped he knew what she wanted to say.

"I…I mean. I want to see you some time," she said.

"Do you mean 'see me' as in go out with me?" he asked.

"Yes. And…we have to talk. Call me later?"

She walked slowly, as if heavily burdened, to her door.

As he ran, Anacleto wondered whether this was a chance for a new beginning, but how could it be? She was not who she had been. Steve, of all people, was her…lover. How ironic and how disgusting! Was she finished with him? Had he left her? Was he the only one? Was he out of the picture now? Was he dead?

His head spun and the familiar hot, uncontrollable anger began to grow.

Why, of all people, did she choose him...and over me? I knew I had done wrong, but my...sins were minor and just thoughtless compared to the ones she has committed.

***

He called Anne that night.

"I've made the biggest mistake of my life," she whispered into the phone.

"What…what do you mean?" he asked.

She was silent for a moment, then she continued by saying, "Oh, just about everything … you…me."

"I've made mistakes too," he confessed.

"I know, but not—"

"Not what?" he asked.

"Listen, Clete, I want to see you…be with you."

"I don't know," he replied. Suddenly, being reluctant and hesitant, keeping Anne off-balance and waiting seemed more important than being back with her.

"What's there to…not know about?" she asked.

"This is not what I want…what I wanted."

"What do you want?" she asked.

"I…I never wanted us to be apart, and now—"

"That's on me. I should have been smarter. It was nothing…what you did. I was stupid," she said.

"I'm not t…talking about whose fault it was. I mean, we were…perfect, and now, I don't know what I feel."

"If you don't know, then you're not sure. Right?"

"I…guess so," he replied.

"Listen, Clete…"

He waited.

"You did wrong, twice...but, as I said, I…made bigger mistakes. I want to start fresh."

How fresh? You're not a virgin. I wish I could say the same about myself.

"I don't know. I think—"

"No. Don't think. What does your heart say?"

Someone else telling me that I think too much. My heart. Which heart? The one that was hot for you? The one that was torn to shreds when you brought Steve to your bed and I stood in your alleyway, wishing I could disappear from this world?

"I don't know. A few weeks ago, I would h…have run to you, but now…"

He was torn between wanting her and wanting to punish her.

"I hate to think I've lost you," she said. "I care about you and I forgive you and I want us to be together. I want us to be closer…physically closer."

"Oh."

Well, if she's finally ready, great. If I don't think I really love her anymore…if we don't stay together...that's okay too.

"Anne…I can't pr…promise you anything."

"That's okay. Remember how you said I was worth waiting for? Well, now I'll be patient because I know *you're* worth waiting for."

He didn't know whether he wanted her waiting.

Anne asked him to come to her house the next morning, Saturday, after her mother had gone out. Francine planned on spending the day at Rita's house. She and her sister had healed the rift. She would be bringing Peter with her. Anne said that her father would not be coming to the house. She concluded the phone call by saying, "One thing, Clete…I'm willing to be patient, wait for you to decide how, if you want us to be together…as a couple, but I don't want to wait to be with you. I want you…I want…to be alone with you very soon...now."

He hung up, feeling more upset than excited, more cold than hot. He knew he had to do this. *Had to do this?* It seemed more like a chore, an unpleasant obligation…a tough gymnastics routine that he had to master, a math formula that he needed to memorize than…what it should have felt like, but he felt that he had to do it...to…make his mark…claim his right.

He tried to organize his thoughts. He couldn't think of any reason why he shouldn't do this. If it didn't feel right, then he wouldn't do it.

Doesn't feel right? Of course, it will feel right...I think.

That morning, he decided that he had to be completely honest with Anne and with himself. Not mostly honest, but completely. He wouldn't tell her that he loved her unless he was sure. He would not promise her…unless he was totally prepared to commit to it. If she wanted to have sex with him, then why would he hesitate?

If she made the first move, he would respond…if he wanted to. He remembered how Ricki had jammed her hand down his pants. Wouldn't that be something? Anne, the reluctant lover, assaulting him. What if she didn't? What if they kissed as they used to, and nothing more? Should he push? No. No. NO! But she had done it all with Steve…and who knew how many other guys?

He looked at the clock, and waited.

***

He knocked on Anne's door. She looked lovely in a white blouse and tight jeans. Her deep, brown eyes were large, and she looked happy.

"How are you?" she asked.

"I'm fine. I'm…so glad to see you," he responded, cursing himself for revealing his feelings so spontaneously.

"I'm happy too…and very excited."

She cupped his face in her hands and kissed him. Then she took his hand and led him to her bedroom. He sat on her bed. She sat next to him and began stroking his hair. She lovingly moved her fingers through his hair and down to his neck. He held her close.

"You're nervous, Clete. I can feel your heart."

"Yeah. Just a l…little."

"I'm nervous too."

He wanted to ask her if she had been even more nervous her first time. He wanted to ask her how many times she had done it, and with whom. He wanted to thrust into her so hard that it would hurt…that it would erase the memory of Steve and whoever else…

Forget it. Accept it. Be grateful for…Santo had said I would be so grateful to the first girl who…How does he know these things? He lives…I think, and I make the wrong choices.

"I want us to forget everything that's happened since last summer. Remember,

I told you that, if you stuck around, we'd be making love?"

Now she was kissing his cheeks and neck. He squeezed her tightly and kissed her.

"Let's pretend we've been together for this whole year with no interruptions," she murmured.

He shook his head in agreement.

They kissed as they used to kiss, deeply, sweetly, but with more urgency than before. His hands roamed over her back; then he tentatively brushed them over her breasts. Instead of stiffening or merely accepting his touch, she moved toward it, moved with it.

She pressed herself to him, saying, "You feel so good."

She unbuttoned her blouse and slipped out of it. He unclasped her bra, pulled it off, and dropped it to the floor. He pushed her down and caressed and kissed her from her forehead to her firm, smooth abdomen. She gently pushed him away and stood up, pulling off her jeans and panties. He sat on the bed, enraptured by the marble-like beauty of her skin…of her nakedness. He stood up and stripped down to his undershorts. They embraced and kissed deeply. His hands explored and caressed the smooth flesh on her back and her round buttocks. She pulled down his shorts and grasped him.

"Oh, Ricki." She froze, and so did he.

"Do you still think of her?"

"N…no. I d…don't know why I said th…that. I don't."

"It's okay. We both have to…work hard to put the past behind us."

She took his hand and moved to the bed. He followed. They kissed and grappled and turned and caressed and explored each other until she said, "Now, Clete. I need you now."

He twisted and stretched down from the bed to reach his pants on the floor.

"What are you doing?" She sounded upset.

"I…have…to get—"

"No, Clete. Now. I want you in me now." She reached for him and began pulling him toward her.

He resisted. "No. I have to get a…you know—"

"No."

She pulled him away from his pants and back to the bed. He complied, aflame with his burning need for her. He lay on his back. She began lifting herself over his body; she reached down.

If she wants me this badly, it has to be right.

Then he panicked.

"No. Are you cr…crazy?" He held her off him.

"No. It's okay…I just finished my period. I want you now."

She tried to press herself onto him, but he twisted aside and pushed her back down.

"No. I h…have them right in my pants—"

"No!"

She climbed on top of him again and raised her torso. He held her body away. Inches from bliss…from…he did not know what.

"Just let me reach down—"

"No!" She shrieked; then, looking at him, she continued, "I…want you now…as you are. No condom. If I get pregnant, then that's what I want. Don't worry. It's on me. It'll be good. It's all good."

"I d…don't understand."

She kissed him and held him down. But his fears, his questions, his doubts weakened his desire.

"Now, Clete. I want you now."

It was too late. He had lost it.

"I'll take care of that." She moved down. Within seconds, she brought him to an astonishing peak of arousal—until an ugly jagged thought tore through his brain. He fought the urge to stop her—he wanted her to go on forever. He exulted in the astounding, overwhelmingly and powerfully warm sensation that was radiating through his body. He floated above the bed, looking down at the young lovers.

Then…he came down; he was back on the bed, looking at her, feeling her urgency. But then, in the midst of this gratifying, stimulating, powerful, and astonishingly electrifying sensation, as if he was a bystander again, he saw a disembodied hand lift Anne's face up and push her away.

She was distraught. "What? Don't stop me. You're ready."

For a second, he was too confused to speak. Finally, he said, "I had to. Why do y…you w…want to become pregnant?"

"Not now, Clete. Later." She bent her head down to him again.

"No. Anne. No." He pushed her away again and sat up on her bed. He was beginning to feel trapped in her little room.

"I don't want to be pregnant. It's just that I want you…so bad, I don't care if your baby is in me," she breathlessly replied.

"Th…that's crazy."

"It won't happen, Clete. I just got over my period."

"That's no guarantee."

"Just this one time, Clete."

His body was still ready, but the harsh, sizzling, rough-edged thought burning through his brain was more powerful now; it seared and cut his consciousness into slivers—then those slivers came together to form a harsh conclusion.

"I th…think you're pregnant."

"No! No." Her eyes were wild...strands of her wet hair were plastered to her forehead. She pushed him down again. He grasped his genitals with both of his hands and turned from her; then he placed his feet on the floor. She slowly moved away from him and sat on a corner of her bed. Then she began crying.

Neither of them spoke. She sobbed and shook and choked. After a while, he moved close and held her. All of the heat was gone. He wanted her to be dressed. He no longer wanted to see her nakedness. After a long while, she became quiet, calm.

Finally, he spoke as gently as he could: "Anne. I won't say…it's all right—"

"I'm sorry," she squeezed out before she was overwhelmed by another long spasm of crying and choking.

He stroked her hair and held her.

"Don't t…talk. Don't talk," he whispered. "I…meant I…won't say it's all right…about being preg…nant. Everybody always tells people 'It's all right' when… things are a disaster."

He was grasping, struggling to find the right words. "I mean…I imagine…I'm sure you're not happy about it."

She put her head on his lap. She cried, her body shaking with her sobs. After a while, she cried more softly. His genitals, where her face was, which just a few minutes before had been the center of his inflamed sense of pleasure and anticipation, were wet with her tears and devoid of all sensation now.

"Look. I understand. I think I do. I'll help you."

She continued to sob and choke and breathe heavily.

"Do you w…want a tissue?" He eyed the box that was on her dresser.

She didn't respond, so he lifted her head, but she clung to him.

"Okay. I won't move."

He sat, holding her for a long time, watching the small rectangle of sunlight on the floor disappear and return and disappear as clouds moved across the sky.

ANNE'S STORY

How many times had he dreamed that he was dead? How often had he attempted to calculate how many years he *had* to live? Anacleto had often wished his time was up. How many mornings had he awakened, wishing he had never been born?

He awoke stiff, perspired, and feeling very protective of Anne. She was still asleep. He didn't want to move, but he needed to use the bathroom. He thought about the strange twists and unhappy turns that his life had taken. The clay of his self always sagged as it was being shaped. It always seemed to emerge from the kiln deformed and disappointing.

Everything involving Anne and Santo always turned out about as far from what he would have wanted as possible. Yet he found himself worrying about Santo more and feeling closer to Anne now than ever before. He told himself that she hadn't done what she had done to hurt him. And…if she had, he had deserved it. Besides, she was the one in trouble, not him.

Finally, he had to get up. He sat up and, as gently as he could, he moved her head from his lap and settled it on the bed. When he returned from the bathroom and began dressing, she stirred. Then she sat up.

"I'm such a mess," she croaked.

He kissed her forehead.

"I don't mean my looks. I mean my life…my choices. I am so screwed up," she whispered.

He resisted the urge to tell her that she was wasn't screwed up, but knocked up because she had screwed around. He knew it wouldn't sound amusing; his anger would cut right through her. Besides, he didn't want to think about that. He was attempting to restrain the hot rage that, once again, was burning inside of him.

"I'll help you."

"Thanks. I knew I should have come straight out with the truth."

She wiped her eyes with a tissue and blew her nose.

"I guess your mom doesn't know."

"No. Nobody does."

Then he spoke the words that he knew, even as he said them, would lead to more pain for both of them: "Does Steve know?"

She was startled. "Oh, no. How do you know who—?"

Because I saw him go into the house with you…the day you couldn't pull your clothes off fast enough to jump into bed with him!

"Does it matter?" His voice had a sharp edge to it.

"No. He doesn't know."

"Why?"

"For one thing, I don't know where he is."

"Otherwise, he'd know and you'd be on your back or on your knees for him every day, right?"

First her eyes widened, and then they narrowed. The heavy silence in the room was suffocating. Then she began to cry again.

"I'm sorry. I shouldn't have said that."

She cried louder and with more desperation than she had before.

"I'm sorry. I h…have to get used to…to…it. To this new situation. I'm sorry," he explained.

"Please don't be mean to me. I'm sorrier than you can imagine. It was the biggest mistake of my life," she said.

He knew he could pull off his pants and jump on top of her and she would either enjoy it or tolerate it. He wanted to hurt her. He wanted her to try to stop him. He struggled with his seething fury and forced himself to think of her.

"Anne, forget about what I said. I'm angry and I'm disappointed and I'm upset. I …I wanted to be the one. I think, in a selfish way, that's what upsets me the most."

"Whatever. I'm not a prize. I'm not any different now. I mean,…obviously, I'm different because I'm…pregnant." She smiled. It was a pitiful smile. "But, my feelings are the same. Having sex didn't change me."

"But I wanted you and me—us—to make love…I wanted us to be—"

"I know. I don't want to argue. I don't have the strength, but I know you were with Ricki. She has a…reputation."

"I…don't know about her reputation. She and I never…" He looked into Anne's eyes. He thought: *truth…no more bullshit.* "She came on like a tidal wave. I wanted to leave. She…She gave me a hand job. That's all."

"That's all! I wouldn't let anyone touch me, not then, except for you!"

"Well, you m…more than made up f…for it!" he accused.

"Nice. Very nice."

He was beginning to feel the familiar, unpleasant start of a head fog episode. He tried to convince himself that this was real. He mentally repeated the usual litany of his name, the day, the place—attempting to keep himself grounded. His thoughts were at war with each other. He wanted to be compassionate and loving and accepting, but he wanted to hurt Anne because…she…shouldn't have let this happen. He needed to make her regret and he needed to burn all traces of Steve…of any other man out of her.

"Do you love him?"

"NO!"

"*Did* you love him?"

"I…thought I did."

"What happened?"

"He just left one day and…that's it."

"Have you c…called him?"

She put her head down. Then she looked him straight in the eye and said, "I tried. He's gone."

"What do y…you know about h…him?"

"I know he knew Santo. That's how we started talking."

Then she told him that her friend, Jenny, had known that Santo had been dealing drugs and, one day, Jenny had pointed out Steve to her as someone who might have known Santo, someone who could help her to find him.

"How…does Jenny know Steve?"

"She went out with him once. She said he was rough and she was turned off by his friends."

"And you weren't?" he said this softly, again trying to be understanding.

"At first, I just asked him about Santo. He said he knew him and he would try to find out where he was. Then he told me that, if I wanted him to put his neck out, I would have to put out."

Anacleto looked at her, stone silent.

"He said he didn't mean it, that he was joking, but I knew he was serious. I thought I could handle him. I sort of liked him. Funny…he's so different from what I think a…guy…a man should be, but I did like him." She looked at Anacleto. "I'm sorry."

"Don't apologize for liking him, although I can't understand it. He's a piece of shit."

"He is. How do you know him?" she asked wearily.

"It doesn't matter. So, you liked him enough to…sleep with…to fuck him, right?"

"No. I told you, I thought I could handle him. He told me that I would have to go to his place. He lives…lived with his brother, but his brother wasn't home."

"So, what happened? What did he do right?"

"He's strong. I don't mean…strong. I mean he knows what he wants and he goes for it. I guess, in a way, he reminded me of Santo."

"He's a drug dealer."

"No. He's not. I know he dabbled. He told me that Santo was in it a lot. Steve only smokes pot. He traced Santo to some place in Staten Island. He went looking for him. He even spoke to Santo once, but he wouldn't come home."

"That's bullshit!"

"How do you know?" she asked.

"I…know. St…Steve's a liar."

"How do you know that?"

"I…can't…I just know it."

Anacleto felt guilty. Once again, he was not being totally honest with Anne. He would give Santo a few more days, and then he would tell Anne and her mother that he had seen him. He was angry with Santo again and torn up thinking about Anne's relationship with Steve. *He* had touched her. She had wanted him to. It hurt so much, but Anacleto needed to know.

"So, how was he able to…get you into bed when I c…couldn't?"

"Stop thinking that way. He was the biggest mistake of my life. He doesn't matter to me. I wish I could go back to that day…it would never happen."

"But it did. Tell me. I was waiting for you to be r…ready."

"I know you were. It wasn't that long, Clete. We only went out for a few weeks. I still wasn't ready."

"That didn't hold you back, did it? Or was it that he chose the right moment?"

"You don't want to know."

"I do."

She opened her mouth to speak, and then she stopped. She rubbed her face with her hands, and then she looked at him. Anacleto was glad he wasn't naked anymore.

"You remember when you came to the house…I was ready to take you back. You accused me of…screwing other men and you…were rough with me." She looked sad and hurt and angry. He felt like a monster. Then she smiled. "Well, I had gone out on a few dates, but I never even kissed any of them. I wasn't ready. I wanted to wait…to see what would happen between you and me."

"So…I bl…blew it even more than I th…thought I did?"

"Yes. You made me feel like shit—like a piece of meat—like a walking vagina. And I thought…if he thinks I'm screwing other guys, why don't I?"

"Good logic," he snarled.

"Well, I didn't. Steve made me feel desired. I know…I know…you did too, but in a different way. With you, it was like you wanted us to make love and then it would be like we were married. I know…you would have wanted to marry me right away if we were older, but since that wasn't going to happen, you wanted to lock me up by getting me into bed."

"No. that wasn't it at all. I wanted you. I loved you and I felt so good every time I even j…just th…thought about you—"

"Well," she continued, "I felt a little afraid of you. Not afraid like you were going to hurt me, but afraid that I was holding your life in my hands. I felt…sometimes…like you were suffocating me."

"Boy, did I ever misun…derstand a situation. I have to tell you, Anne, you're a little nuts." He tried to smile, but, with every word she uttered, she was cutting him up inside.

"I don't feel that way now. I wish I had let you…make love to me. I really did want you; it's just that I was afraid. If I hadn't held you off, none of this awful stuff would have happened." She shook her head sadly.

"Then what happened?"

"You want to hear more? Are you sure?"

"Yes. I want to know what he h…has that I don't. Is he more macho? Is that it?"

"That's a stupid question. Forget it."

"I guess that means you think he is. Boy, are you shallow."

"And you're an idiot. I could love you for the rest of my life…but you have to worry about…nonsense."

"Forget that...L…last question: What got you to stay with him?"

"He made me feel secure, and I knew I could never hurt him. I was angry at you and I thought I'd never be close to you again. Instead of fighting for me, you gave up."

He knew she was right. He wondered how he could have made so many poor choices.

"Is that it? You know it all now." She stood up. She reached down to the floor for her bra and panties.

"No. I don't. I want to know how he got you in bed…without protection."

"That last part's easy. He doesn't worry about a thing. He got me to feel that whatever he told me was true. He wouldn't wear a condom, no matter what."

"So, I'm the j…jerk for worrying about getting you pregnant."

"No. I'm the jerk for being with him instead of sticking with you," she said.

"That's one p…point in my favor. Finish."

"He made me feel invulnerable. We smoked pot and—"

"You smoked pot? I don't believe it!"

"We did. I got high. Next thing I know, he was pulling off my clothes and…I felt helpless and…he…pushed into me."

"You mean he…forced you?"

"No. I didn't really try to stop him. I just wanted him to give me a chance to clear my head, but…I…sort of liked it. I didn't have to think. I was this source of… gratification for a guy…I liked that…and I just lay there and waited. I guess…I was glad when it was over…like I had crossed a bridge and left part of me behind."

"After that?"

"Don't you know enough?"

"I guess you l…liked it after that."

"It was okay. No fireworks, but…I thought I loved him and he was my…link to Santo. He said he would find him. I had to be patient."

"Smart guy. He gets you high. He screws you and keeps you with him by lying about l…looking for your brother."

Anne's eyes narrowed. "You know where Santo is."

"I don't know any…thing about any…body—and that includes you and it includes me."

He went home after that.

The rest of that day was a bleak, lonely waste of hours. He stayed in his small, stuffy room, trying to read, thinking, mourning. He pushed away his confusion. Then he called Anne to tell her that he needed a day or so to digest everything that she had told him, but he promised that he would help her.

WHAT WOMEN DO

Anacleto awakened to a dark, chilly, wet day. He called Anne on the phone, but she wasn't home. Francine said that she had left the house without telling her where she was going. Anacleto panicked, thinking that she had gotten in touch with Steve. He asked his mother for the use of her car. She wanted to know why he needed it.

"Can't you, for once, Ma, just let me do something that I w…want to do without giving me a hard t…time?"

"It's my car. I need it. What am I gonna do if you wreck it in the rain?"

"I'll buy you a new one," he told her.

"With what money?"

He told her that he had two thousand dollars saved up.

"You don't have that much. I saw your bank book."

"It's not in a bank account. I have the money."

She let him take the car. He drove for hours, checking all the parks, bus stops, and subway stations in his neighborhood. He passed all of the popular hangouts. He parked, and looked in pizzerias, restaurants, candy stores. Each time he saw a girl or a group of girls, he slowed the car and cranked down the windows for a better look. Finally, soaked, tired, disgusted, depressed, he gave up.

He called Anne when he got home. She answered the phone.

"Where have you been all day?"

"Out." She sounded tired.

He resisted the urge to ask who, where…

"Do y…you want to talk?" he asked.

"Yes. Please. Meet me outside."

The rain had stopped. They sat on lounge cushions on the stoop of his house.

"So, wh…what are you going to do?" He didn't know what he hoped she would say.

"I need you to believe me, Clete. I need you to promise that you'll try."

"I'll try." He waited, anxious, nervous.

"I wanted you to believe you made me pregnant, that it's your baby I'm carrying, but you know that already," she whispered.

"I know you wanted to tr…trick me into thinking I got you preg…nant."

"I'm sorry. It wasn't malicious. I love you. I wanted it to be your baby."

"It doesn't work that way. He got to y…you first," he sneered.

"I know. I'm sorry. I'll be sorry for the rest of my life."

"I'm sorry too." Then softening, he looked at her and said, "I'm listening."

"I want to believe that it's your baby. If we love each other and we love the baby, then it will be yours and mine. Do you believe me?"

"I don't know."

"I…" She stopped, looked around, moved closer to him and spoke even more quietly. "I want you to believe it's yours…"

"I don't know—"

"I need you. I'm not asking you to marry me or to support me. I just…I need you now and for the long run. I realize now that you are for me and that I am yours."

"I...have always wanted that. What about the pr ... pregnancy?"

She was quiet for a moment. Then she looked directly at Anacleto and said, "I hope you can understand this...I wish I wasn't pregnant, especially since...he...you know...he did it, but I can't have an abortion. I have to have this baby."

"Why? You don't go to church anymore."

"I still think I should go, but I don't. I don't really believe in any of it. There's so much hypocrisy. I don't...I guess—"

"Confession. Right? That used to worry me when I was a kid, when I went to church."

"That's part of it. I can confess that I had sex with Steve, but that isn't really a sin. I mean, at the time, I was confused and I thought I loved him—"

"You're sure you don't now?"

"Please…" She smirked. Then she became thoughtful. "I want you to understand…I can't believe I should have to confess that I'm sorry that I want the man I love to love me physically."

Anacleto stiffened.

She looked at him. "I mean you, of course," she said.

"Oh. It's hard to keep track of who you love," he replied.

"I understand how you feel, but I want you, and I have to keep this baby."

"Are you sure you've th…thought this over carefully?"

"Yes. I can't…I have to have it. I hope I don't lose you. I hope you can understand."

"I understand that you w…want to keep it, but…it's Steve's…I mean he's the father, not me."

"He's not in my life and I don't want him. I can't do this without you. I…need you to be here for me."

"I'm here. Your mom will be too," he reassured her.

"My mom and I are going through a rough patch now. She hated Steve."

"She'll get over it. Go to her."

"It's not that. You don't understand. All my life, she's told me to be careful. She drilled into me not to get pregnant. She says that being pretty, attracting men, my father, having Santo…ruined her life."

"Oh. What do you think she m…means?"

"She means, if she hadn't been pretty, my father wouldn't have fallen in love with her and, if he had anyway, but she hadn't had Santo and the rest of us, she would have divorced him long ago. She's unhappy. They just barely get along."

"You're sure that's what she means?"

"I guess. I can understand that. Girls try so hard to be alluring; then they attract men, and their lives are ruined."

"You really feel that way?"

"Well, look at me now. My mother knows what she's talking about. I mean, I don't have to wear a scarlet letter, but my fate is pretty much sealed now."

"I guess you're sort of right. So, you're afraid to tell her."

"I'm not worried that she'll be mad at me. I just feel I can't look her in the eye and tell her that some guy who's a…mistake made me pregnant."

"And, if she th…thinks I'm the baby's father, she can—"

"She'd accept it. She knows you love me, that you'll be here for me. But it's more than that. I know this baby could keep us apart, make you feel like it's a stranger, a hindrance to our relationship...or, you can think of it as yours, as I am yours, as I always will be yours."

Anacleto stood up and walked to the curb. He looked down the street, to the corner. He tried to play out in his mind how he would feel when people, neighbors, his family, his mother found out that he had made Anne pregnant.

He sat next to her again.

"If it was mine," he whispered, "I would accept the situation and take responsibility. I've never even made love to you. I'm still a virgin."

"I'm sorry. I told you that. If I could take back every second I spent with Steve, I would. But I can't." Her sad, desperate eyes implored him.

My fault...her fault...my disgusting, pitiful life.

"I am yours," she promised. "I will always be yours. You never need to worry that I will say no to you again…about anything. We'll both forget he ever existed."

"I have to think about this. And you won't consider an abor…tion?"

"No. It's too much for me. I feel I'm being punished enough. It's my baby."

"It's not a baby. It doesn't even look like a t…tadpole yet."

"It's a life and I'm Catholic, even if I don't really believe in the Church any more. I know you don't believe."

"I believe in a lot of things. I believe in God. I think I do. I don't even know if

I could handle an abortion either, but not because of what the Church says. I mean…I'm not encouraging y…you to have one. It's not something I want you to do. I don't even know how you find someone to do it. I wouldn't want you to have to go to some doctor's back door late at night, but—"

"But it's not a good thing. I can't do it."

"How about letting a piece of shit drug dealer get you into bed—when you wouldn't let me? Was that a good thing?"

"I…can't apologize to you…for the rest of my life," she sighed.

"The rest of your life? It's only been a couple of days…that I know about it," he replied.

"I know."

"I understand…you think you have to keep it as part of your penance."

"I don't know. I don't need penance for the reason you think: that I had sex before marriage. I don't care about that."

She sat silently, holding her head in her hands.

Then she spoke: "I do deserve punishment for letting him touch me and for hurting you, but I don't think that's why I have to…keep it."

"Then why? Why should you let priests and bishops and a pope tell you what you can and can't do with your life? It's all made up. You think these restrictions are from God? Hah! A group of men, mostly old men who were afraid of sex, who thought they knew what God wants, got together in councils and made up these rules back in the middle ages to control women, to control people. God has nothing to do with it."

"I know. You're right about that. That's not why."

"Then why?"

"Partly, it's because this is what women do: we grow babies."

"You really think that way? I mean, of course women become pregnant, but they should have a choice."

"I do. This is my choice. I wish I had other choices, but I don't."

"Why?"

"It's hard to explain."

"I want to understand. Why must you keep it?"

"I think because it's...the baby is part of me, and keeping it somehow makes this terrible situation mean something good. It will grow up to be a good person, someone who lives a good life."

"You're sure about that? Th…that hasn't been my life."

"Oh. You're wrong. You're just about the best person I know."

"That's because you're comparing me to shitty and screwed-up people."

"No, Clete. I want this baby to be like you, smart, considerate, kind—"

"Confused, odd, never knowing what to do, a loser."

"That used to be you. You're just about perfect the way you are now."

"Really? Too bad you feel that way now, and not back when you took Steve into your bed."

"I've told you I'm sorry. You have to forget him. I have."

"You really can't expect me to forget so quickly, you know," he explained with bitterness in his voice.

"Listen, Clete. All I know," she sighed, "…is that I regret everything about everything. If I could put us back to where we were when you came back to me, after you were with Ricki, and I knew then what I know now, I would have kept my mouth shut."

"I'm sorry about her, but I did not have sex with her and I did come back to you."

"Letting her do to you what she did is sex," she replied.

"Yes, okay, but not as much as what you did over and over again with Steve."

She was silent.

"How many times, Anne? How many times did you screw him while I waited home alone and while I was at school and at work. How many times?"

"Oh, God. Stop it! He's a shit! It was a mistake. I don't know how many times. Not many…one time was too much! I need you, not him."

"I need to worry about me. You weren't thinking about me then, were you?" he asked.

"That's not what people do. They don't think about…someone else when they're…in bed with…Oh, God!"

"That's what *I* did. When Ricki wanted me to be with her, to stay with her, I thought of you. I should have been stronger. I should have run out and gone to you. I gave in to…the feeling…the grat…gratification,…but I wanted you! I wished it was you touching me."

"And now *I* want *you* and I need you. I don't ever want to be touched by anyone else again," she said.

"You're trying to use me. I don't even know whether you really love me."

"No. I am not using you. I love you. I never stopped…even when I was angry with you. I know you love me. I am…hoping that you love me and trust me enough to help me keep this baby. It will be ours—I wish it really was yours—but it will be ours because I know that we'll be together for the rest of our lives."

"I don't know how to say this; I feel bad that it's....that piece of shit's baby. I'm sorry. I know it's yours too. He's such a piece of crap, and you let him——"

"Enough! You're going to drive yourself crazy—and me too!" she shouted.

The door to the house opened suddenly—Lucia stood there and glared at Anne. She had been in the foyer, trying to hear what they were saying.

"Hi, Ma. We're talking."

"I know you're talking. I heard you screaming," she said to Anne.

Anne put her head down.

"She wasn't screaming, Ma. We're just talking."

Lucia didn't take the hint, so Anacleto took Anne by the hand and led her down the steps.

"I'll see you later, Mom."

Lucia stood there, guarding her home, undoubtedly wishing that she could protect her boy from the evils of women and the world in general. They walked. The sidewalk was empty.

"I don't know. I need time—"

"Clete. I'm…more than a full month late. I'm going to start showing soon. I need you to make a decision."

"I'm sorry. Why do you need to know now? You're not going for…you know…an abortion, so why does it m...matter what I say?"

"You don't understand. I want this to be our baby."

"You tr…tried to trick me…I was supposed to believe it's…but it isn't. We haven't even…made love yet."

"Is that the problem? Come on. Let's do it now. In my room—my mother won't bother us…in your mother's car. Wouldn't that be a scream? If your mother only knew." Her smile was angry and bitter.

"You make it s…sound so simple—"

"It is! It's no big deal. You're so damned concerned about Steve screwing me first. It's nothing. It doesn't change you. He's nothing to me."

"Well, he might be nothing now—"

"Come on, Clete. Forget about him."

"I can't…not so fast. You don't understand. I've come a long way in my life. I used to…hide…I used to put my hands over my eyes and hide."

"I know. I remember. You don't do that now. You're great."

"Hah…I'm a mess. I stopped doing that because I wanted to live my life like other people…out in the real world…the crappy, dirty world…not seeing it from between my fingers."

"I know that…I knew you were in pain."

They were both quiet.

"Let me tell you something else…I used to see…things."

"What do you mean?"

"I used to see people and think I knew how th…their lives would turn out."

"Oh. You mean like seeing into the future."

"No…I don't know…I used to see glimpses of…things."

"And you saw something about me?"

"No. I never did because I didn't look at you that way."

"That's good."

"No. It's n…not good. Maybe, if I had looked at you that way, I would have been able to warn you."

"I wish you had."

"The really sad part is I was j…just starting to feel good about myself for the first time in my pitiful life, but now, I feel like a loser…again."

"You're not. I want you…I want you always."

"You should have wanted *me* then…not him."

"I know."

"Now, he's part of you, and I'm not."

"That's not true."

"No? You wanted him…he got what I wanted."

"Is that what's bothering you? Fuck me now. Get it over with. We can do it three or four times a day if you want. If that will make you feel better."

"You're n…not being help…ful."

"It doesn't change you, Clete. You and I will look the same afterwards."

"Th…that may be true, if you don't count the pregnancy."

"Well, that brings us back to the real problem, doesn't it? The pregnancy," she sighed.

"St…Steve's baby."

"It's not his. Sure, his…his sperm made it. But…he's nothing. Forget him. I have."

"Where did you go today?"

"Why?"

"Are we g…going to be per…perfectly honest with each other?" he asked.

"Yes. I want to be," she whispered. "Okay. Listen, I went looking for him again. Not because I want to see him, but…but, I wanted to tell him to stay away. I don't want him to see me in a couple of months and think…know that it's his."

"How d…do I know you're telling the truth?"

"Because I can never feel for him what I feel for you. I want to be a part of you."

"I can't claim to be…its father. I'm not."

"Okay. How about this? I know you don't trust me, but you will, in time. The only one I care about in this whole mess, besides you, is my mother. I want her to believe it's your baby. I won't tell anyone else. If anyone asks, I won't answer."

"It's not that. I'm not worried…Well, maybe I am a little worried about what my mother will think…No...I'm not...that's not it."

"Explain to me, then," she said.

"If I ran a race and lost, I wouldn't want the medal, even…even if it was offered to me."

"I'm not a prize, Clete."

"But, you are. Not the way you th…think I mean. I don't mean like I won you and you're my possession."

"Thank God for that!"

"I mean…this is hard to say—"

"Say it."

"I wanted you before we began go…going out. I thought about you. I cared about you before you seemed to notice me. And…"

Anne waited. Her eyes were wet.

"And…he w…was deeper in your heart than I was—"

She paused and dabbed her eyes with a tissue. Then she said, "That's not true. I was confused. He was strong. You were too gentle and too confused. And I was angry."

"How was I too gentle? I tried to force myself on you."

"But you stopped. Don't get me wrong. I'm glad you stopped. I was still a virgin and I didn't want you—or anybody then."

"I don't get it."

"You stopped. You didn't want me badly enough. He did."

"He's a selfish drug addict pig! He's probably screwed and left a couple of dozen girls. Who knows how many bastards he's created?"

She put her head down, leaned against a parked car, and cried.

"Sor…ry. I'm so upset and angry," he said.

"I know," she sobbed.

"We're supposed to be honest, right?" he asked.

"Yes," she whispered through her sobs.

"I guess I…I mean…I know…I'm hurt so much I don't know how to h…handle it."

"But you have to try…or else tell me you can't. I need to know."

"I can't tell you now," he replied.

"Okay. I'll say this one more time: I can't change wh...what happened. I wish to God I could. If I could change everything from last summer to now, I would…and not just because I'm pregnant with the baby of a guy who doesn't deserve me. If I committed a sin...if there's any such thing as sin, that's it: that I gave myself to him and not to you. You deserved me, not that I'm such a prize. I was stupid. I was hurt by what you and that tramp did and I was stupid when you came over that day…when you were…so ready for me. I think…I'm not sure…I think I was ready to make love, but I was angry still and I didn't want to give you the satisfaction."

"The two of us have been stupid."

"Yes. But this is our chance."

"How do I know you won't change your mind…go back to him some day?"

"If I even think about that, please, please put a bullet in my head."

TRYING TO DECIDE

Anacleto wanted to believe her. Believe what? That she had tried to trick him so he would act as the father of Steve's baby because she loved him and not Steve? Or, because Steve was gone, and she needed a replacement? Anacleto asked himself whether he wanted this new complication in his life. Would he be the baby's father. Would it call him "Daddy"? Would he resent the baby because it wasn't his? Did he want to be a father? Did he want to just stay in his house and hide?

He wanted Anne—more now than before. Why? Did he want to fill her up so that it would…that it would make the baby his? Did he want to overpower Steve's genes, hoping that the baby would have his? That didn't make any sense.

He had told Anne that he would decide by the end of the week. He had trouble sleeping. When his alarm clock rang on Monday morning, he concentrated on getting ready for school and work. All that day, he thought, he questioned, he fought a mental battle that resulted in a pounding headache and a case of stomach-churning indigestion. By the time he reached his house that evening, he was as confused as he had been when he first began thinking about the decision he had to make. If it had been his, after the shock of finding out that Anne was pregnant, he would have gone along with her decision to keep the baby, no questions asked. After all, if he wanted to be with her, then, having a baby, even though it would have been inconvenient and embarrassing, would have been…part of the package, maybe even a nice thing. If he had to, he would have gotten a full-time job and gone to college at night, and they would have gotten married. Despite his insecurities, he knew he could land a good job and support a wife and child.

The draft…the damned draft…the stupid, wasteful war…

That would be a problem. Without a college deferment, he might be called up. The new lottery system had assigned the number 182 to his birth date. How typical of his life! Neither here nor there. Almost exactly half of 365. Without a deferment, once the men his age who were born during the 181 birthdays on the list before his had been drafted, his number would come up.

And, still, he couldn't get past the thought that it was Steve's baby—the same son of a bitch who had urinated on him…and done so much to Santo. And…that he had been her lover. Was he a lover or did he use her? It didn't matter. Steve had her while Anacleto had sat in his mother's car across the street, eating out his guts. And…how many times and in how many different ways?

He knew he would have been even more upset to have seen them walking, Anne pregnant, Steve proud. But Steve wasn't that kind of guy. To him, girls were just…commodities. And, so, there he was…agonizing over a situation—it was almost funny—a situation that any guy with any amount of survival instinct would have walked away from. Of course, if he really did love her, he would grasp this opportunity to be her savior and solidify their relationship. If Steve never came around, and he probably would not, the baby would be Anne's and his.

His mother. How would he tell her? When had she ever accepted a choice that he had made or sympathized with a problem of his? Of course, he did not have to tell her. She might assume he was the father. He wouldn't answer her, if she asked. It was Francine who Anne wanted to reassure. She wanted to come to terms with her mother and not cause her more grief. Francine would be upset at the thought of Anne being pregnant, but believing that Anacleto was the father would comfort her.

That was a bit of irony: Anne following in her mother's footsteps, but, of course, she did not know about that…and this was different because Anacleto wasn't already married to someone else.

He decided he needed more time.

He and Anne went out that night to visit her friend, Jenny. She lived with her boyfriend, Keith. She was clearly surprised to see Anne and Anacleto together.

Later that evening, when he walked Anne to her door, she asked him to come into her room with her. He told her he wasn't ready.

"No strings." She whispered in his ear, "I really want you to make love to me."

"I…I can't. I don't feel it. I'm…too nervous and frazzled."

"I can help you. Come on."

"No. I'm sorry. I'm probably the only guy in Brooklyn who's turning down an offer like this, but I—"

"I understand. You're afraid that, if we do it, you'll feel obligated to do what I want."

"No. Not ob…obligated…I think I want to make the decision first. Then we can move on with our lives."

"I really do want you, Clete. If you can forget the decision, I won't bring it up…not tonight."

"No. I guess…in the same way th…that I'm still upset that you…that you're not—"

"What?"

"That you did it the first time with someone else, that it won't be our, your, our first time together. I guess I don't want this fir…first time for us to be…in the middle of this decision…this problem. I want a clear head. It…making love to you is a big deal to me. You say it doesn't change a person. I want it to change me. It has to be, for me, for us…much more than just…pleasure."

"What if it's not?" she asked.

"I…don't know. I guess I'll be very disappointed because I want it…to…be more than...I don't know."

"I know. I do know. You want it to affirm our love for each other," Anne offered.

"Yes. That and more."

"It will because I love you completely. More each day," she said. "And, if you can't ever think of the baby as yours, that will be sad, but I will accept it."

In the alley, he turned to look at the door; she was there, looking back at him through the little window. He smiled. Then he turned and walked to his house, knowing there was something wrong with him: no normal guy would walk away from a chance like this and, at the same time, still entertain the thought of taking title to another man's baby.

He wondered whether he would ever reach the point in his life in which he would make decisions based on what was best for him. Why did he find it so difficult to do what came so naturally to everyone else?

ANACLETO'S DECISION

"It's time," Anacleto said when Santo picked up the phone.

"Whadda you talkin' about?"

"You said you would call them and tell them you're alive. So?"

"So, I…I don't know," he answered.

"Okay. Tell me what's holding you back. You're out of prison, you're clean, you're working…Right?"

"It's…the longer I wait, the harder it is to make the call. I don't know…what to say to them."

"Do you want me to write it out for you? I will," Anacleto suggested.

"No. I guess, if I was coming home from the army or from college or something good, it would be easy. They'd smile and kiss me and be all happy to see me, but—"

"Santo, your mother prays for you every day, and Anne…she…every so often, two or three times a day, no matter what she's doing, a little cloud darkens her face, and I know she's worrying about you."

Santo was silent.

"And Peter…he's a year and a half. He knows he has a big brother…your mom shows him your pictures all the time."

"Would you tell them? Tell them about me. Tell them the bad stuff."

"No, Santo. I won't. They won't care about that. They just want to know you're among the living and that they're going to see you."

"I'll call. Soon."

"I'm going there as soon as I hang up with you. I'm going to tell them…just that you're alive and well. That's all."

"Okay," Santo said.

"After that, it's up to you—be a man, Santo."

"Okay," he said, sounding like a little boy.

***

Anne answered the door.

"Hi," she murmured as she kissed him, and then led him into the kitchen.

"You look…beautiful."

"Thank you. I put on fresh makeup, hoping a handsome man would knock."

"Oh? Should I leave?"

"You know it's you, silly," she teased. "I meant what I said. I want you…only you… forever. Nothing else matters."

"Is your mom here?"

"Sure. Why?"

"Call her." His heart was racing; it isn't every day you can tell a mother that her son is alive and well.

When Francine came into the kitchen, Anacleto smiled and told her to sit. She looked at Anne. Suddenly, he realized what Anne must have been thinking.

Oh, no. I screwed up again! She thinks I'm going to tell Francine that Anne's pregnant and I'm the father…

Francine was smiling, but she looked nervous; Anne looked anxious.

"Francine…I spoke with Santo. He's okay."

She screamed, and grabbed Anacleto, pulling him down to her on the chair. He fell on her and, if the chair had not been backed by the kitchen table, the both of them would have fallen to the floor. She cried and hugged him and sobbed and then she laughed and kissed his head and cheeks. Then they heard Peter crying. Francine released Anacleto, and he stood up. Her tear-stained face was aglow with happiness. Anne was standing where she had been when he made the announcement. She was smiling, wiping tears from her face.

"Go…get Peter. I don't care if he doesn't sleep now," Francine said. "Santo's okay. Thank God."

Anne went to Peter's room, what had been Santo's room.

"Where is he? What happened to him? When is he coming home? Tell me," Francine said.

"Well, I can't tell you more than what I s…said. He sounded fine. He did…didn't stay on the line for more than a minute. I don't know where he is."

Anne returned with another smiling, tear-stained member of the family. She handed Peter to her mother and embraced Anacleto. Then she pulled back a little and looked at him questioningly.

"But, he must have said more than that," Francine said, kissing Peter.

"No. Sorry. He s…sounded great, but he hung up right away."

"When will he be here? Is he in trouble?"

"I don't know...I d…don't th…think he's in trouble."

"I'm worried," Francine sighed.

"Look, Francine, I under…stand," he said, smiling at her reassuringly, "b…but he's alive and…he sounded great."

Just then, the door opened, and Mr. Faricola entered the apartment. When he reached the kitchen, Francine announced, "Leo, Santo's okay. He's coming home soon."

She stood up and, with Peter in her arms, she hugged Leo. After a few seconds she started to cry again. Leo held her lightly, his hands on her sides. His hard, dark face betrayed no emotion. Francine repeated to him everything that Anacleto had told her.

"That's all you know?" he asked Anacleto.

"Yes…That's it."

He walked off to the bathroom.

"Would you like something to eat?" Francine asked Anacleto.

"No…no thank you. I ate."

Anne caught his eye and looked at the door.

"We're going out, Ma."

"But, what if Santo comes home?"

"We're just going for a walk. We won't be far."

"Francine, I h…have to tell you…he didn't say he'd be home soon."

She shook her head gravely. Then she smiled again.

"Santo's alive. Thank God," she murmured.

They walked down the alley and onto the sidewalk.

"I'm sorry. You must have th…thought I was going to announce your…the situation to your mom, right?"

"I sort of thought that. Yes."

"I'm so stupid. I—"

"No. Whatever you say or do is all right with me," she said.

"I…I don't know."

"I've been thinking. Only two things are important to me now. I have to keep the baby and I have to keep you, if you want me."

"I do."

"I'm not asking you to say anything. What I'm trying to say is, when I start to show, I won't tell my mother it's your baby. I won't tell anyone it's yours."

They walked in silence for a minute. Then Anne continued: "Could you accept that? Being with me, pregnant. People knowing that we're together and me not saying it's your baby?"

"I th…think so."

"Good. Then it's settled."

"I don't want th…this situation to be worse for you. Give me a little more time to get the idea into my head," he said. "I'm over the worst part...I mean...I think I can do this now."

"There's plenty of time now. You see, people will all assume it's yours, even if I deny it, which I will, if you want. If you ever decide, anytime, that you want to claim that you're its father, then that's what we'll say. It's as simple as that."

"Okay. I guess we can do that, for now," he agreed. "I think, little by little, I'll be able to call the baby mine. I love you and I want us to be together."

"You make me so happy," she said.

***

He knew he had to tell Anne how he knew Steve and what had happened that night. It would be wrong to keep that from her. But he was worried that, upon telling her how he had hurt Steve and how he had left him there, bleeding, her eyes might betray concern for him. He lay awake for hours, many nights, trying to decide how and when to tell her about this last, ironic chapter in their shared history.

LIFE CAN BE VERY GOOD SOMETIMES

Lucia announced that she was going to visit George in Virginia.

"He told me to come. I wrote it down, here," she said, handing a scrap of paper to Anacleto.

"Fort Belvoir, Alexandria, Virginia," he read.

"How are you going to get there, Ma?"

"I'll take the Greyhound tomorrow morning. Frank will drive me to the Port Authority. I told Georgie that you and Frank and James couldn't come. He understood. He knows you're all working and that you're going to school. Besides, he says he should be home soon."

***

"Did you speak to Santo again?" Francine asked the next day as she let Anacleto into the apartment.

"No, I didn't."

"He hasn't called us." Then, in a plaintive voice, she asked, "Why doesn't he just come home?"

He didn't know what to say.

"I don't understand," Francine said, and then she began to sob.

He held her. "Don't cry. He's alive and he's okay. I guess h…he needs time. You sh…should be happy."

Peter sat in his playpen, gurgling and shaking a rattle.

"I know. You're right. I have to convince myself that he's okay. I just…I'll feel better when I see my son."

"Where's Anne?" he asked.

"She should be home soon. I'm making dinner. I want you to stay."

He told her about his mother's visit to sec George. Francine said that she was pleased for her. Then he sat on the living room floor and played with Peter. About a half hour later, the door opened. Anne's face brightened when she saw him.

"You look like hell," she remarked.

"I know. I'm tired. I haven't been sleeping well."

"Poor baby. What's the matter?" she asked.

"I don't know. I'm just tense, I guess."

Tonight, he decided, he would tell her.

***

"Well, thanks to George, I am finally in your house. This is a real treat," Anne exclaimed as they walked into the foyer. "Show me your room."

"Okay. It's not much. Once I finish college and have a job, I'll move out."

He led her up the stairs. It was warm in his room and the air was stale, so he opened the one window. The night was cool and dry; a refreshing breeze floated in.

"You should feel honored. Nobody's ever been in here, except for Santo—once."

"It's austere, but nice," she proclaimed.

"Nice word…*austere*," he joked.

"Only the best words when I'm with you," she responded.

"Thank you. I love your mind," he said.

"Only my mind?"

"No. Not just your mind. I'm not a fool."

She swiveled her hips and playfully fluffed her hair, holding it above her head. Then she put her hands on his shoulders and kissed him. He returned a quick kiss. For a second or two, he thought he might wait to tell her.

I want her so bad...this is the right moment...But...

"I have to tell you something," he said.

She searched his face, anxious.

"It's not anything bad. Not really. Don't worry." He moved her away and held her two hands. He led her to a chair. Then he sat on his bed, across from her.

"Listen...I want to be very honest with you…about everything. I don't want us ever to have secrets. That's what's caused us so much tr…trouble."

She waited, her face displaying the fear that was running through her at that moment.

"No…it's not bad…not really. Listen. I can't tell you everything because Santo has to be the one to…tell you about…How can I say this? I don't think I have the r…right to tell you about things that happened to him."

"I don't understand. What happened to him?"

"I mean things that happened last year. That's for him to say."

"Just tell me: is he really all right?"

"Yes. He's all right."

He explained to Anne that Santo had disappeared because of his drug dealing. He told her about two men beating up Santo and sending him packing. He told about meeting Santo and his plans to resolve the issue. Then he gave her the details of what had happened that night in the courtyard of the building. She started to cry. He knelt by her and held her.

"He's really okay. But there's one more thing I have to tell you."

He moved back to his bed. He needed distance from her for this next part. If this revelation was going to destroy their relationship, he didn't want her to have to push him away.

"The guy…the one who beat up and then shot Santo, the one I punched and then kicked in the balls…it was Steve."

Her eyes widened; then she cried and hit her knees with the palms of her hands.

That's it. I screwed up again. I've lost her…Idiot!

After a few seconds, her crying subsided. Then she wiped her eyes with her hands. He searched for a tissue. When he couldn't find one, he pulled a clean tee shirt from one of his drawers and handed it to her. She dabbed at her eyes with it. He sat on his bed again.

"You can blow your n…nose on it. It's okay."

She laughed. Then she said, "I hope you can forgive me."

"Forgive you? For what?" he asked, baffled and relieved.

"For letting that horrible piece of shit ever touch me."

"You didn't know. I forgive you for everything as long as you forgive me for being such a jerk."

"You're not a jerk. You're wonderful."

No more secrets…there is one…the gun…the gun that I shouldn't have ever touched…ever brought out of the attic…the place of dust and darkness and my family's secrets…

"I want to tell you—"

"No more talk." She stood up and approached him, placing her hands on his shoulders. She looked down at him with soft, glistening eyes; strands of her midnight-black hair brushed his face. He knew she was all he would ever want.

They kissed and held each other. Within seconds, their clothes were on the floor of his little room and they fell into a long, feverish embrace that ended in an explosion of joy that left them perspired and drained and content. They lay in each other's arms. Neither one wanted to move.

***

Happily fulfilled, Anacleto lay on his bed staring at the cracks on the ceiling and drifting into sleep until Anne said, "Thank you, Mrs. Roosevelt and the United States Army."

"Do you want to speak to Santo now?" he asked.

She shook her head. He dialed the number. Roseanne answered the phone.

"Roseanne…it's Clete. How's he doing?"

"Hi, Clete. He's good. Here."

Santo came on the line. "How you doin'?"

"I'm fine, Santo. You don't have to call your house."

"No. How come? They okay?"

"Sure," he said. "Hold on." He handed the phone to Anne.

She talked and laughed and cried. After a few minutes, she handed the phone back to Anacleto.

"You had no right," Santo complained.

"What can I say? I'm glad I did."

"Yeah, but—"

"But nothing, Santo. Now, when are you going to call your mother?"

"I…I don't know."

"Santo, she's not going to judge you. She's home alone with Peter. She said your father wasn't coming home tonight. Call her. She worries every day."

"I don't know."

"I do know. Call her now!"

"Okay. I will."

"Now…not tomorrow."

"I promise. As soon as I hang up."

Anacleto lay down next to Anne and rested one hand lightly on her arm.

"Life can be very good sometimes," she whispered in his ear.

***

When Anacleto walked Anne back to her house later that night, Francine ran into the kitchen, beaming. Anne and her mother embraced and laughed. He walked out quietly, and went home.

He lay in bed for a long while, remembering their lovemaking. It had been exhilarating and heady and joyous. He had been swept away by a tsunami of desire and delight. Anne was wrong. Anacleto did feel changed. He felt bound to her; he was a part of her…and of her baby. But he felt lonely afterwards; when he withdrew from her when they were finished, it was as if he was losing a part of himself. He knew that he would never again be complete without her.

FRANCINE THE REALIST

One night, a week later, when he went to her house after work, Anne said, "Don't come in. Not tonight. I have to tell my mom. I can't hide…it any longer."

"Of course. Right," he said, trying to hide his disappointment.

"I wish we could make love tonight, but we can't," she said.

"Call me. I'll sit by the phone and get it on the first ring."

"Wouldn't want to disturb your mom," she said, smiling.

At home, sitting next to the little telephone table, he tried to study. He didn't want Anne to be upset and he hoped that Francine wouldn't be too unhappy. He thought about how strange it was going to be…walking with an obviously pregnant Anne, meeting people they knew. He wondered at what point they would have to stop making love. She had told him not to worry about that.

He and Anne knew three couples around their age who were married. Tommy and Joyce had gotten married within a few months of their high school graduation. Their baby was born right after that. They both worked, but they lived with Joyce's parents. Sal and Annemarie waited a year after high school—their baby was a year old when they decided to get married. He worked in his father's plumbing business, so they had enough money to rent an apartment.

Then there was Stan and Edie. They had had a big wedding. Stan worked part time and attended City College. Edie left her baby with her mother during the day. She worked for the telephone company.

Anacleto had told Anne that he would marry her. She told him they shouldn't think about until they had both finished college and had good jobs. She said she didn't care about what people thought or said about them.

Anacleto worried about what to say to his mother. If he said nothing, she would surely think of and, most certainly, refer to Anne as a tramp. But…how could he tell her he was the baby's father? She would, of course, become wildly hysterical, scream, and pull her hair and curse. He had reached the point in his life at which her irrational behavior no longer bothered him, but…who wanted to see it? Or hear it? But he had to tell her; at some point, she would have to accept Anne and the baby.

What if it had blond hair, like Steve? Anacleto's father's hair had been dark brown, as was his. His mother, who had dyed her hair auburn for years to hide the gray, used to have mousy brown hair. In all of the early photos of his grandparents, they seemed to have had dark hair also.

He waited a long time. He thought about calling Anne, but decided against it. He wondered what was happening.

The jarring ring of the telephone interrupted his thoughts; he picked up the receiver, but not before Lucia called out, complaining that "…nobody who's any good calls people this time of night."

"How d…did it go?"

"You won't believe it: she said she knew I was pregnant and was hoping I would tell her before it became obvious."

"Really?"

"Yup. But…" Now Anne whispered, "…she doesn't believe you're the father."

"What? It's my baby…I mean…"

Anne was quiet. Then he heard sobs.

"What's the mat…ter? Are you upset? Should I come over?"

"No. You said…it's your baby."

"Oh. I did…Of course it is. Everything about you is m…mine and everything about m… me is yours."

She sighed.

"Is she angry? Is she upset with you?"

"No. She never gets angry; in fact, she's surprisingly…placid."

"Well, you said that…you s…said she would be okay if she thought I was the father… b…but she doesn't believe I am."

"No. She didn't say anything except that she knew."

"Then what makes you say she doesn't believe I'm the father?"

"I know my mother's looks. This one said, 'I know better.' I guess she knows more or less how far gone I am…like I said, about six weeks, I think, and that you and I started going out after that."

That word "about" bothered him. It shouldn't have, but it brought to the surface, once again, the fact that she and Steve had been intimate many times—enough times that she could not pinpoint when she conceived.

He worked at suppressing his anger and his sense of humiliation.

"Clete…Clete? You there?"

"I…Wait a sec…second. I n…need to do some…thing."

He put the phone down and pushed the poisonous thoughts to the perimeter of his consciousness. He breathed deeply and told himself to think about the here and now only. Then, under control, he said, "Oh, so I guess your mom fig…figures—"

"I guess she figures you're here for me, so she doesn't need to ask questions."

"I am. I always will be."

"My mom's a realist. She's had to accept a lot of crap in her life."

"I know. How are things with…between…them?"

"I don't know. Shaky…not good. He hasn't been around for a week."

"Where do you think he is?"

"I don't know. Maybe he has a girlfriend or something."

"Does that upset y…you?"

"Yes, but only because of my mom. If she didn't care, then I wouldn't, I guess."

"Are you going to tell Santo?"

"Oh…I meant to tell you: he came by right after you left…before I told my mom."

"Good. Your mom must have been happy."

"Yes, but he didn't stay long. She's upset that he won't live here, but he told her he won't be running away anymore either," Anne said.

"Did you tell him, or should I?"

"I didn't…I don't know. It's a hard thing to tell to a brother—especially one like him."

"Let me."

"Are you sure?" she asked.

"I'll call him now."

"Okay. You sure?" she asked.

"Yes."

"See you tomorrow?"

"Anne, you never need to ask me that. You…you're going to see me every day… unless…Oh, never mind. Good night."

He hung up the phone, and breathed deeply. He read for while, assuming Santo needed about forty-five minutes to get back to Queens. Then he picked up the receiver, counted to ten, and dialed Roseanne's number. Santo answered the phone. Anacleto asked him how he was.

"Good. My job is good. I got money. I got my girl. And…I seen my ma. I just got back here."

"I know. Anne told me. Sorry I missed you."

"You humpin' my little sister?"

"Santo, I don't talk about her that way."

"Oh? It's a match made in heaven. He loves her, but he won't slip his sausage into her," he laughingly replied.

"Very funny. I'm not saying yes or no. It's private." He tried to sound amused.

"I'll take that as a yes. You take care of her."

"You never need to worry about that."

Clearly, this was not the time to tell Santo about Anne's pregnancy.

"By the way, you didn't believe that shithead's lies about Anne, right?" Santo asked.

"Not for a second. Say, Santo, you want to meet me tomorrow?"

"How come?"

"No reason. I want to see you."

"Okay. I guess we can—"

"Should I come to Roseanne's apartment?"

"You know…why don't you and Anne come here? Friday night. Roseanne will make lasagna."

"Are you sure?"

"Yeah. Be here at…six."

"We'll be there."

He called Anne.

"I hope I didn't wake Peter."

"No. My mom is playing with him. I think she's so happy about seeing Santo that she can't sleep."

"Maybe she's too upset about you."

"Nope. We talked some more. She says she wishes I hadn't 'gotten that way,' but, she's okay with it. You know, I think my mom and dad had Santo before they were married."

"Really?"

"Yeah. You know, I've never seen a wedding picture or a marriage certificate or anything," Anne whispered.

"Oh."

"I've asked my mom. She said they got married quick. No party and no pictures. They were dirt poor. And the marriage certificate got stolen when their first apartment got broken into."

"That's too bad," he consoled.

"Who would want to steal a marriage certificate?" she asked.

"You never know…By the way, we're going to Roseanne's apartment on Friday night for dinner."

"Oh. So…you told him. Is he okay with it?"

"I didn't tell him. It'll be better then. When we're there. He'll see us together. He'll know that I'm in this for good."

"Oh. You're right, I guess," she said.

"I hope I'm right."

AFTER DINNER TALK

Anacleto pressed the doorbell to Roseanne's apartment a little after six. Roseanne answered the door.

"Hi. Roseanne; this is Anne."

The women greeted each other. He handed Roseanne a bouquet of flowers. She sniffed them and smiled.

"Santo's in the shower. He'll be right out."

She led them to the couch in her small, tidy living room. The apartment was bright and very clean. They sat. There was a bottle of wine and some soda and a bowl of potato chips on a small glass-topped coffee table in front of the couch.

"It's a lovely apartment," Anne said.

"Thank you."

"You work for your father, right?" Anacleto asked.

"Yes. I'm a kind of bookkeeper and office manager. The office is in Ozone Park."

"What kind of business is it?" Anne asked.

"It's construction—commercial mostly. I'm on the phone all day long. It's hectic, but I like it and he pays me well."

"Really? I need a job," Anne said.

Anacleto looked harshly at Anne.

"I thought you were going to college," Roseanne said.

"I am, but,...as it turns out, I've decided I want to work for a while and go back to college in a couple of years," Anne explained.

"That would be a mistake," Roseanne said. "Everybody always says if you drop out, you never go back."

"She's hasn't really decided," Anacleto interjected.

"I have. I'm ninety-nine percent sure. I want to...I really need to work now. I'll think about college after...later."

"I can arrange an interview for you, if you want. Call me at work tomorrow. I'll write the number down for you."

Santo walked into the room wearing a perfectly pressed shirt and a pair of sharply creased jeans. He and Anne hugged and kissed each other and patted each other's shoulders. Anne alternated between crying and laughing. Santo smiled, but his eyes were wet. He had a small red bruise on his temple. The remnant from that night.

They talked and sipped wine. Anne drank Seven-Up. She asked where the bathroom was.

"I'll check the dinner," Roseanne said as she stood up and walked to the kitchen. She walked with the grace and dignity of someone who demanded respect.

"This is great, Santo. You're really settled in."

"Yeah. I think I finally got myself where I friggin' want to be."

Anacleto laughed.

"I gotta watch my language. Roseanne don't like me to curse," Santo confided.

"Well then, watch your fucking language, shithead," Anacleto hissed.

That broke them up.

"What's so funny?" Roseanne asked.

Anacleto and Santo looked at each other, and then they laughed even harder. After a few minutes, Anne emerged from the bathroom.

"You took so friggin' long, I thought you died in there," Santo teased.

She smiled, embarrassed, and looked at Anacleto. She wondered whether he had told Santo yet.

They ate salad and lasagna. Santo talked and laughed and the others basked in the glow of his happiness.

"I'm gonna join the ironworkers union. Then I'll get training and I'll be making a good income. Between Roseanne and me, we do all right." He smiled at her. Then he said, "I don't understand, Anne. How come you're quitting college? You got the brains. Why do you gotta work?"

Anne looked at Anacleto. Roseanne, sensing that the discussion was a family one, stood up and began clearing the table. Anacleto asked her to sit.

"Santo, we h…have to…tell you…something."

Santo looked from Anne to Anacleto and back to Anne again.

"You s…see, Santo…we are together and we're st…staying together. It's not just like…like we're going st…steady—"

"Come on, man. Get to the friggin' point," Santo demanded.

"Okay…you see—" He couldn't get the words out.

"I'm pregnant, Santo."

They all watched Santo's face: first it was expressionless; then he seemed to be baffled; finally, he shook his head and closed his eyes as if he were about to cry.

"It's okay, Santo. We love each other and we're going to be happy," Anne said reassuringly.

"You're not keeping it, are you?" he asked in a husky voice.

"Yes," Anne replied.

"You don't know what you're doin'," Santo responded.

"Clete's here for me," Anne said, reassuringly.

"I am, Santo," he promised.

Santo's face took on a hard, bitter expression as he said, "Clete, you're my best friend. We been through a lot. You know I trust you with my life, but…you don't know you're gonna be there for her."

Anacleto looked Santo straight in the eye. Then he said, "Santo, the way you trust me with your life, you can trust me with Anne and our baby."

"You getting' married?" he asked.

"When I finish college," he replied, looking at Anne.

"This is the same fuckin' thing…" Santo began.

They all waited. Roseanne, who had remained silent, did not react to Santo's language.

"You don't know what the hell you're doin'!" he shouted.

"Don't be so upset, Santo," Anne pleaded, beginning to look frantic. "We're together. We didn't want this to happen, but it did. Clete is here for me. If we were a couple of years older or if he had a good paying job, we'd get married. I mean—"

"We would," Anacleto repeated.

"You're fuckin' liars, the two of you. You'll end up with a baby or two babies and he'll be somewhere the fuck else…or he'll visit you a couple of times a week and give you money for milk and bread. Don't have the baby!"

Santo stood up and bolted from the table, knocking over his chair. He strode off down the hallway of the apartment.

"I'll talk to him," Roseanne said, and she followed Santo.

Anne and Anacleto looked at each other sadly.

"Why…I mean, I understand he doesn't want me pregnant when I'm not married, but he seems so angry…like he knows what's going to happen to us…I…I don't understand," Anne said.

Of course, Anacleto did.

***

Santo came back a few minutes later, followed by Roseanne.

"I'm sorry. I guess the shock got to me."

"It's okay. We knew you wouldn't be happy, but don't worry. We're a team." Anne smiled at him.

"Yeah. I know. Clete's the best man I know," Santo said.

"Anne, would you help me with the dishes?" Roseanne asked.

Anne picked up all of the plates and silverware while Roseanne gathered the glasses and the leftover food. They walked to the kitchen.

"Clete, you gotta know why I'm so fucking pissed off," Santo snarled.

"Of course, I know. But…you have to try to understand that I am not leaving her. This is it for me. I feel empty and lonely when I'm away from her. She and I will have a life together. I'm crazy about her."

"It's not just the pussy you're crazy about?"

"Don't talk about her that way."

"I ain't talkin' about her, you jerk. 'Pussy' means getting laid. Jeez, sometimes I can't believe you were born and raised in Brooklyn—you don't understand the language of your own people," Santo said, shaking his head in disbelief.

"I might have been born in Brooklyn, but I didn't have a chance to learn a thing until you became my friend," he responded.

"Yeah? Oh. I guess that's true, but, you're some slow learner," Santo said.

"I've always thought so too."

"Okay, but you know what I mean. Right?"

"Yes. Santo, I'm not your father. She's the only girl I've ever…had sex with; she's the only one for me. I want a chance for a life with her."

"I hope so," he said.

"Case closed."

"Does my ma know?"

"Yes. She's okay with it. She was so happy to see you that…nothing could bother her now."

"Yeah. It was good to see her."

"So…what's with you and Roseanne?"

"Well, she ain't knocked up, if that's what you wanna know," Santo answered.

"No. I mean are you serious about her?"

"I'm not like you, Clete. I banged more girls than I can remember." He thought for a second. Then he continued, "But she's special. She's smart. She coulda went to college, but she don't get along with her step mom so she wanted to move out and work. She don't drink. She don't smoke. She don't let me smoke in the apartment. She won't never cheat on me. And drugs…that's out."

"Thank God."

"Yeah…thank God," Santo repeated. "Now, if you two jerks—"

"It's fine, Santo. We're together."

"I know, man. I trust you."

"You should invite your mother here, Santo. She'd feel good seeing you settled," Anacleto suggested.

"Yeah, maybe I will. I sure as shit don't ever want to go to my mom's house unless I know my friggin' old man ain't there."

"Here's one more bit of advice, Santo: start fresh; make peace with him."

"Not so easy," Santo said, shaking his head. "He don't accept me. I hate his guts. We're gonna fight. I'm gonna say somethin' to him, and that'll just make it harder on my ma. I'm gonna kill that bastard some day."

Anacleto shivered.

"He ruined my ma and he ruined me. I wish to God—"

"You know," Anacleto cut him short. Then he hesitated because he wanted to make his next observation gently, without ruffling Santo's sensitive feathers. "You know, your mother accepts the s…situation. It's not your problem. She knows what she got herself into a long time ago, and sh…she…lives with it."

"Yeah, but she'd be happier without him. I gotta get her out," he said, gritting his teeth.

"Santo, take this the right way: you got into all of the crap that happened to you because you thought you needed money to get your mother out."

Santo looked angry for a second. Then his face softened. "You're right about the trouble, the drugs, the incarceration," he whispered.

Anacleto waited.

"But, if I had the money, she woulda been long gone," he said.

"And you and Roseanne wouldn't be together and I wouldn't have Anne."

"You're my friend, Clete, but I gotta add to that: my sister wouldn't be knocked up."

Everything Anacleto thought of saying seemed wrong.

Anne and Roseanne returned with ice cream. They talked a while longer. Santo and Roseanne said they would walk Anne and Anacleto to the subway station. Santo and Anacleto walked together, behind the two women.

"You have to keep up with your mother," Anacleto reminded him.

"Yeah. I will. I'll find out when my old man's not gonna be there."

Anacleto leaned toward Santo and whispered, "And that knife. I should have taken it tonight. I don't want it in that apartment."

"Hey, don't be talkin' to me like that," Santo growled.

"I'm not the one on probation and I don't have a temper like yours."

"Yeah. You're right, of course. I'll get rid of it."

"Get rid of it soon, Santo."

"I will," he said, "but don't forget…you can use anything to kill a man."

THE DIRTY WORLD

On the subway ride home, they agreed that, despite Santo's initial reaction, he had accepted the news of Anne's pregnancy reasonably well.

"You're not quitting school," Anacleto stated, trying to sound forceful.

"Ooh…I like it when you act caveman," she responded with a smile.

"I'm serious. I'll support you and the baby."

"Not tonight. Can't we discuss it tomorrow?"

They got off the train and walked, hand in hand. They tiptoed into her house.

"I need to pee," she said.

"Yeah. Me too."

"But you have to be quiet," she said.

They went to the bathroom together. They covered their mouths with their hands, trying to suppress their laughter as they took turns at the bowl.

When they were in Anne's room, he asked her why she felt they had to be so quiet.

"I don't know. I guess…it's sort of respect. I mean…my mother never knocks on the door now when we're in here because she doesn't want to know what we're doing. She's always treated me more like a younger sister than a daughter. You know, we've never had a fight. She's always just let me do my thing. In any case, if she knew we were in the bathroom together, I think that would embarrass her. She and my father would never do that."

"No? I thought couples—"

"Well, my mom and dad don't."

"Ok. Let me see that sexy body of yours," he teased, sitting on her bed.

"I don't know how sexy it is now," she replied, patting her abdomen.

Then she slowly undressed, shook out her hair, and posed provocatively.

"Beautiful. You're a goddess."

"No. I'm fat. My belly's growing."

"I don't see it. If you've gained weight, it's nothing. But look at those boobs!"

"I know. They're sensitive," she complained.

"They don't seem to hurt when I touch them."

"Of course not," she said.

They kissed, gently at first. Then, as he became more aroused and as he felt her becoming excited, he pulled her closer as if he was trying to merge their bodies, their souls. They made love as if they knew it was to be their last time ever. They grasped and writhed and pushed against each other with hot ferocity, climbing to an incredibly feverish highpoint of excitement. Then they both shuddered and moaned.

He lingered, drained and exhausted, for a few quiet, warm moments. He did not want to separate himself from her. Then they lay side by side. She gently stroked his arm.

"You know, the first few times, I was nervous and unsure, but I felt satisfied, but then I felt…lonely when we were finished," he said.

"Really? Why?"

"I don't know. Maybe it was because I didn't know when we would do it again and I missed you when I went home."

"We do it all the time," she reminded him.

"I know, but, at the beginning, I…didn't know we would."

"I told you: I will never say no to you," she stated, matter-of-factly.

"But, you see, I had to learn what to make of this…uh…of this…sex thing."

That made Anne laugh.

"I mean it," he continued. "I knew I wanted to…make love to you. I thought about it all the time. When we're making love…the most important thing in the world to me is…really…it's you…Anne…the person who I want, who I need, who I think about when we're not together. And…when I think about you, it's usually just picturing you looking at me or talking to me or laughing. It's not…sexual. Is that making you feel claustrophobic?"

"No. I like it. It turns me on when you talk that way…because I know you love me. That's one of the things I love about you: we make love…but, when we're done and you've gotten what you want—and I've gotten what I want—you're still here. And when you go home, you're still here. I don't know what I was thinking when I said I felt suffocated."

"Good. I don't have that…I don't know…that instinct that a lot of men have to want to… dip into a lot of wells…and disappear."

"That's very poetic," Anne teased.

"Ha. Maybe I read it somewhere. Anyway, I just want you…every day. I wish we could sleep together one night."

"That would be lovely," she remarked.

"Actually, I wish we could sleep together every night," he said wistfully.

"That would be wonderful. Everything with you is wonderful."

"And it will stay that way. I promise."

***

A week later, on a Saturday, he had breakfast with his mother; then she went through her weekly ritual of cleaning the house. He studied. Then he worked out in the basement. When she finished cleaning, he told her that he had to speak with her.

Trembling, in a shaky voice, he said that Anne was pregnant. Her eyes narrowed. He thought he saw the beginnings of an insult directed at Anne forming on her lips, so he told her that he was the father.

"That son-of-a-bitch-bastard! That tramp! She won't ruin your life!"

He waited. Repeated, painful displays of his mother's bizarre view of life and her extreme fits of anger had taught him that he had to wait until she was finished spewing her blazing hot invectives before he attempted to interrupt her. No sense trying to hold back a volcanic eruption. He knew he had to wait.

After a minute or so, Lucia calmed down; she had cursed, pulled her hair, squeezed her face, and stamped her feet to the point of exhaustion.

Anacleto calmly explained that he was happy. He assured his mother that they were not planning on getting married…at least, not now, and that he would stay in school. In response to her agitated but relatively calm questions, he assured her that he was the father and that Anne had been a virgin when they had first had sex. He rejected her notion that Anne was now "used goods" and, therefore, unfit for him.

He concluded by telling her that, as much as she might not like it, and he could understand that, she had better accept it and she had better treat Anne with respect and dignity because, if push came to shove, he would choose Anne over her.

That led to a renewed eruption.

"I knew I shoulda kept you in the house—there's nothing good out there for you," she cried out.

"Ma, the whole world is out there. I'm nineteen."

"Your brothers never did this. Why did you have to let that tramp do this to you?"

"Ma, I'll b…be patient for a while, b…but don't ever call Anne a name like that again. I love her."

This led to yet another round of hysterics, during which his mother's glazed eyes rolled in her head and she alternately cried and mumbled about how "…the world, the dirty world ain't for you…"

As Anacleto waited, observing her frenzied display, he felt nothing; then he felt bad for her. Actually, he was upset with himself because he had very little real sympathy for her. He put an arm around her shoulders and kissed her because he had to do that.

Then he ventured out into the dirty world.

***

He told Anne about his mother's reaction to the news; he prudently deleted the epithets that his mother had used to refer to her.

"So, it's about as bad as you thought, huh?"

"I guess so."

"Don't feel bad. She'll get used to it," Anne said, with very little conviction.

***

When he got back from his regular Saturday morning run, his mother was waiting for him on the stoop.

"Georgie's on his way home. He's getting discharged tomorrow! He just called," she cried out.

He hugged her and told her that he was very happy.

"He said Ronnie's on his way back home from that place too. He's gonna be, you know, discharged soon too. We'll have a party. All the relatives. Everybody."

"Sure, Ma. That sounds great."

"All my sons are gonna be together!"

He stayed with her for a while. An hour later, James and Frank drove up to the house. When James heard the news, he said that he would stay at the house overnight, and not return to Manhattan.

Lucia went into the house to call the relatives. Anacleto told his brothers about Anne.

"You knocked up skinny little Annie Fanny?" James asked, incredulous.

"You and Anne?" Frank seemed even more surprised than James. "I knew you were going out with her, but…gee, I guess I still think of you as a kid."

Anacleto assured them that they had both grown up and that he loved her.

"And…you're going to marry her?" Frank asked.

"Not yet. Only because I'm in school and we d…don't have enough money. That's all that's holding us back. She's the one for me."

His brothers smiled and shook their heads.

***

Later that day, as Anacleto and Anne traveled by subway to the Museum of Modern Art, he tried, one more time, to convince her to stay in school. She insisted that she had made up her mind.

"You're really doing this? Going for a job interview where Roseanne works?"

"Yes. I want to. My head is not into studying and I want to earn money, so I might as well make a clean break now, and get a job."

"I said I would give you money."

"Don't worry. I still have the money you gave me when we first went out, but I'm going to need more. I won't need your money. Concentrate on school."

"Don't ever say 'your money' again," he said, more harshly than he had meant to.

Anne, not the least bit ruffled, smiled and said, "My man. He wants to provide for us."

He pretended to be grumpy.

"Did I tell you my father called?" she asked.

"No. When?"

"Oh…last night. I didn't speak to him."

"So…what's the deal?"

"I don't know. My mother just said he's been busy, but he would come around tomorrow."

"Tomorrow? He never comes over…I mean he's usually away on Sundays, right?"

"Usually," she answered. Then she continued, "I don't believe him anymore. I'm sure he has a girlfriend. It doesn't make sense that he spends so much time on the road."

"Oh?" That was all he could think of saying.

"I've been lying to myself for years. I've always suspected that something fishy is going on. My mother either believes him or she's a good liar too."

"Let it be, Anne. You…we have a bigger problem now."

"I know. But, you know what? I don't give a damn what he thinks. He's my father and all, but he's not part of my life. I don't give a damn."

"I understand, but he has a temper. It's worse than Santo's, you know."

"I don't want you there when I tell him. He might decide to take it out on you, and I couldn't stand that," she said.

"I'm not afraid of him...or anybody anymore."

"I know."

And she nestled her head against his chest.

A TIME FOR REUNIONS

The next day, Sunday, was a time for reunions. George breezed into the house at eight in the morning, awakening everyone. Lucia beamed with pride and joy. Anacleto held back as Frank and James hugged and kissed George. Then George looked at Anacleto and rubbed his eyes.

"Anacleto, you're so big. You're a man. Come here," and he gripped his youngest brother in a bear hug. Anacleto's eyes filled with tears.

"I got a big announcement," George declared. "I spoke to Ronnie last night. He'll be here today."

"Oh, my God! Oh, my God!" Lucia held her arms up and repeated, "Oh, my God!"

When everyone had quieted down, George, still smiling, added, "But, he was hurt."

Before any of them could ask George any questions, he continued, "He got burned…over there …in Nam. He was in a hospital. He's okay now. That's why he's coming home. But he was burned."

"Burned where?" Frank asked.

"A lot of places…his back, his arms, a little on his face."

"Oh, no, God, no!" Lucia fell to her knees and hit the sides of her head with her palms.

Frank picked her up and put her on a chair.

"It coulda been a helluva lot worse, Ma. I saw guys die. I saw guys with arms and legs blown off." He hesitated, looked at her, then he said, "He's alive, Ma, and he'll be all right. He just needs to go to the VA for rehab."

"And you, Georgie, you okay?"

"Yeah, I'm all in one piece, Ma. Say, what's for breakfast? I'm starved."

She pulled herself together, and made scrambled eggs, toast, and coffee for everyone. George told some funny stories about some of the men he had met in the service. He didn't say anything else about his tour in Vietnam except that "It was hell every day."

Anacleto called Anne and told her the news. A couple of hours later, he managed to get out of the house. His brothers had decided to visit some friends, saying they would be back soon; they invited Anacleto to go along, but he told them that he would rather stay around and wait for Ronnie.

Anacleto and Anne waited on his stoop.

"My father's coming today," Anne said.

"I know. You told me."

"I know. I guess I'll wait until he's had a chance to talk to my mom and play with Peter before I drop the bomb on him."

"You know, you don't look pregnant. I mean, your breasts, but that's all."

"You're being kind. I show," she complained.

They sat there, talking, watching the slow traffic on the street.

When Leo Faricola drove up and parked, Anne got up and walked to him. She kissed him on the cheek and talked to him by his car for a minute.

"Why didn't you come over?" she asked when she returned to her spot next to Anacleto.

"I don't know. I don't usually say hello to him. He doesn't like me," he replied.

"That's not true. He's just one of those You Have To Say Hello To Me First kind of people," Anne explained.

"Well, I'm just one of those You Can Screw Yourself Before I Run Over To You kind of people," he rejoined.

"He may be a shit, but he's my father. You have to try to be nice," Anne said petulantly.

"I'm sorry."

"It's okay. You can say whatever you want, but, please try to get along with him…for me."

"Of course," he promised.

The third homecoming was, of course, Ronnie's. A khaki-colored Army sedan pulled up to the curb. Anacleto opened the house door and called his mother, and then he and Anne walked to the car. The car door opened and Ronnie slowly stepped out and stood on the sidewalk. He smiled at them, probably not recognizing Anne, and he reached for Anacleto. It was obvious that any kind of stretching was painful for him. The right side of his face was pink and Anacleto could see redness on his neck.

As Ronnie put his arms on Anacleto's shoulders, he warned him to be careful. They kissed each other lightly on their cheeks. The driver, a young private, and an older man, a sergeant, stood nearby and watched.

When Lucia got to Ronnie, Anacleto grabbed her first and reminded her to touch him gently. She stood there and examined him. Then she stood on her toes and kissed his cheek. She took him by the hand and led him, limping, to the house.

Anne smiled sadly at Anacleto; then she went home.

Anacleto invited the two soldiers into the house. They followed. While Lucia helped Ronnie to walk to the kitchen, Anacleto asked the two soldiers what they knew about him.

"All that we know, sir, is that your brother has been discharged from active duty. Here are his papers. One set is from the doctors who treated him."

Anacleto thanked them and asked if they would like to have a bite to eat or a drink. They declined. Then they left.

The reunion with Ronnie was bittersweet. He was happy to be home, but, although he tried to hide it, his fears and anxieties came through. It was obvious that he would need a great deal of medical treatment and rehabilitation before he would be able to return to a normal life, if ever.

When George, James, and Frank returned, they greeted Ronnie without touching him. George had warned the others to be careful.

Anacleto was happy that his brothers were all home, especially because his mother was so pleased. They stayed in and kept her company for the rest of the day.

When they all decided to go to a neighborhood bar, and asked Anacleto to join them, he felt he couldn't say no. He thought it was ironic that, during all the years he had craved their companionship, he had been rejected; now that he didn't need them, they wanted him.

Frank drove. Ronnie had the front passenger seat to himself, while George, James, and Anacleto squeezed into the back. Ronnie squirmed uncomfortably the entire time he was in the car.

At Monahan's, Anacleto sipped his beer, while George, James, and Frank guzzled away. Ronnie, after a couple of beers, looked more relaxed. He said that he was on pain killers, so he had to limit his alcoholic intake. The other brothers polished off three or four beers each and then they competed to see who could down the most shots of whiskey. The more they drank, the sillier they became…until they decided they needed to get laid.

A group of girls had smiled at the brothers early in the evening. One had even sent an air kiss to Frank, who had always been a magnet for women. By the time George, James, and Frank approached them, however, they were sloppy drunk. The girls, who had struck up conversations with some other men by this point, made it clear that they were no longer interested in talking with the brothers.

"Why…not?" asked George, his speech slurred and his gaze unsteady.

"You're very nice, I'm sure…when you're sober. Not tonight," one of them said. She had the fluffiest teased blond hair that Anacleto had ever seen.

George leered at her. James and Frank were almost as drunk, but they held back, hoping, somehow, that George could persuade the girls to overlook their condition and take them back to wherever they lived.

The other men at the bar decided that they had given George enough time to back off, so they pushed him. He stumbled and almost fell.

"What the fuck?…What the fuck?" was all George could say, as he searched for a place to sit.

James and Frank cursed, but they realized that they were too incapacitated to uphold George's honor. Only Ronnie and Anacleto were sober. At midnight, Anacleto convinced his intoxicated brothers to get into Frank's car. He drove.

"If An-a-clee-toe didn't have a steady lay, he woulda hustled those babes today," George sang.

Anacleto ignored him.

"Anne…little Annie Fannie Faricola…Santo's sister," Frank said. Anacleto could see him, in the rearview mirror, smiling and shaking his head.

"Yeah. She's turned into some nice piece of ass," James contributed.

Anacleto kept driving, knowing what was coming next.

"And…guess what?" James sounded as if he was half asleep.

"What?" Ronnie and George asked at the same time.

"He…knocked her…he knocked her up!" James and Frank blurted out.

George smiled his silliest smile.

Ronnie looked like he was in excruciating pain.

"Should I stop, Ronnie? Do you have to get out or move or something?" Anacleto asked.

He shook his head and whispered through his agony, "It's…okay…Drive."

"What the hell? You…stink!" James complained from the backseat.

"Whoever smelt it, dealt it," George answered.

"I was…talking to Frankie, but…I guess you did it," James said to George.

They began hitting each other and belching and laughing.

"Some things never change," Anacleto said.

"Yeah, well, some things…do," Ronnie replied, as he tried to find a position in which his injuries would not cause him as much pain. "My Vietnam souvenirs," he said through gritted teeth.

***

The next morning, Anacleto walked Anne to the subway station.

"Sorry I didn't call you last night to hear how it went. My brothers and I went out drinking and—"

"Drinking?" Anne could not suppress a smile.

"Yeah, I know. I was the sore thumb there. In any case, we didn't get in until after midnight. How was it?"

"Besides the abuse I had to take from my father, of all the damn stinking luck, Santo dropped by for a visit."

"With your father there?"

"Of course. He's never home on Sundays...and Santo brought Roseanne to visit. He had called my mom earlier in the day to tell her he was coming, and she never said a word about my father," she complained. "She just doesn't think sometimes."

"So, what happened?"

"It was bad. My mother and I just finished telling my father about me...about us. He was furious. He wanted to go to your house, even though I told him you're sticking by me. He cursed and screamed. I'm surprised you didn't hear him."

"I guess we were making a lot of noise too," Anacleto said.

"Tell me about Ronnie."

"There's a lot to tell, but finish your story first."

"To make a long, terrible story short, my father was in the middle of his ranting and raving when Santo walked in. My dad didn't say hello or show that he was happy to see him—my mom had told him that she had seen Santo—he just started grilling Santo about where he had been and what he had been doing and—"

"That's a normal thing for a parent to ask."

"Yes and no. He wasn't looking for answers; he was...trying to catch Santo in a lie. He wanted a chance to yell at him," Anne remarked sadly.

She sighed.

"He wasn't cool about it—Santo. He blew up. He used my father's anger... his hostility? No, that's not the word," Anne said.

"Enmity?" Anacleto suggested.

"Oh, that's a good word," Anne teased. "No. I keep thinking of *bell* or *ante...bellum* or..."

"Oh...you mean...belligerence."

"Yes. He used my father's belligerence to argue instead of answering him."

"I'm sure that was nice."

"I don't know who was the bigger idiot," Anne remarked disgustedly.

"What about your mother?"

"She was horrified, especially because Roseanne was there. And Peter, he cried and cried. My father actually told me to shut Peter up."

"Well—"

"I took him out of the house and went for a walk with Roseanne," Anne said. "I was worried the whole time that Santo and my father were going to kill each other."

"I understand."

"So, when we got back, Santo told Roseanne that they were going. He said he wouldn't come over again unless he was sure my father wouldn't be there."

"I guess that's the best thing."

They had reached the subway station. Anacleto turned away from Anne, fearful that his eyes might reveal his fear of impending doom.

"I guess it could have been worse," she said. She suddenly looked tired and ill.

"You're not feeling sick, are you?"

"No. I've been lucky. I told you, I've been sick only a couple of times. I'm just sad. We're back together, and there's so much…hostility. So, tell me about Ronnie."

"He has trouble moving because of his burns, but you saw that. He's going to need lots of rehab. I hope he'll be all right."

"We all have to live with our consequences," she said. "But he didn't deserve that."

***

Ronnie was scheduled for rehabilitation sessions three days a week. Since James lived and worked in Manhattan, Frank and George worked long hours, and Anacleto was busy with classes, work, and studying, Lucia was the one who drove him to the VA hospital most of the time. George had filled out an application for the police department; he knew he wouldn't be called for the test for months.

Frank had been told by the doctor who had examined him for his induction physical that he had a heart murmur and that he would not qualify for the service. He patted his chest and thanked God for his defect.

Ronnie was relieved to hear the news.

"You know, before I got drafted, I thought I'd become a fireman," Ronnie reflected during dinner one evening. "How's that for a laugh?" he said as he painfully reached across the table for milk to pour into his coffee.

Lucia was happier than she had been in years, since before her husband had died. She did not ask about Anne, which was fine with Anacleto.

Anne got the job in the construction office with Roseanne. She took a leave from Hunter College, and started working immediately.

Anacleto hadn't seen Santo in a couple of weeks, but he had spoken with him on the phone a few times. He said he was working hard, pleased to be drawing a steady paycheck. Each time they talked, Santo carried on about his father.

"Do you believe the balls on that guy? That bastard that goes home to his wife every night, he's got the balls to talk about Roseanne. I swear to you, I will kill him if he ever says anything about her again."

"Santo, don't do this. Calm down. You're not killing anybody."

"And you and Anne. He said she was a tramp and you're a lowlife. What balls!"

"Santo, it's all right," Anacleto assured him before he hung up.

Then he tried to reassure himself.

THE STANDOFF

Late one misty evening, Anacleto looked out of a window, and saw, through the haze, a car with two men sitting in it parked across the street from Anne's house. It was a Mustang. In the dim light of the street lamps, the car appeared to be blue, but he wasn't sure. He walked down the stairs and carefully opened the door. He still couldn't tell. He told himself it was probably a different car with different people, but he needed to be sure, so he walked up to his room to get his shoes. Then he walked down the stairs again. When he opened the house door, the car was gone.

***

A few days passed. Anne saw it before Anacleto did.

"Oh, my God," she whispered.

It was early evening. They were walking home from the movies. There was the blue Mustang. The driver's side window rolled down.

"Hello, Annie. How you doing?" Steve called from across the street. He studiously avoided acknowledging Anacleto.

"What are you doing here?" she asked angrily.

"I'm waiting for you, babe," he replied.

Anacleto told Anne to wait, and he walked to the car. He tried to look more sure of himself than he felt.

"Sh…she's w…with me, Steve."

"Used merchandise." He laughed. Darren, next to him, smiled and lit a cigarette.

Ignoring his taunt, which was chewing up his insides, Anacleto asked, "What d…do you really w…want?"

"I c…come to s…see my old g…girl…friend." Steve's imitation of Anacleto sent him into a fit of raucous laughter.

Calmly, Anacleto suggested to him, "You don't w…want her now, Steve."

"Yeah? Why not?"

"She's dif…ferent. Believe m…me, you don't want her," he repeated.

"Well, I'll tell you what: I'll settle for a chance to talk to Santo. You seen him lately?"

"Not for a long time. I think he m…moved upstate."

"Oh, yeah? What's his address?" Steve challenged.

"I…don't know." Anacleto concentrated on speaking slowly so that he wouldn't stammer.

"Well then, it's a standoff. I want to speak to Santo, but he ain't around, so me and Darren, we'll just wait."

"That's okay," Anacleto said, and walked back to Anne.

"Hey, Annie, you're lookin' good. How's about we go to your room?" Steve opened his car door and started getting out.

"Don't waste your breath, Steve. I wouldn't let you near me…if we were the last two people alive on Earth," Anne called out.

By now, several neighbors were watching the scene from their windows.

"Gee, you used to love it. You forget?" he said, as he approached them.

Anacleto moved in front of Anne, blocking Steve.

"Oh. You're brave now?" he said, going nose to nose with Anacleto.

"You m…mean like you were br…brave that t…time, when you had a gun in your hand and Santo didn't?" Anacleto didn't move.

Glaring at Anacleto with a venomous look, Steve said, "Yeah. Well, you gotta know the fuckin' rules. By the way, in case you think I forgot, I owe you, you piece of shit! These little scars on my face are from you."

"You, get outta here. I'm calling the cops!" Mrs. Albanese called out from her door. A couple of other neighbors came out of their homes.

"Drop dead, lady!" Steve called out.

"Hey, you, watch it!" That was Mr. Weisenberg, who was a retired high school principal.

"Screw you, baldy!" Steve yelled.

Anacleto continued to stand between Steve and Anne, his arms down, attempting to appear resolute and unafraid, but not aggressive. Steve pushed Anacleto. He held firm; then he quickly turned and nudged Anne out of the way. Steve pushed him again; he lost his balance and fell to the sidewalk. Steve laughed and told Anacleto to get up. At that point, Darren stepped out of his car and walked toward them.

If the sight of a dissolute-looking stranger, cursing and pushing a neighborhood resident upset the observers of the scene, the appearance of a tall, powerfully built black man set off alarm bells. Before Anacleto could stand up to face Steve, Mr. Caspari, Mr. Santoro, Mr. Shannon, Mr. Cohen, who was a Holocaust survivor, and a man who Anacleto didn't know approached Steve and Darren. They told the strangers to leave. Steve stood his ground, but Darren understood the neighborhood boundaries of Brooklyn. He knew he would receive more than his fair share of punishment, if it came to that. He took a few steps away from the confrontation.

Anne returned to Anacleto's side. She was ghostly white. He told her to go to her house, but she shook her head no.

"We just need to have a friendly talk. That's all. We're buddies. Annie used to be my girl," Steve explained to the neighborhood men in mild tones.

"This don't look friendly to me," said Mr. Santoro.

Two more men from the neighborhood joined the group. One of them, Mr. Woodmere, was a police officer. He told Steve and Darren to leave and said that he would be running a check on the license plate of the blue Mustang.

"Really, sir," Steve said, civility and respect dripping from his tongue, "we're just here to talk to Santo. If he ain't around, then I gotta talk to this guy, his friend, and her, his sister."

"Go home now," Mr. Woodmere repeated.

"I will. We don't want no trouble. I just wanna talk," Steve implored, acting, for all the world, like a peacemaker.

Darren had gotten back into the car. Mr. Woodmere looked at Anacleto.

"It's okay, Mr. Woodmere. I'll l…listen to Steve."

"Look, officer, you can run my plates. It's my car. I don't owe no tickets or nothin'. Just let me talk to the man."

After looking at Anacleto again, Mr. Woodmere told Steve that he'd be watching. Then he and the other men walked to a spot a short distance down the sidewalk.

"Look, punk. I will kick your ass some other time. I'll break your fuckin' back, but not now," Steve snarled.

As he said the word "back," Anacleto felt his spinal column tighten and snap.

"I want Santo. In fact," he whispered, "if you tell me where he is, I'll keep it my secret and I won't fuck you up or Anne or her mama or that little boy."

Anacleto wanted to lunge at Steve's skinny neck and squeeze the life out of him. He knew that Darren would stay out of it. And, with Mr. Woodmere there, Steve wouldn't pull a weapon, if he had one. But there had been too much of that. Anacleto decided that he had to remain in control.

"That doesn't sound very fr…friendly, Steve."

"Yeah? It's friendlier than what you guys did to me." He held up a scarred, inflamed hand.

"I th…think you hurt your hand when you shot Santo in the head."

"Yeah, that's right. I put one in his head, but he ain't dead. Ha. I'm a poet and don't even know it." He smiled a dirty smile.

"Look, I d…don't know where Santo is. He doesn't come around. I don't even know if he re…recovered from the gunshot. And…if I did know, I wouldn't tell you, so…go h…home," he suggested.

"Okay, but I gotta tell Annie something first."

"No!" Anacleto said, louder than he meant to.

Steve smiled. "You're afraid she might wanna kiss me, right?"

"A piece of sh…shit like you might just hurt a girl—right?"

"Naw. I still like her. I wanna talk to her."

He began walking around Anacleto to reach Anne, but Anacleto blocked his way; he kept his arms crossed so that he didn't touch Steve.

Steve looked at the group of men, twenty feet away, and stopped.

"Hey, Annie, I wanna talk to you. Then I'll go," he said.

Anne came from behind Anacleto.

"No, Anne. Don't—"

"It's okay," she said, standing next to Anacleto and looking at Steve. Steve kept his eyes on her and pretended not to have noticed her placing a hand on Anacleto's arm.

"Naw. I gotta talk to you alone…just for a second," Steve whined.

"You're not going to," Anacleto vowed.

"It this gets him out of here, I'll talk to him alone," Anne said.

Steve smiled, and walked across the street to his car, beckoning Anne to follow him. She walked slowly, keeping her distance. Steve opened his car door and pushed his seat forward so that Anne would be able to get in the back. She froze in her tracks; Anacleto's heart jumped. He took a step forward. Steve smiled, pushed the seat back and got in. Then he closed the car door. Anacleto moved back.

Anne stood next to the driver's side door, talking to Steve, who sat behind the steering wheel, lighting a cigarette. Anacleto saw Steve's hand reach for her; she took a step back. Then he said something and she moved closer. When he reached for her again, she did not move. Anacleto couldn't see where Steve's hand was because Anne was blocking his view. Steve's hand stayed where it was for what seemed an eternity. Then Anne turned away from Steve and began walking back to Anacleto. Steve started his car, gunned the engine, and, without checking for oncoming cars, peeled out and sped noisily down the street, racing through the intersection. Anne had to jump to avoid being sideswiped.

Why couldn't a truck have been coming through the intersection at that moment?

He would have clapped and cheered along with Mr. Caspari this time if he had called out, "Sounds like a good one, boys! Let's go!"

Anne was shaking and crying. Anacleto walked her to her door. The crowd of neighbors remained where they were, talking and pointing to the intersection.

"Hi, there," Francine called from the bathroom as Anne and Anacleto passed by. They heard water splashing and saw Peter laughing and playing in the tub as

Francine bathed him. Anacleto called out hello to Francine. Anne went straight to her to her room, threw herself on her bed, and sobbed.

"What did he say? Why did he touch you?"

"He says he has to talk to Santo. He's going to come back every day until he sees him. He says nobody's going to stop him."

"I'll talk to Mr. Woodmere. I'll tell him to check Steve out. Maybe he can get him arrested."

"He said more, Clete; he said he'll hurt Peter or my mom or me if he doesn't talk to Santo."

"It won't happen, Anne. I know where he stays. I'll…take c…care of him."

"No! You'll get hurt or in trouble. And…you can't tell Santo. No."

"Don't worry. Why did he touch you?"

"He…just tried to…to…make me like him again, I guess."

"Where did he touch you?"

"Oh,…don't be so possessive. He wanted to…touch my breasts, but I wouldn't let him, so he put his hand on my wrist…maybe, just to make you jealous."

"I wasn't…I'm not jealous. I thought he was hurting you. That's all."

"He didn't hurt me. He disgusted me and he scared me." Then she turned over and sobbed into her pillow.

SIGNED, SEALED, DELIVERED...

Anacleto did not tell Santo about Steve's threats. If Santo had known, he would have taken the bait and fallen into the trap. Anacleto and Anne gave Francine a sanitized version of the confrontation with Steve. They warned her to steer clear of him.

"I never liked that boy…" She stopped herself.

"It's okay, Ma. Clete knows I went out with him."

Francine looked sick.

***

"What if the baby is horrid and crazy like Steve?" Anne asked Anacleto the next day.

"I think Steve must have had a bad home life. Your…our baby won't," he reassured her.

"But Santo had a…good home life. Well, not good, but not bad, and look at him," she replied.

"Santo's not Steve. He was a tyrant when he was a kid…because your father's always been hard on him, but your mom more than made up for that. I think he didn't feel good about himself, so he always tried to appear tough. That's why the guys his age re…jected h…him. Now, he's tough and he's fiery and…he's made bad choices, but he's not a bad guy…and he's straightening himself out now."

"But…how did he…why did he get involved in drugs…selling them?"

There it was again. Anacleto felt that he and Anne were as close as two people could be; he couldn't imagine how their bond could be any more intimate and loving, but this involved her father and mother and brother. He had to hold his tongue.

"I know this much," he said. "Santo wanted your mom to leave your father. He wanted money for that. He said your mother had nothing and that she would be better off without him."

"I know he feels that way. I do too, but it's her decision, not mine and not Santo's."

"I know. I'm just telling you…he sold drugs to get money for her to leave him."

"He's got a girlfriend. I'm sure of it, and my mom knows."

"How…do you know?"

"I answered the phone a couple of weeks ago. I've tried to push this from my mind, but I can't. I answered it. I hoped it was my father. That was when he wasn't coming home. A woman was on the line. She asked for Francine. Then I heard my mom talking to her, even though she pulled the phone into another room so I couldn't hear."

"And you think she was—"

"It had to be a girlfriend. All I could make out for sure was my mom saying something like, 'It's up to him' and 'He has three children' and something strange. I mean those other things are strange too. It had to be my father she was talking about… 'three children.' What else could that mean? I mean who else? She had to be referring to him."

"I guess…it sounds like it," he said. "What's the other strange thing…she said?"

"She said…it was like my mom didn't resent this woman…She said something like, 'We're in this together' and 'All I need is money for my rent and food and for the kids.' I was upset when I heard that."

"I understand. You shouldn't have to be upset, ever. You put up with so much shit."

"You do too," Anne sighed. "Sometimes I think life is just one long…pointless slog through shit."

***

"He's a dr…drug dealer, Mr. Woodmere."

"How do you know that, Anacleto?"

"I know somebody who knows…"

"Well, I ran the plate. It belongs to a Stephen Larrison. It's clean. He's clean."

"That just means he's never been arrested, right?"

"Yes."

"Well, he still deals drugs. I know where."

"I gotta know this first: Are you part of this?" he asked.

"No. He used to go out with Anne. He's very poss…possessive. He threatened her and her mother and Peter."

"Then she has to have an order of protection taken out against him."

"Okay, I'll tell her that, but…he wants to hurt Santo."

"Why?"

"I'm telling you th…this as a fr…a neigh—"

"You can say 'friend.'"

"Thanks. Santo served some time in jail…upstate. He was involved with St…Steve…but Santo's clean now. He has a good job and a girlfriend."

"Does he know about this thing with Steve?"

"No. If I told him…if Anne told him, he'd be looking for Steve. That would be bad."

"How do you know so much, Anacleto?"

"Santo's my friend and Anne and her mom and Peter are important to me. I've l…learned a lot."

"I'll check it all out," he promised.

"You can do more than that…I know where Steve deals drugs."

"You have the actual address?"

"No, but I can show you."

"Now you're worrying me. Why were you there?"

"It…it's not important. I don't buy drugs and I d…don't use them…ever."

"Why were you there? If you want me to trust you, I have to know," he insisted.

Anacleto hesitated for only a second before he told the story, with some minor variations from the truth.

"So, let me get this straight...you and Santo went to this building in Flatbush and had a fight with Steve and that black guy, right?" He wrote notes on a pad.

"His name is Darren, but I'm not worried about him. Steve's the dangerous one. I hope this doesn't get Santo in trouble," Anacleto fretted.

"You should worry about yourself," he advised.

"Right."

"Why were you guys there?" Mr. Woodmere's stare was hard and dispassionate.

"Santo wanted to tell Steve something…about how he was clean and not dealing anymore."

"Why did he have to tell him? Why not just steer clear of him?" he asked.

"That doesn't work. When Steve wants to find you, he does. That's why he was here the other day…to find Santo."

"Why?"

"I don't know. Maybe to try to convince him to deal drugs again. I really don't know."

"I'll look into it. Meanwhile, tell Anne and her mother to file an order of protection," he advised.

"What about where he sells drugs? I can show you."

"I don't know," Mr. Woodmere responded.

"It's twenty minutes from here. I can find it. I'll show you the building; then you'll have the address. Please."

"Okay, but I can't promise you anything."

Mr. Woodmere drove. Anacleto didn't remember the exact street on which the building was located, but he knew which subway station they had exited that day, so they started from there. After a couple of wrong turns, during which time Mr. Woodmere sighed and Anacleto became panicky because he thought he might not recognize the building, he spotted it. Mr. Woodmere wrote down the address.

Then they drove home.

Sitting on Anne's bed, they talked about his conversation with Mr. Woodmere and about the order of protection.

"I didn't get Steve's address from Mr. Woodmere. He probably has it…from the license plate check. I can ask him, and you can file that order."

"I don't know. I don't think he lives there anymore. I told you...it was his brother's place."

"Right. I forgot...you told me." Anacleto was surprised that the thought of Anne and Steve alone in his brother's apartment...the fact of Anne and Steve together as a couple didn't bother him anymore.

"I guess I could fill out the order. Do you think that will work?" she asked.

"Truthfully…no. He'd probably still prowl the neighborhood, waiting for a chance to catch Santo…or you or your mom or Peter."

"I'm scared."

"I know. Let's see if Mr. Woodmere can arrest him because of the drug dealing."

"I can't stand this," Anne cried.

"I won't let him hurt you."

"I'm not usually so quick to worry. It's my hormones. I'm beginning to feel different," she said.

"Different? How different? About what?"

"About me. Everything seems different. Food even tastes different."

"What about…other things?" Anacleto asked.

"Now, you have to stop worrying. That will never change," she assured him.

***

The next day, Mr. Woodmere told Anacleto that he had asked a couple of police officers who worked in the precinct where the building was located to check out the courtyard. They said they knew the building. It was one of several abandoned buildings in that neighborhood that had become outlets for illegal drugs. It had been raided in the past.

"Nobody was there. Plenty of evidence of drug dealing in the courtyard, but nothing to tie it to Steve. Sorry," Mr. Woodmere said.

"But…the neighborhood people…they could identify Steve, I'll bet," Anacleto suggested.

"They talked to some of them. They confirmed that dealing was going on. They had called with complaints. I told you…it's a known drug center. Trouble is, right after a sweep, somebody new sets up shop."

"But…they could identify Steve, and then you could arrest him."

"It doesn't work that way. We have to catch them in the act." He thought for a second. Then he continued, "You weren't straight with me, Anacleto. There was a call to that building a few weeks ago. There was a fight…a gunshot. Witnesses described Steve and Darren, but they also described two young men who sound an awful lot like Santo and you."

"I said we were there, but there wasn't any gunshot."

"Really? The one who sounds like Santo had a wound to his head and he was being helped by the one who sounds like you. And a shattered pistol of some kind was found in the courtyard."

"I…I…I guess—"

"Look—don't tell me anything else. If I can pick up this Stephen Larrison, I will. Keep your nose clean."

"Thanks."

"And…give my best to Anne. I hope she feels all right," he said.

Anacleto wondered what he meant by that.

***

Nobody in Anacleto's family had asked a thing about Anne. He had not expected his mother to tap a vein of sympathy or understanding that she did not possess, but…his brothers...None of them asked about Anne.

He couldn't bring Anne to his house. The only times that she had been there were those three wonderful days when his mother had visited George in Virginia.

Santo called his mother one Sunday morning to make sure his father would not be there. When Francine promised him that the coast was clear, Santo said he would be there at noon. He had asked his mother to wait outside for Roseanne and him. Francine asked why, but all he would say was that it was a surprise. She waited with Peter; Anne and Anacleto were there too.

They heard it before they saw it. A shiny, red Pontiac Catalina rumbled to a stop in front of the house. The radio was blasting. Santo opened his window and smiled proudly at them.

"I decided…I work hard…Roseanne works hard…so what's the money for?" Santo asked.

He took Francine and Peter for a ride while Roseanne stayed with Anne and Anacleto. She asked Anacleto how he was doing. He told her that he was working lots of hours at the college library and carrying a full course load.

"And," Anne added proudly, "he saves all his money for the baby."

"You're quite a guy, Clete," Roseanne remarked.

"Well, there's nothing much I need right now," he answered.

"I wish I could say the same about Santo. He's a hard worker too, but he spends his money before he has it," Roseanne complained.

"The car," Anne said.

"Yup," Roseanne agreed.

Just then, Santo sped down the street and screeched to a stop. Francine got out, carrying Peter.

"Very nice, Santo, but I think I'll walk from now on," she said, catching her breath.

"Come on. Get in," Santo commanded.

Anne and Anacleto climbed in the back seat and Roseanne sat next to Santo.

"Be back later, Ma," he said, as he gunned the engine, put the car into gear, and peeled out from the curb.

He drove dangerously fast on the local streets. They reached the Belt Parkway in half the time it should have taken. He drove east, toward Queens and Long Island way over the speed limit. As they shot past Jamaica Bay, the air that swept into the car through the partially opened windows felt damp and cold. Anne clung to Anacleto for warmth and protection. He held her close.

"Santo, slow down," Roseanne pleaded.

"You only live once, babe," Santo bellowed. He turned up the volume on the radio, and they all sang along with Stevie Wonder: "Signed, sealed, delivered…I'm yours."

Then Santo slowed down and pulled into a rest stop along the highway. They got out.

"So, whadda you think?" Santo asked.

"It's great. It's a beauty. I'm glad for you," Anacleto replied.

Santo beamed.

"When you gonna buy a car, Clete?"

"Not for a while. I have to finish college and start a job. Then I'll think about it."

"You're working. I'll connect you to my guy. I paid almost nothing for this baby," he announced proudly.

"If you call two thousand dollars almost nothing," Roseanne interjected.

"That's a good price. You know what they go for new?"

"It doesn't matter, Santo. I thought we were going to look for a bigger apartment or save money to buy a condo some day," she complained.

"Sure…we'll do that," Santo said.

"No we won't. You don't save anything," Roseanne said.

"Don't break my balls. I'm makin' good money. I just wanted a car."

"Whatever, Santo," Roseanne said, throwing up her hands.

Anacleto changed the subject by telling Santo about his college classes. Santo seemed genuinely interested. They walked away from Anne and Roseanne, toward a bench under some trees.

"I always said you were smart. I wish you coulda taught me how to be," Santo said.

"And I always wished you could've taught me how to live."

"You're doin' great now."

"Well, I wouldn't call it great, but I'm okay. It's t…taken me long enough."

"Nobody gave you a chance—that's what it was," Santo said.

"You did. You know, you're still my only friend."

"I always will be."

"How's work?" Anacleto asked.

"It's great. I'm in the union and makin' good money, just like I said before."

"Good. I guess we're all okay."

"How about Annie? She's lookin' nice. People ain't askin' yet, right?"

"No. I don't think she really looks pregnant," Anacleto said.

"Naw, but soon. You better get ready for a shit storm."

"I already went through part of it with my mother. She had a fit,…as I knew she would. Now, she won't even look at Anne. And my brothers…they didn't pass judgment, but they never ask about her."

"You know how it is…guys look down on women…like Anne—not that they should. There we are…all of us—except for Saint Anacleto—we're all banging every broad we can get and, when one turns up…you know—knocked up—we call her a tramp. It ain't right, but that's how it goes."

"Is that how you feel?" Anacleto asked.

"You gotta be kiddin'. Me? Anne and my mother—both of them knocked up and not married? Me—I'm that kid…just like the one inside of Annie. But that little guy is luckier than me—he's got you for a father. I got a piece of shit for a father."

"You know, Anne suspects something." Anacleto told him about the phone call from the woman who Anne suspected was Leo Faricola's girlfriend.

"That sounds like his…wife. Tell me again what Anne heard my ma say."

Anacleto repeated as much of it as he remembered.

"I think he must be getting pressure from her—his wife—to stay away."

"He hasn't been around as much as usual lately," Anacleto added.

"Yeah—except that one Sunday I dropped by for a visit."

"Too bad. No sense having a confrontation with him."

"Next time he gets in my face, I'll use that knife on him!"

"Then he would be dead and your mother wouldn't have any money…and you would be in jail—for life."

"Yeah. You're right. You're always right."

Anacleto smiled, and then he couldn't resist saying, "And don't you forget it."

RONNIE'S STORY

Lucia had wanted to have a Welcome Home party as soon as George and Ronnie were back, but Ronnie kept asking her to put it off. Now, almost a month later, she couldn't wait anymore.

"And we'll have it next Sunday. And all the family will be here—both sides, and you can invite your friends. I'll make macaroni and roast pork and I'll bake," she excitedly told her sons.

"I'm bringing Anne," Anacleto told her.

"No! No, you're not. No!"

"If she can't come, I won't be here," he calmly told her.

"But they're your brothers," she said, pointing to George and Ronnie.

"And she's my girlfriend. And, we're going to get married as soon as I finish college."

"But…it's not right. She's…used—"

"Ma, don't say that. She's my girlfriend. I'm not going to have another one…ever. I know this is hard on you, but either she comes and you treat her right or I won't be here."

"But, people will know."

"They're going to find out sooner or later."

"Oh, my God…such a shame!" She shook her head in resignation.

***

Anacleto had asked his brothers to reach out to Anne during the party, and they did…a little stiffly, except for Ronnie. His injuries and his pain had turned him into a quiet, morose man who accepted whatever came his way. He expected very little, so he was never disappointed. He viewed Anne as a fellow sufferer, someone else who had been damaged by the vagaries of life. As such, he felt a special closeness with her. They talked a lot during the party.

Lucia was formal and coldly polite to Anne. She was grateful that Anne was wearing a thick sweater. No one asked her about her condition.

Toward evening, after everyone had consumed large quantities of food and beer and homemade wine, the conversations became more boisterous and expressive. Anacleto sat with Anne and his brothers and a group of relatives who had gone into the backyard. It was unseasonably warm for early April. The only illumination came from a hurricane lantern on a nearby table.

"We should drop an H bomb on those yellow Commie bastards," Carmine, one of Lucia's cousins announced.

"That would kill all of our guys there, Carmine," Ronnie commented.

"No…I don't mean in the South. They should drop it on Hanoi," Carmine explained.

This led to an argument between those who, at this late stage of the war, were still hawks and those who saw the writing on the wall.

"There's going to be a negotiated settlement. There has to be," intoned Uncle Richie.

"Oh, listen to the diplomat—a ne-go-she-a-ted settlement," teased another cousin.

"We shoulda dropped the bomb on North Korea…back then. I was there, you know," said Carmine.

Everyone quickly told him that they knew. They had all heard his war stories over and over again.

"What do you think, Georgie? How's it going to end?" asked Aunt Felicia.

"How? I don't know. I thought we were doing the right thing, but…" He looked at Ronnie, who was trying to put off taking his pain medication. "Now I don't know. I wish there was no such thing as war."

"Everyone agrees on that," said James.

"We have so many problems in this country. Who needs the friggin' war? Who gives a damn about the Vee-et-na-meeze anyway?" asked Richie.

"You're damned right. We got problems with the coloreds in this country—not that they're all wrong," Uncle Joe commented.

"They're mostly wrong," joked Carmine.

"No, they're not," Anacleto said before he realized it.

"Oh, the young liberal. You'll see…You'll become more conservative as you get older," Richie said.

"But, how did it start? After emancipation, those Jim Crow laws. What did Martin Luther King want? He j…just wanted people to accept each other," Anacleto nervously countered.

"They don't want to accept us and we don't want them," Carmine interjected.

"That's not true, Carmine," Anacleto said. "If people only—"

"Naw. You gotta feel bad for those white people down south in…I don't know …Mississippi. They're always having to deal with this integration bullshit," Carmine said.

"Let me tell you all something," Ronnie said. Everyone turned to him. He shifted uncomfortably in his lawn chair and pulled his jacket more tightly up to his exposed neck. Then he continued: "I met a lot of guys in the Army—white men, black men, Puerto Ricans. Some were guys like us. Others were from the west…like Arizona and Utah. Some of them were from the south. They came from little towns in Mississippi and Alabama and Georgia." He stopped talking, and winced. Then, slowly, painfully, he sat up a little straighter.

"You okay?" Frank asked.

Ronnie did not say anything.

"Finish what you were saying, Ronnie," George urged.

Ronnie looked around at the dozen or so people sitting near him. Anacleto held Anne's hand and looked at her because he couldn't stand to see his brother in pain.

"I saw guys get killed. I looked at their bodies. They looked surprised, like they couldn't believe what happened. Guys I knew lost arms and legs or suffered spinal cord injuries. They'll never be able to control their pissing or shitting…ever again. Guys saved other guys. Some of them were so brave. We got along well…out there...in the bush…in the shit. White guys from Arkansas who never even knew black people and black guys from Chicago who never had a white friend were…like brothers."

He stopped talking for a few seconds, and lit a cigarette. His drawn, tired face looked ghostly in the pale light of the match.

"But, you know what?" he continued. "As soon as they had leave—R & R—in some clean, American place like Hawaii or even in Japan, those white guys talked about 'nigger this' and 'nigger that.' I'm sure the black guys talked about 'crackers.' I don't know…they had their group and we had ours. This country is so sick…it's not worth fighting for. This thing that happened to me…if I knew then, when I went in, what I was fighting for..."

He took a long drag on his cigarette and finished his beer—one of the many he drank that night.

"I'm sure you were a brave soldier, Ron," Carmine suggested.

"Brave? Stupid? What's the difference? I did what I was told. You want to know how I got hurt? I'll tell you: we were told to enter a little village…a hamlet actually. If it had a name, I don't remember ever hearing it. Our job was to find the village leader, an old man, and bring him back to our forward base for an interview. He was supposed to be the one who could convince the rest of the villagers to spill their guts to us about where the Viet Cong were."

He opened another can of beer and took a long gulp.

"Oh, yeah…the interview," he continued. "You want to know what the interview was? An intelligence officer would offer the head man money, televisions, whiskey, anything. He would get rich and then he would be more powerful and influential and he would tell the poor slobs in his crappy little town to tell us whatever the hell we wanted to know.

"So, we walk into this disgusting, muddy place and we ask where the village leader is. A little girl who we ask tells us she can take us to him, but first, she tells a little boy something in her language. It wasn't Vietnamese. The ARVN interpreter didn't understand a thing she said. So, the little boy runs off and the girl takes us through the village, looking for the headman. We're stepping in pig shit and babies are crying and it's hot and wet like you can't believe. By the time the girl smiles and tells us that the next hooch belongs to the headman, we don't give a damn anymore. We just want to get back and take baths and drink until we pass out.

"So, we walk to the hut and knock…not that you can really knock…" Ronnie looked at all of them, slowly, one by one, catching each person's eyes. "Then, there's a loud pop and a big blaze in front of us and all around us...and pain—I don't complain about this pain because it's nothing compared to what I felt that day and for three months after. I'm lying there, in the mud, in the pig shit, and I'm burning up like I'm a high school bonfire. And I hear screaming and crying and crackling flames and I smell my flesh burning."

He took another long gulp of his beer.

"That's how fucking brave I was."

Everyone was silent.

Then Carmine said, "You survived. That's bravery. Bravery under enemy fire."

"No," Ronnie replied. "That was my brain and my heart and rest of this mass of cells and organs surviving. I didn't make it. I died back in that shitty Mekong hamlet."

No one, not even Carmine spoke now.

"Oh, yeah…one more thing: it wasn't enemy fire. It was the little boy…the one the little girl spoke to. He threw gasoline on us and the little girl lit a match."

LEO PROTECTS HIS FAMILY

It starts out as a spark falling on dried grass or brush in a distant forest. It may have been the result of a lightning strike or a stray match or an ember from a campfire. That spark gives birth to a flame which may die out right away or after it has consumed all of its fuel, leaving a smoky, ashy residue. Or it may feed on nearby leaves, twigs, or other forest debris and take strength and grow.

***

Steve returned a few times. He parked his car across from where Francine and Anne and Peter lived, and waited. He always left after an hour or so. If Anacleto spotted him first, he would stand next to Steve's car door, and stare at him, silently. Steve didn't dare make a move. He knew that someone was always looking out of a window somewhere.

One day, when he saw Anne, he took a long look at her rounded abdomen and asked her how many months pregnant she was. She told him to screw himself. He smiled and told her that he would be back.

If this had happened years before, when they were kids, the boys from the block would have straightened Steve out. But, now, they were all either in the service, working, or going to one of the local colleges. Albie was the only one who was away at college; he was in West Virginia.

Once or twice, when Anacleto wasn't around, Steve approached Anne and talked dirty to her. Once, she thought he was going to put his hands on her, but he just stared at her until she pushed him away and ran home. She begged Anacleto not to fight with him. He told her he wouldn't if she took out the restraining order. She said that she would talk to her mother about it.

"There's nothing to talk about. Just do it."

"I…can't. I keep thinking that, no matter how bad he is…I don't want to see Steve in jail."

"Why the hell not?" Anacleto asked.

"It's not Steve I'm worried about. I did this. It's all my fault."

"No, no, no. It's not you. He's using you to get to Santo. You know that."

She said that, if he came around again, she would go the police station with her mother and they would file a complaint.

One Saturday morning, Anacleto approached Leo Faricola and told him what had been happening. Anacleto knew that he knew people. Leo didn't care about Anne and he had no interest in Santo, but his face grew darker and angrier as Anacleto repeated what Steve had said about hurting Francine and Peter.

"My wife didn't tell me."

"I guess she hoped he would go away."

"So, what have you been doing to protect them?" he asked.

"What *can* I do? It's not me or Anne or Francine he wants. It's Santo."

"So, tell him where that sonofabitch lives," he suggested.

At that, Anacleto lost it: "You know, Leo, you can be p…pissed off at Santo, but he's still your son, and you should pr...pro…tect him."

"Oh, the little shit is talking," he sneered.

"If I'm a sh...shit, what does that make you?"

"What?" he demanded.

Leo's face turned red and his nostrils flared and he raised his big fists, but his curiosity and fear got the better of him.

"What the hell do you mean by that?" he asked.

"Think about it."

"No. Tell me," he demanded.

"I know where you are when you're not here with Francine and Peter and Anne."

"Oh. You think I got a girlfriend. Well, I don't. I swear I don't. You don't know what you're talking about."

"I know you don't have a girlfriend. I know who you d…do have, who you go to when you're not here."

Leo fumed, but he remained silent.

"Listen," Anacleto said. "I'm not interested in you. I care about Santo. I need your help. He needs your help. One of these days, he might just run into Steve, and then—"

"I don't see where you chime in," he said.

"I…I just got in the middle of it. If you want to take care of it without me, that's gr… great, believe me."

"No. Not so fast. If I gotta stick my neck out, you gotta be there too. And Santo. He gotta clean up his own shit."

"You don't understand…Santo has to stay out of this. This guy wants to kill him. And, if he doesn't hurt Santo, Santo might hurt him, and he'll end up in jail."

"Maybe you'll end up in jail," he asserted, pushing his finger into Anacleto's chest.

Anacleto grasped Leo's finger and slowly pushed it away.

***

The next day, Anne told Anacleto that her father had decided to move them to a new apartment.

"I told my mother I wouldn't move with them," she said.

"What…are y…you going to do?" he asked.

"I don't know. I'll get my own apartment, I guess."

"You can't do that. Who'll take care of the baby…when…it comes?"

"We could live together…you and me," she said.

"We'd use all of our money for rent and food, and that doesn't solve the babysitting problem."

"So, you think I should move with them?" she asked.

"If it's not too far away, we can work it out."

She started to cry.

"What's the matter?"

"You…you're glad I'm moving away…I won't see you again," she bawled.

"How can you think that? I couldn't get along without you. You know that."

He held her.

"What does your mother say?"

"What can she say? My father decided. He won't pay rent here…once he finds another place."

"Where's he looking?"

"I don't know. He doesn't tell her anything."

***

Anacleto went to Anne's house right after class the next evening. He had a couple of hours before his shift at the library. Anne let him in. Leo was sitting at the kitchen table with a mug of coffee and the *Daily News*. Anacleto told him that they needed to talk. He ignored Anacleto, and turned the pages of his newspaper.

"Leo, show me s…some courtesy. Come outside and talk."

"Leave me alone. I know what you want. Forget it," he said.

Anacleto gestured to Anne that she and her mother should leave the room. He waited for them to walk out before he began.

"Listen, Leo,…I don't think I have the r…right to tell you what to do, but—"

"Then don't. Go take care of your pregnant girlfriend."

"You mean your daughter?"

He pretended to concentrate on an article in the paper.

"Listen, I know more about you than you think. I know, for one thing, that your wife calls here and gives Francine a hard time."

At the word "wife" Leo sat up and looked to see if anyone else had heard. Then, with a poisonous look, he said one word: "Don't!"

"Don't what, Leo? Don't tell Anne? Don't tell Santo? Don't let Francine know that I know?"

"Shut up!"

"Somebody had to t…tell me about the phone calls, so it's not a secret."

"Who?"

"I won't t…tell you that. I'll say this…it's still a secret…for the most part. I plan on keeping it to myself—"

"So…now you're gonna blackmail me? Is that it?"

"No. No. I want to protect your family."

"I am. I'm moving them outta here."

"And…you don't think Steve will find out?"

"No. How's he gonna find out where they're going?" he asked.

"He comes by here two, three times a week…maybe more. I'm not home that much."

"So…I'll look out for him," Leo said.

"And…what about neighbors? Francine's been here for…what is it? About seven years? Don't you think they're going to ask her where she's going?"

"She won't tell them. You're just worried because you don't want Anne to move away," he sneered.

"That's part of it," Anacleto agreed.

"You don't wanna have to travel to get what you want, huh?" he asked, smiling.

"That kind of talk is wrong, and you know it."

"Are you gonna tell me you didn't make her pregnant?"

Anacleto hesitated for a second. "…No. Of course not."

"She's a slut and you're a loser."

"What makes her a slut? She's not married and she's pregnant. But I'm not married. At least *I'm* free to marry her."

"You're lucky I'm not wringing your fucking neck," he threatened.

"I don't want to fight with you. I always hoped you and I would be able to get along, but…listen, let's not fight."

"Then leave my wife and my baby alone."

"Okay. I want to protect Anne. You care about Francine and Peter. You and I should work together to protect all of them."

Leo yawned loudly and then he smiled.

"I'm listening. I haven't found a new apartment I can afford yet."

***

Two nights later, Anne called Anacleto at work.

"Steve's car is here."

"He just get there?"

"I think so. He wasn't here when I got home from work."

"What about your father?"

"He's here."

"Good. Tell him I'll be there in twenty minutes."

Anacleto hung up and told his supervisor that he had to leave. When he reached his street, Steve's car was gone. So was Leo's car. Anne was waiting at her door.

"What happened?" Anacleto asked.

"He...my father didn't want to wait for you. He said he had to get going," she answered.

"So, he just went…he just left?"

"No. He talked to Steve. I heard them arguing. Then Steve took off and my father followed him."

"Shit! Shit! He couldn't wait for me?"

Anne looked stricken.

"Do you want to come in?" she asked.

"Just for a minute."

It was quiet and dark in the apartment.

"I see your mom began packing," he said.

"My father said she should start."

They walked into Anne's room and sat on her bed.

"How are you feeling?"

"Fat. I'm okay," she replied brightly and patted her round abdomen.

"Good."

They sat in the darkness and listened to the street noises.

"Do you think your father will be here tomorrow?"

"I guess so. Why?"

"I want to know what happened. The plan was for the two of us to be here when Steve came around, and then try to follow him…maybe to where he lives. Then we could have…I don't know."

"I'm scared," she said.

"I know. And your father…he couldn't wait to go…to get on the road."

She looked crushed. After a few minutes of heavy silence, Anacleto left.

***

Santo called Francine on Sunday morning to invite his family to Roseanne's apartment for dinner. He said he wanted Anne and Anacleto to come too. He told his mother that he would come by to drive everyone to Queens.

Anacleto could not take that much time from studying, but he told Anne to let him know when Santo arrived so he could see him. She called at two o'clock.

As he entered their apartment, he could hear Santo complaining.

"What are you movin' for? Whaddaya mean, 'Dad thinks it's a good idea'?"

"You know your father, Santo. When he makes up his mind, he just starts things going. It'll be all right."

"Do you wanna move?" he asked.

"Well, we didn't…but…it's fine."

"What about you?" he asked Anne. "This okay with you?"

"No, but what am I supposed to do?"

"Where are you going?"

"We don't know, Santo. When he finds a new apartment, he'll let us know," Francine answered.

Santo turned to Anacleto.

"You knew about this, Clete. Right? Why didn't you tell me?"

"What's the difference, Santo? Your father decided."

"There's something fishy about this," Santo fumed.

"It's fine. Let's go to your place for dinner now." Francine smiled brightly, but her lip was quivering.

"No, it's not fine. I'm gonna talk to him about this."

"I don't think that's such a good idea," Anne warned.

"There's something else going on…He'll tell me," Santo said.

Francine and Anne looked to Anacleto.

"Let's talk, Santo," Anacleto suggested.

They went outside and sat in Santo's car.

"What do you know about this?" he asked.

"I don't know a thing," Anacleto lied.

"Then what do we have to talk about?"

"You know what's going to happen when you and your father talk; he'll insult you and Roseanne, and you'll fly off the h…handle, and—"

"I gotta talk to him. I swear, this is it. I'm gonna straighten him out one way or the other."

THE WORDS THAT BURNED IN HIS EAR

That forest blaze may enlarge, only to be snuffed out by a sudden storm. If it is not subdued by rain or man or lack of fuel, it may move out, threatening to consume an even larger area.

***

When Anacleto arrived home from school and work the next afternoon, Anne was waiting for him on his front stoop.

"Santo's here," she informed him. "And my father."

"I know. I saw their cars. What's happening?"

"Just some arguing. Dad told him all about Steve looking for him."

"I th…thought he would. That's why I tr…tried to con…vince Santo not to come here to talk to him."

"Santo says he has to find Steve and settle it once and for all," Anne said.

They talked a while longer. Anacleto told Anne that he had to go into his house for a minute, but that he would be back. Ronnie and Lucia were eating dinner. Anacleto said that he wasn't hungry.

"Come on; you gotta eat. You been out all day," his mother informed him.

"It's okay, Mom. I ate at school."

"You spend money like it's water," she said, as if it were a new thought.

He asked Ronnie how he was. He looked stronger and his color was better.

"Like I said yesterday, the therapy is finally working. I'm better. Thanks."

Anacleto put his books away. Then he went to Anne's house, dreading the confrontation. He walked into the kitchen. Only Santo and his father were there, talking quietly at the table.

"There he is—Judas," Santo snarled.

"I could…couldn't tell you," Anacleto said.

"Why the fuck not?"

"Because I'm trying to…I'm trying to—"

"If you're gonna say 'protect you,' forget about it! I can take care of myself."

"I know you can, but I thought…you're working, you have Roseanne, you don't need this …complication."

"Did you ever stop to think that I can take care of my own shit?" he asked.

"Yeah," Leo interjected bitterly, "…you done a good job so far."

"Look who's talking," Santo retorted.

"I never been in jail and I never used drugs."

"No." Then Santo lowered his voice, and said, "You just lied to everybody you know about your life and your families."

"I don't know what you think, Santo, but—"

"Don't even try. Like I said before, somebody told me the whole story."

"Who told you? They're lying."

Then Leo looked at Anacleto and said, "Santo here, he's been telling me that somebody, some lying skunk told him…some cock and bull story about me…having another family."

Anacleto felt himself shrink. He stood, sweaty and cold and numb, watching them as they looked at him.

"Anacleto here, heard the same bullshit story. He was hinting at it the other day," Leo informed Santo.

"Yeah. I told him. He's my friend," Santo asserted.

"Some friend. He makes your sister pregnant and he won't marry her."

"You son-of-a-bitch. He loves her and he takes care of her and they're gonna get married when he finishes school."

"Yeah. Right," Leo said.

"Well, at least Anne knows she has a shot," Santo whispered, remembering that his sister and his mother were in one of the other rooms of the apartment.

"We'll see. My money is on him finding a college girl and turning tail," Leo asserted. "Then I'll have another mouth to feed."

"No you won't." Santo put his mouth to Leo's ear, whispering, "He's gonna do the right thing—not like you."

Leo moved away, Santo's words burning in his ear. Then he looked at Santo and started to say something, but stopped. Then he said, "There ain't no use talking to you." He turned to Anacleto and said, "So, you got something to say?"

"I do, actually—"

"I love the way you say 'actually,' like a college faggot," Leo snorted.

"What I w…want to know," Anacleto said, trying to counter Leo's insult by sounding assertive and sure of himself, "is why you didn't w…wait for me to come home the other night…when Steve was here. That was our p…pl…plan, remember?"

"I take care of my family," he stated, and turned from Anacleto.

"Oh, yeah…he did a great job," Santo hissed. "He told me he exchanged words with Steve and then Steve, he drove off and my…father, here, he went after him."

"I followed him to Manhattan, through the Battery Tunnel, but I lost him," Leo said. "I think I scared him."

"I doubt that," Santo said.

"You were supposed to wait for me, Leo," Anacleto reminded him. "I missed you by five minutes."

"Yeah? Well, I took care of it. He's gone," Leo said.

"I doubt it," Santo repeated.

"Well, in the meantime, I found a good apartment for my family. I'm movin' them next month, after it gets painted," Leo said.

"Where is it?" Anacleto asked.

"It's in Queens—Jamaica."

"Is that closer to where you live...with your wife?" Santo whispered.

"You're crazy, you lying weasel!" Leo bellowed.

From another part of the apartment, Anacleto heard crying...Anne or Francine or both.

"I'm not the crazy one!" Santo shouted. "Mom loves you and you treat her like shit. You ignore Anne or else you insult her, and...and...you've never been a real father to me, you piece of shit!" Santo spit out, his eyes burning red with anger and revulsion.

"I been a good father, even to you!"

"Even to me? You think...you ever think the trouble I been in is because you always put your hands on me?"

"No. I put my hands on you because you needed it—every time! I was trying to turn you into a man!"

"Well, well, is that because you're such a good man? Tell me, does your real wife think you're such a good man? What about your other kids?"

Anacleto felt sick...the black, venomous cloud of choking, virulent hatred that was pouring from these two men spread out and pushed the air from the room.

"Let me tell you something..." Leo started to say, but then he looked toward the part of the apartment where Francine, Anne, and Peter were, and he stopped.

"What? What do you want to say? That you're father of the year? That you always took care of your family? You've never been here when we needed you and you never treated me like a son, like you love me. I wish you dropped dead before I ever got to know you! You're a shitty excuse for a father!"

Leo, swinging one of his big arms, slapped Santo across his face, knocking him off his chair and onto the floor. With a screeching curse, Santo sprang up and lunged at Leo, knocking him and the chair on which he was sitting to the kitchen floor. They grappled, punching and choking each other and grunting and cursing as they rolled on the linoleum. Then Santo was on top. He pushed down on Leo with his body and held down his arms. He repeatedly, viciously, slammed his forehead into Leo's. Anacleto grabbed Santo and attempted to pull him up from Leo.

Santo held tight and continued to press his forehead against Leo's.

Anne and Francine ran into the room and began to shriek.

Then, in the midst of the bestial struggle, Leo put his mouth against Santo's ear. Santo stiffened and then moaned. He slowly relaxed his grip on Leo and allowed Anacleto to pull him up. Leo put his hands to his forehead. Santo sat heavily on a chair and leaned on the table. Leo stood up, holding a handkerchief to his forehead with one hand and rubbing the back of his head with the other. He looked at Francine, who turned away from him.

"Let's go out, Santo," Anacleto whispered, shakily. "We'll go for a walk."

When Santo didn't move, Leo straightened out his clothes, smoothed his hair, and started for the door.

Santo sat up and yelled, "Wait!"

Leo stopped and turned.

"What did you just whisper in my ear?" Santo asked.

"Nothing. Forget it," Leo replied, and turned away again.

"No!" Santo stood up, reached for Leo, and grabbed his arms from behind; he roughly turned Leo around so that they were facing each other, inches apart.

"You said something. I think I know what you said, but I gotta hear it again to be sure."

"No," Leo said.

"Listen, you never done nothing for me. At least tell me the truth now."

"You don't wanna hear it. You're not man enough for the truth," Leo replied, smiling bitterly.

"I wanna hear it, or I'm gonna kill you, you lying piece of shit!"

"You're gonna want to kill me if I say it again," Leo replied. Then he added, "Not that you can…you're not man enough for that either."

Santo pushed Leo against a wall, his hands holding the older man's arms to his sides, and held him there. Leo's smile was cold and bitter with hatred.

Pressing his face against one of Leo's ears, Santo repeated his threat. Anacleto approached them and told Santo to let go. Francine and Anne stood nearby, sobbing. Peter was in his room, crying.

"I'll kill you, you old bastard…I swear I will. Tell me what you said," Santo hissed into Leo's ear.

"All right. Let go of me. I'm too tired to fight."

Santo released Leo and stepped back.

"I don't want them here…any of them," Leo said.

"They stay. Talk!"

"No."

"What the hell did you mean? When I had you on the floor,…I think you said 'I'm ain't even your father.' What the hell?"

Francine moaned and turned white. She walked from the room. Anne looked at Anacleto. Then she followed her mother. Anacleto started to go after them, but Santo gestured that he should stay.

"You know I'm gonna tell you what he said," he told Anacleto. "Sit down."

Anacleto moved away from them and sat at the kitchen table, wishing, once again, that he were somewhere, anywhere else.

"Talk, or I'll smash your ugly old face in!"

Leo looked Santo straight in the eye and smiled again. He slowly pulled a cigarette out of a crushed pack that had been in his pocket, and lit it.

"You know, every time you got in trouble in school or in the neighborhood and every time you screwed around and didn't do what your mother or me wanted you to do, I wanted to tell you, but I didn't. I tried to be a father to you, but I couldn't do it. You're not mine. You got bad blood."

"What do…do you mean?" Santo's eyes were wide and his skin looked sallow and loose.

"I'm talking about how, when I met your mother, she was already pregnant. Some guy, some kid she knew, he's your father."

Santo looked down.

"I gave her a place to live. She was living in a shithole when I met her. I gave her money to go to a doctor I knew, but she wanted to keep the bastard. I loved her, your mother. She was beautiful."

"I don't wanna hear no more," Santo whispered.

"I tried to treat you like a son, but you were always…fighting me, like you knew I wasn't your father, like you thought I couldn't tell you what to do."

"I never thought that…I always wanted you to treat me like a son…like all the other dads. I…loved you," Santo spoke softly, sadly.

"You never showed it. You been a crappy kid from the day you were born."

Santo sat, his head down on the table now.

"I tried. I did. You were always a hard kid. I figured it's because you had some other guy's blood, not mine."

Anacleto looked down at the floor, at spots of blood. He was hoping a hole would appear. He would have gladly jumped in.

THE MAN WHO SHOULD HAVE BEEN HIS FATHER

Later that night, about an hour after Anacleto had gone home, Anne rang his doorbell. He came out and they walked.

After a few minutes, she spoke: "You must hate me now."

"What? No. I…feel b…bad for Santo…for your mom, and for you. I know this is all a big shock to you."

"Yeah. My head is killing me, but, you probably think this is something that runs in the family…like the sins of the mother."

He held her shoulders and looked straight into her eyes, and said, "Your mom had a crappy home life and some boy made her pregnant. Your father took care of her in his way. It happened. Our life together will not be like theirs, I promise you."

"But, my mom and me…It's almost like we followed a pattern."

"Who knows how many other women have b…been down that s…same road?"

"But—"

"No. Shush. It's different. Our situation is different. We don't need to talk about this again...unless you *need* to talk, that is."

"I can't believe it. They're not married, you know," she said.

"I know."

"You've known for a while, right?"

"Yes," he hesitantly answered.

"You thought I couldn't handle it, right?"

"No. That wasn't it. Santo asked me to k…keep quiet. I…I don't know."

"It's okay, I guess. You did right," she said. "I can't believe it. I guess you know he has a wife and three grown kids."

"I didn't know the de…details, but I knew he was married."

Then Anne looked at him with teary eyes, and said, "Life can be shit."

***

The woodland blaze has no mind, no conscience, no sense of restraint. It moves slowly, without purpose, consuming all in its path. Unless someone or something stops it, it continues on its destructive rampage. Finally, when it runs out of fuel, having killed everything it has touched, it also dies.

***

Anacleto parked his mother's car and watched as Ronnie slowly, but with very little obvious discomfort, climbed out. They had returned from his therapy session; Anacleto had time before he had to go the college library to start his five to eleven p.m. shift.

Lucia would not be home from work for another hour. Ronnie settled in front of the television while Anacleto reviewed some class notes in preparation for a test the next day. Then he went out.

He assumed Anne was not home yet, but he knocked on the door anyway. Francine told him that she expected Anne any minute. He checked his watch, and walked out. He would have walked to the subway station to meet her, but she alternated between the two nearby lines. There was no point in going to one station if she had taken the other line, so he walked to the corner and waited. After a few minutes, he saw her coming his way. He walked to her. They kissed. Then they walked along the sidewalk toward her house.

Just as they reached Anne's house, Steve pulled up and parked. Leo's car was nearby. Anacleto wrapped an arm around Anne, and they turned into the alleyway. Steve exited his car and ran to block their path.

"Well, if it ain't the stuttering loser and the knocked-up girlfriend," Steve spit out.

"L...leave us alone," Anacleto said. "It's over. We don't know where Santo is."

"Bullshit! You and I know he lives in Queens. I'm gonna get him. Maybe I'll kill you first or I'll get this bitch to go down on me—just like she used to."

"Hey, watch it. Leave Anne out of this," Anacleto warned.

"What you gonna do? I could hurt you bad...one-two-three, but I want Santo more. Why don't you tell me where he is?"

"I don't know."

They edged around Steve and, to their surprise, he did not try to stop them. They walked quickly to the apartment. Anne went to the bathroom. Leo was sitting at the kitchen table, sipping from a big coffee mug.

"This is our chance to...double-team him," Anacleto breathlessly told Leo.

He sipped his coffee, ignoring Anacleto.

"Do you hear me? He's outside, Leo."

"It ain't my problem," he said.

He gulped the last of his coffee, put the cup in the sink, and left the room. Francine was playing with Peter in the living room. She held the last piece of a wooden jigsaw puzzle in her hand, preparing to move it into its place, ending the mystery, revealing the picture. Anne emerged from the bathroom.

"Oh, no!" Francine cried out. She was looking out a front window. Anne and Anacleto looked. They saw Santo arguing with Steve. Anacleto ran to the sidewalk.

Anne followed. Francine, holding Peter, followed them.

As Anacleto approached Santo and Steve, he was relieved to see that, although they were talking angrily, they were keeping their hands at their sides. Anacleto stood next to Santo. Steve looked at him with dead eyes.

"Santo, I need to end this with you. I need some respect," Steve asserted.

"You don't deserve no respect," Santo countered.

"You see, that's what makes this so hard—you don't wanna settle this," Steve said.

"What do you want? Tell me. How *do* we settle this, Steve? Do we have a fuckin' duel?"

"Yeah. Something like that. We go to this place I know and we fight it out—man to man. Nobody else. You don't bring nobody and I don't neither."

"What's wrong with right here?" Santo asked.

"You think I'm crazy? You got your friend here and all these nosey neighbors. Uh uh…No."

"It's here or no place, Steve. Clete will keep out of it."

"There's another way, you know." Steve looked around to make sure no one else could hear before he continued. "You pay me back for all the product and all the cash you stole from me—nine bills should do it."

"Oh, sure. I'll do that…after you pay me back for the product and cash you stole from me twice," Santo replied.

"What?"

"Yeah," Santo said. "First, what that girl stole that you ended up with and then when you and Darren beat me up and took my property and my spot."

"That was sanctioned, Santo. You gotta know that."

"If it was sanctioned, it's because you lied about me."

"No. They told me you hadda be replaced."

"Bullshit!" Santo yelled.

By now, a number of neighbors had come out to witness the confrontation. Mr. Woodmere, the police officer, was not among them.

"Okay, Steve," Santo said. "We end this now. You leave and you stay away or I cut you down now."

"What you gonna do? Kill me in front of witnesses?"

"I don't need to kill you." Then he moved closer to Steve and whispered, "I'll hurt you so bad you'll be in the hospital for months. Remember, I got the witnesses; you don't."

Anacleto sensed that someone was behind him. He turned, and saw Leo looking at Steve; his expression was one of curiosity, not anger.

"Look at this, Leo," Steve said. "He don't wanna be reasonable. He don't wanna end it."

"Be a man, Santo. End it," Leo said.

"I wanna end it, but not by going off to get jumped." Then, turning around to face Leo, he asked, "And, how is it he knows your name?"

"He and I talked once," Leo replied. Then he walked over and stood next to Steve, facing Santo and Anacleto.

Santo's eyes bulged. He licked his lips and swallowed. "Why are you standing there?"

"I'm tryin' to settle this…peacefully. I'm tryin' to be an…arbitrator," Leo replied.

"Is this what you call tryin' to be a father? For cryin' out loud, stand over here with me."

Steve smiled.

"You son of a bitch…You piece of shit excuse for a father…You don't give a damn about me or mom or Anne or anybody."

"I love your mother," he replied. "I'd protect her with my life."

"You're a liar, and you and I know it. You treat her like shit and she shoulda walked out on you years ago. You're a piece of dog shit!"

"You watch your mouth. You better—"

"Better what? Listen to you? Because...why? Because you're my father? Hah!" Santo's laugh was cold and angry.

"I tried to be your father, no matter what kind of dirty blood you got from who the hell knows where!"

Santo's face was contorted by rage. He jabbed a finger at Leo's chest. Leo slapped Santo across his face. Santo stumbled back, twisting an ankle, and falling against the sharp spindles of the rusty wrought iron fence in front of the house. He painfully pushed himself up and rubbed his back; then he bent over in agony. Within a second, Leo was on him, leaning over him, brutally slapping his face and the top of his head over and over with his massive hands.

In a panic, Anacleto grabbed the back of Leo's shirt and tried to pull him away. At the same moment, Anne rushed over to shield her brother. Leo savagely pushed Anne away, knocking her roughly to the sidewalk, and then he pivoted and punched Anacleto in his gut. Anacleto held his abdomen, gasped for air, and fell to his knees next to Anne. After a moment, he forced himself to his feet and reached down to help Anne. Just then, Steve approached and swung hard and low, smashing into Anacleto's ear. Pain shot through Anacleto, from the side of his head to his tailbone. Hot, dazzling pinpricks of light sizzled and flashed as he fell to the sidewalk, a ferocious ringing in his ears disorienting him for a few seconds. He looked up to see an unfocused image of Steve standing over him, smiling. He turned his head: a neighbor had helped Anne up and was walking her away from the brutal scene. She was holding her abdomen with both hands. Anacleto turned his head to the other side: Leo was savagely punching Santo, who covered his face and the top of his head with his hands. Each time Santo attempted to rise, Leo punched him down. Finally, Santo dropped to his knees, as if in prayer, tucked his face down, and held his hands over his head. Leo continued to viciously punch him.

Further down the sidewalk, Anne, frantically running her hands through her disheveled hair, wailed in anguish. Francine, with Peter in her arms, held her daughter.

Anacleto called out to Anne, but his voice sounded as if he was underwater. He looked at Leo and Santo again and attempted to stand up, but his head was spinning, so he sat down.

More sickening than the violent beating, which was more brutal than the one that Anacleto had witnessed years before, was Santo's reaction: He looked up for a few seconds and loudly cried out, "Stop, Dad! Stop! Daddy, please stop!" Anacleto could not hear the words clearly, but he saw the grief and the little-boy sense of loss and defeat that contorted Santo's face.

A few neighbors hesitantly approached Leo and told him to stop.

Steve kicked Anacleto's leg. He looked up at Steve, bewildered. He had forgotten that Steve was there. He tried to stand, but Steve kicked him again, this time connecting with his inner thigh. Then Steve pulled Anacleto up, forcing him to stand on shaky legs.

Steve smiled and hissed something; through the violent ringing, Anacleto thought he heard, "You're shoulda stayed in your hole, where you belong."

Then Steve made a fist and drew back his arm. Before Anacleto realized he was doing it, he plowed into Steve, knocking him down and landing on top of him. Anacleto tried to scramble to his feet, but Steve grabbed the front of his shirt, pulled him down, and rolled on top of him. Anacleto wrapped his arms around Steve and rolled him onto his back; then he seized Steve's wrists, pushed his arms down, and pinned him to the sidewalk. Steve rocked from side to side, attempting to free himself. He angrily rolled and pushed, grunting and twisting and spraying saliva, and finally managed to slip out of Anacleto's grasp and thrust him off to the side. Then, sitting up, Steve swung at Anacleto, who was trying to stand, connecting with one of his hips. Enraged by the pain, Anacleto reached down and swung wildly, missing Steve. Then he hobbled away from Steve and forced himself to stand straight; he held his fists in front of his face. Steve lunged from his sitting position and barreled into Anacleto's legs, knocking him down. The back of Anacleto's head collided with the sidewalk. Then Steve leaped onto Anacleto's chest, sat on him, and began punching his face. As Anacleto frantically attempted to seize Steve's wrists, his attacker continued to swing at him, connecting over and over. The sharp pain from the blows and the metallic taste of blood flowing in his mouth infuriated him. Summoning all of his reserves of strength, Anacleto arched his back, braced his body with his feet, and, grasping the front of Steve's shirt, he pulled Steve to the side, rolled him over, and sat on *his* chest. Undeterred, Steve continued to punch up at Anacleto, repeatedly connecting with glancing blows to his face and chest. Then, tucking his head down to protect his face from the blows, Anacleto reached down blindly and grabbed Steve's neck and jaw and violently slammed the back of his head to the sidewalk. Without thinking, propelled by ferocious animal instinct, Anacleto punched Steve's face…and then again and again until Steve stopped moving.

Two of the neighbors pulled Anacleto off Steve and sat him on the sidewalk against a parked car. Others grabbed Leo and, with great difficulty, pulled him from Santo. Leo thrashed and howled, but the men held tight.

Anne and Francine and Peter were screaming.

The same men who had pulled Anacleto up forced Steve to his feet and roughly walked him to his car. They opened the door, shoved Steve into the car, and slammed the door shut.

Leo, infuriated, struggled to free his arms. He kicked at the men who held him. Santo was crouching and leaning against the spiked fence, holding his head. He was crying and shaking.

Then, with an enormous burst of savage ferocity, Leo broke free of his captors, knocking them both to the ground. He slowly pulled off his belt and, doubling it, he approached Santo. His face was bestial, contorted by rage; he blew out a whale-like mouthful of spit. Then he viciously slashed down at Santo with the belt, grunting with each blow. He stood on his toes and savagely hit Santo's head and face and shoulders. Santo did not raise his hands to protect himself.

Instead, he called out, "Dad, please don't! Dad!"

"I'm not…don't want...to be…your father!" Leo bellowed.

Then, in an instant that Anacleto's eyes could barely follow, Santo shot up and straightened out. With a look of uncontrollable, brutish hatred in his red-rimmed eyes, he lunged at Leo, wrapping his arms around him and spinning the both of them around. With bull-like strength and propelled by rage, he pushed Leo, thrusting him hard against the pointy top of the spiked fence. Leo shrieked, dropped the belt, and pushed Santo off him. Santo stumbled back. For a moment, he looked at Leo writhing in pain and slowly extricating himself from the spikes. Then, before any of the neighbors could stop him, he barreled forward and slammed against Leo, forcing him down on the sharp spikes; he grasped the tops of the spindles on either side of Leo and pressed all of his weight and all of his fury and all of his sorrow down on the man who should have been his father. Leo frantically pushed against Santo. His eyes bulged. He roared in pain and anger. Santo stood on his toes and pressed down harder on Leo with all of his furious, maddened strength; as he did so, he cried.

A low, gurgling, choking sound escaped from Leo's mouth.

It did not happen. Anacleto closed his eyes. When he opened them, Santo was lifting Leo from the fence and hugging him. Anacleto felt relieved and was comforted to see that all of the onlookers were crying tears of joy at the sweet reconciliation of Santo and his father.

Anacleto could not understand why a ragged, splotchy line of red was slowly spreading across the back of Leo's white shirt, so like the time-lapse films of blooming flowers that he had seen on nature shows on television, or why blood was bubbling out of Leo's mouth and dribbling down his chin. After a few seconds, Santo broke the embrace and Leo sank to his knees, kissing Santo's shoes. Leo lay on his back on the sidewalk, twitching and laboring to breathe, blood oozing from his mouth. Then he stopped moving; his open eyes focused on heaven. A small blossom of blood unfolded and grew on the front of his shirt. There was a similar but smaller red blot, like a diminutive flower petal, on Santo's shirt front.

Anacleto's eyes took it in, but his brain did not comprehend the meaning of the blood that coated the pointed, rusty spindles of the fence or the puddle that spread out beneath Leo, like a peaceful, glistening pond.

***

Leo's lifeless body was wheeled into an ambulance. As the driver was preparing to move out from the curb, one of the police officers on the scene pointed to a flat tire. Twenty minutes later, another ambulance arrived. Leo's body was transferred to it and taken away. Santo had been handcuffed and placed in the back of a police car. He sat frozen, seemingly detached from reality. Then he was driven away. Anacleto climbed into a second police car. Francine and Anne stood on the sidewalk; Anne was holding Peter. Anacleto hoped the neighbors would comfort them.

LIVING WITH THE CONSEQUENCES

Santo insisted on accepting a plea deal, even though it meant a stiff sentence. His attorney had tried to persuade him to let the case go to trial. He believed a sympathetic jury would acquit Santo of the most serious charges.

When Anacleto tried to convince Santo, shortly after he had been processed, that he had been defending himself, Santo said he knew he was going to kill his father one day and he was relieved that he done it.

"I did what I hadda do," he explained, the black circles under his eyes making him look like an old man who was tired of living.

After that, he refused to see any and all visitors.

On that appalling day, after a neighbor had helped Anne into her house, she became hysterical. Then she began hemorrhaging. At the hospital, they called it a spontaneous abortion. Anacleto sat by Anne's bedside and held her hand. He didn't know how to feel about the termination of her pregnancy. She broke her self-imposed silence only once during the time of her hospitalization: she asked Anacleto whether he thought her father's body was still in the basement morgue of that same hospital. Then she turned away from him and slept.

The next day, Anacleto found, in Leo's car, a phone number for Sonia, his wife. He called her. She listened in silence as Anacleto briefly explained what had happened. The only question she asked was, "Where is he?"

***

Francine fell into a bottomless depression. On a few occasions, she lost her way when she went grocery shopping and, sometimes, when Anne came home from work, she found that Peter had not eaten all day. Anne, Francine, and Peter moved in with Francine's sister, Rita, in her apartment in Park Slope, not far from the zoo. Visiting the animals seemed to soothe Francine.

Anacleto found a large, airy, rent-controlled apartment a few blocks away and convinced Anne to move in with him, along with Peter. Aunt Rita agreed to watch the boy when Anne was at work, saying, "This way, he can see his mother a bit. Having him around at night is too much for my sister."

Anacleto took the rest of the year off from school and worked, full time, first at Joe Zitto's Auto Body and then for an insurance adjuster he met there.

Months passed before Anacleto's hearing fully returned, but the bitter memory of that horrifying day did not vanish or even begin to recede into the background of his daily existence. Nor did his sense of loss, of guilt. He was overwhelmed by the waste of so many lives and by the fact that he had been unable to act in time to prevent the tragedy.

Anacleto's brothers told him not to trust the draft lottery system, so he returned to college to maintain his student deferment and he worked at night. He promised them that he would not allow himself to be sucked into the bloodletting in Vietnam.

***

So much misery. So much pain. So many lives destroyed.

Anacleto had spent years of his life avoiding life or, rather, accepting his place as an outsider, not even trying to look in. Not wanting to be let in. Then, when Santo reached for him, Anacleto grasped his hand and allowed himself to be pulled into the world, just a little. And Rudy, crazy Rudy…Anacleto's short, troubled friendship with Rudy helped to bring him a little further into contact with others. And Mr. Randazzo—he believed that Anacleto had a gift. And Ricki—she enflamed his passion. His relationship with her also helped him to see, once again, that actions have consequences. He accepted those consequences and continued to move on.

Anne. With Anne, he had exulted in life...for a while.

***

During quiet moments of the day, Anacleto wonders what would have happened or not happened if he had not gone with Santo to the courtyard to confront Steve that night.

What if he had not shown the guns to Santo? What if he had not allowed Santo into his house that day? What if he had never climbed into the attic? Perhaps none of the misery would have occurred. Or, perhaps it all would have happened anyway or in a different way. Maybe a different spark would have ignited some forest debris in another place at another time, causing a different set of equally appalling calamities.

So many months later, Anacleto and Anne are both still too damaged by what happened that day to enjoy what they once shared. Neither of them is able to laugh or smile or love—not as they once did.

They try to take pleasure in each other, but they cannot do it in the abandoned, explosive, jubilant way that they had before that hideous black afternoon. They agree that they have an obligation, as the survivors, to attempt to be happy. They try. They know they have to continue to attempt to balance out the grief and the despair that is the stuff of their shared existence with at least a modicum of happiness.

If not for themselves, then for Peter, the gentle boy they are raising as if he were their son, they have had to learn how to seek out and attempt to enjoy the pleasures of life; they understand that if they don't, he will grow up feeling despondent and hopeless and unloved.

***

I made choices long ago, and now I have to live with their consequences. I could have stayed in my house, where I was safe and cut off from the dangers outside. Instead, I went out. I wanted to live like other people. I took chances. I enjoyed life...and I got hurt. It is what it is. Even if I wish I hadn't done what I did, it's too late now. I decided that I no longer wanted to live as an outcast, despised and alone, looking at the dirty world through the spaces between my fingers.

The End

Made in the USA
Charleston, SC
11 September 2012